A Gentleman 'til Midnight

A Gentleman 'til Midnight

ALISON DeLAINE

HARLEQUIN® HQN™

ISBN 978-1-61129-064-6

A GENTLEMAN 'TIL MIDNIGHT

Copyright © 2014 by Alison Atwater

For my husband, Tom.
I love you.

CHAPTER ONE

East of the Strait of Gibraltar
April 1767

A WAVE SWELLED and broke over his head, and for a moment Captain James Warre couldn't breathe. His fingers dug into the wet wood beneath him, but there was nothing to grasp. The churning water choked him, nudged him, smothered him.

With a massive effort he shifted to his side, then let his head fall in a fit of coughing. The seawater left his mouth brackish and dry. Closing his eyes, he let himself slip away.

"Lavender's blue, dilly dilly, lavender's green." Nap time, young Master Warre, and I'll hear no more of your sorry excuses.

Nap time. The sun shone warm on his back as he pitched and bobbed with the chop.

Then suddenly, a shadow.

There was a bump, a scrape. Wood met wood, jarring him. His eyes flew open as he braced for a cannon's roar. Fluttered closed again when it didn't come.

A female voice drifted to his ears. "...alive, do you think?"

The soft, lilting sound wrapped around him like a melody.

Bump, bump, bump.

"...bloody well dead, or close enough." A male voice now.

Bump, bump, scrape.

"...haul him up?" Female again.

Bump, bump— He opened his eyes and stared straight at the wet hull of a ship. Another wave engulfed him and left him gasping, straining to see the deck in a moment of clarity. He hadn't the strength. His gaze swept the ragged length of the raft keeping him afloat— No, not raft. Broken decking. A memory threatened to pull him under, but he fought for lucidity and kept his gaze moving, turning, sweeping upward. She was a brig.

"...any manner of disease. We cannot afford the risk." Through a haze he recognized the words as English. But then a string of shouted words, this time unintelligible—but not unrecognizable.

English and Moorish together, on a Mediterranean brig.

Renegades. They would not look kindly on the captain of a British ship of the line.

The muffled snap of cloth in the breeze kept him fighting to see the stern. If he could just see her colors... The curving hull blocked his view of all but a bright red corner wafting in the wind.

He fixed his eye on that corner, waiting, clawing against an invisible undertow.

Nap time, young Master Warre—

No! He had to see that flag.

A wave broke over him. His mouth filled with seawater and he gagged, choking and sputtering again as he re-fixed his gaze. Finally, a gust whipped the greater part of the flag into view.

A slender, yellow arm stretched out against the red background, its fist curled around a black cutlass.

Bloody living hell.

He didn't need to see the rest of the flag to know that shapely arm was attached to a woman's shoulder and breast. He let his head drop against the wet wood.

"Lavender's blue, dilly dilly..."

Bump, bump, bump.

The next wave swept him from consciousness.

CHAPTER TWO

It was a pathetic sight—every bit as pathetic as the day they'd fished Mr. Bogles out of the harbor at Malta, but Mr. Bogles was a cat. A man offered none of the same benefits, yet presented dozens of dangerous possibilities. Captain Katherine Kinloch forced herself away from the railing.

"He could have any manner of disease," she said flatly. "We cannot afford the risk."

"Aye, Captain." Her Algerian boatswain headed toward the fore, shouting a reprimand to three deckhands gawking over the side. Even bathed in the Mediterranean sunshine, she shivered.

Lower the net! The order strained on her tongue, but she clenched her teeth and lifted her spyglass toward the strait. Nobody aboard would have survived if she'd let herself succumb to emotion each time the winds blew contrary.

"Terrible way to die," her first mate commented, looking down at the water from where he lounged against the railing. His tone delivered reproof the way syrup carried a tincture.

"Every way to die is terrible, William." The words were cold. Awful. She felt a little sick. "I doubt we could do anything but make his last moments an agony by dragging him up."

"Suppose he's perfectly healthy? Just dying of thirst?"

"Suppose he carries the plague?" she snapped. One deck below her feet, Anne was happily teaching Mr. Bogles to string beads. Some dangers to Anne were unavoidable, but this one wasn't.

A tremble made the horizon dance in her field of view, and she steadied her grip. As soon as they passed through the strait, she would be in unfamiliar waters, sailing with a skeleton crew toward a homeland she hadn't seen in over ten years. Doubts about that decision already kept her pacing the decks during others' midnight watches—this was no time for more potential folly. Damn Cousin Holliswell and his greed, and double-bloody-damn Nicholas Warre for helping him. But then, Warre men could be counted on to be merciless.

An inky length of her hair flew over the spyglass, and she snatched it away. "For all we know," she added, "he is a Tunisian corsair."

"Or a subject of the king," William countered conversationally. And then he added, "I don't recall you having so many qualms when we took Phil and Indy aboard."

"Of course not. And you know the reason."

He leaned over the rail and called down to the near lifeless form below. "If you've got breasts, old boy, now's the time to show 'em."

"Enough!" She lowered the spyglass. William's blond beard glinted pure gold in the sun, the exact shade of the hoops gleaming from both ears beneath his scarlet turban. His loose white tunic fluttered in the breeze above black linen trousers and bare feet. "I should have thrown you over years ago. Your sense of humor leaves much to be desired."

He raised a brow. "As does yours. It has disappeared entirely, along with your compassion."

The accusation struck hard. "That is entirely unfair. We know nothing of him," she said. "Not his nationality, his occupation, his loyalties, his morality—"

"Irrelevant."

"—nor his history. All of which is relevant with so few of us left on board." She caught her boatswain's eye from the lower deck. For God's sake, she could barely trust her own men. She raised her chin at Rafik and stared him down until he looked away.

Familiar tension coiled in her gut, screaming that there was no room for error. No room for any but the most calculated risk. "I'll not be made to feel guilty for mitigating danger," she added. But guilt crept in anyhow, and not only about the unfortunate in the water. This voyage was the biggest risk yet. If it turned out to be a mistake, Anne would be the one to suffer most.

She felt William staring at her. "It's not too late to turn back," he said quietly.

"Bite your tongue."

The sound of angry footsteps on the stairs warned of Millicent, who stepped onto the upper deck with her expression locked in the glower she had adopted the moment they'd sailed for Britain. With her slender body enshrouded in a shirt and breeches, her hair pulled severely beneath a misshapen hat and her conventional features, Millicent passed for a young man to those who weren't looking closely. "Philomena is beside herself," she announced, "and India is ready to go over the side.

This isn't sitting well with the crew." She awaited Katherine's reply with lips thinned.

"We'll be underway as soon as the tide turns," Katherine told her.

"And leave him to his fate?" Disbelief raised the pitch in Millicent's voice.

"Katherine Kidd," William quipped, pushing away from the railing. "I shall go see what I can do to quell the riot."

Katherine looked over the rail, hoping for confirmation that it was too late and there was nothing they could do. As she watched, a wave rolled over the man below. One of his hands moved, reaching, then stilled. Devil take it, watching him die was intolerable.

She thrust her spyglass toward Millicent. "Come here. Look at him. Is there any sign of disease?"

Millicent, the eldest daughter of a country physician and an excellent surgeon in her own right, pointed the instrument downward. "There are no sores on his face that I can see," she said after a moment, "but it's difficult to tell with several days' growth of whiskers. I don't see any jaundice. I see nothing on his hand except raw skin." After another moment, she returned the spyglass. "Assuming he was clean-shaven before disaster struck, he's been adrift at least three days. It is very unlikely he would have survived this long if he also had a sickness. I can't be sure, of course. Not without examining him. But I believe he's as safe as any to bring aboard."

Safe was patently the wrong word. Reason advised that one man could pose little threat, but experience warned otherwise. Katherine stared down at him. A shipwreck survivor? They'd seen no evidence, and the weather had been clear except for some high clouds.

A Barbary captive attempting escape? The possibility stirred a sympathetic rage inside her.

"I don't speak lightly, Captain," Millicent added stiffly. "I would never endanger this crew, or Anne."

"I haven't the least suspicion that you would." Another swell covered the motionless form on the raft. On the main deck, so many hands had gathered at the rail it was a wonder the ship did not list to starboard. Young, impulsive India gestured wildly to William. Philomena—never one to turn a blind eye toward any man—looked up at Katherine as though to say, "Well?"

The tension in her gut coiled so tightly she wanted to vomit. The uproar from the main deck buzzed in her ears as precious, lifesaving moments ticked away. Some mistakes should be easy to avoid. If she acquiesced, and he turned out to be the danger she feared…

Yet if she left him to die…

"Very well." The words tumbled out, ejected by the sick pit in her stomach. "Haul him up. If there is any sign of disease, any sign at all—" But Millicent had already spun away, practically flying down the steps to relay the order.

Katherine Kidd, indeed. She inhaled deeply and tried to still her trembling hands. Already her stomach eased, but it shouldn't have. Even if the man was healthy, he could bring trouble.

If he did, he would spend the voyage in chains.

Alone on the upper deck, she held the spyglass to her eye and carefully focused it downward. A striking face came into view, close as breath in the lens. Her belly quickened in a sudden, visceral reaction. The man's complexion must have been swarthy before, but now a pallor made him seem ghostly. A strong, perfectly sculpted nose extended from an angular face with sharp cheekbones. Wet, black lashes lay against the hollows beneath his eyes. His jaw hung slack, dusted by a thick stubble of whiskers that nearly hid a dark slant of mustache above firm, lifeless lips. Water plastered his hair to his head in careless black waves streaked with silver.

For a long, hypnotic moment the world contained only him.

And then the ship rolled with a wave, tearing him from her view. She inhaled sharply and lowered the glass. Surely it was too late. His large hands lay motionless against the boards that supported him. She hadn't seen any movement through the glass.

Rafik's staccato shouts barked up from below while the crew threw the nets over the side and clambered down. She held her breath as several crew members tried to lift the man off his raft but only succeeded in nearly capsizing it. They shouted for a boom, and soon the crew on deck fashioned a sling and lowered it down. Within minutes they hauled the man's listless, sodden form into the air.

Quickly she made her way to the quarterdeck and then to the main, just as they brought him aboard. Crew members crowded in around the rescuers. "Give them room!" she ordered, and they backed off instantly. "Is he alive?"

"He was half an hour ago," India said insolently, brushing past her to help remove the sling. Her blond braid hung like a rope over one shoulder as she deftly undid the hooks. Rafik hacked away the man's white shirt and tan breeches, while two deckhands doused him with fresh water from the mop buckets. Now the orders came from Millicent, who forced everyone away except those who helped wash him.

"Phil went to find some toweling," William said, moving in beside Katherine.

After a moment Millicent called over her shoulder. "He lives!"

Katherine exhaled.

The man lay naked and facedown on the deck as they continued to douse him until Millicent was satisfied that no salt remained. Phil returned with two lengths of linen and crouched by his side. His legs were long. Muscular. Katherine slid her gaze past solid buttocks to the broad expanse of his back and shoulders.

"A fine form of a man," Phil purred, drying him carefully.

India snorted and snatched one of the towels from her hand. "Auntie Phil, he's in his dotage!"

Phil laughed at her niece. "In your eyes, any man over twenty-five is in his dotage."

"Exactly so." Eighteen-year-old India smiled wickedly from beneath her tricorne hat.

Millicent rolled the man over, revealing a sprinkle of dark hair on his chest, a rippled stomach and—

Katherine looked away, straight into William's laughing eyes. "I'll wager you side with Phil this time," he said.

"He will need clothes," she snapped. "Something of yours will do."

William leaned in, lowering his voice to a mock-whisper. "Are you sure? Because I rather had the impression you might prefer him without."

"Devil take you. You're as bad as Phil."

"I heard that," Phil called. "And I resent it deeply."

But Phil had been right about one thing. The man was definitely not in his dotage. The ordeal may have nearly killed him, but he looked strong, and he was large. Commanding. "I don't want him in the infirmary," she told William under her breath. "Too close to the crew. We can clear out André's cabin and put him there, but in the meantime—" she hesitated "—put him in mine."

As expected, William's brow ticked upward.

"One word, and you'll meet the end of my cutlass," she bit out, but the threat had no effect on William's amusement. "As soon as he's been seen to, everyone will resume their duties or punishment will be meted out."

"Captain Cat-o'-nine-tails."

"If behavior warrants." But they both knew she owned no instruments of torture. It was far more effective to offer good food, high pay and commendations for good behavior. "Fortune has smiled on him today," she said, a bit too sharply. "We shall see if that changes once he is awake." She looked once more at the newest person for whom she was responsible. The man was handsome—too handsome, with features that bordered on aristocratic and a stubborn, angular jaw.

"We could use another man on the crew," Phil pointed out.

"True enough," William agreed. "But then, we've no idea whether he knows his cock from a bowsprit."

In that same moment, the man's eyes fluttered open. He looked up, straight at Katherine, piercing her with depths as green as a backlit Mediterranean wave. Something hot and liquid and unexpected shot through her, and a shiver feathered her spine.

He knew the difference. She'd wager the entire year's take on it.

CHAPTER THREE

JAMES WRITHED RESTLESSLY beneath cool linens.

He was drowning—dragged beneath black water, sucked into frigid numbness. Wood splintered. Cracked. A timber shot from the water, and he made a desperate lunge. Grabbed hold.

Wood turned to flesh beneath his hands. Cold became hot. Water became woman. The curling waves unraveled, tumbling, becoming hair like black walnut silk in his hands. Her body wrapped around him. Engulfed him. He gasped, tasting the wild sea on her skin.

From somewhere far away, sultry voices pierced his dream. "…and have you try to bed him while he's yet unconscious? Absolutely not."

"You offend me grievously, Katherine. I'm quite through with affairs. Tedious things. Besides, he could be anyone."

The voices threatened to tear him away. He strained to keep the woman alive, wanting. Needing. But she began to fade, slipping away.

The voices broke through, stronger now. "For the moment, Philomena, he is our captive."

"Honestly, he hardly warrants such status." A door closed. Footsteps tapped against wood. He awoke as if fighting the churning sea.

"Nor does he warrant any other. Help me put this shirt on him before he awakes."

He opened his eyes to a sky-blue ceiling edged with gold scrollwork. His gaze swept over an ornate dressing table with an oblong looking glass, two armchairs upholstered in sapphire velvet, a chest of drawers inlaid with mother-of-pearl. He turned his head.

A woman stood by the bed with a maroon tunic in her hands. Silken walnut waves fell to her hips from beneath a length of ochre cloth tied around her head in a makeshift turban shot through with shimmering threads. High cheekbones. Straight, finely sculpted nose. Statuesque profile, silhouetted perfectly by the light from a small bank of windows he recognized as belonging to a ship.

He was on board a vessel. In the captain's cabin.

"Katherine. Look."

Her face snapped toward him. His gaze locked with glittering topaz eyes, and his pulse leaped. He struggled to think. To remember. He tried to lick his lips, but his mouth was powder dry.

Someone else pushed in next to him—another beauty, this one with sable curls and wide, blue eyes. He felt a hand beneath his head, lifting, and a glass against his lips. Cool water slid over his tongue and he tried to gulp, but the blasted woman pulled the glass away.

"Not so quickly," she purred, and the glass returned. "Careful, now. Just a bit."

He sipped, then sipped again before she pulled the glass away.

"More." His voice croaked. The vessel rolled and creaked, lolling with the waves. And suddenly, he remembered. A storm. A wreck. Days upon days adrift at sea.

A red flag with a yellow arm.

"You speak English," the bewitching one said. He watched her mouth move, could taste those sumptuous lips as if she'd been the woman in his dream.

"Aye." He tore his gaze away, only to have it veer to her breasts, covered only in the richly colored hues of Ottoman textiles draping her body. A blue jacket threaded with silver hung past her hips over a knee-length chemise, covering lighter blue, flowing trousers. A red sash tied around her waist held a gleaming cutlass.

The image of her flesh burned in his mind as sure as if she'd laid herself bare.

"You are a subject of the Crown?" she demanded.

"Aye." Beneath the covers, the idiot between his legs pulsed against soft linen, stubbornly holding on to the dream. He was naked. And chained, he realized when he tried to reach for the glass. Heavy links clanked against the bed, and iron cuffs banded his wrists. "Is this necessary?" he rasped.

"I want to know who you are," she said. "Your name. Where you're from. Were you aboard a ship?"

"Let him drink again," the other one said, offering the glass once more. She eyed him curiously as he sipped. "There will be broth coming, and when you're ready, some bread to sop it with."

The news made his stomach rumble. If the prospect of such a meager meal piqued his hunger, no doubt he'd been adrift a very long time. Already the idea of food began to tame the desire that gripped him.

His name. His origin. Of course. His mind churned

as if racing through mud, reaching for a false identity. "Thomas Barclay." The lie fell roughly across his tongue. "I was aboard the man-o'-war *Henry's Cross*. Went down—" he swallowed, his mouth already dry again "—northwest of Gibraltar. Near Cadiz." That last, at least, was true.

"When?"

"April 10."

"Four days ago," she said to her companion. "The current must have pulled him through the strait."

"Where are we?" he managed.

"Anchored east of Gibraltar, awaiting conditions for passage west through the strait. You are aboard the brig *Possession*, and I am—"

"Corsair Kate." The irony of the situation snuck through the mental fog. Three years of quietly subverting orders to put an end to what the admirals considered her questionable seafaring activities, and now here he was. All that was left was to inform her that her ship was now the property of the Crown and declare victory.

Those topaz eyes narrowed, and those lips curved ever so slightly. "You may call me Captain Kinloch," she bit out in a voice both sultry and liquid. Fresh desire surged through him.

This lust was unacceptable. He needed to regain control, but he was so weak he couldn't lift his head—at least, not the one that knew better than to dally with the likes of Corsair Kate, who—since her father's death six months ago—was also countess of the Scottish seat of Dunscore.

The lady beside her laughed. "It's a grand thing to have earned a pseudonym of such notoriety, Katherine. I rather think you should sanction its use." This beautiful companion was most certainly the scandalous young widow Philomena, the countess of Pennington. And somewhere aboard would be the countess's young niece, Lady India, daughter of the Earl of Cantwell. The tale of their rescue had become legendary: taken captive by Barbary corsairs during an ill-fated voyage to see antiquities in Egypt, and subsequently liberated when the *Possession* in turn captured the marauding ship.

Captain Kinloch crossed her arms and pinned him with an assessing look. "The *Henry's Cross*," she said thoughtfully. "Captain James Warre's command?"

His own name on her lips caught him by surprise. "Aye."

Her lip curled. "You have indeed met with improved circumstances, then. What was your rank?"

Improved circumstances? "Midshipman."

"Midshipman! You're too old for that."

Hell. The real Thomas Barclay, of course, had been just the right age. "I was...demoted. Problems with the captain." It took all his strength to hold her gaze.

"With Captain Warre? What kind of problems?" she demanded.

"Any number of things." Devil take it, he could barely think.

"I want details."

Damn the woman! "It was...a misunderstanding," he rasped.

In a heartbeat she whipped out her cutlass and laid it against his neck, leaning over him. "What *kind* of misunderstanding?" Those topaz eyes blazed, and the ends of her hair pooled on his chest.

His body reacted as though she'd straddled his hips.

"Katherine," Lady Pennington warned.

"Insubordination," James managed through gritted teeth. He knew men who paid for this kind of treatment, but damnation! He wasn't one of them. "I've been known to have difficulty with authority." Another grain of truth.

"And Captain Warre tolerated you at his side? The good captain must have favored you." The blade's pressure increased by a fraction. "Understand me well, Mr. Barclay. You will display no insubordination aboard this ship if you wish to see its destination."

"You would not murder a British subject," he breathed. God, he needed more water.

Her lips curved into a terrifying yet seductive half smile. "A British subject who by all accounts perished at sea."

Their eyes locked in silent battle. But her blade lay cool against his neck, and her chains sat heavy on his wrists. "I assure you of my utmost respect," he said, and forced a half smile of his own. "Captain."

IF THOMAS BARCLAY'S utmost respect included a perpetual salute from his male organ, he would find this a very long voyage indeed. "This is unacceptable," Katherine said, storming into the great cabin, already guessing the next words that would fall from Philomena's lips.

"I daresay the situation suits *him* well enough." Amusement colored Phil's voice. "I don't suppose you noticed—"

"I noticed!"

"Noticed what?" William asked, looking up from the charts spread out on the table. Anne sat in a spear of sunlight on the floor, jiggling a length of twine for Mr. Bogles to attack.

"Never you mind," Katherine said. "It was nothing." The pressure she'd felt earlier in her gut had traveled to her head. She needed a nip of wine, morning hours be damned. She went to the cupboard and poured a tiny slosh. He hadn't been as close to death as they'd assumed.

She raised the glass to her lips and tasted a blend of guilt and ire. She'd been wrong about his condition, but absolutely right about his temperament.

Phil settled into one of the plump chairs at the table. "Oh, I wouldn't call it nothing. Suffice to say our guest seemed rather...*pleased*...to meet Katherine."

William arched an amused brow. "Oh?"

Phil's lips curved mischievously. "I would almost say...excited."

The brow arched higher. "Oh."

This was her reward for mercy. Thomas Barclay had no more been a midshipman on the *Henry's Cross* than she was a cabin boy on the *Possession*. More likely he was an officer, and a high-ranking one at that. The lie had been there on his face, although if he'd been stronger, he would certainly have been able to hide it.

His utmost respect! Even with her blade at his neck, he'd defied her with his eyes.

"Is he quite recovered, Mama?" Anne asked.

"Not quite, dearest," Katherine replied. "He's still very weak from lack of food and drink." Weak, yet everything about him screamed of power. Her blood still hummed with it. A man like that would have a difficult time with his superiors, indeed. Even a captain as ruthless as James Warre must have feared for his own authority.

This was exactly why they should have left Thomas Barclay in the water.

Worry lines furrowed Anne's innocent brow. "May I go in and hold his hand?" The ball of twine fell out of Anne's hands and rolled with the ship's sway, and Katherine quickly set her glass aside to retrieve it, this time ignoring that she shouldn't.

"My little angel of mercy," she said, putting the twine back into small hands while Anne, blind since a fever took her sight three years ago, stared in the area of Katherine's shoulder. "Not now. We know too little of him." Not ever, and they knew enough. Anne would never be allowed in the same room with that beast. Pressure throbbed in Katherine's temples as she smoothed Anne's dark hair from her small, upturned face.

"Yet he suffers, Mama."

Suffer was perhaps the wrong word. "He is comfortable for now. You mustn't worry." Anne would not pay the price for Katherine's misjudgment—not ever again. "Be a good girl and take Mr. Bogles into William's cabin for a while. You can play him a song on your bells. Are you hungry? I shall have cook send you some *kesra*." The warm, soft flatbread was Anne's favorite.

"Yes, please, Mama." Anne stood up with her ball of twine and found her way out of the great cabin with practiced pats on this chair, then that one and then on the side table, then the doorjamb as Mr. Bogles darted past her into the passageway. Katherine resisted the urge to help, and the pressure intensified.

Devil take it, there was no time for a headache. She had to figure out what to do about the insubordinate in her bed.

"Do I need to run him through?" William asked the moment Anne was gone.

Phil laughed. "Katherine nearly did a good enough job of that herself. I feared she would slit the man's throat."

"He will learn to respect his superiors," Katherine said, moving to inspect the charts herself, "or he will reap his reward accordingly."

"Well, you certainly had respect from *part* of him."

"Aha." William leaned back in his chair. "A man can't always control these things, you know. Poor fellow. Faced with the two most beautiful and powerful women on the sea, his humiliation was all but certain. Were you able to find out anything?"

Thomas Barclay would not compromise this voyage in any way. She would kill him first. "He survived a wreck of the *Henry's Cross* outside Cadiz," she said. "A midshipman, demoted by Captain Warre for insubordination—or so he says. It seems your friend dealt lightly with him."

"Growing up on neighboring estates hardly makes James Warre a friend. The *Henry's Cross* went down? God—unthinkable."

"It would seem Captain Warre's cannons aren't as effective against Mother Nature as they are against wood and sails." A memory snaked down her spine. When corsairs had captured the *Merry Sea* ten years ago and taken her captive, she'd thought Captain Warre would prove her savior. But Captain Warre hadn't cared about saving anyone. His cannons had sunk the *Merry Sea* and one of the Corsair xebecs, while the other xebec slipped away with Katherine bound and gagged in its hold. There was no doubt he would have sunk it, too, if he'd been able. "Pity it wasn't the good captain himself who washed up against our hull," she added. "I would have relished the opportunity to finally meet him."

"Ha!" Phil leaned forward. "To slit his throat, more likely, and then where would you be upon our return? Dangling from the end of a rope, that's where."

Upon their return, she would already be dangling— at the end of Nicholas Warre's bill of pains and penalties. The Lords might well strip Dunscore from her before she could set foot inside those ancient walls again. Cousin Holliswell would smugly accept the title and the estate, and she would have once again failed Anne.

That would not happen. Not if Katherine had any say in the matter.

"Poor sod's been through a hell of an ordeal," William said, standing. "Suppose I'll go talk with him. Probably beginning to wonder if he's the only man on board."

"Assure him we shall see to it that he suffers no more," Phil said.

William laughed. "Still waiting for you to ease *my* suffering, Philomena."

"The moment my desperation becomes that unbearable, I shall certainly let you know." There was nothing between them, but William found no end of amusement at suggesting there should be.

"I won't have you turning sympathetic with the prisoner," Katherine called after him.

"Course not." He grinned from the doorway. "I mean only to tighten the shackles—hold down the circulation and all that. Might solve the problem for next time."

Next time. Good God. "My bed, a haven for deviants," she muttered, and called after William, "See that you do!"

"Shackles aren't all *that* deviant," Phil commented after he left. "If you don't want him chained to *your* bed, I'll happily allow you to chain him to mine. Even in this sorry state, that man has more virility in his little finger than most men have in their—"

"Enough! As soon as we're through the strait, he won't be chained to anyone's bed."

Just then, India stormed into the cabin. "Millicent says she hopes we're captured by Barbary pirates in the strait!"

"Millicent is a fool," Phil snapped. "Does she think *they* would return her to Malta?"

"She's just angry." India plopped down at the table. The dark waistcoat she favored fell away from her hips, revealing the gleaming pistol that was her prized possession.

"She'll thank Katherine one day," Phil said.

Katherine doubted that—not after she'd resorted to trickery to force Millicent to return to Britain with them. Even had Millie succeeded in her plan to gain admission to Malta's School of Anatomy and Surgery by applying as a young man, eventually the truth would have been discovered. She would have been expelled from the school and left to fend for herself on Malta, and Katherine refused to be responsible for that.

"We shall sail on tonight's tide," Katherine said.

A smile spread across India's face. "Just imagine how infamous we shall be in London."

"Just imagine how *ruined* you'll be," Katherine said. The thought of returning to Britain turned the screws on every nerve. Society would accept neither her nor

Anne. All the reasons why she had shunned her homeland after escaping Algiers still existed—all but one.

When you are countess of Dunscore, Katie...

She slammed the door on Papa's old, familiar words.
Dunscore meant nothing to her now except a means to
Anne's security.

India gave a haughty shake of her head, managing
to look regal even in her ridiculous tricorne. "I am the
daughter of an earl, and still a virgin, and my chaperone
has been ever with me," she said. "I am not ruined—
just well traveled." Katherine looked at Phil. Life aboard
the *Possession* would not be regarded merely as travel.

"How is the castaway?" India asked.

"Not still a virgin, I daresay," Phil answered slyly.

"Blech!" India made a face and covered her ears.
"Auntie Phil, you're disgusting. I'll wager he's fifty if
he's a day!"

"Certainly not." Phil's blue eyes twinkled like the
sea on a clear day. "Do you think so, Katherine? Fifty?"

"I shall leave such judgments to your expertise."
Thirty-five or forty, more like. And judging from the
smile playing at Phil's lips, bound to be a distraction.
Of all the dangers she had considered, that one was easily addressed. As soon as Mr. Barclay recovered, she
would either lock him in the brig or put him with the
crew under the boatswain's supervision.

Either way, Mr. Barclay and his virility would be out
of sight and out of mind.

CHAPTER FOUR

"Boy-o, James." The sound of the door and a familiar voice jolted James out of near sleep. "Sounds like you could use another dunking—perhaps in the waters of the Arctic. Got the ladies all in a tither."

A blond, blue-eyed corsair stood grinning at him. James took in the turban, gold earrings and billowing trousers. "Good God. Jaxbury?" A slightly apprehensive relief eased through his weak body. "Haven't seen you since..." His mind raced to remember. "Good God. That time in Marseille." And before that, not since their youth.

"Ah, Marseille. Fine wine, finer women." Jaxbury dragged a small chair closer to the bed and straddled it backward. "Devilish good fun we had. Must have had—I barely remember it."

"Had no idea you'd taken up—" James dragged in a breath "—with Corsair Kate."

"Don't let her hear you call her that," Jaxbury laughed. "Things won't go easy. Of course, you haven't heard. Those of us of the masculine persuasion aboard the *Possession* aren't the stuff of wild stories. Nothing interesting about us at all."

James tried to raise his hand but couldn't fight the iron. "I don't suppose you've come to unlock these shackles."

Jaxbury shook his head. "Never hear the end of that one. Especially not after the show you put on for the ladies."

Bloody hell.

"Nothing to worry about," Jaxbury said. "Weakened state, some things hard to control—don't have to explain it to me, old boy. I'll sound you a caution, though—Phil's been two years without an *affaire d'amour,* and she's getting damned restless."

James looked at the sky-blue ceiling. "This is a bloody nightmare."

"Is it? I can think of any number of men who'd be contemplating how to turn the situation to their advantage. Won't work with Katherine, though, and of course, I'd have to kill you if you tried," Jaxbury said conversationally. "But Phil—damn me if you wouldn't be doing us all a favor."

"Are you and Captain Kinloch—"

"Good God, no. Like a sister to me."

A sister. Only a corpse or a blood relative could look at Captain Kinloch and feel that way. His disbelief must have been evident, because Jaxbury laughed. "You'd feel the same if you'd been the one to deliver her child." Her *child!* Jaxbury made a face. "Bloody disgusting! At the same time, a damned miracle. Never look at her the same. May as well be the Virgin Mary."

"So you haven't told her my identity." But Jaxbury's other revelation still had him reeling. Captain Kinloch had a child. Whose child?

"Wouldn't want your blood on my hands. I'll give you fair warning, she holds no affection for you." And James knew why. Even ten years later, the sight of those Corsair xebecs butted up against that British merchant ship was as fresh as if it had happened yesterday. He'd let loose with everything in his power to save it, knowing full well what awaited those on board if they were captured. If he'd succeeded, he might have saved Katherine Kinloch, as well.

"So sorry about the *Henry's Cross*," Jaxbury said solemnly. "Tragic."

A strangling grief ripped his chest. Memories of the recent wreck swarmed like bees, and for a moment he relived the terror—giant, nighttime waves, splintering wood, the invincible *Henry's Cross* pulled under like a bit of flotsam. Had any of his men survived? "We were headed back to Britain," he managed. And it would have been his last voyage. The moment his feet touched land, he'd planned to go directly to the Admiralty to tender his resignation.

"You're in luck, then, on that count," Jaxbury said. "We, too, sail for Britain."

"Britain!" He said the word with too much force and ended up in a fit of coughing.

Jaxbury filled the mug and held it for him. A simple necklace of mismatched beads on braided twine peeked out from beneath his tunic. "Aye. The captain has business to attend to in Scotland. No doubt you're aware of her change in status."

James managed a drink of water and nodded once. "Nothing to drive a person home—" he coughed again and inhaled deeply "—like a title." It hadn't worked for him, but it should have.

Jaxbury leaned forward, his eyes glinting with a seriousness James would never have believed his carefree childhood friend capable of. "Do not presume to understand her."

"I wouldn't dare." God, they could not reach Britain quickly enough. Perhaps he would not spend even a single night in London. Perhaps he would go directly to Croston Hall. The sooner he could shut himself away in the library with every bottle of cognac in Croston's reserve, the sooner he could forget how much he'd once loved the sea, and that sometime in the past year—two years? three?—life had seemed to turn gray.

Perhaps he'd stay foxed for a month.

"Katherine is first and foremost a captain," Jaxbury went on, "and until we reach London you'd best not forget it."

"Not sure how I could." He imagined a voyage spent in chains and briefly considered revealing his identity to Captain Kinloch just to exercise its leverage. But his identity was the only weapon he had, and it would be a shame to play that card too soon.

"And make no mistake—she's a damned fine one. Taught her everything I know, but some things cannot be taught, as you well know. She's got a sixth sense for the sea, and it carries her on its bosom like a babe on a teat."

The image was entirely unhelpful. "Then I shall consider myself in the most competent of hands."

Jaxbury leaned back, smiling once more. "Precisely."

HOURS LATER, JAMES opened his eyes to a pitch-black cabin and realized two things: the ship was being tossed by a squall, and someone was crying. Crying and squeezing his hand.

"Who's there?" he rasped into the darkness.

There was a sob and a sniffle. "It's Anne," came a tiny, muffled voice from a small figure hunched against the side of the bed. Wood creaked and groaned with the ship's heave and fall. The cabin echoed with the crash of waves against the hull. "I c-can't find Mr. B-Bogles!" she sobbed. "The big waves came, and I was s-scared, so I went into William's cabin, and I thought he c-came with me, but then…but then…" Despair wracked her little body and stole her words. The ship heaved. Crashed.

This had to be the child whose birth had raised Lady Katherine to saintly heights in William's eyes. And it was a good guess this Mr. Bogles walked on four legs, not two.

"Where is your mother?"

"On deck with the others," Anne said in a trembling voice. "Usually somebody stays with me when the big waves come, but Mama said they need all hands going through the strait!"

The strait—in a squall, at night? Bloody hell, he'd survived one wreck only to perish in another. The ship crashed harder than the last time, and Captain Kinloch's daughter pressed her face into the bed.

"I don't like it when the big waves come," she said into the linens. Her hand tightened around his and he felt it in his chest. He reached for her with his other hand, but the yank of the chain stopped him. "Please help me find him," came her tiny voice.

"Can't, little one. The chains." And even if he were free, it was doubtful he could walk.

"I will unlock them!" she cried. "And then you will find my kitty!"

Unlock— Good God. "Anne, your mother—" Would likely cut off his balls.

"Please," she begged pitifully. "Please, I know you aren't well, but if I unlock them, will you please find him?" Heave. Crash. A wet face pressed into the back of his hand.

His balls for a cat. An excellent exchange. "I shall try," he breathed, holding out hope that she didn't know where the keys were kept. But her shadowy figure moved away. The ship heaved and she stumbled, crossing to the other side of the cabin. In the faint light from the windows he saw her feeling her way along the dressing table. Wood slid against wood—a drawer. And then the heavenly clang of keys.

Never had freedom rung with such impending doom.

She returned, still sniffling. Her hands felt for his arm, slid up to his wrist. Her fingers circled the shackle, feeling for the keyhole, then let him go. He heard her sorting through the keys. Sniffling. She was so small the bed only came up to her belly.

Heave. Crash. She grabbed for him, nearly losing her balance. Fumbled with the keys. Tested them with a small child's clumsiness. And then—

Click. The shackle popped open. "I did it!" she cried. "Please hurry!"

He loosed the key and unlocked the other shackle. The moment both arms were free he struggled to sit up, and blood rushed from his head. He leaned forward with his head in his hands. He felt her touching him, patting his arm and shoulder.

"Oh, no—you're not well at all, are you?" Desperation returned to her voice.

"Sat up…too quickly," he managed. Carefully he swung his legs to the side. The tunic and trousers they had put on him were light and loose, and his feet were bare.

"I'm terribly sorry. I know I shouldn't bother you—

Mama says I'm not supposed to—but...but..." The tears started again.

James stood, nearly toppling with the movement of the ship. "Tell me where to look."

"You'll need a lantern."

Of course. A lantern. He'd seen one hanging on the wall and in the darkness he managed to find and light it. His tiny liberator, he now saw, was a miniature sultana. Her dark hair hung in a braid down her back, and tiny jewels flashed against her olive skin at her ears. Fabric of a rich blue draped her from neck to toe. She had the darkest eyes, and they fixed strangely on his chest while her tear-streaked face trembled.

"I'm afraid he might have gone into the hold," she said pitifully.

The hold. Bloody hell, this was a fool's errand. The ship continued to pitch, yet he managed to lurch out the door and into the passageway. "Which way?"

"Left!" she cried.

He didn't know this ship, but he'd known a great many, and he found the stairs quickly. He started down and she followed him, clinging to the railing.

"Mr. Bogles!" she cried. Her voice trembled. "Mama says I'm never to go in the hold."

Excellent. He may as well remove his balls now and save Captain Kinloch the trouble. He reached the floor and glanced around. It was an upper hold, full of everything from casks of wine to bolts of textiles. How much legally gained was anyone's guess.

"Mr. Bogles!" Anne called again, reaching the bottom of the stairs.

"Stay here," he ordered. James hung on to a stack

of crates held in place by a timber frame and stumbled farther into the hold, shining the light this way and that.

"Wait," Anne cried. "I have some dried fish. He loves it more than anything!"

A bribe ought to increase his chances, which as things stood, were zero. Light-headed, he hung the lantern from a hook on an overhead beam and went back. The ship heaved and crashed and some cargo on the starboard side shifted noisily as he struggled to find his usually reliable sea legs.

Anne was already holding out the dried fish when he reached her, but something wasn't right. She faced to the side without looking at him. "He'll come for this," she said, as though speaking to an invisible third person. "I know he will."

"I'll give it...a try," he said, out of breath. Immediately she turned toward him with her arm still outstretched and her eyes fixed on his belly. He paused. "Anne?"

"Yes?"

He held out his hand. She didn't seem to see it, and a hole opened up in his gut. "Anne," he said sharply. "Can you see?" There wasn't time for niceties.

"I hear him!" Her face lit up suddenly and she pointed past him. "Mr. Bogles! Oh, do hurry!"

Blind. Anne was *blind*.

Hell and damnation, he'd led a blind child into the hold. Damn Jaxbury for not saying something. He lurched forward and grabbed her arm. "We're going above." Mr. Bogles could fend for himself.

"No!" Anne screamed and struggled. "We can't leave him!"

"You can't be down here."

"Please. *Please!*"

Her desperation cut him to the bone. She struggled, and he hadn't the strength to fight her. He wrapped her hands around the stair rail. "Wait here. *Do not move.*"

"I won't. I promise!"

"Give me the fish." He took it from her fingers.

"I hear him again! Please hurry!"

James didn't hear a bloody thing, but he went in the direction she pointed. He grabbed the lantern from the hook and finally heard a faint meow from among the cargo. A rat scurried away. Whatever Mr. Bogles was up to down here, he was not doing his job.

"Mr. Bogles!" Anne cried.

Meow, came an answer from the direction of a pile of large rope coils that had slid sideways with the waves. James willed himself forward, holding up the lantern. *Meow!* came another complaint from beneath the pile. Through a gap he saw two glowing eyes and part of a white, whiskered face.

The ship heaved and rolled. Somehow he managed to hang the lantern and reach for a coil. His arms rebelled, buckling like wet straw, but he tried again. He shifted one coil this time, then another. The rough floor scraped his soles as he sought purchase with his bare feet. His legs burned, threatening to give out.

"Do you have him?" Anne called from much closer than the stairwell. A glance over his shoulder showed her making her way through the cargo.

"Anne, stop!" He barely had the strength to make himself heard. "Go back!" He stretched forward, half lying across the pile now, and shoved at another coil. More coils towered above him. With all of his strength he propped up the coil that trapped the cat, but Mr. Bogles cowered somewhere in the recesses. Blast it all, he'd dropped the dried fish.

"Come out, damn you," he said through gritted teeth.

The ship heaved.

"Anne!" Captain Kinloch's voice shot through the hold.

The ship crashed. James lost his grip on the rope and a white flash shot past his shoulder.

"Mr. Bogles!" came Anne's joyous cry.

James fell forward, and the coils he'd moved tumbled on top of him. He grunted in pain, crumpling beneath their weight, and his hand closed around something leathery. The dried fish.

"Anne! What are you doing down here?"

James said goodbye to his balls and let his head fall.

DRENCHED FROM THE rain and waves above, Katherine flew down the stairs with her eyes fixed on Anne and swept her into a fierce hug, ignoring Mr. Bogles wiggling between them. "Anne Kinloch, I told you *never* to come into the hold!" She ran her hands over Anne's face, hair, shoulders. No injury. Already she could imagine half a dozen ways she would kill Thomas Barclay when she found him.

Farther into the hold, the lantern from her cabin swung wildly from an overhead beam. Bloody cur— *this* was her reward for caving to pity and hauling him aboard. "Anne, quickly," she said, rising. "Upstairs."

"But the man, Mama— I think I heard him fall!"

"Shh…we shall find him and he won't hurt you again. I promise you that." By God, she would kill him slowly and feed him in pieces to the fish.

"Mama, you mustn't be cross!" Anne shook her head

frantically. "It was my fault. I couldn't find Mr. Bogles, and I begged him! I know I shouldn't have unlocked him, but—"

"*Unlocked* him?"

"I'm sorry, Mama. There was no one to help." She tried to turn out of Katherine's grasp. "Oh, why don't I hear him? He was just here!"

At precisely that moment, Katherine spotted a pair of bare feet sticking out from among the cargo.

Anne's lip trembled. "I know I shouldn't have taken the keys from your drawer. I was so scared."

Katherine hugged her tightly. "I'm sorry, sweetling. I'm so sorry." She *never* left Anne alone in high seas. Never. But they'd needed all hands on deck, and she'd promised herself it would just be this once, and she would come down to check…but she should have come sooner. She should never have left Anne in the first place. Wicked, wicked man, taking advantage of a little girl's fear.

"Do you see him, Mama?" A tear tumbled down Anne's cheek.

Katherine stared at his feet. "Shh…I will find him. Quickly, now, upstairs to safety. Give Mr. Bogles to me." Sweet Anne was too innocent to know a man in Mr. Barclay's condition did not rouse himself for the sake of a cat. Her jaw tightened. With any luck fate had already punished his attempt at insurrection, and she would no longer have to bother with him.

With Anne and Mr. Bogles safely shut inside Philomena's cabin, Katherine hurried back to the hold. The ship heaved and rolled as she made her way quickly through the cargo and there he was, half-buried beneath a fallen pile of rope coils. If he was alive, she would shackle him more securely this time. And hide the keys more quietly.

She planted a boot on the pile and wrested the coils off him. "Mr. Barclay," she called sharply. Perhaps he'd hoped to find munitions here in the hold. Distract the crew with his disappearance and gain the upper hand by threatening Anne's life.

It would not have worked.

He lay sprawled on the coils with William's tunic stretched a bit tightly across his shoulders. His tousled black hair with its silver streaks fell across his cheek and over his eyes. *"Mr. Barclay."* She bent to check his pulse.

At her touch, he groaned and tried to rise. "Bloody hell," he said, collapsing once again into the ropes. At least she would not have to explain his death to Anne.

"Get up! You've been foiled, and I haven't the time to play nursemaid." They needed her on deck. Punishing his foolishness would have to wait.

"For God's sake, cut 'em off quickly," he mumbled into his sleeve. He was delirious again, and little wonder. His eyes opened slightly. "Anne?" he rasped.

"Is upstairs and none of your concern. Now get to your feet— I want this lantern out of the hold before it shatters and sets my ship ablaze." She grabbed hold of his arm and pulled. The ship rolled and he lurched to his feet, nearly toppling over. He was taller than he'd seemed. Broader. She braced herself against the water casks with his weight crushing her against them as the ship's pitch threatened to throw them both to the floor. His breath labored near her ear and one large hand curled around the edge of a cask above her.

"Foolish man. You haven't the strength to carry out this kind of plan."

"Can't insult a man—" he exhaled sharply when he finally found his feet "—with the truth." He backed away from her and steadied himself against the casks. "Little bugger got free, then." His breath came hard, as though it took all his strength to stand. "Didn't—" he inhaled, exhaled "—take his prize, though." He held out his other hand.

He held a strip of Mr. Bogles's dried fish.

It wasn't possible. In his condition, merely leaving her cabin would have been a feat. He would not have done this for a cat.

She didn't want to consider that he might have done it for Anne.

She tried to slip the dried fish into her pocket, but her clothes were soaked so she tossed it aside. His eyes met hers, then dropped. Darkened. Shot away as he dragged in another breath.

She glanced down. Her sea-drenched clothes clung like a second skin to her breasts, and her nipples jutted hard through the wet fabric. Good God—even a brush with death wasn't enough to cool this man's lust. She allowed her lips to curve. "There's no time for your lechery now, Mr. Barclay. You'll have to control yourself. Can you walk?" He tried a step, but the ship's heave and roll threw him off balance immediately. She caught him beneath the arm and tried to help.

"I've got it," he said sharply, trying to steady himself as the lantern swung noisily from its hook above them. "Only let me hold...the casks."

She let go. "Did you think you could hide from us here and gain some advantage?"

He worked his way along, out of breath and fighting to stay on his feet. "My plan to lure you into the hold… and ravish you…has gone disappointingly awry."

"Insolent bastard." Her clammy skin flushed unaccountably hot. "It's no wonder you had trouble with Captain Warre."

He grunted. "Stodgy old cuss…" They made it to the last of the casks, and he lurched toward the stairs. "Never did approve—" he dragged in a breath "—of ravishing." His hands curled around the railing and he rested there, ashen-faced.

"Can you climb the stairs alone?"

His eyes swept their length, and he gave a nod.

"Then above and to bed," she ordered in a tone she might have used with Anne. The man had lost his mind as well as his strength.

He pulled himself up the first step and glanced at her. "A tempting offer…Captain."

A tempting— "Above!"

This was no demoted midshipman. He was an officer, or she'd swallow her cutlass. As soon as they were safely through the strait, she would instruct William to lock Mr. Barclay in the cabin André had occupied. And then she would force the truth from him.

CHAPTER FIVE

THE TRUTH HAD to wait for two days while the lecherous Mr. Barclay, now occupying his new quarters, slept. Millicent fed him broth four times a day and ruthlessly shooed everyone else away.

They were safely through the strait with the storm long behind them, but the story of Mr. Barclay's heroics would not die. Anne insisted on retelling it to everyone. Multiple times.

"Mama, may we go see him now? Please? Millicent says he's awake." Anne tugged on her sleeve. "Please, Mama. He's better now."

Apparently that was supposed to be good news. "In a moment, dearest." Katherine dipped her quill, started to scratch another coordinate in her massive logbook, but veered away at the last moment and added another name to the scrap of paper that held the short list of people in Britain who might be able to help her. Lord De Lille. Hadn't he been one of Papa's friends?

Her father's voice echoed in her mind: *Damn me, Katie, there's not a soul in all of England or Scotland that can outwager De Lille.*

She rubbed her forehead, trying to remember names and relationships from more than a decade ago. But Papa had had so many friends. The only one she truly remembered was his best friend, Lord Deal, and according to the solicitor's letter, he was already working to fight the bill that threatened her inheritance.

Her fingers tightened around the quill. What if Mr. Allen's letter hadn't found her? The bill was unlikely to pass, he'd written. That it had been read once in the Lords meant little—that the second reading had been put off six months was far more telling.

"Mama, *please*. What if he goes back to sleep?"

Then the inevitable would be delayed a few pleasant hours longer. Perhaps Mr. Barclay's actions had been—in the most attenuated sort of way—laudable. And as galling as it was, she could no longer deny that his folly in the hold had been for Anne's sake. Midshipman or officer, he would have known a one-man insurrection would fail.

Katherine would have been happy to ignore his sacrifice for Mr. Bogles. But it was not to be.

Anne's dusky lips pursed a little with impatience, and small, dark brows dove with frustration. Sometimes she looked so much like Mejdan's mother it was hard to know whether to laugh or cry.

"Very well," Katherine said, finally setting down her quill. "Come along." With all the enthusiasm of a convict on his way to the gallows, she led Anne into the passageway.

"I can give him the scroll, right?" Anne whispered outside the door to André's old cabin.

"Yes, sweetling."

"But you'll tell him."

"I will tell him." Many things, but most of them not until Anne left. Mr. Barclay may have yet been unwell—she knocked once and turned the key—but she intended to have the answers to her questions. "Mr. Barclay—"

The bed was empty. There was a splash, and her attention shot to the bureau. He leaned over the basin with his hair slicked back and water dripping off his face, wearing only a pair of William's trousers.

"Mama, ow!" Anne tugged at her hand.

Katherine eased her grip. "Perhaps we should—"

"Mr. Barclay," Anne called into the cabin, "we've come to pay you a special visit."

Return later. "Anne…"

He reached for a towel and—devil take it—caught Katherine watching him in the looking glass. One of his brows edged upward. "An honor indeed," he said. His gaze shifted to Anne. "I see you're not letting that errant cat of yours go far, Miss Anne," he said. Katherine felt a push against her leg and realized Mr. Bogles had followed them in. Mr. Barclay ran the linen over his face, neck, shoulders. Muscles rippled beneath his skin with every movement.

"He's better now that the big waves have stopped," Anne told him.

"I'd say that describes every one of us."

Anne gaped. "You don't like the big waves, either?"

"Nobody does." He reached for a shirt—one of William's tunics, dark blue with long sleeves—and pulled it on as he came toward them, a head taller than Katherine and fully lucid.

Katherine silently exhaled. "You seem much improved," she observed.

"A short-lived burst, I fear."

Anne tugged impatiently on Katherine's hand. "Mama, may we tell him now? Please?"

Mr. Barclay glanced down, raising a brow.

"Yes," Katherine said. "Go ahead." The sooner she swallowed these bitters, the better.

Anne let go of her hand and reached for Mr. Barclay, patting his leg as she held out the scroll. "This is for you."

Comprehension dawned in those damnable eyes as he took the scroll, and amusement tugged at the corner of that hard mouth. "Thank you."

Devil take Millicent and her restorative broth.

"*Now,* Mama," Anne said.

At least he could be in no doubt as to whose idea this had been. "Thomas Barclay," Katherine began solemnly. "As captain of the ship *Possession* I hereby commend you for your actions of bravery and sacrifice—" she absolutely refused to look at him "—on behalf of a most valued member of our crew, being that you did, during high seas, risk your life to save one Mr. Bogles, in service to Anne and everyone aboard this ship. For this, you have earned the highest level of respect and appreciation aboard this vessel."

Anne could no longer contain her excitement. "It's a commendation!" she cried.

"You do me too much honor," Mr. Barclay said. It was an understatement of epic proportions.

"Did you look at the scroll?" Anne asked, with an achingly huge smile.

He untied the ribbon and glanced over the words Anne had insisted Katherine pen last night. "I will treasure it always," he said, touching Anne's cheek. "Thank you for recommending me for what I am convinced is a very coveted award."

The temptation to soften her opinion of him wormed

its way into Katherine's mind, but she stopped it quickly. After all, two things remained unchanged: he was lying to her about his rank, so he'd served—no doubt very closely—under Captain Warre; and he remained every bit as virile as Phil had first claimed. The first she could simply force him to disclose. The second could not be remedied.

"Come now, dearest." Katherine steered Anne toward the door. "Back to the great cabin while I speak with Mr. Barclay."

"You mustn't commend him any more without me, Mama. I want to hear."

"There will be no further commendation. I promise."

Moments later Anne was settled at the captain's table with her box of beads, and Katherine returned to Mr. Barclay's cabin. "Now," she said, shutting the door. "You will tell me your actual rank aboard the *Henry's Cross,* and this time you will tell the truth."

He opened his mouth to speak but faltered, turning pale. "Do you mind if I sit? I'm feeling a bit—" He reached for the bed and sat down without waiting for her answer. He leaned forward and braced his head in his hands. "Told you it would be short-lived."

She much preferred him weak and seated. "Should I send for Millicent?"

"God, no. She'll only force me to take more broth."

Katherine almost smiled. "Your true rank, then, Mr. Barclay."

"What makes you so certain I'm not a midshipman?" he said to the floor. Solid forearms supported large hands with strong fingers that disappeared into damp, dark waves lightly salted with silver. Whatever his true rank, he clearly had the strength to do any job a ship required.

"Answer the question. I've had enough nonsense for one day."

"Nonsense?" He looked up. "Please, Captain—I've only just received my first commendation aboard this vessel, and already you're making me doubt its sincerity."

"You need not doubt my sincerity when I tell you that you will regret withholding the truth."

"I don't doubt *that* in the least. And if I refuse, what will it be? The lash? The dreaded cat? Perhaps there's a medieval rack hidden away in some lower hold."

"You are not lying about having been under Captain Warre's command," she replied. "That much is evident. To date I have never found a need to resort to physical punishment aboard this ship—although there could always be a first time, I suppose." She propped one knee on the bedside chair, where his borrowed waistcoat hung neatly across the back. "My crew and I enjoyed the most delicious pie at yesterday's dinner," she said conversationally. "Succulent gravy, tender beef and vegetables, topped by the lightest, flakiest crust. You know the kind, I'm sure? Melts on the tongue? Such a wonder what can be done with dried beef." His eyes narrowed, and she knew she'd hit her mark. "What a shame that Millicent says you're to have broth for at least another week—no, I take that back. She did say you could have a few bits of meat in it, I think, so under the strictest definition I suppose that isn't *broth*. And of course, I faithfully defer to Millicent in all things medical." She smiled. "Except when I don't."

"The depth of your ruthlessness, Captain Kinloch, has been wildly understated."

"I'll not deny it." She held his gaze while he weighed his options. His penetrating stare teased a nerve in her belly.

"Very well," he finally said. "I was a lieutenant. The captain's third in command."

A flutter of something—foreboding, probably—ran across her skin. A lieutenant. Of course. No wonder he hadn't wanted to reveal his identity. "That carries a good deal of responsibility," she observed. To Captain Warre especially.

"It does."

"Tell me about your relationship with Captain Warre."

He considered that. "I'm not sure we had a 'relationship,' per se."

"Don't be obtuse," she said irritably. "You must have worked very closely with him."

"I suppose you could say that."

"Did you consider him a friend?"

"I wouldn't use that word exactly, no."

"You disliked him, then."

"At times."

"Disobeyed him?"

"Never."

"You agreed with his decisions?"

"I'll admit to having reservations about a great many of them, but generally, yes."

Of course he had. "You are as ruthless as he was, then." *Lieutenant* Barclay looked ruthless. And hard, and uncompromising, and shrewd. The half-delirious unfortunate they had pulled from the water was gone.

"I suppose we shared certain traits, but I'm not sure ruthlessness is one of them. Resolute, perhaps."

She made a noise. "If you call Captain Warre's tactics 'resolute' then you most certainly do share his penchant for ruthlessness. The captain's reputation for being unmerciful at the helm is well-known."

"I should hope so, given that his job was to win battles—not lose them." He rose to his feet and went to the bureau for water. "I have the distinct impression you don't care for Captain Warre," he said, watching her in the looking glass. "Do you know him well?"

"I know enough."

He drank deeply and set down the mug. "Have you met him?"

"You could say I've had an encounter with him."

One of his dark brows ticked upward.

"A *maritime* encounter," she said sharply.

"Naturally." He came toward her, reached past her for his waistcoat. His arm touched her knee.

She put her foot on the floor. "You must have been a terrible thorn in Captain Warre's side."

"Eternally."

That made her smile. Just as quickly, desire began to smolder in his eyes. He did not back away as he shrugged into the waistcoat. Her smile faded, and that renegade nerve quickened in her belly again. She glanced brazenly at the front of his borrowed trousers but found no inappropriate salute to her authority.

"As you can see, Captain," he drawled, "along with my renewed strength has come a measure of control." His eyes wandered over her, and she felt them like hands.

She looked him in the eye and allowed the corners

of her lips to curve upward. "I'm relieved to hear it. I would hate for you to spend the entire voyage in a state of torment."

"Indeed," he said dryly. "It's been clear from the beginning that my comfort is your utmost concern."

"Your lack of gratitude makes me wonder if I should have left the shackles on, after all. And let me be clear on one point—certain kinds of comfort are not available aboard this ship."

"I will endeavor to contain my disappointment." Boredom dripped from his tongue, but his eyes burned hot. He may have succeeded in controlling his anatomy, but in his thoughts he was doing with her exactly as he pleased.

She laughed derisively to suppress a shiver. "You will contain much more than that, or you will meet the end of my cutlass." She went to the door. "I shall send up some pie."

"Wait." The command shot across the cabin—not a request, but a demand.

She spun on her heel. "Do *not* speak to me in that tone, Lieutenant Barclay." She was across the room in a heartbeat, face-to-face with him. "You are no lieutenant here, and *I* am your captain now."

"If I am your prisoner, then you are my gaoler," he countered. "Not my captain. I only meant to ask whether I may expect to spend the entire voyage locked away."

"Perhaps you will, and for good reason," she said, even though she'd already decided there would be little point to it. "For one thing, since we took you aboard my ship, you have demonstrated a difficulty in controlling your baser instincts."

He gave a laugh.

"Moreover, you've shown yourself to be a liar. But most damning of all, far from being the insubordinate you claimed, it would seem that you and Captain Warre were practically of one mind. You are therefore complicit with him, and that alone makes me wish I *did* have a rack in the lower hold."

"It sounds as if I should be thankful that you at least removed the shackles." He raised his wrist, rubbing it. The motion brought his hands a hairsbreadth from her breasts, a closeness she wished she hadn't noticed.

"There was *some* sincerity in that commendation."

His calculating gaze narrowed. "What if I told you that Captain Warre was the soddingest bastard I ever set eyes on, and that if he were here right now I would heartily recommend that you do your worst?"

Katherine laughed and took the opportunity to move away. "I would say you're a very smart man indeed, Mr. Barclay, with high marks in self-preservation." He reeked of danger, but at least he was entertaining.

"Then consider it my unswerving opinion, and leave the door unlocked when you go."

"I will give it my most thoughtful consideration. Good day, Lieutenant Barclay." She let herself into the passageway, closed the door and paused, recovering from the effects of his smile. He would never succeed in overthrowing her command even should he attempt it. And he wasn't a threat to Anne. No, the danger he presented was more in the area of Phil's expertise.

Soddingest bastard, indeed.

She walked away without bolting the latch.

CHAPTER SIX

"IT'S THE MOST reckless thing you've ever done," Phil declared the next evening as they lounged in the great cabin. "He left his door propped open all morning, and the sight of him lying abed was a terrible torment." The gleam in her eyes made it clear she hoped to bait Katherine into acknowledging Lieutenant Barclay's appeal. It wouldn't work.

"It's astonishing that your duties took you past his cabin so frequently," Katherine said, swirling the wine in her glass. *She,* of course, had only walked by in order to reassure herself that she had not made a mistake allowing Anne to finally go in and play nursemaid.

"Indeed," William laughed. "Astonishing." He leaned across the table toward Phil. "My door is always open, too, you know."

"Perhaps Lieutenant Barclay needs a lock on the *inside,*" Katherine suggested.

"Auntie Phil, you're not *listening,*" India complained, propping her feet on the table as she popped a date in her mouth.

"I *am* listening, dearest. To *you,* anyhow." Phil poured herself more wine and shot a look at William. "But what you're saying is so far-fetched that my mind naturally drifted to more realistic possibilities."

India made a noise. "I have no intention of sitting

idly by doing needlework and learning sonatas on the pianoforte after our return."

"I daresay you'll have little choice in the matter," Philomena scoffed. "Your father will lock you away the moment you arrive."

"If he tries," India said, pointing at Phil with a date, "I shall simply move in with you."

"Ha! I've quite had my fill of looking after you."

"Then I shall live with Katherine."

"Living with a pariah would do little for your marriage prospects," Katherine said, reaching for the basket of *kesra* and tearing off a piece of the bread even though she was already full.

Phil rolled her eyes. "I don't understand why you persist in this notion that we shall be outcasts. Mysterious, certainly. Even scandalous, but that rarely does any real damage. I have yet to discover what a widowed countess cannot do and still receive more invitations than she can reasonably consider, and as for you—well, I daresay the same will hold true for a countess in her own right. Even a Scottish one. They will expect you to eat dainties and applaud their daughters' mediocre musical accomplishments at more gatherings than you will be able to count."

William shuddered. "Hate those gatherings. Nothing to do a fellow in like a marriage-minded girl in command of a pianoforte."

"I don't need marriage prospects," India said, "because I have no intention of marrying."

Phil laughed. "You'll be fortunate if your father hasn't already paid some poor young man an offensively large amount to secure an arrangement."

Katherine rose to get another bottle of wine and

raised a brow at India, who sprawled in her chair like a man. "Would have to, given the prize."

"You're both insufferable!" India huffed, and bit into another date.

William reached for a piece of fruit. "I resent being left out of that. Katherine, I fancy an apple. Slice it for me?" The apple sailed in her direction and she whipped out her cutlass, slicing it in midair. The halves fell to the table with a satisfying thud.

"You're insufferable, too, William," India said. "You all are." She shook her head defiantly. "If Father has arranged something, I shall run away," she warned. She thought for a moment. "Or perhaps I could be a kept woman."

"I wouldn't advise it," came Lieutenant Barclay's voice from the doorway. Katherine's attention snapped toward him as if he'd fired a pistol. "All the drawbacks of marriage with none of its benefits." A smile played at the corner of his mouth. "Well, very few."

India turned bright red, and Phil laughed. "Well put! Just look at you, Lieutenant, up and about. You appear quite recovered. Do you not agree, Captain?"

Katherine watched his gaze sweep across the giant Italian table she'd fallen in love with in Venice, the Spanish walnut cabinet that kept her wine and glasses safe from the waves, the intricately inlaid Turkish chest where she kept her logbooks. It came to rest on the painting of three veiled women tending children in a Moroccan courtyard. Discomfort edged through her, as though he could see her own memories in that painting.

"Improved, if not recovered," she said. "The power of broth should never be underestimated."

"I confess to having a thirst for something of a

slightly different nature." He glanced around the table. "Perhaps, since your surgeon isn't here..."

"Lucky thing!" William said cheerfully, sliding a chair out with his boot. "Wine? Rum? Cognac?"

Lieutenant Barclay eased into a chair next to Philomena. "Undoubtedly the cognac."

Katherine gave the apple halves to William and met Lieutenant Barclay's eyes across the table. The wine that already warmed her blood rose a degree. Indeed, Millicent would have objected strongly if she hadn't been holed away in her cabin, studying her anatomy text.

"An impressive display, Captain," Lieutenant Barclay said with a nod toward the fruit.

"Katherine's a virtuoso with the cutlass," India informed him. "She's done oranges, pears, figs, plums—"

"Enough, India," Katherine said.

"—and even grapes."

Humor flickered in Lieutenant Barclay's green eyes. "Point taken."

India frowned. "Point?"

"The ladies were just discussing their futures," William cut in, lips twitching. "Young India plans to become a courtesan, as you just heard—"

"I said no such thing!"

"—while Phil expects to embrace the freedom of an eccentric widow, and our good captain anticipates complete social ostracism."

"Does she." Lieutenant Barclay sipped his cognac and gave her a look that was ten times as intoxicating as any liquor. "I have a suspicion you'll be more sought after than you expect, Captain."

"Oh, I expect to be highly sought after—by lechers with insulting propositions." Or alluring lieutenants with dangerous eyes. "But as for the rest of society, your esteemed captain must not have told you of the bill his brother Nicholas, Lord Taggart, has introduced in the Lords."

"Pillock!" India spat. "What business has he, trying to strip you of your title? He just can't stand that you should accede to an earldom when he has merely been granted a barony."

"Except that he, too, is an earl," Phil pointed out, "if James Warre perished on the *Henry's Cross.*" Her eyes shifted with delight between Katherine and Lieutenant Barclay. Katherine wanted to reach across the table and yank her hair.

The lieutenant frowned. "A bill of pains and penalties?"

"Precisely," Katherine said, and curved her lips to hide her fear. "I stand to lose both my title and my estate."

"But not your liberty?"

"A telling sign that they lack evidence of any 'high crimes and misdemeanors,' would you not agree?"

He considered that with a thoughtful lift of his brows. Katherine swirled the dark red liquid in her glass. "Captain Warre never spoke of his brother, Lieutenant?"

He reached for the plate of dates India had been slowly diminishing. "He was never one to share personal information with subordinates."

"Naturally." She watched him sink his teeth into the date. They were white teeth, perfectly straight. "That would risk the kind of friendly bonds that a sodding bastard such as Captain Warre would never tolerate."

"Such language, Captain," William said, crunching into his second apple half.

She smiled. "The lieutenant's words, not mine."

"I propose a toast," India declared, raising her glass. "To Nicholas Warre's eternal ruin!"

"Hear, hear," Katherine agreed. But Lieutenant Barclay, whether out of fear for his soul or respect for his dead captain's family, polished off the rest of his date without joining the toast.

JAMES WAS STILL pondering that toast to his brother's eternal ruin three days later when he finally felt well enough to venture on deck. God only knew what Nick was up to with this bill Captain Kinloch spoke of. She'd told him the Lords had put off the second reading, which meant the bill was as good as dead. James rubbed his hand over his unshaven jaw and tried to ignore the voice telling him that if it wasn't, he would need to do something about it once they arrived. After all, he owed the woman his life. But when his little brother got his teeth into something, he did not let go easily.

The weather had turned balmy as they sailed north along the coast of Spain. The *Possession* was an average brig—two-masted, square-rigged. But making do with a crew of ten, counting Lady India, Lady Pennington and the captain herself, when she would have done better with at least eighteen. The ship had sixteen guns that could prove deadly to a larger, less agile foe. Not that he was aware of the *Possession* taking deadly action against any kind of foe except in circumstances where James himself would have done the same.

If the Admirals wanted Captain Kinloch's shipping activity stopped merely because she was an able female captain, without proof of more, they could bloody well come to the Mediterranean and stop her themselves.

He rested his arms on the railing of the upper deck, instinctively studying the horizon for ships, trying to adjust to being a passenger without a single responsibility. It should have been more difficult than it was. But the emptiness inside him that had begun long before he'd nearly drowned with the *Henry's Cross* dragged him like a fierce undertow. All that was left was to resign his commission upon their arrival in London and set out immediately for Croston. Once there, he would face nothing but endless days of...nothing.

Perhaps he would become a pigeon fancier.

The one thing he would bloody well *not* need to do was assert himself on behalf of Katherine Kinloch. It would be enough to report to his superiors that he'd personally observed the protocols aboard the *Possession,* as well as the goods in her hold, and that—as he'd suspected—there'd never been any reason to question her legitimacy in the first place. His celebrity ought to be good for that much, at least, and a positive report ought to discharge his debt to her in spades.

The devil it will.

A wave crashed against the hull and a fine, salty mist caught him in the face. The feel and the taste of it stirred his old exhilaration for the sea, but the feeling was snuffed out almost immediately. An image of the *Merry Sea* rose in his mind as if the entire scene had happened yesterday and not ten years previous on a day much like this one.

They're coming about! Fire!

His own order shot through his memory. They'd been so close he hadn't needed his glass to watch the grisly fighting between the *Merry Sea*'s crew and the Barbary corsairs intent on capturing her. He'd unleashed everything he could, knowing full well what awaited the seamen once hauled away as slaves to Barbary. There hadn't been so much as a glimpse of petticoat to indicate the presence of a woman—not that it would have made a difference, except that he might have unleashed less, not more. And then there'd been the currents, the wind... Hell. In the end, there'd been nothing he could do, and his inability had cost Katherine her freedom.

He didn't want to think of it, nor any of the other mistakes he'd made during twenty years of a supposedly glorious naval career. Every misstep, every miscalculation, every failure—they dogged him like a pack of wolves closing in on midnight prey. There would be no peace until he reached Croston.

But you'll still owe her for that day. And now for your life, as well.

The *Possession*'s heavy canvas sails thwacked in the wind, and the calls of her small crew carried above the gentle crash of waves against the hull. Sunshine glittered off the water like diamonds scattered on the sea. Every inch of burnished wood gleamed softly. Clearly the *Possession*'s toilette rivaled that of any great beauty who spent hours in pursuit of perfection. She was a brig, but detailed carving on the rails and stern gave the ship a Moorish exoticism to match that of her captain. Across the deck, that captain stood tête-à-tête with Jaxbury, conferring about some detail of the voyage.

"Spot any threats, Barclay?" Jaxbury called over to James.

Just one. James let his gaze linger on her. The breeze played with Captain Kinloch's loose trousers and tunic, fluttering and molding the cloth to her body in brief glimpses that presented a very credible threat to his sanity.

"I'm merely a passenger," he called back. "Got an eye out for porpoises—nothing more."

The two of them conferred a moment longer, and Jaxbury descended to the quarterdeck while Captain Kinloch— Damnation. From the corner of his eye James watched her come closer and join him at the railing. By the time she took the spot next to him, his breathing had gone shallow.

"Do sound the alarm if you spot anything, Lieutenant Barclay," she said. "I'd like to think I may benefit from your vast naval experience."

Her smile alone had alarm bells clanging painfully, but only he could hear them. "It's gratifying to know you consider me of potential value, Captain. Shall I notify you of possible targets as well as threats? Perhaps you could engage in a bit of last-minute marauding before we approach England."

She laughed, and the wind whipped a strand of her hair into his face. He brushed it away and felt his control slip a notch. "Clearly the depth of my ruthlessness *has* been overstated. I've never been one to maraud entirely unprovoked."

"What a pity I won't get to see that famed cutlass arm in action." He hadn't failed to notice that the British flag had replaced her colors flying at the stern.

"You have only to displease me, Lieutenant Barclay, and you shall see it firsthand." She closed her eyes to the wind and tipped her face back. He let himself notice the way her hair shone in the sunlight, the fine sculpture of her cheekbones, the sensuous curve of her lips.

She was, without a doubt, the most alluring woman he'd ever seen.

"I shudder to think of the terrifying woman Anne will become with you as a model." Except that sweet, vulnerable Anne would never be able to defend herself with a cutlass. It crushed him to watch her navigate the cabins by memory, patting her way from one chair or table or wall to the next with those tiny hands. He'd noticed that under no circumstances was any piece of furniture to be moved. Every critical door remained open, held in place by heavy anvils that would not budge. Textured tiles marked each room, mounted outside each door at just the right height. "She is a remarkable child," he said.

"Yes, she is. She's had to be." Worry shadowed Captain Kinloch's eyes, and it annoyed him a little that he wanted to ease it.

"Already she shows signs of your deviousness. I suppose you are aware that your keys are not the only objects whose hiding place she has discovered."

A smile touched Captain Kinloch's lips, and he watched the way it softened the lines around her mouth. Under other circumstances, would she smile like that more often?

"She's found the doll," she said. "Yes, I could tell. Do you suppose my lower drawers are not the most effective hiding place for a birthday gift?"

He could tell by the laughter in her eyes that she'd meant for Anne to find that doll. "I think she enjoys the search more than anything," he said. Against his better judgment he'd thought of an idea for a gift for her, but he would need access to the ship's carpenter in order to find the necessary materials.

"The doll I let her find, but I've a small mandolin hiding elsewhere that she won't receive until her birthday arrives."

"A mandolin is an excellent idea."

"You may not say so after listening to her endless practicing." She laughed.

"Oh, I imagine I can tolerate it." It was hard to imagine what he wouldn't tolerate for Anne's sake.

Captain Kinloch looked at him. "The attention you've shown her has been much appreciated."

"She's an endearing girl." And that was the problem. All the plea rolls in England did not contain enough parchment to list the reasons why it would be a mistake to form any kind of attachment with Katherine Kinloch's daughter.

"I'm told you are an accomplished storyteller," she said.

"Hardly." He had to laugh at that. "I never told a story before in all my life—except to the governess."

"Never?"

"Not many children aboard a frigate." The hypnotic lure of Captain Kinloch's eyes snared him. Mysteries lurked there—dark ones likely rooted in her years as a captive, and softer, spicier ones that suggested she was aware of him as a man. The possibility had an unwelcome effect on his baser instincts.

The remainder of the voyage taunted him with the prospect of interminable weeks of temptation. It was a prospect that would change very quickly if she somehow discovered his identity.

"Captain." Her Moorish boatswain called from the top of the stairs, and James caught himself a heartbeat before he responded to the title. The boatswain waited with his arms crossed and his gold earrings and shaved head gleaming in the sunshine. A string of beads like the one William wore was tied around his neck. All the crew had them. It was their mark, he'd learned, fashioned by Anne.

Captain Kinloch stepped away from the railing. "Excuse me a moment, Lieutenant."

"Of course." It took all his willpower not to watch her hips sway in those damned trousers as she walked away.

KATHERINE FORCED HERSELF not to look back as she left Lieutenant Barclay standing at the railing. But she hardly needed to look when her body still hummed with his presence. "What is it, Rafik?"

"Young rigger Danby wants to see you."

"Send him up."

"He will not come. He is afraid."

Katherine frowned. "That's ridiculous."

Rafik only regarded her with that expressionless stare that silently let her know he thought he would make a better captain than she.

Katherine brushed by him and descended the stairs, finally allowing herself a glance over her shoulder. Lieutenant Barclay stood with his eyes on the horizon and the wind toying with the hair at his temples. She forced her attention away. "Did he give you no hint of his concerns?"

"It is best for you to hear it from him, Captain."

Fears of returning to England had plagued the crew since the moment they'd set their sails north. No doubt he feared the impressment gangs, but there was little she could do to protect him from that. Perhaps he wanted permission to go ashore before they reached England. *That* was out of the question.

They made their way toward the stern, where Danby was partway up in the rigging. The moment he saw her he climbed down and whipped his hat off his head.

"What is it you have to say, Danby?"

His hat crumpled in his hands. "I—I should have told you before. I know that. But I was afraid...well, I was afraid you wouldn't hire me."

"Told me what?"

"That I was aboard Captain Warre's ship. When we put in at Gibraltar, I snuck away. I know it was wrong, Captain, and I'd never do such a thing to you. I swear. I'd die first."

"I believe you. But why tell me now?"

"I'm afraid, with him here—him what we pulled aboard."

"Lieutenant Barclay?" Her thoughts filled with his smile—the creases at his eyes, the lines around his mouth, the subtly wicked angle of mustache above his lips. White teeth against sun-browned skin. If she were a different kind of woman—

Danby frowned and looked past her toward the upper deck. "Aye, but...that ain't Lieutenant Barclay, mum." He gripped his hat in his hands. "That's Captain Warre."

CHAPTER SEVEN

CAPTAIN WARRE.

Katherine stared toward the upper deck where he stood laughing with William. William, who surely knew the truth about their visitor. Captain Warre looked her way, caught her watching him.

An accomplished storyteller, indeed. Her blood began to pound. "Danby, are you certain?"

"No doubt on it, Captain." Danby still worried his hat in his hands. "No mistaking the likes of him."

She turned her back on the upper deck. "You've no cause for concern. He cannot punish you here, and with the number of sailors on a man-of-war, it's doubtful he'll remember you. You may rest easy."

Danby exhaled and replaced his hat. "Yes, Captain. Thank you, Captain."

"Have you told anyone that you recognize him?"

"Not a soul, Captain."

"Good. See that you tell no one else." Danby bobbed his head and hoisted himself back up the rigging, while Katherine exchanged looks with Rafik.

"I shall take him now and lock him in the brig," Rafik said.

"No."

"Then what do you wish me to do?"

Her stomach clenched fiercely. In her mind, Captain

Warre's cannons exploded. She could almost smell the acrid gunsmoke drifting across the water. The girl inside her tried to propel her forward to confront him, but the woman she'd become kept that urge in check. She may have been helpless then, but she bloody well wasn't helpless anymore.

She glanced at the upper deck, and the past sucked at her with its violent whirlpool of fear and helplessness. For a moment she thought she would be sick. "For now," she said slowly, "nothing. He can do little, being only one man." Except that Captain Warre had the presence of ten men.

"That is dangerous thinking," Rafik said too sharply.

"It is not for you to question," Katherine shot back. "For the time being, we shall let him continue to believe we have not discovered his identity." The significance of that identity could not be ignored. "And I shall place him under your supervision."

Only a slight narrowing of his dark eyes told her he might find that acceptable.

"You shall assign him every menial task," she told Rafik. Oh, yes, the great Captain Warre would swab decks and polish cannons and slop buckets of filth. "He will be one of the crew—just another sailor. And I expect you to treat him as such."

"Aye, Captain." A slight curving of his lips betrayed his opinion this time.

"Not more harshly, Rafik." She would need Captain Warre alive and well when they arrived in London.

"I will treat him as the rest of the crew."

"Excellent." She shifted so she could see the upper deck once more. Soddingest bastard he'd ever set eyes on, was he? As she watched, he put his hands behind his head and stretched his shoulders. Her body went soft and liquid deep inside, and she clenched her teeth. Ten years she'd nursed her hatred for this man, and now it took an effort to tear her gaze away from him.

This was unacceptable.

"Tomorrow," she decided. "You will move him into the berth with the crew. He is still weak, so give him only small tasks at first and keep an eye on him for signs that he is not as recovered as he seems."

Rafik nodded.

"And report to me regularly about his activities. I want to know at the first hint of insubordination." It would likely come moments after he received his first assignment.

Rafik returned to his duties, and Katherine turned toward the upper deck. Her hands shook with the desire to whip her cutlass from its sheath and confront the bastard.

Captain James Warre. Here, on her ship, eating her meat pies and drinking her wine and sleeping on her linens. She watched him shift his weight from one foot to both and brace his hands on the railing. Her eyes followed the angle of his legs past his buttocks and across the broad expanse of his back, over his shoulder and down the line of his arm to the fingers that curled around smooth wood. She didn't need to be any closer to know exactly what those fingers looked like. Strong, solid, lightly callused. Gripping the *Possession* as though he owned it.

A hot lick of sensation shot through her belly as though he touched *her*.

Captain Warre. He was Captain *Warre*. Perhaps if she thought the name enough times, her body would stop reacting to him. To think that if Danby hadn't recognized him, before the voyage ended she might have been foolish enough to—

Good God.

Petrels soared above the sails as Katherine returned to the upper deck. The sound of the waves and the familiar shouts and laughter of her crew were a comfort, but everything had changed. William still chatted with India, but she would deal with him later. Oh, yes. She would deal with William. But for now, she rejoined Captain Warre at the railing.

"Everything all right?" he asked. His scent—Turkish soap borrowed from William, plus some musky undertone that was uniquely him—wafted over her on the breeze.

"A misunderstanding among the riggers." She put her own hands on the railing and tried to cleanse her lungs with sea air, but his subtle spice lingered.

"That required your intervention? I would have guessed your boatswain capable of handling such problems."

"Rafik is capable of handling any number of problems—" as Captain Warre would soon discover "—but my crew is free to speak with me whenever they wish. No doubt that seems strange to you. I'm sure your Captain Warre would have abhorred such a policy."

He made a noise. "To the extent it would have meant five hundred men queued up outside his cabin, I'm sure you're correct."

No doubt he planned to play the role of Lieutenant Barclay for the entire voyage. He probably reasoned that once they reached London and he rejoined the upper echelons of society, it wouldn't matter if she finally discovered his true identity. Hot anger simmered beneath her skin, so much easier to tolerate than the attraction. And infinitely more acceptable than that old vulnerability.

Her life held no room for weakness, not when so many depended on her strength.

Captain Warre, hiding like a coward behind the persona of a dead inferior officer. How many lies would he tell to protect his identity?

"You were about to tell me a little more about yourself, Lieutenant," she said, deciding to find out. "Are you the eldest son?"

"Hardly." One lie. "My eldest brother, Theodore, will inherit the baronetcy." Two. Three. According to Philomena, Captain Warre was an earl by virtue of his older brother's death five years earlier.

"I merely wish to leave the sea and all its tedium behind and live a quiet life," he continued.

Without a doubt, four. "Leave the navy? But surely you would become a captain soon."

He nodded. "In a few years, I likely would have had my own command." Five. The real Lieutenant Barclay may have had a few years to wait, but the renowned Captain Warre had risen quickly through the ranks and attained his first commission twelve years ago.

"That seems an excruciatingly slow wait," she said. "Surely you've been at sea twenty years now."

The corners of his eyes creased when he glanced at her. "You pull no punches about a man's age, Captain. Just shy of half that, I'm afraid." Which, for the real Lieutenant Barclay, may have been true. Six lies. The only thing she didn't know was whether Captain Warre was hiding his identity for fear of her reputation or because he knew she'd been aboard the *Merry Sea*. More likely the former. He would hardly remember one violent encounter among the hundreds that spanned his career.

"I can't imagine Captain Warre approved your plan to leave the navy, battle-hardened as he must be," she said. "With his record and reputation, I've no doubt he'll order 'Fire the cannons!' with his dying breath."

He laughed, full and real with a smile that gleamed white as the sails and creased his cheeks with wicked merriment. "First, there would have to be a war on."

"Which there undoubtedly will be again."

"Bite your tongue. And second, he would have to remain in the navy. The reason the captain approved my plan most heartily was because he planned to resign his own commission as soon as our voyage was over."

He did? "For what reason?"

His smile dimmed. She refused to be disappointed. "Fatigue," he said. "Jadedness, perhaps. Battle-weary, rather than battle-hardened. I fear you would have been sorely disappointed had you met him—he was hardly the bloodthirsty predator you imagine."

Seven. If the calculating bastard standing next to her was fatigued and weary, it was only the lingering effects of his ordeal at sea. "He could hardly have attained such notoriety otherwise," she said. His actions against the *Merry Sea* supported that opinion.

He turned his head and looked straight into her eyes, piercing her with a memory. As she stared back, suddenly she knew. He had not forgotten the *Merry Sea* or his own hand in her fate.

"Even the most driven of men make miscalculations, Captain Kinloch."

"Do they." She was speaking to Captain Warre now, not Lieutenant Barclay. Desperately she fought back an onslaught of emotions and memories. "I rather wonder if they don't simply become complacent with regard to any unfortunate consequences of their actions."

"I can assure you, they do not." For a heartbeat those green eyes looked as weary as he claimed. "If he were here, I have no doubt he would tell you he has many regrets."

And she would tell him to go to hell. "If Captain Warre were here," she said, "I have no doubt that he *would* have many regrets—and none would have to do with his naval career."

KATHERINE WAITED UNTIL William had retired to his cabin that evening and knocked once on his door. Captain Warre was not the only one who would have regrets.

"A word, please," she said tightly when William opened. He'd removed his turban, and his golden hair glinted in the lamplight. She stepped into his cabin and waited until he shut the door. An atlas lay open on the desk against the wall.

"Thought I'd see where I might go after you've claimed your title," he said. "What do you think of Madagascar?"

"You betrayed me," she said. William was her best friend in the entire world, and he'd lied to her. Was *still* lying to her. Her chest felt tight and hot as though she'd been speared.

William studied her for a long, quiet moment. Everything in his cabin glittered—the gold in his ears, the gilded scrollwork on the bedstead and dressing table he'd purchased in the Levant, the bejeweled waterpipe he'd taken from a ship bound from Tangier. "I would fall on my sword before I would betray you, Katherine." There was no trace of his usual humor. His blue eyes glittered, too—hard, like sapphires. "Protect you, yes. Betray? Never."

"Explain how lying to me is protecting me."

"I suspect the punishment for mistreating the captain of a first-rate ship of the line would be most unpleasant."

"You think me so stupid?"

"I think anger could blind you to the consequences of revenge, and I think you've spent your entire adult life in a world where the rules are nothing like those where we're headed. It would be easy for you to underestimate the value of our latest cargo."

"I assure you, I fully appreciate Captain Warre's *value*."

"That is precisely what I'm afraid of."

"He's got two hands like everyone else on board," she said harshly, "and a strong back." An image of that strong back leaped unhelpfully to mind, rippling with muscles beneath white linen.

"Katherine, you cannot—"

"Cannot what?" She rounded on him. "Cannot put him to work? Demand that he earn his passage?"

"You cannot mistreat him."

"Beginning tomorrow, he will be under Rafik's supervision. He will receive the same *mistreatment* as any other member of the crew. If the good captain perceives honest work as mistreatment, then I will gladly stand accused."

William exhaled and rubbed the back of his neck. "Did he disclose himself to you?"

"Hardly. A *loyal* crew member recognized him and

saw fit to inform me. But you—" She swallowed past the tightness in her throat. "You would have let me play the fool the entire voyage."

"I have far too much respect for you to play you for a fool," William said, his voice low and harsh in a tone he rarely used. He stepped close, framing her face in his hands. "You know that."

"It was your duty to tell me his identity." Because his identity changed everything.

Not everything.

Yes. Everything. Whatever misguided attraction she'd felt for Lieutenant Barclay—good God, for *Captain Warre*—was at this moment shriveling in her bosom.

William brushed her cheek and tucked a strand of hair behind her ear. "It's my duty to protect you, pet, and everyone aboard this ship. Can't think of a worse time for you to finally come face-to-face with him. Too many uncertainties."

When you are countess of Dunscore, Katie, men will bow at your feet like pagans before Isis.

Papa's declaration reached out from a past she'd long since abandoned. If the Lords had their way, she would never be countess of Dunscore at all—never mind see anyone bow at her feet. Not that it mattered, except for Anne. She was doing this for Anne's future, not her own.

"I never thought I would count you as one of those uncertainties," she said.

"Couldn't risk you dealing with him irrationally. Regardless of what you think, he knew from the first where my loyalties lie."

Bah. "And now I know, as well," she said, even though it wasn't true.

"You don't believe that."

The touch of her dear friend made her want to lean into him as she'd done during those early days after their escape, when she'd been pregnant with Anne and terrified by an unknown future. Returning to Britain with a half-Moor child in her belly had been out of the question. So had been staying in Algiers. But William had found their solution. He had been her rock—at least, until she had learned to be her own rock, thanks to him. It was William who'd suggested she act as captain. William who'd stood to the side, teaching her everything he knew, knowing the independence it would give her. She owed him her life for that.

She stepped away from him. "If you ever lie to me again, I'll run you through and toss your carcass to the gulls."

"Agreed." He watched her through eyes that knew her too well. "We were both captives, Katherine. I know only too well how badly the finger itches to point at someone other than the true culprits." He paused. "I also know how easily old resentments can be intensified by more recent aggravations."

The slightest tick of one dark gold brow told her exactly what he was thinking. "I assure you, my resentment toward Captain Warre needs no intensification," she said. It was her own fault that William suspected she'd found Captain Warre attractive. She'd been too unguarded, too seduced by broad shoulders and sea-colored eyes.

She would have no trouble resisting them now.

CHAPTER EIGHT

HENRY'S CROSS WRECKED.

Nicholas Warre, Lord Taggart, stared numbly at the printed words. A fire crackled in the fireplace, but a chill shivered across his skin.

All hands lost...

The news screamed at him from the paper. He'd stared at it all afternoon. He'd stared until a cavern of emptiness hollowed out his body and sucked his mind dry.

First Robert, now James. His only brothers, dead.

Nick felt dead, too.

He leaned over James's desk—his desk, now, though he didn't deserve it—and cradled his head in his hands, fighting to breathe through a throat that felt swollen shut. Images darted through his mind—dark imaginings too easy to conjure of gigantic waves, splintering wood and the screams of drowning men. He squeezed his eyes shut, then pushed back suddenly from the desk, springing to his feet, turning toward the fire.

Bates's knock sounded at the door.

Nick stared into the flames. "Come in," he said woodenly.

"Lady Ramsey has arrived, your lordship."

"Send her in."

The rustle of yards of fabric and lace preceded Honoria into the study. "Snuffboxes, Nicholas!" his sister declared as she entered the room. "They're hawking *snuffboxes* with his likeness on the lid!"

"Oh, for God's sake." He gripped the mantel and dropped his head to his forearm. There would be no such thing as a private mourning.

"Is there nothing we can do to preserve the family's dignity?"

"I'm little match for the adoration of the masses," Nick said.

"A pox on the masses! James hates snuff." Her skirts swooshed as she walked up behind him. He felt his sister's hand on his back, smelled her familiar perfume. "La, Nicholas," she whispered. "I don't know how I can survive it."

He wanted to turn into her arms, but if he did, despair would open a chasm inside him and he would be lost. He returned to the desk instead. "Been all day with Fortescue," he said. "Nothing's changed. Not one damned thing."

She followed him to the desk, all powder and jewels and black lace. Modest, by Honoria's standards. Grief had dampened her usual high spirits and killed her quick laugh. "I keep having to remind myself it's really true," she said quietly. "With him at sea nearly all of the time, everything seems so...usual."

It did. But it shouldn't. They'd all been so close, once— God, it had been ages ago. He, James, Robert, riding hell-bent through the countryside, staging mock battles on the lawn, enraging Honoria with their merciless teasing.

Two brothers dead, and they'd all grown so far apart

it was as if nothing had changed. "It's very hard terms for a title," he spat.

Honoria reached across the desk and took his hand. "Tell me Fortescue had a solution for your problem, at least."

"Oh, certainly. It's not as though there isn't a solution. But I can't burden the Croston estate with my debts."

"It's your estate now. You can do with it as you wish."

"Indeed. Just as I've done with Taggart." His own barony sat mortgaged to the tune of over forty thousand pounds—an act of desperation as one after another of his shipping investments met with disaster, and that would have been worse were it not for insurance, but that hardly made a difference now. He'd become Bertrand Holliswell's puppet, and the fact of it made him sick.

"Tempests are not your fault," Honoria said sternly. "Nor pirates, nor any of the other disasters that befell your ships. La, Nicholas, will you blame yourself next for—" She broke off abruptly.

James's death. That's what she'd been about to say. No, at least he was not to blame for that.

He exhaled and looked at the papers on the desk as though they held some kind of answer. "I've got to get that bill through, but it looks like the bloody thing has been put off indefinitely."

"For heaven's sake, I cannot abide the idea that you're willing to throw that poor girl to the dogs to satisfy a debt that could be paid with the stroke of a pen."

"Poor girl?" He stared at her in disbelief. "The woman is practically a pirate."

"Don't you remember her at that garden party at

Lolly's, pining after McCutcheon like a lost puppy? No, of course you wouldn't. Such a spectacle, but then, we were young. We all gave our hearts recklessly at that age." Honoria sighed. "Poor thing."

"Poor thing?" Incredulous, Nick put his hands on the desk. "She took a corsair prize!"

"Defending the Barbary reign of terror, brother dear?" She arched a brow at him. "She freed twenty English captives, which is a good deal more exciting than anything I've done this season."

"Will you join your dear friend Lady Pennington aboard that pirate ship? Oh, yes, I can just imagine you with a mop in those dainty hands, swabbing decks."

"I highly doubt Philomena is swabbing decks. And it is *not* a pirate ship. The last letter I had from her told of glorious adventure—which, though I'm not well-versed in the law, I know to be perfectly legal." Her green eyes turned worried. "I only hope the tempest that caught our James did not find them, as well." She pried one of Nick's hands off the desk and held it in her own, and he felt like a cad for picking a fight with her—the only sibling he had left. "When the only person standing with you is Yost," she said, "it's a good sign you're going the wrong direction."

"They'll come around."

"Lord Dunscore was well loved."

He didn't need her to tell him that. He pulled his hand free and paced back to the fire. "I think he even befriended the parliamentary rats with stray crumbs," he said in disgust. The terrible thing was Nick had liked him, too. Always ready with a laugh, always up for a night of drink and debauchery, always offering use of his horses, carriage, houses—the man would have done anything for anybody. Poor fellow had tried like hell to ransom his daughter out of Morocco after her capture, but the dey had given her as a gift to a cousin in Algiers who had not been interested in ransom money. It was only when a handful of captives she'd rescued had come home with their tale of a Scottish virago sea captain that anyone knew she had escaped captivity. Lord Dunscore had disappeared up north for months drowning his sorrows. "She broke his heart not coming home," Nick added.

"But he didn't disinherit her."

"In England she never would have inherited in the first place."

"Be that as it may, the estate is in Scotland, and harridan though she may be, she *has* inherited. As a matter of principle, it's not the House of Lords' place to interfere."

The irony of Honoria calling someone else a harridan was almost too much. "This has nothing to do with principle. Only with satisfying Holliswell."

"And marrying his daughter, although you already know my opinion on *that*."

"Yes. And I'll thank you not to repeat it." It wasn't enough that Holliswell held Nick's debt. Holliswell's daughter held his heart. The moment Nick had set eyes on her, it was clear that the lovely, gentle Clarissa Holliswell was a helpless pawn in Holliswell's lustful quest for connections. Holliswell wanted the Dunscore title for himself, yes—but failing that, he'd made it clear he would marry Clarissa to even the oldest, most licentious beard splitter in England if the man had the right title.

Baron, Nick had already discovered, was not the right title.

"If this business is keeping you from happiness," she said, "it has everything to do with principle."

Dear Honoria, loyal to a fault and impervious to shortcomings. He smiled a little, only to have the rudimentary curve shrivel on his lips. Happiness. It was a ravenous beast, insatiable, incapable of satisfaction no matter how much one fed it.

"Just use the money from the Croston estate," she said sadly. "The title belongs to you now, and it's what James would have wanted."

It was out of the question. "I incurred this debt of my own doing, and I shall discharge it the same way." Once this bill passed, it was all but certain the Dunscore estate and title would be settled on Holliswell. And once Holliswell became the Earl of Dunscore, he would forgive Nick's debt and bless his union with Clarissa.

Or so Nick hoped.

WHATEVER JAMES MIGHT have wanted, what he'd received was a demotion of monumental proportions.

Deep in the hold, he pushed the end of a broom into the crevice between a stack of crates and raked out a wad of rats' nests. Five days of emptying slop buckets, carrying water, cutting biscuits, swabbing decks—it should have made him furious. He tried for something like outrage when he shoved the next handful of disgusting mess into the bucket, but all he did was scrape his knuckles against the wood.

He yanked his hand away with a hiss.

That he couldn't work up a good fury over something like this was proof he wasn't himself. Perhaps he was ill. But then, he'd been wondering that for months now with no sign of physical manifestation. His ship's surgeon—God rest his soul—had suggested malaise. If nothing else, all this work had him sleeping like a babe in that creaking, knotty hammock he'd been relegated to. But his joints ached like the devil.

The menial tasks, of course, were punishment for being "practically of one mind" with the supposedly ruthless Captain Warre, whose merciless brother threatened her family estate. But poor Lieutenant Barclay wasn't being punished for Nick's sins, that much was clear. He was being punished for Captain Warre's.

Wouldn't she be disappointed to know that the impassioned naval captain for whom she cherished such a special hatred had been dead for at least a year, perhaps two. The tenacious, single-minded man he used to be had gone missing as completely as the bodies of the men aboard the *Henry's Cross*. All that was left was a man who, he could assure her, was much less satisfying.

But if this was Barclay's penalty for simply knowing him, he preferred not to know what his fate would be if she knew his true identity. Incarceration, probably—and he'd be damned before he let her know he preferred menial tasks over idleness. He wanted his idleness on his own terms, preferably with a generous glass of something expensive and strong.

Briskly he swept out the crevice, shined the lantern to see the result and repeated the process until not even a mote of dust remained. He scooped the mess into a bucket and got on his hands and knees to reach around the side of the crates and into another corner. The little buggers had met their fates at the paws of some of Mr. Bogles's relations, but before the massacre they'd turned this lower hold into a city the size of London.

He breathed in a puff of nasty dust and coughed, wiping his face with his wrist.

Devil take it, *this* should have been enough to cool the fever she stoked in his blood. But there was no sign of relief from that. Malaise definitely did not afflict him where she was concerned.

At least the tight quarters in the sailors' berth kept him from becoming more closely acquainted with himself than he ought to.

"I see you're surprisingly adept with a broom, Lieutenant," came her smug voice into the hold.

Bloody *hell.*

Protocol demanded that he stand. Instead, he reached farther around the crates and came up with another handful of dusty, feces-riddled nesting. "I'm adept with any number of tools, Captain." He didn't even try to keep the double-entendre from his voice, although there was no doubt it hurt him more than it annoyed her.

"Versatility is a useful quality in a sailor." Her heavy boots thumped across the planks as she moved in to inspect his work. "My boatswain says your strength is increasing. I thought I would see for myself how you're managing."

As though she hadn't been observing him these past five days at every task he'd put his hands to. He'd felt her eyes on him, caught her watching him countless times. "As you can see, I'm quite recovered and managing well." He dumped the mess in the bucket and finally stood, reaching for the broom, purposely letting his chest brush her arm—and then regretting it. "You may satisfy yourself that your nemesis is turning in his watery grave to see his lieutenant doing the work of a cabin boy."

She stood with that arrogant posture, shoulders back and chin up, as though she commanded not just her ship but the sea and everything on it. Her dark hair gleamed in the lantern's light, falling loose over the swell of her breasts beneath layers of Turkish muslin.

"You misunderstand, Lieutenant," she said evenly. He watched her lips move and fought an overwhelming urge to kiss that self-satisfied curve from that sensuous mouth. "Your new duties have nothing to do with my feelings toward anyone else. I'm simply operating with a skeleton crew, as you are aware, and naturally I require the assistance of all hands."

"Naturally."

"I apologize if the position doesn't suit you, but I'm afraid I have all the officers I require at present."

"I have no wish to be one of your officers, Captain." But he could imagine several other positions that would suit him very nicely. Her power was intoxicating, wrapping around him the way her legs might do, and he drank it in. The raw need to touch her surged through his veins. "Given that I've not yet resigned my commission, I am obliged to continue my loyalty to the navy." He shoved his hand in his pocket and encountered the handful of dowel discs he'd recovered off the floor beneath the carpenter's bench.

"I am fully aware of where your loyalties lie, Lieutenant." She looked him up and down, and a pulse jumped in his groin. "Are the men treating you well? If you have any complaints, you are as free to speak with me as any other member of my crew." The gleam in those topaz eyes told him any complaints he had would be met with satisfaction.

"No complaints, Captain." Except that he was on fire, and he needed her to leave.

"Excellent." Her eyes darkened. Good God.

"Although my hammock creaks."

"I'm sorry to hear it."

"And this broom is worn."

"I shall see that you get another."

And I am James Warre. One sentence, and everything would change—though not necessarily for the better. Wisdom dictated that he wait until a more strategic moment to have the satisfaction of seeing the look on her face when he disclosed himself. Or perhaps he wouldn't disclose himself at all. Perhaps he would wait until London and savor the moment when circumstances threw them together.

"You're doing excellent work, Lieutenant," she said, looking past him with a raised brow. "Very thorough. One can only imagine what you could accomplish with a fresh broom." She smiled. "You may well earn yourself another commendation."

On the other hand, perhaps he would prefer to savor his moment much sooner.

CHAPTER NINE

KATHERINE SENT THE fresh broom and hoped the hammock would keep him awake every night, the same way his presence on board was doing to her.

Her attention followed his movements like a compass needle, and she hated it.

By Anne's sixth birthday nearly a week later, the *Possession* had made good time sailing up the coast of Spain toward France. Katherine stood at the railing after the birthday festivities with her hands fisted inside a heavy woolen coat, overlooking the lower decks where Captain Warre swabbed the main deck near the bow.

How vexing that he worked with as much vigor now as he had a week ago in the hold—never mind that he'd been assigned the midnight watch, and a moist drizzle threatened harder rain, and the breeze was chilling. The man was impervious to every hardship.

"The closer we get to England, the more insufferable India becomes," Phil said, joining her at the railing in a billowing, hooded cape. She followed Katherine's line of sight. "Aha. I see the view from here is excellent today."

"The closer we get to England, the more insufferable *everything* becomes," Katherine said irritably, and pulled her coat more tightly around her. He deserved to be vulnerable. To know what it was like to be power-less and expendable.

"I left Anne instructing Mr. Bogles in the basics of draughts," Phil told her. "I have a feeling he'll be a most inept player, but I didn't wish to disillusion Anne on her birthday—especially since Cook put her in charge of meting out the leftover sugar cakes."

"With India around, no one else need worry about leftover cakes."

Phil made a noise of agreement. Below, Captain Warre ran a rag over the railings. Katherine could feel the moment Phil's gaze shifted away from him and back to her. "The draughts board is remarkable," Phil said. "Such meticulous detail. Who would have ever thought of embedding rope into the wood so Anne could feel the squares?" Phil's voice dripped with the answer: Lieu-tenant Barclay, that was who. "I never would have ex-pected him to be so skilled with wood," she said. Her lips twitched with suppressed amusement. "At least—"

"Do not say it."

"Very well." Phil was quiet for a moment that was pregnant with her mischievous thoughts. "I suppose the third son of a baronet learns any number of divert-ing skills."

Apparently so did the second son of an earl. "The draughts board was a gift from the crew," Katherine said tersely.

"Mmm."

'Twere all Tom's idea, Cap'n. He was the one who had thought to adapt the game so Anne's blindness would not prevent her from playing. It was so difficult to find things to make Anne's life interesting, things she could do independently. Now she had one more thing to give her confidence.

It was impossible to hate Captain Warre for that.

A drop of rain fell from Katherine's eyebrow to her cheek and slid down her face. She brushed it away and gripped the dewy railing. The familiar wood, like her sense of control, slipped beneath her grasp. The *Merry Sea* called to her from its resting place beneath the water, tempting her with memories of those terrifying hours when she'd known, without a doubt, that she would die.

Below, Captain Warre had exchanged the rag for the mop. They watched him drag the mop forward and back, forward and back, carefully pushing it around the railing spindles. He bent to pick up some small thing she couldn't identify and flung it over the side.

"Anne is very fond of him," Phil reminded her. "And she misses his stories."

"I tell her stories."

"And now you'll play draughts with her, as well, I daresay. Although one's own mother is vastly less entertaining than an intriguing naval lieutenant—no matter how many similarities you and the lieutenant share."

"Continue, and you'll find yourself swabbing alongside him."

Phil laughed. "Worth the price, if I could but see you distracted from your worries by a fiery amorous liaison."

It was past time to tell Phil the truth. "The longer you persist in this notion that I should have an affair with Lieutenant Barclay, the more severe your disappointment will be when it does not occur."

"The only thing you will gain by such a prudish attitude is a pinched mouth and a crease above your lip."

"I already have a crease." Phil was going to be furious that Katherine hadn't told her. And once she knew, there would be no peace for the rest of the voyage.

"Then you must bed him quickly to prevent more."

"I rather think I shall continue my nightly cream instead."

"What could it possibly hurt? A few stolen moments, a passionate embrace..."

Katherine was *not* going to embrace Captain Warre.

"Let me assure you, lovemaking can be very discreet. If you move him from the midnight watch—"

"Enough!"

Phil raised a brow.

"There's something I haven't told you."

"You *are* having an affair with him." Phil gripped her arm. "I *knew* it."

"No." Katherine dragged her gaze from Captain Warre. "I am not."

Phil's eyes narrowed and her grip tightened. "Tell me."

"You must swear you won't breathe a word to anyone but William."

"William knows? Katherine, tell me *instantly.*"

Katherine did, and Phil went from deathly curious to outraged in a heartbeat. "I should run you through on the spot!" she hissed. "Isn't that what you always say? For heaven's sake, Katherine—how dare you keep something like this from me? It's— It's—" She spun on her heel, stalked a few paces away and stalked back. "Why did you not tell me? Did you not trust me?"

"Perhaps I did not wish to hear about his skill with wood," Katherine hissed back.

"Do you honestly believe I would have said such things if I'd known?"

Katherine answered with a look. Of course Phil would have said such things—and with all the more glee.

"At least credit me with *some* sense," Phil scolded. But already Katherine could see Phil putting the pieces together, realizing that mere moments ago Katherine had been watching Captain Warre—and not because she was merely surveying the crew. Katherine studied a distant ship on the horizon.

"Oh, Katherine. You mustn't be angry with yourself."

It was too late for that. "His identity changes nothing. My plans are the same." Captain Warre was not going to steer her off course. Clearly she was a fool, but she was a fool in command—of both her ship and herself.

"He has no idea that you know? You haven't spoken to him at all of the past?" Someone called to Captain Warre from overhead, and he tossed the rag over his shoulder and climbed into the rigging to put his weight on a rope.

"No. Nor do I wish to."

"Of course not. But— Oh, you should have *told* me." Agitated, Phil pulled her cloak and hood more tightly around her against the annoying drizzle. "Katherine, you've got the Earl of Croston *swabbing* your *deck*."

"It's less than he deserves."

"Most definitely. But you must realize this changes everything. Everything! You cannot keep him with the crew. Oh, if only I'd known, I would have advised you never to have put him there. Don't you see? We didn't rescue just anybody—we rescued Captain Warre. *You* rescued Captain Warre."

"Yes. And I intend to make sure his brother is fully aware of that fact."

"Which is all good and well, but the possibilities are so much larger. You'll be a heroine in your own right. This is exactly the kind of thing that will open society's doors." Phil looked at him once more. "You're absolutely certain he is the captain?"

"Yes."

Phil's lips tightened, and she sniffed. "I always imagined him with a bulbous nose and cruel, twisted lips." The fact that he had neither hung silently between them as they watched him carefully but efficiently wipe down the spindles. "But that's neither here nor there. Regardless of all the reasons you have a right to dislike him, you must remove him from the crew immediately and begin cultivating his good favor."

"*His* good favor!" Katherine stared at her. "He should be cultivating mine."

"Perhaps so, but unfortunately that is an attitude you cannot afford. Your father's friends in the Lords cannot be counted upon to approve of you, and Lord Taggart certainly won't appreciate the news that his brother served as your cabin boy."

"He will appreciate that his brother is alive, and that if it weren't for me, he wouldn't be."

"Will he?" Phil questioned, and for the first time Katherine realized the flaw in her plan. She met Phil's blue eyes, and Phil arched a damp brow. "The new Earl of Croston might not be pleased to lose his earldom so soon."

"And there is Lord Deal."

"So you keep telling me, and I agree that your father's best friend is an excellent champion, but Lord Deal could not do in ten months what Captain Warre could do in ten minutes if he took up your cause."

"I do not want him to take up my cause. I want him to grovel at my feet." Even from here she could see how the drizzle had turned Captain Warre's hair into dewy black waves. That she noticed his hair at all was galling. "I deserve my revenge, and I will have it."

"Is not your *rentrée* into society more important than revenge?"

It was, but— "I shall have both."

"Think, Katherine. With the right kind of effort, once we get to London all of society will praise you as a heroine." Phil narrowed her eyes in his direction. "Unless you capitalize on your acquaintance with Captain Warre, what you will very likely have is nothing."

CHAPTER TEN

WITH THE RIGHT kind of effort, Katherine decided, one could exact a very satisfying revenge.

Over the next few days, she ignored Phil's repeated pleas and made sure that her new cabin boy had plenty to do. There was no end of unpleasant tasks aboard a ship. And conveniently, the most repugnant were those most in need of repetition.

They were also those most likely to be stoking his resentment against her.

Now she stood at the top of the stairs that led down to the hold where they kept a small hen coop and listened to him sweet-talk the hens as he cleaned their straw and collected eggs.

Lord Deal could not do in ten months what Captain Warre could do in ten minutes if he took up your cause. The same would be true if he decided to oppose her cause, as well. What if she was taking things too far?

It wasn't as if she were abusing the man. If he had a complaint, there was little doubt he would make it known.

And he was reaping so much less than he deserved.

But they would reach London in a week, and Phil was right about one thing: she would need all the good favor she could curry.

She pushed her mouth into a curve and started down

the stairs. "I see you've finally found a lightskirt to allow you the liberties you've craved," she said, reaching the coop.

He faced her with a small bucket of eggs in his hand and a piece of straw in his hair. His gaze raked over her. "To what do I owe this pleasure, Captain?"

"Millicent reports that you've made a complete recovery. I wanted to see for myself."

His eyes drove into her. "And what, pray, is your assessment?"

"You don't seem to have come to any harm," she said mildly, but the way he looked at her made her pulse jump. She should have left well enough alone.

"Harm? How thoughtful of you to be concerned for my welfare. Could it be that as we approach England you are regretting your decision to demote me so severely?"

She laughed. "Heavens, no. I only regret that I won't be able to keep you after we arrive. I am convinced you would make an excellent stable boy." He looked like a fallen god, and she clenched a fist to keep from plucking the straw from his hair. The coop suddenly felt twice as small.

"Mmm. I thought perhaps you might be worried that the punishment you've meted out will turn back on you in London."

"I've meted no punishment."

"A matter of opinion." His eyes dropped to her mouth.

Every breath suddenly became a conscious effort. "Do you plan to air your complaints to London at large, Lieutenant?"

"Not at all. But the truth will out, as they say." A

hint of amusement creased the corners of his eyes. He was thinking that truth now—that he was not Lieutenant Barclay at all.

"In that case, I have nothing to fear," she said, but Phil's warning silently screamed at her. "Nobody will frown on a sailor doing honest sailors' work."

He laughed. "You'll not be able to afford such obtuseness in London if you wish to prevent the bill of pains and penalties you mentioned. London society—not to mention the Lords—will not bend to your authority. I suspect that securing your right to Dunscore will be no easy task. What will you do if your dream of becoming a countess does not come to fruition?"

"You overstep your bounds, Lieutenant." Damnation—that came out too sharply. And now he observed her through narrowed eyes that saw too much. "I *am* a countess," she said quickly, before he could respond. "I do not have to become one." She smiled and turned to go. "But I suppose if I'm not successful at acceding to my own title, I shall have to find a desperate earl to marry."

The corner of his mouth curved upward. "I'll be sure to let you know if I hear of any desperate earls in the market for a wife."

YOUR DREAM OF becoming a countess.

Four nights later, his words still chilled her. Mere days out of London, she sat with her feet propped on a chair at the table in the great cabin as evening turned to night. At the far end of the table, Millicent trounced India at draughts.

The hope of seeing Dunscore again—and soon—

clogged her throat with unwanted emotion. And now Captain Warre knew how she felt.

He pitied her. She'd seen it in his eyes.

More the fool her, for expecting something more from him. What a devil that she'd let him upset her. It would be impossible to maintain the upper hand if his slightest references to Dunscore had her succumbing to fanciful girlhood dreams.

She didn't ache for those things anymore. She had new things. She had Anne. If Dunscore had any relevance at all now, it was only because of the future it promised Anne.

"That's not fair," India cried as Millicent captured four of her pieces.

"Beg your pardon?" Millicent said. "I can't hear you behind your 'contribution to fashion.'"

"Très amusant," India said, with a movement that might have been a head toss, but it was hard to tell because beneath her usual tricorne India was swathed from head to waist in a length of turquoise cloth. "I think the English have much to learn from their Ottoman counterparts."

Which may well have been true, but given that India's interpretation of Ottoman fashion made her look more like a turquoise mummy than a modest Ottoman female, was somewhat inaccurate. "If Englishwomen were going to take a cue from their Ottoman sisters," Katherine said, sipping her wine, "they would have done it long ago."

"And they certainly won't do it now from a girl whose father has locked her away in her apartment," Phil added. And then, turning her attention squarely back to Katherine, she said, "You're not listening."

India noisily captured one of Millicent's pieces in retribution. "I think it makes a woman look mysterious." Katherine stared at the game board Captain Warre had largely crafted with his own hands. Too many things aboard this ship were being done by those hands. She could hardly grip a railing without physically sensing that his hands had been the one to clean it. She didn't have to wait for London for her actions against him to turn back on her—she suffered from them now in the smallest details of her own ship.

"Englishmen don't want that type of mystery," Millicent scoffed. "They would have women go about entirely nude if they could."

"Less than a week before our arrival," Phil went on, "though I daresay the damage is already done." She leaned close to Katherine, though for what purpose was a mystery. India's persistent eavesdropping had required the truth to come out days ago. "You *must* move him back to André's cabin." That Phil ignored Millicent's quip about nudity underscored how serious she thought this was. "He is your goose that will lay the golden eggs, and you would do well to keep him healthy and happy—not emptying slop and keeping midnight watches. You must start plumping the goose now if you wish to reap its rewards later."

"One only plumps a goose if one plans to kill it," Katherine said. "You'd best read the fable again."

"In this case, killing the goose would be vastly more satisfying," India said from behind her mummy mask. If nothing else, she could count on India for all the appropriate outrage at their new cabin boy's true identity. "I think you should tell him you've discovered his identity and call him out in a magnificent duel."

"A tempting idea, but according to Phil I need him alive to confirm my heroics. I can hardly go about London praising myself for his rescue."

Millicent made a noise. "Especially since *you* would have left him to die. I can only imagine what London would think of *that*."

"The decisions aboard this ship are mine to make," Katherine said sharply.

"I'm well aware of that," Millicent shot back. "Nobody aboard this ship has any say in matters but you."

"Watch your tongue, Millie," Phil advised. And then, to Katherine, "Trust me, dearest, praising yourself won't be necessary. It will be the easiest thing in the world to innocently let it be known what happened, and in a single morning's time all of London will know."

"And then I shall be showered with invitations and good will," Katherine said dryly.

Philomena laughed. "And then you shall place yourself in proximity to Captain Warre at every opportunity, and let the news work its magic. The two of you together will be a sensation."

"Promise me you won't expose him without me there," India said. "I want to see the expression on his face."

So did Katherine. And she needed to expose him before the voyage was over, when she still had the advantage of being in command. But deciding how and when to do it wasn't easy—except that one place it would *not* happen was in front of India.

She hadn't the means on board to give Captain Warre what *he* truly deserved. But she could at least have the pleasure of exposing him. The timing should be perfect.

Time, however, was running out. Soon—very soon—
she would have to confront him whether the time was
right or not.

CHAPTER ELEVEN

THE MISTY BLUE of midnight surrounded Katherine with an eerie breeze. Beneath her feet, Dunscore rose monolithic above the sea. A man stood on the ramparts with the wind in his hair, looking out as if commanding the mist. She moved toward him. He held out his arm, and she took his hand. Kissed it, as though paying homage.

And she was his. Only his.

His arms came around her, capturing her body, drawing her in. Possessing her. Her head fell back and his mouth came down, down, hard on her lips, branding her. She sank her fingers into dark waves of silver-streaked hair, drank in the smell of the sea on sun-browned skin.

He touched her body and her clothes melted away. Strong hands slid over her skin, closed around her breasts, touched her most secret places. She cried out and pushed herself against him, rocking.

Rocking.

Creak...splash.

Creak...splash.

Katherine's eyes flew open in the dark. She awoke on her stomach with her chest heaving into the bed, gripping her pillow with both hands, being tossed by the pitch and roll of the ship. Heat throbbed between her legs, slick and pulsing.

Captain Warre.

She closed her eyes and breathed into the pillow. The dream fogged her mind, and the blend of damp moor and salty sea air lingered in her nostrils. Misty tendrils of longing curled through her: Dunscore. Home.

Captain Warre.

On a ragged breath she pushed herself up, pushed her hair from her face and felt a damp sheen along her hairline. Her breasts hung heavy and yearning beneath her nightdress. Her lips tingled with the knowledge that his knuckles were warm, his fingers strong and callused. Her skin burned as though his hands had really touched her.

Her heart ached as though she'd really stood on Dunscore's ramparts once again with the wind in her hair and the ancient stones of her ancestors beneath her feet.

Home.

Her cabin was dark. Shadowy. The palest moonlight filtered through the windows, just enough light to see, and she reached for the familiar surroundings as though grabbing a lifeline. She forced herself from the bed, felt the cool wood floor beneath her bare feet.

This was reality. *This* was home. Here. The *Possession*. With Captain Warre merely being ferried to Britain, and she carrying out a plan to secure Anne's future. That was all.

She got a drink of water and stood listening to the ship's soft creak, but still the dream's temptation thrummed in her blood, blurring the line where Captain Warre ended and Dunscore began.

This was unacceptable. As if Dunscore were his. As if *she* were his. Agitated, she paced to the window. His eyes betrayed his desire each time she caught him watching her. He wanted to touch her. To do in the flesh all the things he'd just done in her dream.

Oh, God. If the dream hadn't ended, within moments he would have been inside her.

Her body pulsed hotly, and she fisted her hand against the pane.

It was time—past time—to confront him. That he believed she thought he was Lieutenant Barclay, who would have no reason to hide his thoughts, only made everything worse. Even his berthing with the crew was not enough—not when her eyes still sought him out and her ears still listened for the sound of his voice. If he knew she'd learned the truth, he would be more guarded.

She needed more of a barrier between them than this game of mistaken identity afforded.

You realize this changes everything. Phil's words lilted through her mind. Katherine shivered in the darkness as the night air began to cool her skin. She didn't want to capitalize on their acquaintance. She wanted to exterminate him from her thoughts. And judging from the slice of moonlight on her floor, he was on deck this very moment for the midnight watch.

She turned from the window to her chest and yanked open one drawer, then another, quickly pulling loose trousers over her hips, pushing her arms through silk shirtsleeves, aware of every brush of fabric against her skin as she stepped into a pair of sandals. With gritted teeth she let herself silently into the passageway and climbed the stairs into the cold night air.

The sails billowed in the moonlight, making the *Possession* glow like a ghost ship on a midnight-blue sea. Voices drifted from the bow, but she spotted him on the upper deck. She moved quietly across the quarter-deck, nodding to another sailor on midnight watch, and climbed the stairs. He had his back to her while he put his full weight on a line and made an efficient knot. He worked this ship as though it belonged to him. As though he knew it as well as she did.

As though he were the captain here.

Captain.

That one word would put an end to this folly and erect a barrier between them too thick for illicit yearnings to penetrate.

Yes, she would do it. Now.

"Captain," she said sharply, while she still had the element of surprise on her side. She was not disappointed.

He stopped. Turned. "I fear you must be sleepwalking, Captain," he said. The moonlight let her see his face but not his eyes—not enough to judge his thoughts. "You should return to your cabin."

"I am not sleepwalking, *Captain.*" She took a step closer, letting her tone bite him. "Did you really believe you could fool me on my own ship?"

"You must have been having wild dreams indeed."

Her heart skipped a beat. She mentally reached behind her ribs and squeezed it into submission. "No doubt you'll say you'd planned to tell me eventually," she said.

"I confess, you have me at a loss. Tell you what?" He walked past her, leaving her to follow him to the other side of the deck while he repeated the procedure he'd just done and tied another knot.

"The celebration of your homecoming would have exposed you."

He turned to face her, and she thought he smiled a

little. The sea was an eerie midnight surge behind him, crisscrossed by scores of shadowy lines that shot up to the masts. The dream washed through her like a wave spreading across the beach.

"You do realize the insane are poorly treated in England," he said. "You ought to have a care."

She laughed away both his suggestion and the dream's temptation.

"Tell me, Captain…do you deny it out of self-preservation or shame?"

He stepped so close that his warm breath, tinged with a hint of the rum her crew favored, wafted over her face. "You can hardly blame me for concealing my identity when you've made little secret that I would not be as welcome a guest as my lieutenant."

A shiver coursed over her skin.

"Although I'll admit you've surprised me," he went on. A hint of amusement played at the corner of his mouth, drawing her attention to firm lips accustomed to issuing commands. "I would have expected you to mete out something rather more unpleasant than a cabin boy's duties. That is what you've been doing, is it not? Punishing me, and not my lieutenant. I suspect you've known the truth for some time—William's loyalty is steadfast indeed. Bravo, Captain. You have proven yourself an accomplished actress these past weeks."

"As you have proven yourself an actor." Let him assume what he would about how she had discovered his identity. "Perhaps we should both join a theatrical troupe on our return."

"I fear the *ton* will be shocked enough as it is."

Oh, yes. The *ton* would be shocked. It was difficult to think standing this close to him, so Katherine moved to the railing and breathed a little easier. "Perhaps you hoped to keep the element of surprise on your side so you could have my ship arrested and forfeited the moment we reach England." She raised a brow at him over her shoulder.

He gave a bark of laughter and came up behind her, close enough that his words feathered the back of her neck. "If your ship is arrested and forfeited, it will be none of my doing. Not only do I lack the power, I also lack the desire. I assure you, once we reach England your life will proceed without interference from me."

She forced her attention on the sea, breathing only through conscious effort, inhaling his scent with every breath. Apparently he had not considered that he was her leverage against his brother's bill. "Is it true that you plan to resign your commission?" she asked.

He moved in next to her, and she watched his strong hands wrap around the railing much too close to hers. The breeze fluttered his sleeve against hers, and she felt it like skin against skin.

"Everything I told you about myself was true."

She made a noise. "You told me you have an elder brother named Theodore."

"I was describing Lieutenant Barclay."

"You also said you had never told a fiction except to your governess—"

"*That* was a lie."

"—and that you sometimes dislike yourself."

"Given your lack of regard for me, you of all people should have little difficulty understanding the truth of that."

His voice carried a dark undertone that spoke of regret. She chose to ignore it. "I find it difficult to believe you plan to abandon the glory of the sea when you have yet to reach the pinnacle of your career."

"The glory of the sea," he repeated thoughtfully. In profile he looked like chiseled stone except for the breeze ruffling his hair. Her fingers warmed with the knowledge of what that hair felt like, as though the dream had not been a dream at all. "And what, exactly, would that glory be?" he inquired, staring out at the sea. "The French prize I took in '59, and then recaptured twice after she was taken back, only to have her sunk by the Spanish? Or perhaps the cholera outbreak in '61 that killed nigh on half my crew. Or certainly you don't mean the wreck of the *Henry's Cross*—glorious indeed."

If his bitterness had been a whip, she would have bled.

"Glory," he said again, turning to look at her. "Perhaps you refer to the merchant ship I stumbled across ten years ago. I found her in the hooks of two xebecs, like a fly already half-wrapped in a spider's silk."

Katherine tensed. The *Merry Sea*. "And so you sank her."

"I attempted a rescue," he shot back.

Her mind filled with the smell of blood, the terrifying clash of swords, the screams of the *Merry Sea*'s crew, the bite of rope around her wrists. The explosive roar of Captain Warre's cannons. "Was I supposed to catch a cannonball and float to safety?"

"I didn't realize there were women aboard," he bit out.

"Would it have made a difference?"

"The fate of European men taken to Barbary is well known." The relatively few women, however, were usually ransomed quickly and returned home.

It took her a moment to realize the implication. "So you assumed they would have preferred to *die?*" she asked in disbelief.

"A quick death in the sea versus a slow, tortured one being sodomized and performing heavy labor under the whip? Yes, I think they would have. The fighting I witnessed aboard the *Merry Sea* attests to that."

"Self-preservation is a different thing from being murdered," she said coldly.

"Murdered?"

"Would you prefer to call it mercy killing? I can assure you, from where I sat there was no mercy in it at all." But honestly she didn't know which had been worse—the destruction wreaked by his cannons, or the calm that had settled over that xebec after it made its escape and the cannon fire died. Her own screams dying in her throat after she'd given up tugging uselessly on the ropes. The terror of being brought ashore, captive, in Salé—a foreign city that was the furthest thing imaginable from either London or the Continent—and having no idea what to expect.

He was quiet for a long moment—affronted, no doubt, by her lack of gratitude. "You have a flair for the melodramatic," he finally said. "And a righteous view of naval warfare for one who has plundered so many ships."

"I only plunder those that have already plundered."

"That's putting a rather fine point on it, don't you think?"

"If you're implying there is no difference between making a prize of a pirate's take and plundering a trading vessel sailing under legitimate colors, then no, I don't think so. Besides, my marauding is greatly exaggerated. I've made most of my fortune running perfectly legal trade goods." She kept her eyes on the sea but felt him watching her. Assessing. Judging. Wondering. Pearls of moonlight danced on the waves.

From the corner of her eye she saw him reach out and capture a strand of her hair. Her breath caught. The fire that had torn her from sleep ignited instantly. Her gaze flew to his hand, and she watched him smooth the inky curl between his fingers. Then she met his eyes.

He dropped the strand as though it had burned him. Common sense screamed at her to step back, but this was her deck, not his. Her ship. Her command.

"Thanks to my failures," he said roughly, "you were fed to the Barbary dogs."

Annoyance raced through her veins. "To call them dogs would be to say that Anne is half-dog," she managed calmly, "and that I will not do."

"No." A muscle tightened in his jaw. "Of course not."

"Have you spent any time in the Barbary states, Captain?"

"A little."

"And how did you find the hospitality?"

"The *hospitality?*" Something in him seemed to snap. "You've run mad. After everything that happened to you—not days, or weeks, or months, but years. *Years,* of living with al-Zayar, of being his—" He broke off and shoved his hands through his hair, then gripped the railing again. "I understand escape is a dangerous risk," he said tightly. "Undertaken only by the most desperate."

He looked at her then, and she saw the questions in his eyes. The wild imaginings. But more than that, she saw in his eyes the reason why she had not returned home after her escape.

In his eyes, her life was a tragedy. And he blamed himself.

"People become desperate for many reasons," she said sharply. "Do not presume to know something you cannot possibly understand."

"Explain it to me."

His thoughts were as easy to read as the stars on a clear night, and her heart swelled with bittersweet memories no Englishman could possibly understand.

Explain it to him? As if he could possibly comprehend the terrible emptiness of knowing without a doubt that one will never go home again, that one's life had been changed forever. The dreadful anticipation in that moment when the caravan had finally arrived at the gates of her new home—where the air had been thick with the delicious scent of orange blossoms and rang with the shrieks of delighted children somewhere inside the walls, along with deep male laughter she would soon learn belonged to Mejdan al-Zayar.

The crushing relief of finding kindness where one had expected cruelty. And then, a few short years later, the terror of having it all torn away.

Captain Warre thought she should hate Mejdan. But it would have been impossible for anyone to hate him. He was too full of smiles, of love for those around him. Yes, Anne was Mejdan's daughter, along with all that implied. But Captain Warre would not appreciate how long Mejdan had waited when he hadn't needed to. How much she had grown to adore Mejdan during that time, how much he was admired and respected by those both in and outside of the household.

That going to Mejdan's bed had been tolerable.

Captain Warre would never believe any of that. All

he would see—all any Englishman would see—was the fact of her captivity.

"You need not grieve over my virtue, Captain." She would explain nothing, to him or anyone else. "I need no one's pity. As you pointed out yourself, I've built a successful enterprise." The memories of Algiers were *her* memories—hers alone—and she would guard them the way a shipwreck guarded its treasure. Already she could feel her homeland trampling on them.

"And yet now you are going home."

"This ship is my home," she snapped.

"To Dunscore, then."

"Which, were it not for your ineptitude, I would have done years ago."

But the fatigue and weariness he'd once spoken of colored his voice, and doubts about him began a subtle attempt to lure her away from her outrage. The breeze blew a strand of hair in his face, and she clenched her fist against the urge to reach for it. "I shall leave you to your watch, Captain," she said tightly. "Good night."

SOMETHING RAW AND alive and terrifying surged through James's veins as he listened to her walk away. It burned through him, a hot and painful imposter of the life that had once animated him, reminding him that he'd once had a fire. A passion. That he'd once felt that glory of the sea she spoke of.

He gripped the railing and inhaled the cold sea air, gaining a little relief when the sound of her footsteps finally disappeared.

Where had that passion gone?

Perhaps she was right, and all he'd ever had was the

brutality that characterized life at sea. Ruthlessness masquerading as honor.

The guilt of not having been able to save her gnawed at him like a lion tearing into fresh prey. Countless times he'd gone over it in his mind. If he'd only moved in a hundred yards closer, turned more sharply to starboard. Come around their bow a bit farther to cut them off and avoid the line of fire from their cannon. If he'd held off his own orders to fire by another minute or two. Judged the current differently.

Something. There should have been *something* he could have done.

He couldn't even chalk it up to youth and inexperience. He'd already been on the sea ten years before it happened. He simply hadn't known until weeks later that the *Merry Sea* had been anything but an ordinary merchant ship. Bloody hell, it *was* an ordinary merchant ship—one that just happened to be carrying Lady Katherine of Dunscore on a passage from Italy, where she'd been stranded after her chaperoning aunt had died, to Gibraltar, where family friends awaited.

If she'd made it to Gibraltar, she would have returned to Britain, married and borne children like any other woman. She would have attended soirees and discussed the merits of French lace over Spanish or whatever it was ladies discussed. If he'd been successful in his attempt to save the *Merry Sea,* her life would have been normal.

Instead, she had become one of the most adept sea captains on the Mediterranean. She would never have an ordinary life now. She would likely never marry— who would have her? She would never plan garden parties or fret with other ladies over the introduction of a daughter into society, because Anne would never be introduced into society.

Anne. His chest tightened, and he fingered the beads around his neck. They were not mismatched, after all, but rather, symmetrically placed according to size and shape. She could not match them with her eyes, but she matched them with her fingers.

A part of him wanted to yank the necklace away and toss it into the sea in defiance of the sweetness that was beginning to collar him as surely as the twine on which the beads were strung. Her trust in him made him feel when he didn't want to feel. Care when he'd given up caring.

And Captain Kinloch—

God. He'd come so bloody close to pushing her against that railing and doing everything he'd been imagining, never mind who else was on deck. But his guilt for failing her stopped him.

Even now his chest felt tight. Raw. Damn it to hell— he didn't *want* to care what she'd endured. Didn't want to care what happened to her once they reached London, or whether she would manage to secure her title.

The only thing he wanted to care about now was the wine reserve at Croston.

CHAPTER TWELVE

AFTERNOON SUNLIGHT STREAMED into Katherine's cabin. She stood at her chest, waiting for Captain Warre to respond to a summons, remembering their conversation from the night before.

Dunscore was hers by right. Did he imagine she would allow it to be stolen, when it could be used to Anne's advantage?

The top drawer of her chest held little that was fragile save a few pieces of glass and a porcelain dog with a pale coat, friendly face and inquisitive ears. She took him out, cradling him in her palm. He looked just like the harem dog, Zaki, and a pang touched her heart.

This was not the kind of Barbary dog Captain Warre had meant.

After everything that happened to you...

He imagined she had lived as though in a bordello. Fool. Mejdan's mother would never have allowed anything so wanton.

She closed her hand around the figurine and squeezed her eyes shut, remembering the harem with a joy so fierce it hurt. The serenity of it on a warm morning with the desert breeze making silk curtains undulate and book pages flutter. Peals of laughter as Mejdan's daughters speculated about potential husbands. The comforting taste of mint tea in the afternoon, the excitement of comparing new cloth and trinkets and bangles after a day at the market.

They'd given her a home—Mejdan's mother, Riuza, his wives, daughters, children—when they hadn't needed to. If Mejdan hadn't died, she might have stayed forever.

All the reasons she had taken to the sea instead of returning to Britain after escaping Algiers coiled in a painful urge to order the ship back to the Mediterranean. All those reasons still existed. Nothing had changed. Captain Warre's words proved that much.

Nothing, except one very crucial truth: Dunscore was hers.

She replaced the figurine, shut the drawer and listened. No footsteps yet.

Her accession to Dunscore changed everything because of what it meant for Anne. Unlike the *Possession,* Dunscore could never succumb to pirate attack or wreck on a dangerous shoal. Unlike a house Katherine might purchase in France or Italy or the West Indies, Anne had roots at Dunscore that would lend legitimacy—however small—to her illegitimacy. Anne would be safe there, even after Katherine was gone.

But only if Baron Taggart's bill of attainder did not succeed. Which was why Phil was right—Captain Warre could be very, very useful.

The glory of the sea. His bitterness whispered a quiet testimony she did not want to acknowledge. The great Captain Warre was not the man she'd expected.

Thanks to my failures...

She could not afford to think of what he considered his failure. That he apparently blamed himself for her fate only worked to her unexpected advantage. It was far easier to extract a debt from a man who understood that he owed one. That he appeared almost tortured over it only made exploiting him that much easier.

She stopped in front of the looking glass, remembering the fury in his eyes. On an entirely different level, his remorse made everything more difficult. She watched herself lift a strand of her hair and caress it between her fingers.

She dropped it as quickly as he had.

For a long moment she simply stared at herself— her gold-brown eyes, her straight nose, her too-pinched mouth. The sea had weathered her skin so it was far from the creamy ideal expected in London. She leaned closer, examining a few fine lines around her eyes and the little crease above her lip.

You're so beautiful, Katie. Just like your mama. Papa's opinions had always been biased. Mama had been exquisite. Everything a lady should be.

On impulse Katherine unwrapped her turban and lifted her hair into her hands, twisting, holding the mass of it atop her head. In London there would be no more wearing her hair loose. A maid would concoct elaborate coiffures decorated with jewels and ribbons befitting a countess. She turned her head to one side, then the other, imagining the effect. She let her hair fall and picked up the shimmering ocher cloth, but dropped that, too, when a knock sounded at the door. She hadn't heard the footsteps.

She turned her back to the looking glass. "Come in."

Captain Warre opened the door and stepped inside. His gaze swept over her, darkening. "You asked to see me?"

"Yes." And her cabin was the only place that would

assure privacy. She gestured him inside and shut the door behind him, ignoring a frisson that snuck up her spine. His gaze lingered on her more intensely than usual, and she cursed herself for removing her turban when she'd known he was coming. "I've thought of a way you can repay your debt to me," she told him.

"Oh?" A trace of humor on his lips told her his control would not slip today as it had last night. That was good because she didn't want his pity or his remorse. She also didn't want the desire smoldering in his eyes, but by now she knew better than to think it would disappear.

The smile she gave him felt predatory, and she reveled in it. "No doubt it has occurred to you that you may be in a unique position to help me, given that your brother is the force behind the bill pending against me."

"It has occurred to me. But if the second reading has been put off—"

"Can you guarantee the Lords won't approve the second reading and quickly pass the bill?"

His answer was a flash of irritation in his eyes.

"But you could speak with your brother, Lord Taggart. Explain to him of the error of his ways."

"I assure you, Captain Kinloch, I have no objection to using my influence on your behalf. But nothing so tedious will be necessary. A word with Nick and any of his supporters, and I have no doubt the bill will be long forgotten."

"You think it will disappear so easily?" She fought back the desperation that threatened to creep into her voice.

"I think it very likely that someone has devised a

plan to take advantage of your absence and notoriety. Your return will likely cut the bill off at the knees."

Hope bloomed, but she didn't dare snatch it up. "Or breathe new life into it," she said. She went to her dressing table, shook her hair back and began rewinding her turban. "In which case, you will use your influence to make sure I am invited to all of the best events," she told him, watching him in the looking glass. "Once we are there, you will dote on me most solicitously. We will tell the story of your rescue to everyone who wishes to hear it—" she smiled again "—and you will praise me endlessly as your savior."

His laughter was a devilish sound that resonated through the cabin. "Will I."

She continued winding the cloth, twisting and tightening as she went, ignoring his amusement. "If they are still sitting, there won't be much time. The letter took nearly four months to find me, and we will have been over a month in sailing to England."

"I won't need a month to help you resolve it."

"You can't be certain of that. You know nothing more about the bill than I do."

"But I know a good deal more about the Lords, and about my brother." He came up behind her, close enough that her stomach dipped the way it had when he'd touched her hair, but not close enough for him to do it again. "If my initial efforts seem unavailing, I will agree to your intriguing plan. And if I fail entirely, which I cannot imagine—" he paused "—I will provide assistance." The look he gave her was the same one she'd seen last night when he'd spoken of his debt. The same one she'd seen in the hen coop. And she hated it.

"Assistance?" She finished the turban and turned her back to the looking glass.

"If you lose your estate, you will have my protection until other arrangements can be made."

His *protection?* The word and all its implications fell carelessly from his lips. She met it with a laugh and raked him with her gaze. "I assure you, Captain Warre, I have no interest in your...*protection.*"

His mouth curved. "My apologies. It was not my intention to offer you a position as my mistress." He returned her brazen physical assessment, his eyes lingering where they had no right to linger. "But the idea does have a certain appeal."

A throb of heat pulsed uninvited through intimate places. "I have a fortune independent from Dunscore," she said, waving away his offers of assistance and protection. "If I lose the estate—" the possibility struck her momentarily mute "—Anne and I will have no reason to stay in Britain at all. And your debt will remain unpaid."

He closed the distance between them, all lithe muscle and power, his sea-blown hair giving him a ferocity she would likely never see again once they reached the civilized world of London. "If it doesn't work—and I'm not saying it won't—I'll not live under this debt forever. My efforts will have to suffice, or you'll have to accept some other form of payment."

"There is no other form of payment," she scoffed, laughing. "You have nothing that I need, Captain— except your celebrity." She started to turn away. "If you're not interested in my plan—" She cut off when his hand curled around her arm.

"If I am satisfied with my repayment," he said with a tight smile, "it won't matter what you need."

"Let go of me."

His green eyes bored into her, holding her as tightly as his hand. "This entire bargain is driven by my own sense of obligation."

"Which I should have guessed was false." Except she could see in his eyes it ran bone-deep, and even now he couldn't quite hide it.

"Some debts cannot be repaid."

"An excellent excuse for default, Captain," she snapped. It was impossible to wrest out of his grasp, so she pushed him instead.

"Devil take it—" He lost his balance as the ship listed starboard, and for a moment she reeled with him, but almost immediately he regained his footing. In the next moment he pushed her against the wall and his mouth came down on hers with all the fury of an ocean tempest. She fought him, even as she opened her lips to drink him in. His kiss was half-crazed, fierce and possessive as the sea itself, surging through her blood in waves of desire unlike anything she'd ever felt.

She tried to tear away and they knocked over a chair. He crushed her to his body, backing her hard against the wall. He felt magnificent, and she hated him.

"Damn you!" She wanted him on her. Over her. In her.

Away from her.

He pushed up her tunic and found her breasts. She grabbed his shirt and felt the fabric tear, but the pleasure ripping through her body drowned all reason. She cried out with frustration. Outrage. Desire.

Something—maybe his knee—banged against the wall. His mouth seared into hers, out of control. They stumbled against the fallen chair and he kicked it out of the way.

Suddenly her cabin door flew open and crashed against the wall. She barely realized what was happening before William was there, tearing Captain Warre away from her.

"Bloody he—" Captain Warre's furious oath was cut off when William's fist landed across his jaw, sending him reeling.

"Bloody cur!" William caught Captain Warre by the shirt before he could fall and landed another hit across his jaw.

"No!" Katherine shouted her reaction an instant before regaining her senses. "William, stop! Enough!"

But William was beyond reason, and now it was Captain Warre whose back was to the wall as William drew his knife and held it to Captain Warre's throat.

"William!" Katherine commanded sharply. "Let him go."

Phil and India crowded into the doorway. "Katherine, are you all right?" Phil asked, her voice for once free of insinuation. Good God. They all thought he'd attacked her.

"You filthy bastard," William spat, nose to nose with Captain Warre, who silently stared at him. "You couldn't wait a few more days to slake your lust on someone who's willing?"

"William!" Katherine repeated. "That's enough. You misunderstand."

Finally William looked at her. Only the ship and Captain Warre's breathing made a sound as she met

William's eyes. She raised her chin a notch, but still a wash of heat spread across her face.

Phil's comprehending voice filled the cabin. "Oh, dear."

CHAPTER THIRTEEN

"NOT A SINGLE WORD." Katherine marched to the upper deck with Phil on her heels. "Not one." It was probably the most futile order she'd ever given. Besides, Phil didn't need words. Everything she was thinking was written plain as ink on her face.

Which was why Phil's obedience was worse than anything she could have said. The silence stretched out, brimming with what had just happened below. Deep breaths of sea air didn't cool the fire pounding through Katherine's veins, and her body screamed to go downstairs and finish what Captain Warre had begun.

Captain Warre. Captain Warre. The reality of what she'd just done was a battering ram forcing entrance into her mind. She craved him the way Papa had craved fast horses—recklessly and without regard to the consequences. If William had not interrupted—

She would not think of that. Looking at Phil was out of the question, so she held her spyglass to her eye.

Finally she couldn't stand it anymore. "Say it."

Phil was silent a heartbeat longer. "I confess I don't know *what* to say." Humor edged Phil's pretend dumbfoundedness. "Does this mean you'll be moving him back to a cabin, after all?"

"It's not too late to throw you overboard," Katherine snapped.

Phil only laughed. "Yes, it is. I could swim to England from here." The spyglass jolted as Phil tucked her hand into Katherine's elbow. "You mustn't be angry with yourself, dearest. Despite your better judgment, you find Captain Warre attractive—and understandably so."

"He tried to *kill* me." The resentment she'd clung to for years sounded ridiculous with his taste still heady on her tongue.

Phil ignored her. "The question is, what will you do about it once you arrive in London?" She lowered her voice. "An affair may work brilliantly to your advantage. What better to motivate him into championing your cause? Keep him hungering after your charms and see if he doesn't press your case most urgently."

"Your imagination has run wild."

"Was it my imagination, or did Captain Warre have his hands inside your—"

"Enough!" Katherine pulled her arm from Phil's grasp. "What you saw was not part of a master plan to whore myself for Dunscore. It was an accident." A moment of weakness, after she'd worked so hard to be strong. She focused her spyglass on the distant ribbon of land they'd been paralleling. "I hate him." She hated what he stood for, what he made her remember—the person she'd been when he'd fired on the *Merry Sea*. Vulnerable. Terrified. At the mercy of others, in so many ways.

"Then use him and be done with him," Phil suggested in all seriousness.

The desire to see him, to touch him, seemed to have a life of its own. The kiss had turned the whole thing into a damnable mess that had to be stopped before it went any further. She lowered the spyglass. "He believes a few words to the right people will turn the bill under. There will be little reason for us to see each other after we reach London." Questions she wished she didn't have fought to be asked.

She felt the lightest touch as Phil brushed a strand of hair from her shoulder. "I meant it when I said you mustn't be angry with yourself," Phil told her. "Sometimes our bodies have minds of their own, no matter how harshly we try to command them into submission."

Katherine raised a brow at her. "When have you ever tried to command your body into submission?"

Phil laughed prettily. "It isn't that I haven't tried, dearest."

"Where Captain Warre is concerned, I can't afford to fail." Even now, his touch smoldered on her breasts and his spicy maleness wafted from her skin.

Phil squeezed her arm. "It's the most unfair thing imaginable for him to turn out to be so—"

"Useful."

"—desirable. For heaven's sake, Katherine. You're a woman grown, and he is a very tempting man. You needn't take it to heart. Desire is just…desire. There's no rhyme or reason to it."

"Is that what you learned in Paris?"

"Yes." Phil looked away and pushed at her hair. "Yes, precisely. Things happen in Paris—all kinds of things that go against reason. It's not for nothing that they call it the City of Love." She waved her hand. "But that's neither here nor there. We'll be in London shortly, which hasn't near the magical quality of Paris, and if you're not going to have an affair with him—"

"I'm not."

"—you'll need a different plan because I daresay even he won't be able to make the bill disappear that easily."

HE NEEDED TO get away from the sea, and it couldn't happen quickly enough.

James stalked through the lower gun deck, snatched up the oil rag he'd been using and attacked the salt clinging to the hinges on the nearest gun port.

The sea had addled his brain—he'd seen it happen to better men. God, what had he *done?*

He licked his lip and tasted drying blood, just as a splash of salt spray hit him in the face. Damnation—he swiped his eye with the back of his wrist and heard William calling him.

"James."

"Go away." Instead, William came over and stood next to the cannon. James stood, too, and the motion made his face throb. "Don't take directions well, do you?"

"Not from you." William stood with his feet shoulder-width apart and folded his arms. "I came to apologize."

"Sod off." James turned away to oil the next hinge. There wasn't a trace of apology in William's voice, not that James wanted an apology. Or deserved one. She'd pushed the limits of his patience until he'd boiled over. Christ, he was a disgusting wretch, on fire for the very qualities her ruination had produced—a ruination that was his own damned fault.

The sooner this bloody ship docked, the better.

"What are your intentions toward Katherine?" William demanded.

"My *intentions?*" James tossed the rag aside and turned back, disbelieving. "You catch us in a compromising position and now what? You think to force my hand? I can't imagine your captain approves this approach."

"She may be the captain, but she's still a woman. A very vulnerable one with little experience fending off men who try to seduce her."

When an Englishman wearing a Barbary costume and gold in his ears demanded that one do the right thing, it was a sure sign the world had turned on its head. James felt his lip crack and pressed his fingers to it—too hard, though, and he flinched. "I begin to wonder how well you actually know Captain Kinloch, for all your professed friendship. Perhaps you've failed to notice the cutlass at her side, and her willingness—nay, her *eagerness*—to use it?"

"And the fact that she didn't." William's eyes hardened. "If you lure her into an affair, I promise I won't be so gentle in my next dealing with you."

"I have no intention of luring Captain Kinloch anywhere—least of all into an affair. Captain Kinloch is the last woman I would *ever* contemplate having a liason with." That was a bloody lie.

"Your actions half an hour ago prove otherwise."

"The only thing my actions prove is that I'm a man who's been too long at sea, and Captain Kinloch is a very beautiful woman who, apparently, has been too long at sea, as well."

William got right up in James's face, but this time James was ready. William would not strike him again. "If you make her fall in love with you," William said, "if you break her heart, I swear on all that's holy you'll regret it."

Fall in *love* with him? Good God. "Such pretty romantic notions, Jaxbury. For God's sake, all I want in the whole world, all that's driven me for months, is the prospect of consuming large volumes of cognac in front of the fire. I assure you, breaking Captain Kinloch's heart has no place in that plan. *She* has no place in that plan." Never mind that at this particular moment he would give up all the cognac in France for a single rut with her. God.

"That's just fine," William said. "But if it's true, then I would suggest you stay the hell away from her."

As soon as he repaid his debt, it was a suggestion James had every intention of following.

CHAPTER FOURTEEN

OF COURSE, IF the debt depended on his own sense of obligation, he could simply forgive himself and be done with it.

The idea had no small amount of appeal several short days later, standing with Captain Kinloch and Miss Germain in front of the late Lord Dunscore's towering house in St. James's cloaked by the rank London evening, with an impatient hired hack in the street and no answer at the door. He held Anne against his chest to shield her from the damp and contemplated whether it would be possible to break down the door.

"Perhaps they assumed you were never returning and closed the place up for good," Millicent hissed into the drizzly night.

"And left the lights burning?" Captain Kinloch shot back in a tight whisper. "There must be servants here."

"Deaf ones."

Meow! came Mr. Bogles's outraged protest from inside a lidded basket.

"If we can't get in," Captain Kinloch snapped, "we'll go to Philomena's."

James was just about to risk an almost certain nighttime spectacle by rapping the knocker a third time when the door finally cracked open on silent hinges. A skew-wigged servant scowled out at them.

"Dodd—" Captain Kinloch started, but James had no patience for that.

"Do excuse us." He pushed past the old servant into a grand marble foyer that left no doubt as to the extent of the wealth Captain Kinloch had inherited.

"Now just wait," the man sputtered. "You can't—"

"Please tell your footmen to bring her ladyship's trunks from the carriage."

"I beg your pardon!" came Mr. Dodd's indignant protest. "I—" Then suddenly he sputtered, "Lady Katherine?" Comprehension dawned. "I—I mean, your ladyship! I had no idea. That is to say, we had no word— We weren't informed of your arrival." He swept into a deep bow.

"The *trunks*," James ordered, and was instantly sorry when Anne roused in his arms. "Go back to sleep," he tried to murmur, but it came out more like a muttered command.

"The trunks. Of course. Of course!" The man finally spurred into action.

Millicent carried Mr. Bogles's basket inside, while his repeated meows echoed through the foyer as footmen finally began carrying trunks up the great, curved staircase. Captain Kinloch stood frozen beneath a blazing silver chandelier, looking as vulnerable as Anne felt in his arms.

"Your ladyship is aware," Mr. Dodd started, but paused. "That is to say, does your ladyship intend..."

For God's sake, this was more than James could tolerate on a few moments' sleep snatched during a pothole-ridden coach ride that had lasted an eternity. He glanced around for somewhere to put Anne and spotted an upholstered bench against one wall.

"Intend what?" Captain Kinloch came to life suddenly. Sharply.

"Does your ladyship intend to—" Dodd swallowed visibly "—evict Mr. Holliswell and Miss Holliswell, then?"

Her ladyship's head whipped around. *"Holliswell."* Her tone sliced through the air like her beloved cutlass.

Bloody hell. James went to the bench, fighting an urge to hold Anne closer rather than put her down, but Millicent gathered Anne away from him before he could decide otherwise.

Mr. Dodd wrung his hands. "He and Miss Holliswell have…set up residence, you see, and—"

"In my *father's house?*"

"We did protest, your ladyship. Let me assure you!" Dodd's eyes traveled from Captain Kinloch's turban, down the length of her loose hair and over her woolen wrap, to the billow of Barbary trousers peeking out below and the boots that had served well on a ship's deck but were unspeakably outlandish here. "But it's well-known that Mr. Holliswell is to acquire… That is to say, he expects to receive…"

"He is to acquire nothing." Those glittering topaz eyes flicked toward James just long enough for him to see fear developing behind her outrage. His gut tightened, and he was relieved when with angry strides she went to peer into a sitting room. He could see from here that it was strewn with gilded sofas and chairs that looked as though they belonged at the French court.

"What furniture is this?" she demanded.

"Miss Holliswell has been…redecorating, your ladyship," Mr. Dodd said faintly.

Her hands fisted at her sides. "I want the Holliswells' things thrown into the street."

And wouldn't the gossips have a frenzy with *that*. "Where are the Holliswells now?" James asked irritably. He would explain the folly of her plan later.

"They are out for the evening, sir." Dodd eyed him with mistrust. "I believe they went to dine with Lord Croston."

Devil take it. "*I* am Lord Croston," he said sharply. By God, he would find Nick tonight and put an end to this.

"But…" Dodd's eyes grew wide, and he paled.

There was nothing pleasant about the tight smile curving Captain Kinloch's mouth as she turned her back on Holliswell's painfully distasteful furnishings. "I daresay this would be an excellent time for you to effect your miraculous return," she said, stopping in front of him. "And when you see Mr. Holliswell, you may tell him not to step foot in my house again unless he wishes to be gelded."

"I fully agree with the first." The fact that hearing her speak of gelding aroused him even the tiniest bit made it even clearer this business could not end quickly enough. "As to the second, I may not phrase it in exactly those terms."

"I will find it very hard to stand paralyzed by the strictures of politeness while Holliswell steals my estate," she warned.

Meow! Mr. Bogles agreed.

This, from the woman who thought *he* was ruthless. An accusing voice reminded him this was all his fault, but the fact that he owed her did not make her any less impossible. "If you don't grasp some concept of the strictures of politeness, Parliament will hand your estate to him on a silver platter before you can toss a single gilded footstool into the street."

COME MORNING, KATHERINE fully intended to throw an entire sitting room suite into the street. She tried relaxing her fists, but curled them tightly again to keep Captain Warre from seeing how badly she was shaking. "It would seem he's already been handed my estate on a platter. But if he does return tonight, he'll not step through the door."

The door. It rose high, topped by a sweep of carved marble and flanked by great stained-glass panels whose lead canes she used to trace with small fingers. The last time she'd been here, servants had streamed out that door with her trunks as she bid a numb farewell to Papa and his new wife.

The adventure will do you good, Katie. And when you return, I've no doubt you'll trounce us all at hombre.

The cold chill of powerlessness iced through her and settled in her stomach.

"As long as there's no bloodshed," Captain Warre said with irritation, "I don't care what kind of reception you give him. But I'll thank you not to make my task more difficult by losing control of your temper when I'm not present to tame you."

Her attention shot to him. *Tame* her. She forced a smile. "Find your brother tonight and solve the problem, Captain, and you need never concern yourself with my temper again."

"Nothing would please me more, I assure you."

She glared at him, tempted to continue goading him

simply as a distraction. But behind him a wispy memory lighted on the staircase—Mama with her hand on the banister, glittering and laughing before an evening on the town. *One more hug, Katie, but then I must go or your father will throw me over his knee.*

The great entrance made her feel small. She could not do this. She was not like Mama, sparkling and polished to London perfection. She was more like the wood the *Possession* was made from—burnished and solid, but showing the effects of many storms.

London would tolerate nothing less than sparkle and polish.

"Then by all means, Captain," she said, "be on your way. We have no further use for you here." One word and their trunks could be loaded back onto the hack and returned to the *Possession*. Everything inside her screamed to give the order.

He stood watching her, tight-lipped, studying her too closely. "I shall go speak with Nick and Holliswell. I'll send word of the result."

"Excellent."

"Do try to refrain from anything rash in the meantime."

"I have no idea what you could mean, Captain."

"It's too soon to go careening back to the ship and sailing away in the night."

"What an imagination you have. I—"

"Mama?" came Anne's small voice through the hall.

Katherine's attention snapped to the bench, where Anne clung to Millicent with her feet dangling to the floor, trying to stand. "What is it?"

"I don't feel well."

Just that quickly, Katherine abandoned any fantasy

of returning to the ship. She rushed to Anne's side with Captain Warre a step behind her, a heartbeat away from ordering Dodd to send for a doctor.

"What hurts?" she demanded, finding Anne's forehead and cheeks cool to the touch.

"She has no fever," Millicent said.

"The ground feels strange, Mama." Fatigue and distress mingled in Anne's plaintive voice. "There's no up and down, but I still feel the waves."

Katherine had barely breathed a sigh of relief when Captain Warre reached past her and lifted Anne into his arms. "That's only natural," he told her. "Just as a sailor must find his sea legs when he first boards a ship, *you* must find your land legs."

Anne made a small, whining sound and looped her arms around his neck, letting her head fall into the curve of his shoulder.

It was on the tip of Katherine's tongue to order him to put Anne down, but Anne looked so content she couldn't bring herself to do it. Instead, she brushed delicate wisps of dark hair from Anne's cheek. There was no sense reminding Anne that they went through this every time they went ashore. Already her eyes were closing as Captain Warre rubbed slow circles over the back of her shoulder. She was too tired for reason.

The intimacy of Captain Warre's touch stirred a dangerous feeling inside her. "I'll take her up to bed," Katherine said, reaching for Anne, but Captain Warre started toward the stairs.

"I've got her."

That temper he was so anxious to escape sent up a lick of flame, but she tamped it down and beckoned

Millicent to follow them up the staircase. Soon enough he would be gone.

Halfway up the stairs, her feet slowed. That old, giant portrait still hung where the staircase turned—a wind-swept moor cradling a massive graystone fortress at the edge of a roiling sea. It was a fortress as familiar to her as her own flesh, and the longing to go there—to walk its ramparts once more—poured up from the deepest parts of her soul.

When you are countess of Dunscore, Katie, every stone in these walls will cry out your name.

She tore her gaze away from the painting. She may have been foolish enough to believe Papa then, but she had no illusions now. The Lords could snatch Dunscore from her just as quickly as Papa had married Lady White. Just as suddenly as Mejdan had died in the night.

But Dunscore could secure Anne's future. As soon as Anne was settled and comfortable upstairs, Katherine would begin a list of everything that would need to be done tomorrow.

Deep inside, her spirit shrank from the task.

"Miss Holliswell has taken the north rooms," Dodd told her as they reached the top of the stairs.

"And Mr. Holliswell has taken my father's rooms, of course."

"He has, your ladyship."

Holliswell thought to get himself a title and fortress at her expense, did he? They would see about that. She caught a flash of skirt disappearing through a doorway just as she topped the stairs. "Who is that?"

"Miss Bunsby, your ladyship. Miss Holliswell's companion."

"I want her out. I want all of the Holliswells' servants out."

"There will be time enough for that tomorrow," Captain Warre said shortly. "Where can we put Anne?"

"The blue rooms are vacant, your ladyship."

The blue rooms. She didn't want to see them again, but Anne gave a whimpering sigh against Captain Warre's shoulder. Katherine turned woodenly toward her girlhood apartment. They were only rooms, after all.

She stopped abruptly outside the threshold and let Captain Warre carry Anne inside. Through the door, the shades of misty blue Mama had chosen threatened her with the same melancholia that had consumed her in those last London days after Papa's wedding, a few weeks after her sixteenth birthday, and only days before she had been sent to the Continent. The eleven years that had passed suddenly seemed like eleven days.

Now Papa was gone. Lady White, she'd received word years ago, had died in childbirth. And Katherine had finally returned to claim her birthright.

She reached for her anger like a lifeline. "We'll need someone to move that small trunk into the adjoining room."

"Certainly, your ladyship."

"I'll move it myself," Millicent said tensely.

"You won't," Katherine barked back, more harshly than she'd meant to. A gulp of air didn't quite ease the tightness in her throat. "Put her in the room adjacent."

"Of course."

Captain Warre was settling Anne onto the blue-draped bed where, in the years before Lady White entered Papa's life, Katherine had spent so many nights dreaming of the adventures she and Papa would have traveling the world together. Anne's eyes were closed, as though there were no safer place in the world than Captain Warre's arms, and she protested when he set her against the pile of blue satin pillows. He murmured something in her ear and she sighed.

The bed was too high to be safe for Anne. There was only a small screen in front of the fireplace, and there was a great expanse of empty space in the middle of the room. Later, after Captain Warre was gone, she would move Anne. They would share a room, and tomorrow she would set about having the house changed for Anne's safety.

The thought prompted Katherine to finally find her feet. Long-dead emotions clawed inside her chest, trying to resurrect themselves as she entered the room. She went to the bed and smoothed Anne's forehead, leaning down to give her a kiss.

Katherine straightened and found herself inches from Captain Warre. Lips she remembered too well thinned. "You're going to have to approach this with all the measured precision you would use when confronting a hostile ship," he whispered. "Temper will avail nothing."

"How do you know I ever used measured precision?" she whispered back, focusing all her attention on him instead of on the books, the trinkets, the decade-old toiletries that still lined the dressing table. The collection of artifacts that testified to a girl who—thankfully—no longer existed.

"You may leave now," she told him. But at the thought of him going, a first trickle of panic pooled in her belly. Quickly she put distance between them by moving into the corridor where they would not disturb Anne. He followed.

"Forgive me if I'm hesitant to leave until I have some assurance that you will wait to hear from me before you take any action. It won't help matters if you do something rash."

"I'm not stupid, Captain."

"But you're angry."

"What uncanny powers of observation you have." Like the rising tide, panic lapped higher. She felt it washing her toward him, tempting her to lean on him. So she smiled. "I assure you, Captain, I've never felt more in control."

"Excellent." Those piercing green eyes searched her with a hint of ridicule. "Then I shall go interrupt Nick's dinner party, confident that if Holliswell slips past me, you'll not stain all that lovely marble in the foyer with his blood. The law of the sea does not apply in London."

"Your confidence does me great honor." She forced her feet to carry her toward the staircase. "Of course, if speaking with your brother avails nothing—" she paused with her hand on the banister and faced him "—I will expect you to move forward with *my* plan."

Amusement touched the corner of his mouth. "Naturally. I'll send word tonight."

"Give Cousin Holliswell my felicitations."

His lip curled. "Certainly."

She cocked her head to the side. "Perhaps, when I see him, I shall call him out."

"Good God." Captain Warre's eyes blazed and he shook his head, turning to go. He was still windblown, unshaven, all muscle and prowess—strong and unyielding as a mainmast as his eyes met hers.

I'm afraid. The words winged through her mind and perched on her lips.

His eyes followed them there and darkened with desire. She bit her tongue to keep from spilling out her fears and asking for his reassurance. This was *Captain Warre!* She would use him, yes, to ensure her place in society.

But she would never lay her head in the crook of his neck and let him lull her to sleep.

CHAPTER FIFTEEN

MELANCHOLIA. JAMES CONTEMPLATED the self-diagnosis a short time later as the hack rattled past St. George's and a light drizzle began to fall and he tried to dredge up some kind of emotion about finally being home again but couldn't. His ship's surgeon had never suggested melancholia, but it would explain everything.

By God, as soon as he settled this business tonight he would order his coach and set out for Croston. He would arrive there tomorrow and sink into blessed oblivion, where he would remain for as long as it took to renew himself.

He would forget Captain Kinloch. Forget that he'd ever touched her. Forget that haunted look in her eyes while she stood paralyzed at the threshold of her childhood apartment—

Christ. If he did not end this tonight, she would be his undoing. She drove him mad, made him furious, enslaved him to that baser nature she scorned so mightily, reminded him of the man he should have been but wasn't.

Where Captain Kinloch was concerned, he clung to control by an unraveling thread.

The hack lurched to a stop in front of his town house. It was a devil waiting for admittance at his own door, but Bates opened quickly, and James headed straight for the dining room, leaving Bates standing slack-jawed. He thought of his borrowed breeches and jacket and his wigless, sea-ravaged hair, and he curled his lip. Let them be shocked. That bill would receive its deathblow right here. After tonight, there would be no question who held title to the Dunscore estate and who didn't.

And, for that matter, who held title to Croston.

By the time Bates recovered his senses enough to follow, James was nearing the dining room. From the sound of things, it was a small party.

"May I just say, it's very good to see you, my lord," Bates said from close behind him.

"Thank you, Bates. It's good to see you, as well." That wasn't at all what Bates meant, of course.

He walked into the dining room.

Voices fell silent. There was a heartbeat, then a shriek. *"James!"* Honoria launched herself out of her chair and threw herself at him, wrapping her arms around his neck and sobbing into his shoulder. "James!"

He closed his arms around his little sister, and his throat constricted. There was an uproar of disbelief and the clatter of silverware hitting china as the guests realized what was happening.

"Good God." Nick came ashen-faced around the table, gaping as though James had just emerged from the tomb in his burial linens. He opened his mouth to speak, but no sound came out.

James inhaled deeply past the tightness of his throat, taking in Honoria's tears and Nick's damp eyes. Their mourning clothes. Their grief was part of the equation he hadn't factored in.

The moment he set Honoria aside, Nick hugged him fiercely despite the onlookers. "My God!" Nick said, nearly squeezing the breath from James's lungs. "It can't be!"

"I say!" one of the guests exclaimed. "Extraordinary!"

So this was what resurrection felt like.

Nick stepped back, and Honoria quickly took his arm. "Sit! Eat! La, you look an absolute fright. Tell me you didn't sail all the way home on some awful merchant ship—"

A jumble of speculation went up as everyone began to fire questions at once. James held up his hand. "Enough!" Under his breath to Nick, he said, "I need to speak with you privately." And then, to Honoria, "I have business to take care of, Ree. As soon as it's done, I shall be entirely yours. I promise." He offered a slight bow to the guests. "My apologies. If you'll excuse me." On his way out, he paused to whisper to Bates. "Tell Lord Pennington not to let Mr. Holliswell leave."

In the library, Nick gave him another rough embrace. When they broke apart, James felt a stab of raw emotion that matched the look on Nick's face. It was a face much like his own—hard mouth, sharp cheekbones, dark brows over Mother's green eyes. Nick's wig hid whether the Croston gray had begun to plague him, and there was no trace of the dimple Mother said Nick had inherited from her paternal grandmother. They were all so fragmented now—James at sea, Nick and Ree here, none of them with children. For a moment his throat was too tight to speak.

The slightest change in events, and he might have perished and never seen Nick again.

"By what miracle did you survive the wreck?" Nick asked thickly.

By the miracle of Captain Katherine Kinloch. James inhaled deeply, shoving away thoughts of waves and wreckage.

"The reason I survived," he said carefully, watching for Nick's reaction, "the *only* reason, is because I was pulled half-dead from the water by Katherine Kinloch."

Nick's eyes widened, then narrowed as he made the connections. "Bloody hell."

James stared at him. He tried to keep his voice calm. "It was an amazing coincidence of timing, really. I had been drifting for days on a piece of decking, you see, and she happened to be sailing for Britain to defend her estate against a bill of pains and penalties."

"Bloody *hell.*" Nick turned away, bracing his hip with one hand and his forehead with the other.

"I would have thought 'It's a miracle' would be the more appropriate phrase," James said sharply.

"You think I don't know that? Bloody *hell!*" He raked his fingers into his hair and came away looking as if he were the one who had just spent weeks at sea. "Katherine Kinloch? Are you certain?"

James raised a brow. "After four weeks—"

"Christ, never mind." Nicholas gestured away the inanity of his question. "And so now I have her to thank for your return. This gets more bloody entertaining by the day." He gave a mirthless laugh.

"Explain to me what 'this' is. A debt to Holliswell, I presume."

This time Nick's laugh sounded more like a strangle. "A hurricane in the West Indies, pirates off the horn of Africa, an entire cargo's worth of repairs paid on bottomry to some opportunistic Boston shipwright—the value of nigh on our entire operation and investment, gone in one perfect coalescence of disaster."

James stared at him in disbelief. "And in the time you've believed you had the title you haven't paid him off?"

"You know me better than that," Nick snapped.

"Sometimes I wonder if I know you at all. You're part of the Croston lineage, Nick—not some yeoman's son. Christ. Solving a problem in the most convoluted way possible—never mind throwing an innocent to the dogs in the meantime."

"An innocent!" Nick stalked up to him. "Look here, James. If Katherine Kinloch made a successful escape from Barbary, why did she not go to our consulate? Why did she not write her father? Come home to Dunscore? Not only are her escapades in the Mediterranean disloyal to the Crown, they're disgraceful to society and a downright bad example to our young ladies."

James barked a laugh and hoped it was enough to hide his sudden urge to grab Nick by the throat. So much for the maudlin homecoming. "I hardly think captaining a ship will become society's next vogue for young ladies. Are you trying to repay a debt, or have you launched a crusade for female propriety?" He cut to the chase. "I want you to end this business you've brought up with the Lords. Withdraw your support for the bill and find another way to repay Holliswell."

"Drop my support for the bill?" Nick's eyes darkened with raw emotion, then hardened. "Very well. Just as soon as you find another way to convince Holliswell to allow me to marry Clarissa."

"That had bloody well better be a joke."

"I'd planned to talk to him tonight—" He broke off.

The rest of the sentence, *before I learned I didn't hold the title,* hung in the air. But it was clear the cold single-mindedness in Nick's eyes had nothing to do with the title and everything to do with Clarissa Holliswell.

"If Holliswell's consent depends upon you being an earl, then there's little I can do. I'll not snuff myself out to further Miss Holliswell's cause." He went to the door and called Bates. "Send Holliswell here," he ordered.

"Don't be an ass. Damn it all, James, I don't want to fight with you. Ten minutes ago I thought you were lost forever, and now—" He closed his eyes and cursed again. "If it's a choice between Miss Holliswell's future or Katherine Kinloch's, I don't have to tell you which I'll choose."

"The Dunscore title in exchange for Miss Holliswell's hand and forgiveness of the debt you owe. Is that the arrangement?"

Nick stared at him. "Unlike Katherine Kinloch, Clarissa actually *is* an innocent. And fragile. It would be the easiest thing in the world for a man to crush her." His jaw worked, and his eyes looked coldly through James to some imagined horror beyond. "I always thought men were fools to be taken in by blue eyes and pretty faces, but God—I can't even look at her without wanting to do everything in my power to keep her safe and make her happy, which she bloody well won't be if Holliswell marries her off to someone like Oakley." Nick's lip curled. "I can see you understand my predicament."

Yes. But Katherine was in a predicament, as well. "You really imagine that once Holliswell has the title, he's going to—"

"Uphold the bargain? Perhaps not. But I know for a fact he won't allow the marriage without it."

James went to pour brandy from what he would always think of as Father's snifter. Maybe Nick was right about Clarissa. Probably he wasn't. The effect was the same for Katherine either way. "I could loan you the money," he said.

Nick laughed bitterly. "Exchange one creditor for another?"

"Give it to you, then." Hell. If that was the cost of his debt to Captain Kinloch, it was a small price to pay.

"Even if my pride would allow me to accept, it would avail nothing. Holliswell wants the title."

There was no opportunity to say that he wasn't going to get it, because Holliswell came through the door. He spotted James and curved his mouth into a plump, greasy smile, but his eyes glittered with fury. "Your lordship," he said with an obsequiously deep bow. "I cannot begin to describe our joy at your return."

James moved away from the snifter and toward Holliswell, deliberately failing to extend an invitation to drink. "You will be relieved as well to learn that your cousin the countess of Dunscore has also returned," he said, and fixed his eyes on the hard lines of Holliswell's face. "As it happens, it was she who pulled my half-drowned corpse from the sea. It's no understatement to say I owe her my life."

Holliswell's expression barely flickered. "What happy news. A miracle, no less."

James set his glass on the desk and looked Holliswell in the eye. "You will not return to Lady Dunscore's house tonight." In fact, he would send a footman to follow them and make sure. "Tomorrow, you will send your people to collect your things. And in the future, you will remember that you are not the Earl of Dunscore, and you will act accordingly."

Holliswell smiled pleasantly. "Given Lady Dunscore's lengthy absence, I never expected she would return, nor did I expect she would care about the house. Naturally, my daughter and I will find other accommodations until everything has been settled."

"Naturally," James said coldly.

Holliswell turned to Nick. "You'll understand, of course, if my daughter and I take our leave early. You... didn't have anything you wished to discuss, did you?"

Nick's jaw flexed. "We'll speak tomorrow."

"No doubt we will." Holliswell smiled. "No doubt at all."

THE MANTEL CLOCK in the yellow guest apartment made a tiny chime as Katherine scratched out a list for tomorrow. Half past eleven, and still no word from Captain Warre.

Mrs. Hibbard quietly slipped in with a tray. "I brought you a fresh pot," she whispered, and replaced the tea service on the cart next to the writing desk. Katherine leaned forward to look through the door into the bedroom. Anne stirred a little in the big bed, not quite settled after being moved from the blue rooms.

"And I brought a few slices of Cook's raisin bread. And some butter." Mrs. Hibbard poured Katherine a fresh, steaming cup of tea and stood there with the teapot cradled in her hands, staring at Katherine through brown eyes filled with emotion. "It's such a joy to have you home, Lady Katherine."

"Thank you, Mrs. Hibbard." But this was not home, and she was Captain Kinloch, not Lady Katherine anymore, and if she ate anything now, she would probably throw it back up. "Please go to bed—there's no need to trouble yourself further."

Mrs. Hibbard frowned, and her plump fingers tightened on the teapot. "I intend to stay at your service as long as you need."

"I'll be retiring shortly."

The old housekeeper looked a little distressed. "I'll order the blue rooms cleaned top to bottom tomorrow, Lady Katherine. I assure you, they'll be fit and proper before you're up and about, and your things will be moved first thing in the morning." She glanced at Katherine's outfit. "You'll need a lady's maid—"

"No. I won't. That will be all."

Mrs. Hibbard stepped back. Damnation—this was not a ship, and Mrs. Hibbard was not one of her crew. Katherine softened her tone. "My apologies. I shall occupy these rooms while I'm here. Anne shall take the pink rooms as soon as they are free."

"Of course." Mrs. Hibbard bobbed an awkward curtsy. "Everything as you wish." She set the teapot on the tray and folded her hands in front of her. "If you need anything in the night, just ring."

When she was gone, Katherine inhaled deeply. Exhaled. She did not want to feel sixteen again. Being in London did not mean she had to fall helplessly back into her old life—as if that would even be possible. She'd seen too much of the world since then.

She reached for her tea and took a sip. The aroma was a physical assault from the past—black tea, not the mint she favored now. Turning back to her list, she stared at what she'd already written. *Bed. Fireplace screen. Win-*

dow latch. It was unlikely Anne's small fingers could budge it, but better safe than sorry.

She dipped her pen. *Small metal pitcher and bowl.* Something that wouldn't break if dropped. And— Good God. *Staircase.* Someone would need to stay with Anne at all times, and they would need the same rule about Anne leaving her rooms as they'd had about her going on deck alone.

Furiously she added to the list, keeping her attention squarely on the task at hand, but still old emotions slowly strangled her.

When you are countess of Dunscore, Katie, the sun will shine on this gloomy manse all the year round. Come—I've learned a new trick at cards to show you. It will take our minds off this dreadful weather.

Her hand stilled, and she looked up. The weather at Dunscore was fairer than London, but once Father had met Lady White they hardly left London at all.

As soon as possible, she would take Anne to Dunscore. Anne would like it there. She would be able to hear the waves and smell the surf. She would be able to run her hands across old, craggy walls, and—with help—explore the gardens.

A light knock sounded at the door, and Dodd came in with a note on a silver tray. "This just arrived, your ladyship."

Finally. Katherine shot to her feet and snatched the note off the tray, tearing it open.

Holliswell will not disturb you tonight. All is not resolved—need more time.
JW

Her lungs and throat constricted. "Thank you, Mr. Dodd," she managed. "That will be all for tonight."

Dodd bowed and left, and Katherine stared at Captain Warre's tight, neat writing. Clearly a few words with his brother and Holliswell had not been enough. The note trembled in her fingers. What if nothing he did was enough?

She shoved the thought away, but still she sank back in her chair, blinking back tears. Damn Holliswell, and damn Nicholas Warre. They had no right. No *right*.

She crushed the note in her fist.

All the Lords would see was a shockingly wayward woman who had spurned her father and taken to the sea. They would not understand about captivity, about the finality of fate. About Mejdan's sudden death and what life might have been like if Riuza had not helped her escape the household, or how few choices were available to a slave with a child in her belly. They would not understand about the power of the sea and how powerless she would have been if she had simply come home. None of them had ever tasted true powerlessness. Not one.

She tasted it now, even more bitter and pungent than she remembered.

Slowly she unfolded the note and read it once more. "JW." The scrawled initials taunted her with their informality. Not *Captain,* not *Lord Croston*. Just *JW*. James Warre.

The memory of his kiss scorched across her lips and through her belly.

She forced it away. He was not JW to her. And if he

did not find a way to resolve everything very shortly, she would begin taking advantage of her role as his rescuer and dare him to object.

CHAPTER SIXTEEN

"I DON'T CARE where you put them," she told Dodd the next morning, surveying the gilt-and-floral tangle piling up in the entrance hall. "Just so long as they're loaded into the cart within the hour and returned to the seller."

"Of course, your ladyship." He cast an uncertain eye over her outfit as two servants carried yet another flamboyant chair from the sitting room into the entry.

She cocked her head and looked him in the eye, satisfied when he looked away. No, she had not changed her clothes. No, she had not slept. Yes, she was taking charge of the household.

She may not know how to sparkle like Mama, or how to win support like Papa always had, but she knew how to command a ship, and this could not be much different.

Another servant carried a small chair from the sitting room. "Put it there," she ordered, pointing to an empty space by the door. "Where is the old set?" she asked Dodd.

"The attic, your ladyship."

"Have it brought down."

He inclined his head. "As you wish."

She narrowed her eyes at him. "Is there something you wish to say to me, Dodd?"

His brows shot up. "Not at all, your ladyship."

"I make it my policy that my crew—my *staff*—may speak freely."

"Your ladyship is too kind. Now if your ladyship will excuse me, I shall see that the old sitting suite is brought down posthaste." He paused. "One never knows when your ladyship might receive callers." His eye strayed briefly to her trousers.

"Thank you for enlightening me," she snapped. "And if you repeat 'your ladyship' once more, I shall mete out consequences no other lady would dream of."

His lips thinned, but he acquiesced with a stiff bow and turned to do as he'd been ordered. Resistance was nothing she couldn't handle. Even sweet old Dodd would follow her direction or find himself seeking new employment.

She started up the stairs. Phil would be here within the hour with a dressmaker. Dodd would be happy about that, at least.

But upstairs in the guest apartment, she discovered that Millicent had not waited for the dressmaker.

"There's a wardrobe full of gowns in my dressing room," Millicent told her. "This one fits well enough." It didn't, and it was ugly. Katherine specifically remembered leaving the blue-and-beige gown behind because it wasn't fit for the Continent.

Anne, sitting next to Millicent on the couch, made a face. "It smells awful, Mama."

"Like moths and mildew," Katherine said. "For God's sake, Millie, go put on your other one. We'll all be measured for new gowns as soon as Phil arrives with the modiste."

"I don't need a new gown," Millie said. "There are plenty in that wardrobe I can remake."

"I don't like London, Mama," Anne said plaintively. "I want to go back to the ship."

Katherine crouched in front of Anne and touched her cheek. "You've only been here one night, sweetling. You will love London—I promise."

Her false cheer did not fool Anne. "I don't think I will, Mama." She sighed and leaned against Millicent.

"I shall begin remaking one of the gowns today," Millie said a little crossly. "I shan't need many."

"You will not gad about London in my childhood clothes," Katherine said. "I don't want to hear anything more about it." She went to the writing desk, dipped her pen and signed her name to the last letter she'd written. She glanced up in time to see Millie's mouth tighten, but she hadn't the patience to do anything but ignore it. She folded the paper, let a small blob of bloodred sealing wax pool onto it and pressed Papa's seal into the wax.

"Will I be gadding about London, Mama?" Anne asked tiredly.

When she lifted the seal, the Dunscore coat of arms stared up at her.

When you are countess of Dunscore, Katie, you'll fly her crest from these ramparts, and the ancients will honor it from their tombs.

She turned abruptly from the desk and went to Anne. "You—" she tapped Anne's nose "—will be learning music and dance and poetry and all the things a young lady needs to know."

A tutor. Katherine returned to the desk and added to the list. Yes, Anne would need a tutor.

After answering a barrage of questions about music and dance and poetry and all the things a young lady needs to know, Katherine went to check on the progress of clearing the Holliswells' things from the rooms they'd occupied.

Millie followed her into the hallway, where servants scurried back and forth carrying boxes downstairs. "Lady Dunscore," Millie said from behind her, "when are you going to decide about my position?"

Katherine stopped. Turned. "Do not *ever* call me that again."

"Then pray, what shall I call you?"

Katherine closed the distance between them, keeping her voice low. "Nothing has changed, Millicent. Not one bloody thing. I will not have you in my employ—you are a member of my household, not a servant."

"I was a member of your *crew*," Millicent whispered sharply. "I am not a member of your household. I'd been a governess when I met you, and thanks to you I have little choice but to be a governess again. I'd only hoped to be a governess to Anne and not to some child whose father has wandering hands."

"You don't need to be *anyone's* governess. As soon as I've secured Dunscore, we'll go to Scotland. You'll love Dunscore, Millie. It's right on the sea. You can hear the waves—"

"I could have heard them on Malta, as well."

Always, always it came back to Malta and that damned surgical school. "I was not about to leave you alone on Malta with no protection but a disguise."

Millie's brown eyes flashed. "A bloody effective disguise, and there would have been no reason for anyone to suspect the truth at all. I would be perfectly content to spend the rest of my *life* dressed as a man. Even now I could have been attending lectures on anatomy and physiology, but no. I'm here in London—the last place

I *ever* wished to be—and soon you'll be so busy with masquerades and theater boxes you won't care about the sound of the waves."

"That's untrue." Millicent's words struck like a knife and twisted hard. She would not forget who she was. Not ever. "Disagree with my decisions if you wish, but I will not tolerate disrespect here any more than aboard my ship. Now. Phil will be here soon with the modiste, so you'd best change out of that smelly old gown or I have no doubt Phil will have something to say about it that you won't like."

AT 9:45, A NOTE arrived from Papa's solicitor agreeing to pay a visit that afternoon.

At 9:50, Dodd came to the drawing room carrying a card on a silver tray, turning his nose as though he offered a piece of manure. "A hack from the *Spectator,* your ladyship."

Katherine tore the card in half and tossed the pieces onto the tray. "If he returns, plant his head on a pike by the doorstep."

At 9:55, she went to check the progress in Papa's rooms, where a servant was taking the last of Holliswell's toiletries from the dressing table.

It was harder than she'd expected to see Papa's rooms again. "Are any of my father's things still here?"

The servant's startled gaze hopped from her head to her cutlass to her feet. "Nothing, your…er, your ladyship. His lordship's clothes were packed away into the attic. Everything here belongs to Mr. Holliswell."

Only thanks to Dunscore's coin, no doubt, which meant she should bloody well pack all of *his* things away in the attic and let him find the means to replace it all. Which she absolutely would if it wouldn't create more trouble than it was worth. She stalked through the room and opened the wardrobe, the drawers, the chest at the foot of the bed that Papa had always kept locked. It wasn't locked now, but there was nothing inside.

Katherine left the room, letting the boots that had served her so well on board the *Possession* thump soundly on the polished wood floors. The reality that Papa was gone dragged at her like the fiercest undertow and had her clawing for breath. But there wasn't time to compose herself, because Miss Holliswell's companion waited for her in the hallway.

"Your ladyship." It was a statement, not a question.

Katherine somehow found the means to speak. "Miss Bunsby."

"I would like to request a moment of your time." She was direct—too direct, with shrewd, cornflower eyes in a face pretty enough to exclude her from most positions as a paid companion. Few young ladies would welcome such competition. Even her horrid puce gown didn't hide her beauty.

"A moment is all I have, Miss Bunsby, and I'll save you the trouble of explaining yourself. Your services will no longer be needed. I do not know whether the Holliswells will wish to keep you on, given their change of circumstances, but I will pay you whatever wages you're due and offer you my carriage to go to the Holliswells' new accommodations if you wish." She'd checked first thing this morning to make sure she had a carriage and horses. In fact, there were two—the coach with Dunscore's insignia, and a smaller, newer carriage Holliswell had apparently purchased for his own use on Dunscore's credit.

"I do not wish," Miss Bunsby said flatly.

Katherine narrowed her eyes. "Then you may take your wages and be on your way. Whatever gowns the Holliswells gave you, you may keep." Judging from the shade of this one, nobody else would want them anyhow. "I expect you out within the hour."

"I wish to speak with you about employment."

"I do not need a companion."

"But you need an upstairs maid. You let Polly go this morning."

"And you think impudence will convince me you are suited to the job?" A ruckus from the entrance hall drifted up the staircase and down the hallway, heralding Phil's arrival. "You may tell Mr. Holliswell when you see him that he will not succeed in planting spies in my household. You are dismissed."

Miss Bunsby's hands fisted at her sides. "I am *not* Mr. Holliswell's spy. I simply—"

"Never fear, Katherine," Phil called up the staircase cheerfully, "you shall be properly outfitted for London in no time." A parade of footmen hurried up the stairs with more boxes and bolts of fabric than a ship unlivering on the docks. Katherine left Miss Bunsby standing there and went to meet Phil, who was resplendent in a sunset-colored brocade gown that revealed an intricately embroidered gold petticoat and stomacher. At her side, a dark-haired woman in a stunning gown of pale blue ruched silk surveyed the activity from behind the cooling breeze of a painted fan.

Together, the two of them presented a portrait of everything Katherine couldn't imagine being.

It was an easy guess who the visitor was. Katherine took her time walking down the stairs, knowing it would give full effect to the outfit Dodd disapproved of so heartily.

"All of London is abuzz with news of your ousting the Holliswells," Phil declared as Katherine came down. "Although honestly, Katherine, a bit of discretion might have been more the thing."

"If he wanted discretion, he should not have trespassed in my house." At that, Phil's companion's lips twitched.

Finally reaching the base of the stairs, Katherine looked her straight in the eye. "You must be Captain Warre's sister." The woman's deep green eyes had confirmed it already.

"You magnificent woman," she declared, taking Katherine's hands in her own. She air-kissed Katherine's cheeks. "I owe you my very happiness for rescuing my brother. I do hope you'll forgive the intrusion. I insisted Philomena allow me to accompany her no matter how improper it may be. I want to help you any way I can."

A desperate, awful hope leaped in her breast, and she struggled not to let it show. "You are too kind, Lady Ramsey." Perhaps she would not strangle Phil, after all.

Captain Warre's sister made a face and waved away the formality. "Don't be ridiculous. You will call me Honoria or face the consequences." She glanced at Katherine's hip with a mischievous smile. "Although I suspect your ability to mete out consequences far surpasses mine. I confess to being completely in awe—I am ready at this moment to swear an oath of loyalty, don an eye patch and sail away with you to pillage and plunder in some exotic land."

Good God. "Your brother might have something to say about that."

"James? La, he has something to say about everything! But I adore him, and as far as I'm concerned he can do no wrong."

The new hope dimmed.

"We've brought Madame Bouchard," Phil announced. "She's the best there is. And it's a good thing, too, because Lady Carroll's always-magnificent garden party is tomorrow night."

"You've arrived just in time," Honoria said.

"All the best people attend, and it will be the *perfect* place for you to make your grand debut."

Honoria nodded. "I've already spoken to Lady Carroll. You and my brother should receive your invitations this morning."

"But you'll need the most fabulous gown ever created," Phil said decisively, "and you'll need it by tomorrow afternoon at the latest."

Simultaneously, the pair assessed Katherine from head to toe. "It's almost a shame to replace that outfit with something ordinary," Honoria sighed.

At that moment, a tiny woman who could only be Madame Bouchard swept through the door behind a final wave of textiles. She took one look at Katherine and pressed a hand to her forehead. *"Abominable!"* she muttered. *"Simplement incroyable!"*

An unwise retort leaped to her tongue, but she bit it back. It was impossible to be an effective captain without a skilled boatswain, and it would be impossible to earn London's favor without magnificent gowns.

"I think you look positively exotic," Honoria confessed, and smiled wickedly. "James must have been *undone* with disapproval when he met you."

Phil's lips twitched. "Oh, is *that* what it was. I rather thought—"

"I have the impression your brother is undone with disapproval over any number of things," Katherine said crossly, even as she watched in the glass while Madame Bouchard sorted through a pile of gowns that were already under construction. The last time she'd stood for a London dressmaker, she'd been fifteen and more than a little frightened about her debut. That same worry snaked in now, and nearly for the same reasons.

Honoria laughed. "La, you've pinned it precisely! Poor James."

"Oh," Phil said, "I don't know that 'poor James' is exactly—"

"Bold colors for your complexion," Madame Bouchard declared, circling Katherine and eyeing her critically. "Dark. I have just the thing!" She clapped, and a maid appeared at her side. "Lucy, find the dark red silk."

"Dark red silk!" Honoria exclaimed. "You swore to me last week you had no such thing."

Madame Bouchard regarded her with disdain. "Do you wish your skin to look like boiled fish?"

"Impertinent woman," Honoria muttered.

"You're going to look magnificent," Phil said to Katherine. "There won't be a man in London who will be able to keep his eyes off you," she said meaningfully.

"Phil..."

"Phil?" Honoria chimed in. "Is that what they called you at sea? I *love* it. I only wish I had a masculine nickname, but what's to be done with 'Honoria'?"

Phil thought for a moment. "Horry?"

"Ugh! Leave it to you to think of that." Honoria gave her a swat on the arm. "I haven't charged a fee for my favors yet, you minx. But tell me, Katherine—may I call you Katherine?—it would seem our dear friend *Phil* has let the cat out of the bag. Could it be there is more between you and my brother than a dramatic rescue?"

AFTER TWO HOURS of fitting and pinning and tugging and draping and pulling, Katherine was ready to commit a dramatic mass murder as a result of Phil's and Honoria's relentless prodding and prying.

The whirlwind that was London picked up speed throughout the morning. While Katherine was being fitted into a dark green creation that threatened to push her breasts entirely free, an invitation arrived to dine with a Viscount and Lady Hathaway. Phil advised a polite refusal. While Madame Bouchard had her bundled into midnight-blue watered silk, Dodd came to inform her that Holliswell's men had arrived but that he had not let them in and had instead sent them away with the rest of their boxed possessions. And while Madame Bouchard's apprentice tried to pin together a downright-indecent copper creation, the solicitor arrived.

"So there is nothing I can do," Katherine said half an hour later, pacing back and forth behind Papa's desk in the library, dressed once again in her familiar tunic and trousers.

Mr. Allen watched her through keen, brown eyes that hadn't aged a day in nearly eleven years. His wig sat perfectly straight, and his gaze was unnervingly steady. "Not of a legal nature, no. If they decide to hold another hearing on the matter, I can do my best to argue your case. Your father was the most well-liked Scottish representative member," he added. "Very highly respected. His loss came as a blow to many. The bill may well fail, even under...these particular circumstances."

These particular circumstances. Those, of course, included her tragic fall into shame and her subsequent rise to power and wealth, which, if she'd been a man, would have opened doors—not closed them. "It would seem my acquaintance with Captain Warre truly is my best hope."

"Tactless as it may sound, his misfortune became your good luck. Had you returned without such a feather in your cap, so to speak, the picture would be very bleak indeed."

"The picture is bleak now," she snapped.

"Lord Croston is very powerful. Highly acclaimed."

Lord Croston. Captain Warre. That she should need him, be dependent on his goodwill, was terrifying—never mind her plan to use him for exactly this purpose. Using him and needing him were two very different things.

"There is, I suppose, one other option," Mr. Allen said.

Her heart leaped. "What is it?"

"You could marry."

"Marry!"

"A strategic alliance. Doubtful the Lords would attaint you then, as they'd be unlikely to take another man's rightful property. If you'll forgive me, as highly esteemed as your father was and as vast as your estates are, it should be a simple matter to find an acquaintance of your father's who's willing."

Her mind rejected the idea the way her body might

reject a bit of rancid meat. "Absolutely not. Marriage is out of the question." Even as she said it, Captain Warre's face rose in her mind. "As you said, Father was well loved. Odds are against the bill passing." The ball of rage and fear in her stomach testified otherwise. "And now that I'm here, I can work to curry favor among society." To exploit her connection with Captain Warre, in other words.

"You can," Mr. Allen said, too reasonably.

"I'll not marry a stranger for convenience's sake—someone who cares nothing for me, or worse, for Anne."

"I was thinking Lord Deal might be an agreeable possibility. He is hardly a stranger."

Lord Deal. Her memory conjured up a kindly old face and a ready smile. "He would be Father's age. At least."

Mr. Allen shrugged. "There are plenty of well-situated young dowagers who might tell you that's not such a terrible thing."

Good God. It was a sickening plan. She could never go through with it. Would never *need* to. Would she?

"Marriage is not the answer," she said sternly. "At least, not until it becomes clear the only way to keep Dunscore is to take a husband." And if that day ever came…well, she would marry an ancient bachelor with no backbone and learn how to administer hemlock.

She stared at Mr. Allen, and he observed her passively in return.

Just then, Dodd appeared in the doorway with a note on his silver tray. She met him halfway across the room. "Thank you." She tore through the seal and quickly read the contents. "Speak of the devil," she said to Mr. Allen, and read aloud.

"Your return to Britain brings me much joy. Of course, I will do all I can for you in your dear father's memory. You must do me the honor of attending an intimate gathering at my home this evening—my annual Musicale and Confectionery Extravaganza. Indeed, this will be perfect. Yours, etc.—"

She looked at Mr. Allen. "Perfect?"
He smiled behind steepled hands. "I daresay I am inclined to agree."

CHAPTER SEVENTEEN

"WE'RE DAMNED GLAD to see you, Croston, but we've got one of His Majesty's ships at the bottom of the ocean and a damned infidel on the loose in London, and I've got no patience for evasive answers."

James leaned back in his chair and stared across the table at Admiral Wharton, whose abrasively loud voice was swallowed up in the vast chamber. He'd thought walking the halls of the Admiralty might give him a new perspective. Make him feel something.

It hadn't.

"I've seen no evidence that Captain Kinloch's become an infidel," he told them.

"Devil take it—"

"And do enlighten me as to which points I have evaded. I'll be happy to clarify." James shifted his gaze to Admiral Kenton and raised a brow. The three of them had been seated at this table for the better part of an hour, accomplishing nothing.

Admiral Wharton exhaled and rubbed the back of his neck. "Damn me, but we should have taken the *Henry's Cross* off the line."

"Now is a bloody useless time to admit that," James bit out. And nearly six hundred men were dead because of it. But he wasn't here to repair the navy—he was here to be finished with it.

Admiral Kenton shifted impatiently in his chair and checked the notes he'd scratched. "Did you have an opportunity to inspect the hold?"

"For Christ's sake, Kenton, we've been through this already. I won't sit here and repeat myself." No, the *Possession* hadn't taken any ships while he was on board. No, there was no contraband in the hold. No, he hadn't taken any jam with his rolls at breakfast. This was bloody ridiculous.

Wharton drank deeply from a glass of brandy, set it back on the table and looked at James. "With all due respect, Croston, you've done a damned sorry job of taking that woman to hand."

"There's been no reason to take her to hand," James said.

"No *reason!*" Kenton exclaimed.

"Listen here, Croston. We cannot have a ship of questionable legality captained by a…a *female renegade* loose on the waters of the Mediterranean doing whatever the hell she bloody pleases. You were supposed to put an end to it."

"If I'd seen her do anything illegal, anything even remotely contrary to the interests of the Crown, I would have."

"For God's sake, Croston—"

James leaned forward. "If you thought she was a pirate, you would have had her arrested by now. Someone would have come forward. Filed a complaint, made accusations. The Mediterranean is hardly a remote body of water. But you have nothing, because there *is* nothing."

"Did you get a look at her papers?" Kenton asked. "Bills of lading?"

"And how would I have done that? Asked to see them? She would have laughed in my face. Understand, sirs, that I was little more than a guest on her vessel." Quite a bit less, in fact, but the admirals did not need to know the details.

For a moment the only sound was the scratching of Kenton's quill, and then he snorted. "Suppose there's been more than a few guests in her vessel, eh?"

James's fingers tightened reflexively around his glass.

Wharton noticed, and his eyes narrowed slightly. "Was she truly in command of her ship? Did she have the loyalty of her crew?"

"Yes. Hell, the *Possession* ran with better efficiency than any ship of the line I've ever seen."

Wharton tucked his chin.

"And without a single unseemly activity on her captain's part that I was aware of," James added. "And I don't have to tell either of you that on a ship that size everyone is aware of everything."

One of Wharton's bushy gray brows edged upward. "Defending her virtue, Croston?"

"Virtue!" Kenton exclaimed. "Rumor says she's got some Moor's bastard daughter."

"Irrelevant."

"Not to her virtue, it isn't. Don't believe all that stork business, do you, Croston?"

James quashed an urge to lunge across the table and grab Kenton by the throat. Instead, he reached into his coat and drew out his resignation letter. "I think we're finished here, so I shall give you this." He tossed the letter in front of Wharton. "My resignation."

Wharton's chin disappeared into his fleshy neck. "That's preposterous. You're in line for commodore."

"Let someone else have it."

"No." Wharton shook his head, staring at the letter. "No. We need you."

"What in God's name for?"

"We need that woman under control! If she's attainted, there's no doubt she'll leave England for good. We cannot let that happen—she's been a nuisance long enough." Wharton drummed his fingers tensely on the table. "She needs a husband."

James's heart sped up. "I'll not accept *that* commission, either."

Kenton blanched. "Good God!"

"I'd never suggest anything so preposterous," Wharton thundered. "I have no fear of finding someone willing to acquire Dunscore through marriage. It's her willingness that concerns me." Now Wharton pinned his aging eyes on James. "We need you to arrange a marriage she will accept."

James let out a laugh that felt like a strangle. "You're trying to get me killed."

Wharton scowled. "Are you saying—"

"What I'm saying, Admiral, is that Katherine Kinloch will accept nothing less than her birthright, free and clear." *And that I'll kill any man that touches her.*

No. God. He didn't give a bloody damn who touched her.

"I plan to have her activities in London carefully observed." Wharton leaned back in his chair, studying him intently. "The slightest hint that her loyalties do not lie squarely with the Crown, and she will be arrested."

"What the devil for? She's done nothing."

"So you've reported for three years." He looked at James meaningfully. "And yet we know that during that time she overran at least one Barbary ship. Likely two."

"I reported those incidents when I learned of them."

"And a fine gloss you put on them, too," Kenton said. "An investigation into what you saw or didn't see is not beyond the realm of possibility."

James stared at him. "There's no need to threaten me, Admiral."

"Afraid we won't like what we learn, Croston?"

"Not at all. I simply have business to attend to—" business that involved cognac and solitude and no tempting female sea captains "—and I dread the idea of anything interfering with its immediate commencement." But already it was clear that there would be no immediate commencement.

An investigation. It could drag on for months—years—while they called his honorable service into question and accomplished nothing.

He rubbed a hand over the back of his neck. Bloody hell. Perhaps the admirals' plan wasn't so off the mark. Perhaps if Captain Kinloch married the right man—a peer, and one in good favor—then she would have Dunscore, and he could be done with this entire bloody business.

Right. As if she would ever consent to marry simply because it was expedient. As if any man in London could possibly deserve her.

"By all means," he said irritably, "let me keep watch on Captain Kinloch while she's in London and use my best efforts to barter her on the marriage mart."

Wharton narrowed his eyes. "This is serious business, Croston."

"You've made that clear." James stood up. "Now. If you have nothing else, I must take the helm of my new command."

BY THE TIME Katherine's coach rolled up in front of Lord Deal's that evening, fear had begun to take root.

She held the curtain aside with a finger and looked out. Lord Deal's windows blazed festively in the night, and a line of carriages ejected beautifully dressed members of the beau monde in front of the door. She fisted her hand against the urge to pull the bell and order the coachman to drive past.

Tonight was necessary. She would reestablish her connection with Lord Deal and take note of people's reaction to her—that was all. Lord Deal was well loved and had always been so kind to her. He would be an excellent ally. Yet still dread winged drunkenly through her belly, so she fixed her mind on Anne.

Anne warming herself by one of the fires in Dunscore's great hall.

Anne pushing her fingers into the wet, gravelly sand on Dunscore's shore.

Anne turning her face to the wind atop Dunscore's ramparts.

The coach slowed to a stop. Katherine tried for a deep breath, but the corset prevented it. Madame Bouchard had outdone herself in a few hours' time with the dark red silk and a black, bead-encrusted petticoat and stomacher that created a dramatic effect. Perhaps too dramatic, Katherine thought now. Too dark. The woman in the looking glass just before she'd left for Lord Deal's looked nothing like the starry-eyed girl who had happily tasted the joys of her first Season twelve years ago. The touch of kohl around her eyes, the dark curls lying artfully across one shoulder, the flesh swelling high above her stays—they made her look wicked when she needed to be charming. Fallen when she needed to appear angelic.

The carriage door opened, and for several heartbeats she sat paralyzed by her own vulnerability. And then she forced herself to move. Jet beads sparkled on her red slippered toe as she extended her foot from the coach. Captive inside a prison of whalebone, she needed assistance even with this. Reaching out to the footman, she gripped his hand to climb out.

But the hand she gripped did not belong to the footman. It belonged to Captain Warre.

"A wise decision, leaving your cutlass behind this evening," he murmured, helping her to the ground.

His touch rippled across her skin like a hot gust across a still sea as she stepped into the night, with panniers jutting out stiffly at her hips and stays making it impossible to breathe normally.

"I could hardly win society's approval if I hadn't."

"Approval?" He raked his gaze over her, lingering in forbidden places. "My dear Captain, nobody will *approve* of you. Our goal is mitigation, not acquittal."

The man who had swabbed her decks and polished her cannons was gone. In his place was not even a naval captain in blue, cream and gold, but the Earl of Croston in dark green brocade and a silver-embroidered waistcoat. A white shirt embellished with the subtlest ruffles lay stark against his sea-bronzed skin. At his side hung a Royal Navy sword.

His power hummed through her, and the physical connection of his hand was dangerously comforting.

"I am not on trial," she whispered sharply, pulling from his grasp.

"On the contrary," he said. "Every word that falls from your lips will be entered as evidence in the court of society's opinion." He gave her a look. "As well as every chair and footstool you pitch into the street."

She scoffed. "I shed no blood."

"Commendable indeed. In any case, it would seem I am to be your constant companion, according to the plan you outlined aboard the *Possession.*"

Her eyes locked with his in a mutual memory. Her back to the wall, his hands on her breasts. Her fingers in his hair, his tongue mating with hers. Bodies on fire. Her shove, his push. William's fist.

Even now, a hint of yellowed purple marred his jaw.

"Excellent." She offered her most predatory smile and hoped he didn't see her shiver.

"But there will be no room for your tricks this evening," he warned grimly. "More depends on society's favor than I would wish. My brother will not be moved. His heart is involved, or so he believes."

Her own heart sank. "Clarissa Holliswell."

"Yes."

Already the carriage was pulling away and another was coming up behind it. Captain Warre guided her toward the entrance, where music and light spilled from inside the house. A woman in front glanced over her shoulder and let her gaze sweep over Katherine. Behind them, more carriages arrived and more glittering fashionables picked their way toward the entrance. Their stares burned into her back.

"I spoke with a few men during a brief visit to Westminster," he said under his breath as they climbed the steps. "It seems your unexpected return has sparked interest in the bill. It's a good guess the second reading will be approved."

A light-headed rush threatened her balance, but she recovered quickly. "It would seem your debt is proving more difficult to repay than you once imagined."

His lips tightened to reply just as they swept into the house, and there was no more time for talking. The majordomo announced them. A commotion undulated through a crowd that was too large to be "intimate," and all eyes turned their direction. The room fell silent and suddenly she was fifteen again, shimmering in her first real gown, gliding into her first assembly where every face held the hope of a new and exciting acquaintance.

They held no such hope now. The light-headedness returned with a vengeance.

"Steady," Captain Warre murmured, seamlessly guiding her forward as the crowd found its voice again in a roar and a stately old man came toward them, beaming. The sight of him sent her reeling back even further through time, and for a breathless moment she was eight years old again, being shooed from Papa's library.

"My dear Lady Dunscore," he declared with a bow, kissing her hand. "Words cannot express my deep gratitude and delight at seeing you once again. It has been too long, my dear. Too long indeed."

Mr. Allen was positively, irretrievably out of his mind. Instinct overcame time, and she curtsied deeply. "An honor, Lord Deal."

"And, Croston," he said to Captain Warre. "An honor and a relief, my good man. Ach—an honor and a relief." Turning back to her, he lowered his voice and leaned close. "We have our work cut out for us, but don't you

worry. Too many wafflers not to win over a bare major-
ity, and I don't want that upstart cousin of yours for a
neighbor." He smiled at her with kindly brown eyes and
winked, and the past made another grab for her mind.

"I have every confidence in your ability to persuade
them, Lord Deal," she said, though at the moment she
felt very little confidence of any kind at all. Through
a break in the crowd she spotted part of an elaborate
confectionery display on a table along one side of the
room. In its center sailed a ship constructed of sugar.

Good God.

Already an onslaught of well-wishers presented
themselves to Captain Warre, proclaiming their amaze-
ment at his safe return while the melodious strains of an
orchestra lilted from the far end of the ballroom. Some
of the faces she remembered. Some she didn't.

Furtive female eyes slid her direction from behind
fluttering fans, at once curious and condemning. Less
cautious male eyes appraised her with salacious approval. Their stares assaulted her like cannon fire
from all sides and she felt herself being dragged back,
dragged down, reduced into the small pile of helpless
girl who'd been taken from the *Merry Sea.*

You know nothing about me. The scream pushed into
her throat, but of course, she swallowed it. She waited
for her senses to sharpen the way they did when a ship
engaged her at sea, but instead she floundered beneath
the weight of what they thought they knew. She could
feel them measuring who she was against who she'd
been, drawing conclusions based on their own imagi-
nations.

They didn't know one bloody thing about it.
Someone—Lord Deal—pushed a glass of red wine

into her hands. She took a drink and locked eyes with a devil in red and gold embroidery and a jet-black wig. He raked her shamelessly with his gaze.

"Whatever has put that glint in your eye," Captain Warre whispered, "leave it be."

"I was merely thinking perhaps I should have brought my cutlass, after all. I have a distinct impression that I'm being looked upon as prey."

His eyes shot to the dark-haired rotter. "I shall deal with men like Winston, if the need arises. *Your* job is to appear demure, amiable and harmless."

"Harmless!"

"Smile," he ordered under his breath.

She curved her lips.

"We shall do this on my terms or not at all, my dear lady Captain. I'll not allow your stubbornness to keep me in London a day longer than necessary. In fact, the evening's tedium is lessening my sense of obligation as we speak."

A hint of concern in his eyes belied the bite of his words, and it fueled her with a lick of irritation. "Need I remind you that I saved your life?"

"You say that as if you did me a boon."

He pivoted for more introductions, and more, and more.

"Lady Dunscore!" a Lord Swope exclaimed, letting his eyes rest on Katherine's bosom. "An utter fascination."

"Indeed," declared a Lord Tensy, grinning at Lord Swope's side. "Almost makes me want to be ship-wrecked myself—sorry, Croston. Terrible thing to say. Apologies." He reached for Katherine's hand and kissed it. "I am ever at your service, Lady Dunscore. And you have my deepest condolences. Your father was a capital fellow. Great friend."

"The best," Lord Swope said, and winked at her. "Never got to bed before four when old Dunscore was around."

"Lost five hundred quid to him in one night," Lord Tensy said. "Couldn't begrudge him a'tall. Not a'tall. Never met a better gamer in all my life."

Hopeful speculation in their eyes made it clear they wondered whether she would prove equally entertaining.

Lord Deal leaned close and steered her away. "You mustn't look so grave, my dear. More than a few tight-arses in our company will warm to that stunning smile I saw a moment ago. Ach—here's someone you may remember." They joined a trio that included a wrinkled man in a ridiculous bagwig and purple waistcoat and a silver-wigged woman in an equally silver gown embroidered with a geometric pattern. "McCutcheon!" Lord Deal said heartily, addressing the other man in the group. "Excellent to see you as always. And Plumhurst…Lady Plumhurst. A pleasure indeed!"

McCutcheon. Oh, no. Years ago, she'd thought herself over the moon for him

"Unbelievable turn of events!" Lord Plumhurst cried, clasping Captain Warre's hand. "Simply unbelievable!"

Katherine kept her attention squarely on that bagwig to avoid looking at Lord McCutcheon.

"What a dreadful experience you've had, Lord Croston," the silver Lady Plumhurst said. "It's a miracle you're still with us."

"Not so much a miracle as a very timely rescue,"

Captain Warre told them evenly. "May I present to you my savior, Lady Dunscore."

"Favorable currents were his savior, I'm afraid," Katherine replied, "I merely pulled him from the water." Finally there was no avoiding McCutcheon, and she found him regarding her with a mixture of horror and pity. The face that had sent her fifteen-year-old self into raptures seemed pasty and vapid next to Captain Warre.

"Merely!" cried Lord Deal.

"How fortunate that you possessed the necessary resources to help when needed," McCutcheon said stiffly to Katherine.

Katherine—no longer the blushing debutante—looked him directly in the eye. "I gave the order to lower the nets the moment my crew spotted him floating on a piece of debris against the hull." *Stop looking at me that way,* she wanted to snap. "We had him on deck in a matter of minutes. He was soaked through and nearly lifeless—we pulled him from the water just in time."

"Lucky thing!" Lord Plumhurst declared. "Positively dreadful."

Katherine nodded gravely. "You can imagine our distress."

"And my relief when I realized I had run into the *Possession,*" Captain Warre added with a hint of sarcasm intended for her ears only.

She smiled. "I am only grateful we did not know his identity, or the moments before his rescue was complete would have been all the more tormenting."

"When I saw her colors, I knew I would be well cared for and that my ordeal was over." He turned his lying green gaze on her in a false display of the gravest appreciation. "It's hardly an exaggeration to say that I owe Lady Dunscore my life."

One might even say it was a boon.

"What an irony, after your attempts in Salé proved so fruitless," McCutcheon said, turning to Captain Warre.

Salé. Katherine's attention glanced off McCutcheon, fixed on Captain Warre. A chill ran down her spine.

"Isn't it?" Captain Warre said mildly.

"The would-be rescuer becomes the rescuee," Lady Plumhurst said, fanning herself vigorously. "Astounding."

Rescuer. Captain Warre refused to meet her eyes. But she'd heard all she needed to—she could piece together the rest. *Have you spent any time in the Barbary states, Captain?* Oh, yes, he'd been there. Once. He'd simply omitted that it had been in an attempt to free her.

Her hands began to tremble. "Irony aside," she said to McCutcheon, "you can only imagine how grateful I am to have had the opportunity to repay Lord Croston's earnest efforts." The full weight of what McCutcheon had just revealed bore down on her. She felt herself shrinking, reeling back to those first terrifying days in the dey's palace, hoping she would be ransomed but hearing no news. "Although I daresay my attempts required less effort than his, and certainly met with less opposition."

Lord Deal clapped his hands together. "Oh, but let us not delve into the melancholy past, shall we? What a blessing these two fine young people are both home safe and sound at last. And to think our dear Lady Dunscore was so providently used in such a miraculous rescue... It all smacks strongly of a divine hand, if I may say."

"Divine indeed." Captain Warre smiled at the crowd,

still avoiding her gaze. "Lady Plumhurst, your daughter was recently married, was she not?"

He had *been* there. In Salé. And she was bloody well going to find out why he hadn't told her.

CHAPTER EIGHTEEN

Dear Sirs,
Observed Lady Dunscore at Lord Deal's musicale. Confectionery ship on display. Remained on display after Her Ladyship departed. Perhaps too messy a prize.
Yours, etc.,
Croston

"JAMES, YOU'VE BEEN at sea far too long if you think there is anything acceptable about paying a call at this hour, even to your sister." Honoria stood staunchly in the doorway to her dressing room, but James was in no mood for resistance. "You could at least have waited for me to dress and come downstairs," she complained.

"I've got appointments this afternoon I can't cancel," he said, pushing past her.

"*So* amusing. You're impossible, James. You've always been impossible." All false outrage in a peacock-blue dressing gown covered in ribbons, she followed him into the room. "You may leave us, Mary," she said to her lady's maid. "And have a light breakfast sent up."

"I can't stay," James told her.

"The breakfast is for me." She went through to her bedchamber, and he followed as far as the open doorway. "I haven't been out of bed half an hour yet." Indeed, the bed lay rumpled behind her, and there was a pillow on the floor, and he suddenly wished he had waited for her downstairs. It was likely the same bed she'd shared with Ramsey before he died, and the idea of Ramsey touching his little sister—of *anyone* touching her, even within the bounds of marriage—was more than he could take on an empty stomach. He retreated to the dressing room.

A moment later she returned. "Are you really retiring?" she asked, putting her arms around him and looking hopefully into his face.

He looked down into a sea of misplaced adoration. "Where did you hear that?"

"This is London, James. Oh, please, say it's true. I've missed you so much."

"It's true."

"Oh, I'm overjoyed!" But looking into his eyes, she frowned. "What's the matter?"

Katherine Kinloch was the matter. Nick was the matter. The Lords were the matter. His own bloody conscience was the matter. "Nothing's the matter," he said, and extricated himself from her embrace. "In thirty minutes I shall be taking Lady Dunscore on a strategic round of visiting instead of lingering at my breakfast table with the papers."

And when he did, there would be no more avoiding a private moment with her as he'd successfully done last night. They would be together alone in the carriage, and there was no doubt that he would get an earful thanks to McCutcheon and his wagging tongue.

"James, I've never once known you to linger at the breakfast table. But in that case I forgive you for calling so early—*if* you tell me every detail about last night's musicale. What an aggravation that I'd already accepted that invitation to dine with the Misses Cavely! But I never attend Lord Deal's musicale. The average age of the attendees is above eighty, I daresay." She turned a sly look on him. "I heard Lady Dunscore was fairly well received."

"As well as could be expected."

And now Captain Kinloch knew he'd taken her captivity far more personally than he should have. That he'd thought about her, argued for her, gone out of his way on her behalf. There was no reason he should have done any of that—except that once he'd learned her fate, his mind had conjured up an image of an innocent and terrified young girl in the hands of Barbary captors, and he couldn't let it go.

Last night, on her stricken face, he'd seen that girl as though she'd risen from the dead. He never wanted to see her again. Sooner give him the fury that had burned in her eyes the rest of the evening. *That* he could deal with.

"Lord Deal ought to have *some* influence in the matter, I should think. But rumors run wild, James. La, you cannot imagine the stories I've heard, even just this morning!"

"I thought you'd only just risen."

"There's nothing remotely appealing about pretending to be thickheaded, James. I've had hardly any sleep at all. I received a note from Lady Effy at two o'clock this morning saying Lord Winston seemed quite taken with Lady Dunscore at Lord Deal's—promise me you won't allow *that* to develop—and one from Lady Atwell at half past four saying she heard Lady Dunscore beheaded three Barbary pirates with a single swipe of her blade. That can't be true, can it?"

"No. It can't."

"One pirate, perhaps?" she suggested hopefully.

"Would you like me to go into the particulars of beheading? It takes a good deal of strength because the blade must sever the bone—"

"Never mind!" She covered her ears. "No beheadings, then. I accept."

"This is insanity, Ree. Nothing about Captain Kinloch is worth sending a footman running through the streets in the middle of the night."

She raised a brow.

"I'd hoped to settle this quietly," he said, trying and failing to keep the frustration from his voice.

"You've achieved far too much celebrity for that, brother mine. Perhaps you don't realize? When news of the *Henry's Cross* arrived—" Pain fleeted across her face, but then she smiled a little and disappeared into her bedroom again, returning a moment later holding something out in her palm. "If you tell Nicholas, I shall be forced to think of a very unpleasant punishment for you."

He looked at the object in her hand. "Oh, for Christ's sake." His own likeness stared up at him in brash colored paints from the front of a metal-edged brooch.

"Thank goodness the street hawker had no idea who I was," she told him.

"Street hawker?"

"It's disgraceful, I know. But I couldn't resist it, James. Not when I thought—" Emotion silenced her again, and she curled her fingers around the brooch and held it to her breast. "You may not take it from me. I won't let you have it."

"Believe me when I say the thought of taking it from you never crossed my mind." But she looked so much as she had when they were small that a moment of emotion threatened his composure. He tamped it down. "I need your help, pet."

"I confess I'm relieved to hear it because I've already told Lady Dunscore that I intend to do all I can. She's magnificent, and I adore her."

"Now listen here, Ree. She's no one you should be associating with."

"I'm a widow, James. I associate with whomever I please." She tilted her head slightly. "You seem awfully critical of her, given that she saved your life."

"That I owe her my life changes nothing about her character."

"Which is...?"

"Lady Dunscore is the most damned, belligerent creature I've ever had the misfortune to encounter."

"I see."

"She may not have beheaded Barbary pirates, but she could take a prize with her tongue alone as a weapon."

"Her tongue," Honoria mused, heavy with insinuation. "My intuition is telling me, brother dear, that *misfortune* may not accurately characterize your *encounter* with Lady Dunscore's tongue. Mmm?"

"Damnation, Honoria!" All pretense of patience abandoned him.

She laughed. "I've pinned it exactly, I see."

"You've pinned nothing. I knew it was a mistake to enlist you in this."

"To the contrary! You were perfectly right to come

to me." Honoria's eyes narrowed thoughtfully. "Interesting, though, that she gave no hint there was anything more than a heroic rescue between you."

"That's because—"

She waved him away. "Oh, don't try to deny it, brother dear. It's written all over that menacing face of yours. But never fear—your secret is safe with me."

He contemplated explaining more fully how very mistaken Honoria was in her assumptions, but decided it would only entrench her more solidly in the notion that he harbored something more than begrudging gratitude toward Captain Kinloch.

Something like flaming lust.

"Don't make more of this than it is, Ree, for God's sake."

"Very well. Tell me how I may be of service."

"I need you to help me find her a husband."

"Her— Lady Dunscore? A husband? She said nothing to me about wishing to marry."

He stared at her.

Comprehension settled in her eyes, and her lips curved in a way that made the hair stand up on the back of his neck. She came forward and fingered his lapel. "Never say I'm not helpful, James. I daresay I've found the perfect man already."

He pulled away. "This is serious business. I need someone suitable. Someone she will agree to. I'm beginning to fear she won't secure her estate any other way."

"Such a pessimist. Lady Dunscore is very beautiful, James, and one should never underestimate the power of a beautiful woman. I realize you've always been stuffy, but even you must know there are as many ways to influence politics as there are to cook a goose."

"Captain Kinloch will *not* secure her right to Dunscore with her legs spread. I won't allow it."

"My goodness, what an interesting direction your thoughts have taken. I simply meant that men are very often blinded by beauty, and that she may have more success in winning supporters than she expects—merely by *talking* with people. Talking, James."

Talking. "Of course." His blood pounded, and he flexed his hands. "Perhaps she will at that. But in case she doesn't…"

"A husband. I shall give the idea some thought."

"And while you're at it, you can use your influence to turn Clarissa Holliswell off Nick."

"*Now* you ask the impossible."

"I think not. Only the weather rivals a young girl's heart in changeability."

"You're being unfair. If she believes she loves him, there will be little I can do."

"Tell her he's got a pox if you have to."

Honoria made a face. "That is no kind of talk for a lady's boudoir, James. And I would never spread such horrid rumors about Nicholas. Now out with you. Out! You are a horrid brother, even if I do weep with joy at your return."

"WHAT ATTEMPTS IN SALÉ?" The words exploded off Katherine's tongue as Captain Warre handed her into his carriage for a round of morning calls. He'd made sure she had no opportunity to discuss the matter last night, and all night her questions had built up, waiting, demanding to be asked.

"You seem to have determined the answer to that question yourself." He leaned against the seat across from her and looked out the window, holding the curtain aside as if there was something outside more interesting to see than her own maid sweeping the steps. "And I've made no secret of my regrets."

"No. Only of your visit to Salé."

He allowed that much with a slight inclination of his head.

"Do I understand correctly that you were among those attempting to negotiate my release?"

"Attempting, and failing." He let the curtain drop and turned those damnable eyes on her. A shiver prickled her skin. While she had wept inconsolably in the caravan to Algiers, Captain Warre had been trying to help her.

The reality made her feel vulnerable and exposed. "Thus leaving your sense of obligation unfulfilled," she snapped.

His mouth quirked up, drawing her attention to his lips. "Nothing quite so dramatic as what you're imagining," he said. "I don't blame myself for failing in that regard. I doubt anything could have convinced the dey to break his agreement with al-Zayar. God knows, we all tried."

He had been there, perhaps in the same building. Perhaps mere rooms away.

She did not want this kind of connection to him. It was too personal. It touched a place too deep, made her yearn for him with terrifying need.

"I'm not helpless." Damnation! The words flew out before she could stop them.

"I would venture to say you've demonstrated that quite thoroughly." He observed her a little more intently, as if trying to read her thoughts.

She imagined him in Salé coldly demanding her release. Imagined how his voice would have turned sharp when they refused, how his eyes would have gone flinty with rage.

For her.

"Why did you not tell me?" she demanded, hating how small she felt.

"Would telling you have earned me a promotion aboard the *Possession?*"

"Certainly not," she said.

"I thought as much." In the silence that followed her statement, he studied her from across the carriage. "What are you thinking?"

Memories flitted by: Mejdan, laughing indulgently while his two young daughters draped him with silks to make him look like a woman. Nafisa and Aysha on market day, happily trying on a hundred scarves while the shopkeeper grumbled and huffed. Katherine and Nafisa laughing themselves sick while Nafisa taught Katherine Arabic from the same book the children used, and Katherine's tongue refused to cooperate. Had Captain Warre and her father been successful, there would have been no market days, no playing with the children, no laughter. She would have been brought home to a country that would have seen her as a tragic oddity, where nothing awaited but ruination, isolation and loneliness.

But she made herself raise a brow at him. "That you are by far the most efficient cabin boy I've ever had, and promoting you would not have served my interests at all."

"Touché, my dear Captain." His smile did not reach his eyes, but something else did. For the briefest moment she saw his desire wage war with his guilt.

And then the carriage drew to a stop in front of a town house, and his expression changed to cold calculation. "Here we are," he said. "I would suggest you bear in mind that Lord De Lille is one of the most powerful lords in the House."

She peered out at the house with that same knot in her gut as when she faced an aggressing ship. "I remember. He and Lady De Lille were friends of my father's."

"Then I don't need to tell you to remember your manners in front of Lady De Lille."

She smiled at him. "For shame, Captain. When have I ever not remembered my manners?"

MANNERS, KATHERINE DECIDED a short time later, were a severe inconvenience.

"I've always thought foreign travel was fraught with danger," Lady De Lille declared after Captain Warre had flawlessly introduced a retelling of his rescue. She was a plump froth of lace and pink ribbons, peering out from a frame of heavily powdered gray curls topped by a lacy cap. "I've never once been tempted to see the world's oddities—especially not those where *you've* been." She leveled her eyes at Katherine the way a ship might level its guns and pointed her fan as though it were a pistol. "Not that I haven't been to Paris, mind you."

Katherine clenched her teeth behind the smile she'd pasted to her lips. "Naturally."

"But I would never travel farther south than that." Lady De Lille's mouth pruned disapprovingly. "I have strong feelings about the effect of the Mediterranean climate on one's passions."

"How fortunate that passions are rarely inflamed in Paris," Katherine said.

Captain Warre shot her a meaningful look. *Behave.*

She let her eyes drive into him. *This is preposterous!*

Seated nearby, Ladies Gorst, Linton and Ponsby exchanged looks with each other and with a Mrs. Wharton, who was married to one of the navy's top admirals.

Lady De Lille narrowed one eye, but Captain Warre spoke first. "Hot weather does tend to make people more reactionary," he said pointedly.

"So true!" Lady Gorst agreed. Quickly fanning herself, she leaned toward him to assure a clear view of cleavage her disarranged fichu no longer covered. "A summer in London nearly does me in. I'm sure I wouldn't last above an hour in that hot climate. However did you tolerate it?"

"One quickly acclimates when one has no choice," he said.

"Indeed," Mrs. Wharton said. "The admiral has always said exactly that." The lady looked at Katherine. "*You* must have grown *quite* acclimated to the heat. One can only see how much time you've spent in the sunshine."

"Sunshine is unavoidable in the Mediterranean," Captain Warre said quickly, cutting off the *reactionary* response that leaped to Katherine's tongue. "In any case, I've always questioned whether it can be good for ladies' health to avoid sunshine as studiously as they do."

"Bless me if this isn't the first time any such question has crossed your mind," Lady De Lille scolded. "I've never heard anything so ridiculous in all my life."

Lady Gorst laughed and drew her fan across her

cheek. "And it's hardly a winning argument, as a lady will always sacrifice health for beauty."

Lady Ponsby nodded.

"One can only see how your time in Barbary has affected you."

"Is it true they eat dogs?" Lady Gorst gave a graceful shudder. "Oh, I couldn't bear it."

Lady Ponsby paled.

Katherine thought of Zaki, with his jeweled bowl and his silken pillows, chewing on a mutton bone with nearly an inch of meat still attached. These people were fools.

Captain Warre shot her a glance. "An ill-informed rumor, I assure you."

"Except when the market for kittens is tight," Katherine added.

"Oh!" Lady Gorst placed a hand against her heart.

"My word," Lady De Lille said crossly. "You are in more dire need of a husband than anyone I've ever met. It is only too bad that your age and adventures put you out of the market, though I suppose there is the estate's fortune to sweeten the deal."

Katherine stood abruptly.

"Sit *down*, Lady Dunscore," Lady De Lille ordered.

Instead, Katherine walked away, leaving Captain Warre to make their excuses.

"My heavens," she heard Lady De Lille declare as Captain Warre's footsteps sounded behind her in the entryway, "if her father weren't such an amiable man I would not have her in my house, mark my words, regardless of Croston's good opinion, which is highly suspect in any case under the circumstances given that he is clearly besotted."

"EXAGGERATING MOORISH BARBARISM is a bloody poor way to further your cause," a clearly-not-besotted Captain Warre growled into Katherine's ear four visits later after she told an open-mouthed Lady Someone-or-other that she'd witnessed no less than a dozen beheadings during her first year in captivity.

Katherine stepped into the blessed freedom of the waiting carriage. "This is intolerable." And they saw her not as the countess of Dunscore, but looked at her the way they might gape at some freakish oddity.

"Be that as it may, you will learn to tolerate it or even my most heartfelt endorsement won't help you."

"Heartfelt endorsement!" she hissed. "Was that when you told the odious Lord Bashford that I was anxious for domesticity, or when you told Lord Quinn that my 'accomplishments' may not be traditional but nonetheless should not be overlooked?"

"Your gratitude leaves me speechless."

"As did Lady Moore's suggestion that I should set up shop in Covent Garden."

"She was talking about the theater," Captain Warre said.

"Oh, indeed. That was precisely what she meant."

"For God's sake, I've called you my savior so many times it's beginning to sound blasphemous."

"Croston!" A man unfolded himself from a hack that pulled up behind Captain Warre's carriage. She recognized him instantly from Lord Deal's musicale: tall and broad-shouldered, perhaps a little over thirty, with irreverently black hair that today was tied back au naturel without even a trace of powder. It was the Duke of Winston, shimmering in a dark yellow coat embroidered with black-and-green vines and trimmed at the seams with silver braid.

"How selfish Croston is," he said with a grin, "keeping London's most fascinating new resident all to himself."

A subtle quirk at the corner of his mouth made it clear he assumed the world was a fruit ripe for his picking. Eyes the color of dark coffee lingered just long enough on her breasts to let her know those, in particular, were fruits he would enjoy picking at the first opportunity.

The look in his eyes suggested an especially lurid method of securing Dunscore. She tasted bile but arched a brow at him, anyway. "Perhaps it is I who is selfish," she suggested.

There was a flash of white teeth. "I sincerely hope not." He reached for her hand and kissed it, apparently indifferent to the hard glint in Captain Warre's eyes.

"I should be careful of this one, Winston," Captain Warre said in an amiable tone that she recognized was completely false. "That is, if you prefer your anatomy intact."

Winston barked a laugh. "I do. But you shouldn't believe everything you hear, Croston. Most rumors have no foundation in fact."

"Anytime you'd care to test your swordsmanship with the lovely captain, I would be an eager spectator," Captain Warre told him.

"A unique temptation, but my code of ethics would never allow it." It wasn't difficult to imagine what his code of ethics would allow, and no doubt many ladies had gladly become test subjects for a wide variety of his skills. "Perhaps, Lady Dunscore, we might strengthen our acquaintance in a more traditional manner one day soon. Tell me, do you share your father's penchant for racing? I've recently acquired a magnificent pair that could use some exercise."

"I'm afraid my taste for adventure is limited to the sea, Your Grace."

"Then I shall look forward to showing you my yacht."

"Do not count on it," Captain Warre growled, and shoved her into the carriage.

CHAPTER NINETEEN

Dear Sirs,
Observed Lady Dunscore during morning visits. Cat-o'-nine-tails apparently left behind; ladies escaped unscathed. No Englishman pressed into service.
Yours, etc.,
Croston

"HOLY GOD, CROSTON, are you out of your mind?"

"She's an intelligent woman." In a quiet corner of White's, James kept his voice practically inaudible as he made his pitch to Hollyroot.

"Forgive me, but that kind of intelligence is a quality I could do without. Old Dunscore was sporting good fun, though. Such a shame."

Old Dunscore was a libertine, and everyone knew it. "I think you'll find that Lady Dunscore has any number of qualities that would make her well suited as a wife," he said and hoped Hollyroot wouldn't press him for details.

"Seems more suited to someone like Ingraham, if you ask me."

"Ingraham." If Ingraham so much as imagined himself marrying her, James would kill him. "Listen here. Lady Dunscore is an agreeable woman." In a certain

sense. "Practical. Well-meaning. She needs someone decent. Sensible." Someone like Hollyroot, with a harmless demeanor and an estate that could use an infusion of resources. It was the most efficient way. That bill would have almost no chance of advancing if she married.

It was the logical answer.

A few swallows of liquor sat cold in his gut, along with the full implications of what he was suggesting if this conversation was successful. Hollyroot touching her. Bedding her.

James gripped his glass so hard he felt a twinge in his thumb.

"Suppose I ought to be flattered," Hollyroot said, "but this is a devil of a thing to spring on a fellow." He knocked back a swallow of bourbon and set his glass down, leaning heavily on one forearm propped on the table. "I mean, there's no denying her beauty—"

"She's got more than mere beauty."

"Indeed," Hollyroot agreed grimly. "Rumor has it she's got a child."

Every muscle tensed. "Anne is a sweet girl. Would make an excellent daughter."

"Daughter!" Hollyroot shook his head. "All due respect, Croston, but I think the sea's gone to your head."

Christ. "Very well. Forget I said a word about it. And if you breathe a word of this conversation to anyone…"

"Wouldn't dream of it. Holy God. Do you think I'd want anyone to suspect, to even *imagine*— Holy God. I admire the hell out of you, Croston, but you're barking up the wrong tree."

"HOLD STILL IF you *please,* my lady." A painful tug had Katherine second-guessing her decision to appropriate

Clarissa Holliswell's lady's maid. The girl had developed methods of torture more suited to a medieval dungeon. But piece by piece, Katherine's hair was shaping into a deceptively simple coiffure that involved numerous rolls and braids woven through with copper ribbon.

"A man like that wants his balls removed," Katherine said derisively over her shoulder to Phil, who sat by the window in Katherine's dressing room, reading aloud from the papers.

"I should have warned you about the duke."

"With so many men who require warning off, it's little wonder you overlooked it."

Another tug forced Katherine to face the looking glass. "My *lady!*"

"'*Adventures* in the Mediterranean'?" Phil read aloud. "Insulting. I prefer to think of us as having been engaged in business."

"We *were* engaged in business," Katherine snapped. "And I have the fortune to prove it. I tell you now, if His Grace tries to strengthen his acquaintance with me tonight in any manner—traditional or otherwise—I shan't be responsible for my actions." The maid cast her an uneasy glance in the looking glass. She had no way of knowing how severely Katherine's words contradicted her thoughts.

The morning's disastrous round of visits had made one thing clear: she would need to strengthen her acquaintance with as many lords as she could, in any manner she could.

"I can think of any number of ways to ensure the duke does not misunderstand me," she added anyhow.

Phil set aside the papers. "Sometimes you positively

frighten me. You need to win over the natives, not alienate them."

"At least indulge me some measure of aggravation. Men are such fools." Except one man, but she would not think of that now. Worse, Phil was right. "I've got half a mind to go to Westminster, bare my breasts and see this whole business finished."

Phil laughed. "The situation may be a *bit* more complicated than that, dearest. Though I daresay if you can gain the attention of a man's cock, you've won three-fourths of the battle. All that's left is to influence him in the proper direction. Tonight's party will be an excellent start. Tomorrow night we shall go to Vauxhall, and to the theater the next, until they cannot possibly ignore you."

No, they would not ignore her. She would make sure of that. "I hate that they amuse themselves so well with their impertinences."

"Which you must laugh off as though you haven't a care in the world. All of London is fascinated with you—"

"As they would be with a two-headed ape."

"—and that can't help but work to your advantage, especially with Captain Warre's endorsement. I saw Lady Mullen after I passed you going into Lady Derby's this afternoon, and she had so many questions about how we managed aboard the *Possession* I swear she has a notion of going to sea herself. And she wasn't the only one. And of course, they are all over the moon about Captain Warre." Phil's blue eyes sparkled wickedly at Katherine in the looking glass. "But of course, that wouldn't interest you."

Katherine smiled at her. "No. It wouldn't." But the

smile faded almost immediately. "Captain Warre believes there will be a second reading." It was a struggle to keep the fear from her voice. "After that, will it not be put to a committee? What do you know of committees?"

"Only that they are full of men, which leads back to our original premise. You *must* bewitch them, Katherine. Once you have them all in hand—and I do *not* mean that literally, as that would be counterproductive—they will be falling over themselves to please you."

"With the singular goal of foraging beneath my skirts."

"Of course. That's what men do. And it is astonishing what they will sometimes agree to in pursuit of that goal."

"Indeed." More than one crew member over the years had followed her not out of respect but sheer fascination. Lust akin to slavery. She never kept those crew members long, but she knew very well how to use such motivation to her advantage.

She would bring the men around as if she were maneuvering at sea, using every tactic to keep another ship precisely where she wanted it—and then grappling on with her hooks to take it. She would use their own weaknesses against them.

Fools.

"Your ladyship?" came a voice from behind, and Katherine shifted her gaze in the looking glass. "Pardon me." Miss Bunsby—Miss Bunsby!—poked her head into the room. "Lady Anne keeps asking about a gentleman named William, and I don't know what to tell her. I cannot persuade her off the subject."

Katherine stood abruptly.

"Your ladyship!" The motion pulled the ribbon from the maid's hands.

"You haven't seen William?" Phil asked.

"*What* are you still doing here?" Katherine demanded.

"At the moment," Miss Bunsby said defiantly, "looking after Lady Anne."

"You have been dismissed."

"And I fully intend to leave—" a lie, clearly "—but I cannot go in good conscience if there is nobody to look after young Lady Anne."

"Anne! Where is she? Why is Millicent not with her?" And how could Katherine not have known? Already she was rushing toward the door.

"Miss Germain has been in her room all day feeling poorly. I've been looking after Lady Anne in her stead."

Good God. How could she not have been aware? How could she have sat there having her hair dressed while Anne was unattended? She pushed past Miss Bunsby with half her hair hanging over one shoulder and the maid's outraged protest following her into the hallway.

"Anne!" she called out before even reaching the pink room. "Anne!"

"Mama?"

Katherine rushed through the door and found Anne on the center of an oval rug done in pink and white flowers, playing with the doll she'd received for her birthday. The room smelled strongly of a perfume she recognized from years ago.

"Mama," Anne said anxiously, "when will we hear from William? Why has he not visited?"

Katherine pulled Anne into her arms and kissed her

forehead while Mr. Bogles observed them from the windowsill and the wretched Miss Bunsby watched from the doorway. Anne was all right. Thank God. "There is much business to attend to in London, dearest, and William knows a great many people." It sounded reasonable, but there was little chance it was true. It had been a day and a half, when he'd sent word he would call yesterday. It wasn't like him. She smoothed Anne's soft hair. "I shall tell you the moment I hear from him. I promise."

"But I want to hear from him now, Mama."

"I'm sure he'll visit soon."

Anne dropped her head on Katherine's shoulder. "I don't like London, Mama. It smells awful. Miss Bunsby sprayed perfume and had them bring roses, but it only helps a little."

Only now did Katherine notice a pitcher overflowing with pink, white-and-red roses on the floor nearby. She looked at Miss Bunsby.

"There are any number of good smells in the park," Miss Bunsby suggested. "Flowers, fresh grass, loamy soil."

"I don't want to go to the park," Anne complained. "Mama, when will we go back to the ship?"

Anne already knew they weren't going back to the ship. As for the park, or anywhere else in public…that was out of the question. She thought of Dunscore and wished they could leave London now. Today.

"When will Captain Warre visit us?" Anne asked now.

"He is very busy, dearest."

"But I want to see him. I miss him."

"I know. But just think—Lord Deal has offered to

take us into the country in his phaeton. Doesn't that sound like fun?"

Anne wanted to know what a phaeton was, and what Lord Deal was like, and whether he was as nice as Captain Warre.

"Much, much nicer, dearest. You will adore Lord Deal, I promise. He will be like having a wonderful old grandpapa." She would not think of Mr. Allen's suggestion.

"I've never had a grandpapa," Anne said doubtfully.

"I know, sweetling." A stab of grief for Anne's true grandfather made it hard to breathe.

"Maybe Captain Warre could be my grandpapa, too. Could he, Mama? Would you ask him? I'm sure he will say yes, because he is the nicest man in the whole world!"

JAMES HALF LISTENED to Katherine relate the tale of his rescue to a quartet of baboons especially chosen by his dear sister as perfect matrimonial matches and decided the ideal solution for everyone would be to bind Katherine with rope and stow her in the hold of a ship bound for China.

"My heavens," Marshwell said congenially. "Quite at death's door, were you, Croston?"

It was impossible to take his eyes off the copper creation she wore tonight. It shimmered in the light of hundreds of candles and exposed her breasts nearly to the critical point. *Points.* God.

"Very nearly so," he said tightly. "There would have been a different result had Lady Dunscore not acted immediately." Lilting strains of a string quartet barely floated above the din of a hundred conversations. The cloying scent of a million flowers filled his lungs. The lustful stares of Marshwell, Werrick, Foxworth and Blaine fixed on Katherine's cleavage, and it was a good bet not one of them had marriage on his mind— except Blaine, who likely salivated equally over Dunscore's wealth.

That bloody gown was going to kill him. Or he was going to kill them. Someone needed to kill something, and right now he would be happy to oblige.

"We all feared the worst until we had him safely aboard," Katherine told them smoothly, moving her shoulder in a barely perceptible way that drew all eyes to the curve of her neck. "Pulling an unconscious person from the water is a complicated maneuver."

Not half as bloody complicated as the subtle way she stretched her waist. He remembered putting his hands on that waist—on her bare flesh beneath her tunic— and felt himself come alive in a place that needed to stay dormant.

"Indeed?" Werrick said, wetting his lips a little.

Katherine leveled those topaz eyes at Werrick and shifted them to Foxworth, who had a hundred disgusting hopes dancing behind his slate-gray eyes. "I don't know when I've ever been so relieved to see a man draw breath as the moment I realized Captain Warre was alive," she told them.

"Naturally!" Blaine agreed heartily.

Oh, yes—they were deep in the mire now. "Blessedly the worst was avoided," James said, "thanks to the care and hospitality of Lady Dunscore and her excellent crew." He tried for a pleasant smile, but it felt more like a death grimace. "They set about tending to my needs immediately."

Finally she met his eyes. "Captain Warre's care and comfort were our greatest concerns," she assured them gravely.

"Indeed." He held her gaze in a silent vice. "I could not have received closer attention had I been at home with my own physicians."

"You can imagine how pleased we were to see that he responded to our attentions almost immediately—" her eyes sparked "—and quite markedly."

Two moments alone and he would rid her of that smug expression and perhaps sample what her low-cut décolletage offered while he was at it.

"Such a miracle," Werrick declared. "You must be immensely...*grateful*...to your rescuer, Croston." His eyes, full of calculating imagination, slid from James's face to the cutthroat beauty at his side.

"I would be grateful to anyone who saved my life, Werrick." James inhaled silently and schooled himself. The last thing he needed was *that* kind of rumor flying around London while he was under orders to secure her a husband.

A *decent* husband. Who would treat her—and Anne—with the respect they deserved. Who might need Katherine's wealth, but would nevertheless appreciate her qualities.

At that precise moment, Honoria appeared with a fifth matrimonial offering. "Do excuse me," she interrupted brightly, "but I've got someone Lady Dunscore *must* meet." This time it was Cashen—a middle-aged rakehell Honoria knew damned well worked his way through mistresses faster than most men drank Port.

"Desist," James ordered her under his breath after she made the introductions.

Honoria ignored him. "Why, Lady Dunscore, I am convinced you and Lord Cashen must have a great deal in common. He was just describing the most magnificent pair of Ottoman sculptures he recently acquired."

"Fascinating," Katherine said warmly. "I can't wait to hear about them."

James stared at her. This sensual snake charmer bore little resemblance to the sharp-tongued, cutlass-wielding sea captain who had stood laughing while he swept rats' nests and emptied slop buckets. It was obvious the game she was playing, and it needed to stop immediately.

CHAPTER TWENTY

THE NEW STRATEGY was working beautifully. Fools. She would not have survived one day at sea if she was as easily distracted as these men. Finally free from their cloying gazes—even if only for a moment—Katherine took aim for the shrubbery, where an inviting arbor promised a few moments of solitude.

It was not to be.

"I seem to recall a marked response on your part, as well," came Captain Warre's growl at her side, "a bit later in the voyage."

"Do you? I don't recall." She plunged into the arbor with the captain on her heels and turned on him just in time to see the entire encounter replay itself in his eyes. A nerve pulsed wildly in her belly.

All night those eyes had been on her, touching her the way he so clearly wanted to do with his hands. The way every man here so clearly wanted to do.

But there was only one man whose hands her body remembered too well.

"You must thank your sister for me," she made herself say. "She has been instrumental in introducing me to any number of men whose influence may serve me."

"Has she." The heat in his eyes defied the chill in his tone.

"One must use the resources at one's disposal, after

all." It made her sick that everything she had worked to become counted for nothing here. The power she had as the *Possession*'s captain was gone, and now the only power to be found was pushing dangerously from the top of her stays.

It was a bloody poor substitute.

"Resources," he said coldly.

She smiled. "Phil places great store on them."

"It would seem Lady Moore's comment about Covent Garden wasn't too far off the mark, after all."

"Bastard!" The temper she'd been holding in all night snapped, and she raised her hand to slap him. He grabbed her wrist.

"What will you do if a committee is appointed? Bed them all?"

If she could have drawn on him right here in this arbor and cut him to shreds, she would have. "Perhaps I shall," she scoffed, and yanked her hand from his grasp. "Forgive me if I feel uncomfortable leaving my fate entirely in your hands. I've tried that before, if you'll recall."

His eyes flashed dangerously. "You will cease your flirtations immediately, Captain."

"Or else what? Will you ram your cannons and sink me with a full broadside?"

His mouth tightened. "You need to appear sensible."

"As if any of these men gives a bloody damn for my senses."

"For God's sake, Katherine. You need to appear intelligent. Agreeable. Well-meaning."

Now she smiled. "When have I ever not appeared agreeable, Captain?"

He pointed a finger in her face and, though it seemed

impossible, moved even closer. "Now, you listen here, and listen well. The success of this entire effort depends on your full and complete cooperation. Is that understood?"

The tension in his posture screamed of something besides frustration at her behavior. A hot pulse shuddered through her body. "Explain what you mean by *cooperation*."

He jabbed that finger at her. "I mean that you do every—" jab "—single—" jab "—blasted—" jab "—thing I tell you—" jab "—*precisely* the way I tell you to do it."

"I am not under your command."

"You came under my command the moment I agreed to help you."

"That is quite a fantasy, Captain." Except that it wasn't. In the golden light of a single torch flickering through a jumble of wisteria leaves, his shadowed gaze drilled into her.

Things were no different than they'd been ten years ago. The situation may have changed, but he enjoyed the freedom of his acclaim while she remained imprisoned by her fate.

Voices drifted closer. People were coming. Captain Warre cursed and pulled her deeper into the arbor.

Through the leaves, she saw two men stop near the front of the arbor. "...Holliswell has his way, Dunscore will be off the market," one of them said.

She stood perfectly still, listening, alive to the press of Captain Warre's every fingertip against the small of her back.

"Ingraham," he whispered near her temple.

The other man chuckled. "In the market for that, are

you? Can't say I blame you—Dunscore is no mean estate." In the shadowy light, Captain Warre's expression
turned murderous.

"I'd never have to bow out of a game again," the
first man said.

"And you'd go home to the spiciest quim in London.
Wouldn't mind a piece of that for myself."

Captain Warre's hand tightened against her back.

"...think she's better than Miss Betsey at Mrs.
Blake's?"

The other man snorted. "Gawd, you're a cheap one.
Tell you what—when I'm Earl of Dunscore, I might be
persuaded to turn a blind eye if you want to have a go."

"I'm going to kill Ingraham." Captain Warre's voice
was deadly in her ear.

"Shh!" A sick feeling curdled her stomach.

"...knows what the committee will recommend."

"If somebody marries her, be nothing *to* recommend.
Won't take away a man's rightful property. Besides,
we'd start another war attainting a Scot's estate of that
size." His voice grew fainter. They were walking away.

"I'd lay money old Rayford will— Hell, there's the
wife. She's spotted me. Devil take it, she's waving me
over." The sounds of the party swallowed their conversation. Katherine stood with her heart pounding and
Captain Warre's fingers biting hotly into the fabric of
her gown. Her own fingers dug into his shoulder.

He turned his head, and suddenly she was inches
away from those murderous green eyes. "Ingraham is
a dead man."

It struck her that he was the only person here except for Phil who looked at her and saw the woman
she had become.

Tell me what else to do. How to convince them.

"They can't possibly believe I would consider marriage," she managed harshly, hoping he wouldn't hear the fear in her voice.

"Not to the likes of Ingraham."

"To *anybody*."

He cursed under his breath. "Katherine, surely you realize—" His eyes met hers, those eyes that were green like the Mediterranean on a stormy day. They flicked to her mouth. Darkened.

"Realize what?" His sword handle pressed into her, jabbing through her stays. Beneath her fingers, his shoulder felt like rock.

"That it may become inevitable."

Her hands tightened on him. "It *can't*."

"Katherine—" Whatever he'd been going to say died on his lips. He touched his mouth to hers, and she was lost.

She opened her lips and tasted fire. Touched his face and wanted to melt into him. He turned her in his arms, and already she felt him losing control again.

Oh, God. They couldn't do this here.

Voices. More people were coming.

But she couldn't stop touching him. His face, his neck, his shoulders. She clung to him as if she were drowning, lost herself in the taste of him and the strength of his arms around her.

No. They couldn't—

Voices!

She tore herself away, but not soon enough. Holliswell and a lady had already stepped into the arbor, laughing. He stopped short when he saw them, and the laughter died on his face.

Damn, damn, *damn*.

Captain Warre took a measured step away and offered the slightest bow. "Lovely evening."

Holliswell returned the bow while his calculating gaze shifted from her to Captain Warre. "Your lordship. Cousin." His smile was a razor's edge. "Excellent to see you are enjoying the party."

Katherine reached deep for an air of disdain and somehow clothed herself with it though everything inside her throbbed and ached from Captain Warre's kiss. She glanced at Holliswell's companion and curled her lip ever so slightly. "Likewise, Mr. Holliswell."

Holliswell's companion looked aside awkwardly and, when Holliswell stalked away, followed him into the shrubbery.

FOOL. KATHERINE STORMED up the staircase after the garden party, rubbing her lips with the back of her hand. *Fool!*

She should have returned to the crowd the moment she realized Captain Warre had followed her. Should never have let him stand there touching her. Should have at least pulled away before he kissed her. Could she have been any more reckless? It wasn't as if she hadn't seen what he was going to do.

And now—

"Lady Dunscore."

Katherine's head came up sharply as she reached the landing. "*Why* are you still here? You've been dismissed—more than once."

"Miss Germain has left." Miss Bunsby said shortly, holding out a letter for Katherine to see.

"*Left.*" Good God. What had Millicent done now?

Katherine hurried up the rest of the stairs and snatched the letter from Miss Bunsby's hand, quickly skimming the contents.

Gone. Home to Bedfordshire to live with her brother Gavin.

Gavin. Millie didn't even *like* Gavin.

But Millie was free to make her own choices now. A lump tightened Katherine's throat. Phil was recapturing her London life, India was languishing in her father's custody, William was off doing who knew what and now this. The life she'd built with people she loved—people who knew her, who respected her—was as good as gone.

She swallowed, hard, and fixed her gaze on Miss Bunsby. "You will pack your bags this instant and leave my house, or I will have you arrested and we shall see how your impertinence fares in gaol."

"That is hardly the most efficient course of action under the circumstances." Below, a footman emerged. "Well?" Miss Bunsby called down.

"Madam. Your ladyship." He looked from Miss Bunsby to Katherine and back to Miss Bunsby. "I couldn't find any," he told her.

"Find what?" Katherine demanded.

"We live in the biggest city in England—perhaps in all the world," Miss Bunsby called impatiently. "Do not tell me there is nobody who knows how to make *kesra*."

"*Kesra*—" Katherine started.

"Go back out," Miss Bunsby directed, "and do not return until you find someone."

The footman's mouth tightened, but he turned on his heel and left. At that precise moment, Anne's voice drifted from the pink rooms. "Miss Bunsby? Miss Bunsby, where are you?"

Katherine rushed to her daughter's room, crouching down to where Anne sat with her mandolin on the floor and cupping Anne's face in her hands. "Dearest, are you all right?"

"Mama, I don't like it here. I want to go back to the ship."

Miss Bunsby frowned worriedly. "She wouldn't take any food."

"You know we can't go back to the ship," Katherine said into Anne's hair, and saw the untouched tray at the bedside. "Why have you not eaten?"

"I'm not hungry. Millie went to visit her brother, Mama. I miss her."

"I know, dearest."

"And I want *kesra*." Anne buried her face against Katherine's arm. "Mama, I don't *like* it here."

Kesra. Katherine looked at Miss Bunsby. Helplessness gripped her. "You will love Dunscore, sweetling." *I promise.* "There will be no awful smells, and the sea shall be the only sound, and we shall eat *kesra* every day."

"Will Captain Warre be there?"

Katherine's heart ached a little at the hope in Anne's voice. "Captain Warre has much to do now that we're in London," she said. "I doubt he has much time for visiting, so you mustn't expect him to call."

"But I want him to visit. Will you tell him, Mama? Please?"

"I will tell him." A few more reassurances later, they finally coaxed her to sleep in peaceful exhaustion.

"I tried to stop Miss Germain from going," Miss

Bunsby said outside the room, "but she wouldn't listen to me. I can't say I'm surprised. Two days has been plenty to see she wasn't happy."

"Devil take that blasted surgical school," Katherine said, and refolded the note.

"Is it truly impossible for her to attend?"

"If I believed otherwise, I would have helped her do it." But Millie would try, anyway. There was little doubt of that. She might stay with her brother for a while, but then she would find her way back to Malta. What then? Any number of unpleasant answers flitted through Katherine's mind. At the same time, she felt Miss Bunsby's eyes on her. Waiting.

Katherine assessed her in return. Strawberry-blond hair in a simple chignon. Too-pretty blue eyes. Slender build. Chin raised a notch too far to suggest submission.

She'd already proved well enough that she did not understand the word. She almost reminded Katherine of India.

"Yesterday Anne asked about our friend William Jaxbury," Katherine said, teetering on the edge of indecision. "Has there been no word from him this evening?"

"Not one, your ladyship."

Perhaps Miss Bunsby had proved herself tonight. Just a little. "If he should arrive while I am out," Katherine said, "he is to be denied nothing."

Comprehension—satisfaction—settled over Miss Bunsby's blue eyes, and she smiled.

CHAPTER TWENTY-ONE

Dear Sirs,
Encouraging lack of maritime activity at Lady
Carroll's. Reflecting pool perhaps too small a
body of water. Lady Dunscore unused to land
operations; likely impeded by presence of shrub-
bery. No gentleman engaged.
In your humble service,
Croston

"CHANGED? WHY SHOULD my cousin's arrival have
changed anything?" A blustering, early morning wind
outside Westminster Hall might have threatened to take
Holliswell's peruke with it if the carefully rolled hair
hadn't been petrified with grease, and Nick would have
watched with satisfaction as it rolled down the street
like a ball across a lawn. "Katherine's arrival only
makes the situation more pressing," Holliswell went
on in an offensively mild tone, "especially considering
the circumstances."

The circumstances. That, of course, referred to
James's miraculous return. Nick's throat tightened, but
he quickly gained the upper hand of his emotions. "The
story of my brother's rescue is already on the lips of
every porter and match-seller in London," he said flatly,
"and I doubt if there is a drawing room in all of Lon-

don that doesn't echo with the retelling as we speak. If the Lords decide she's a heroine, the Virgin Mary herself won't be able to convince them to pass that bill."

Holliswell's lips, chapped and pale, curved coldly. "The question will be put this afternoon, will it not?"

"Yes."

"Then let us hope the second reading is approved." He paused. "Lord Adkins has expressed an interest in Clarissa. I'm not sure they should suit, but then, what girl couldn't suit herself to a viscount?"

Adkins.

Nick's vision hazed over. Just last year Adkins had hosted practically the entire *ton* at a masquerade in celebration of his sixtieth birthday, but the real celebration had taken place a week later at Adkins's country estate, where rumor had it the entertainment had included prostitutes playing a unique version of croquet.

His hands ached with the need to curl around Holliswell's lapels and slam the man against the lamppost behind him. Instead, he tightened his lips. "Only the daughter of an earl, I would imagine."

"I'm not sure I like what you're suggesting, Taggart."

"I think you like it a great deal." It was no stretch of the imagination to think that once Holliswell had the title he coveted, he might decide his daughter could make a more advantageous match than either himself or Adkins—although how a marriage to Adkins could be considered advantageous for Clarissa was beyond comprehension.

"I can't imagine the cause is lost," Holliswell said. "There is plenty about Katherine to exploit. You know that as well as I do. God knows how many Moors she's taken between her legs, and I hear she's got a half-Moor whelp as proof. She can't possibly imagine society will accept her this way. In fact, having her here may work to your advantage in gathering more votes."

For God's sake, Nick didn't *want* to exploit anyone. He just wanted this bloody business over with. "If you believe that, you're delusional. I've already heard of half a dozen men lining up to propose marriage."

"Marriage." Holliswell's eyes narrowed, and Nick watched him consider how quickly such a turn of events could change everything. "It would have to be someone powerful enough that the Lords would not possibly consider divesting him of his newly acquired assets. She'll not find anyone of that stature desperate enough to take on such a baggage."

"Perhaps," Nick said. "And perhaps not. I've heard she made a successful debut at Deal's and again last night at Lady Carroll's. She may find someone yet."

"A successful debut indeed—with your brother, in the shadows of the shrubbery."

"Watch what you're implying, Holliswell."

"I witnessed their intimacy with my own eyes," he sneered.

It was a lie. Wasn't it? "It's nothing to me if he's tupping her," Nick said, though it was hardly the truth. If she was more to James than just a welcoming commodity— if *James* got it in mind to marry her—then this damned business with Holliswell would be for nothing.

"Isn't it?" Holliswell said meanly. "If that's the way the wind blows, you've got a bigger job ahead of you than either of us expected."

He felt a little sick, both at the idea of Katherine Kinloch becoming connected to Croston and the prospect of working against James. It grated hard to go against his older brother, especially after believing him lost. From what he'd heard, James had been publicly acknowledging her as his savior. Much more of that, and the bill's cause would be lost anyhow.

"I will do what I can," Nick bit out. "But I fear the tide will soon turn, and no effort to stop it will be successful." Especially if James was tupping her. But if the choice was Clarissa's future or Katherine Kinloch's, he would do what had to be done.

He reminded himself that such a woman had no business acceding to a title in her own right. But for chrissake, he was starting to wish he wasn't the one leading the charge to strip it from her.

THE INVITATIONS BEGAN to arrive before Katherine got out of bed. By the time she was ready to dress, there were twelve.

Winston. Hardly a surprise.

Werrick. Cashen. Naturally.

The number of invitations might have been a sign of spectacular success, but...

Marston, Obbs, Abnersthwaite. Known for their bad luck at the gaming tables, Phil had said.

Blaine. Nicklesdale. Estates mortgaged to the hilt, Honoria had said.

Robert *Prentiss?* The greedy-eyed baronet?

And three more whose names she didn't recognize, but the quality of the paper said everything she needed to know about the state of their finances. Good *God.* They actually believed she might subjugate herself to them in marriage and put Dunscore at their disposal.

Her maid appeared in the doorway to the bedchamber. "Which gown shall I prepare, your ladyship?"

Katherine tossed the invitations on the dressing table and went to her trunk. The only thing these men wanted more than her in their beds was Dunscore in their coffers.

"None, thank you." She unlatched the lid and snatched up a pair of her old trousers. "I shall dress myself this morning."

"Very good, your ladyship." The maid's wide-eyed look said she thought it anything but good.

"But I shall want the pale green this afternoon, and the deep blue for tonight," she added. The deep blue, with its shimmering silk and its revealing cut. Because there was plenty of support yet to be gathered, and she was perfectly capable of exploiting their lust for votes. But *marriage?* She would see them in hell first.

"Very good, your ladyship." The maid bobbed a curtsy and left.

This morning, however, she would do as she pleased. The familiar clothing she'd worn aboard the *Possession* settled around her like a shield, and she smiled at herself in the glass as she slid her cutlass through her sash. Wouldn't it be satisfying to arrive at Vauxhall tonight dressed like this?

Satisfying, yes. Helpful? Definitely not. Katherine sighed at her reflection.

She grabbed up the invitations and went downstairs to study Papa's ledgers. By the time dinner was to be served, seventeen had arrived. Dobbs had just delivered the eighteenth invitation when Captain Warre strode into the library.

"His lordship the Earl of Croston to see you," Dodd said from the doorway, but Captain Warre had already reached the desk, looking windblown and strained, with dark circles beneath his eyes. The mouth that had burned so hotly was set in a grim line.

"Have you heard the news?" he asked.

"What news?" She stood and faced him across the desk, wishing she didn't remember last night's kiss quite so well.

"The second reading has passed. The committee meets on Wednesday next."

Wednesday. "That only gives us six days."

"Your mathematical skill is far better developed than your sense of fashion." His gaze raked over her. "For God's sake, what do you plan to do if you receive a caller—invite them to sit on the floor and smoke a hookah?"

Six days. All the flirtations in the world couldn't win enough support in six days. Could it?

"I rather thought I might call for tea." She tossed the stack of invitations in his direction. "It would seem my company is in high demand. But if these are any indication, any callers I receive will be proposing more than conversation. I've ordered Dodd to burn any more that arrive."

At that precise moment, Dodd returned carrying a card on his silver tray. "Lord Ingraham to see you, your ladyship."

"Ingraham." Last night's conversation in the arbor sprang to life. He thought he would marry her and open their marriage bed to the public, did he?

"Please tell him her ladyship is unavailable," Captain Warre instructed.

"And have him return later?" Katherine scoffed. No. She would deal with this immediately. She strode out from behind the desk and headed for the door. Thirty seconds would be all she needed to take care of Lord Ingraham.

She found him waiting by the door in the entrance hall wearing a ridiculous pale blue coat embroidered with bright yellow leaves. "I am only accepting marriage proposals in writing at this time, Lord Ingraham," she told him before she was halfway across the hall. "If you'd care to send yours, I shall put it with the rest. Be sure to include the exact amount of your debt, of course." She stopped directly in front of him. "Oh, yes—and the number of your friends you will expect me to entertain in our marriage bed." She gave him what she hoped was her most feral smile.

Ingraham's startled eyes dropped to her feet, paused on her cutlass and shot back to her face. "Good God."

Behind her, Captain Warre's tightly bemused voice carried across the hall. "Left you speechless, has she, Ingraham?"

"Croston." Lord Ingraham looked past her, then back. "Lady Dunscore. I—" He paused, then smiled and bowed. "Certainly not. Not speechless a'tall. Though I can see that you are otherwise occupied, so with your permission, I shall take my leave and return at another time."

If he returned again, she would run him through before he crossed the threshhold. "You may state your business now, Lord Ingraham, and eliminate the need for a future visit." Beside her, Captain Warre's animosity radiated off him like heat off a ship's deck in summer.

Lord Ingraham's smile turned brittle. "I see. Well, naturally, my business isn't pressing. A mere social call.

Perhaps you would consider saving me a dance at the Rogersfield ball next week?"

"I will give it my careful consideration."

"Good day, then, madam. Croston."

The moment he was gone, Captain Warre turned on her. "He'll have your eccentricity spread across all of London before noon."

"And by midnight, my breasts will have them all trailing after me regardless. Or have you forgotten our plans for Vauxhall already?"

"Being hotheaded and impulsive can gain you nothing."

"Encouraging the notion that I am available to debtors and wastrels can gain me nothing. But forgive me, Captain, if I did not handle Ingraham *precisely* the way you would have told me." She returned to the library and resumed her place behind Papa's desk. "Who are the committee members?"

Captain Warre took up the invitations and leafed through them while he told her the names.

It was no surprise that several names matched those on some of the invitations. "I particularly enjoyed the Duke of Winston's invitation," she said. "What a delight to hear he will chair the committee. Do you suppose he's especially proud of the luxurious cushions in his carriage, or could there be another reason for his efforts to assure me of their comfort?"

Captain Warre's lips curved like a scratch in ice. "Apparently the man has no care for his particulars." He paused. "I shall deal with Winston."

"I can't imagine how, without giving the impression the only carriage cushions I'll be experiencing are yours."

His eyes shot off the page and met hers, blazing. A pulse leaped in the base of her throat, but it was too late to yank the words back.

"Six days is an eternity in the world of the *ton*," he told her. "Reputations have been made and broken in less—depending, of course, on one's behavior."

"Of course." The time she'd already spent in London felt like an eternity.

Dodd appeared in the doorway once more with his damnable silver tray. "Your ladyship, Viscount Fenley—"

"Tell Fenley she's not here!"

Katherine raised a brow at Captain Warre's explosion. "Yes, Mr. Dodd. Please send him away," she managed evenly. She could not offend every member of the Lords, no matter how little they cared about offending her. A possessive light glowed at the edges of Captain Warre's anger, and a little flutter winged through her belly. She ignored it. "Tonight there is Vauxhall. Tomorrow night I shall attend the theater at your sister's suggestion. I have more than half a mind not to go, as I have the distinct impression she is among those who believe I should take a husband."

"Which, naturally, you have no intention of doing."

A thin edge in his tone gave her pause. "Is that a solution *you* advocate, Captain?"

He tossed the invitations on the desk and exhaled. "I despise the theater. What a debacle this is."

The nonanswer made her a little sick. "A debacle that could be solved if I marry?" she pressed carefully.

"I'll not waste time discussing a subject that has no grounding in reality. I am well aware that you will see Holliswell seated at the head of Dunscore's table before you will tie yourself down in marriage to keep it."

His words hit their mark, and a cold, awful chill snaked its way across her skin. She thought of Mr. Allen, father's solicitor, and made herself voice the unthinkable. "Could it be possible that marriage is the only solution?"

"There is never an 'only' solution. I shall be at Westminster again today taking up your cause. Let us hope I meet with receptive minds."

He looked exhausted, frustrated and patently unenthusiastic. He didn't want to go to Westminster—she could see that much. But he would go because of his guilt.

"I appreciate your efforts," she told him, catching herself—and him—by surprise.

He looked at her a moment, then turned away, rubbing the back of his neck. "I don't like that the committee will meet so soon."

"What could it mean?"

"Anything."

Please keep trying, she almost said. But Captain Warre had seen enough of her vulnerability. He would not see more. "But this nonsense can still be stopped before a third reading," she said.

"I'd hoped to stop it before it got this far."

"Perhaps the quickest way is to accept the duke's invitation, after all, if he is to chair the committee," she scoffed, to hide her fear.

He spun on his heel, leaned across the desk and grabbed her chin in his fingers before she had time to think. "You'll not whore yourself for Dunscore," he bit out. "I won't allow it."

"A joke, Captain."

His fingers burned into her skin. His eyes burned

into her, too—hot and hungry, dropping to her mouth. Her breath turned shallow.

"Some topics don't lend themselves to jest," he said.

A movement in the doorway caught her eye. It was Miss Bunsby, retreating into the corridor. Captain Warre released her chin suddenly and backed away.

Katherine left him standing there and went to see what was wrong.

"One of the upstairs maids let slip that his lordship was here," Miss Bunsby said in a hushed tone, "and now Lady Anne refuses to do anything until she sees him. I've tried to distract her with her doll, her beads, even a game of draughts, but she won't be swayed. She's raising a terrible fuss."

Dearest Anne. Katherine cursed under her breath.

"I tried telling her his lordship was likely in a great hurry, but she is adamant that he will see her."

"Tell her Captain Warre has gone," Katherine whispered. Guilt clawed at her, but nurturing Anne's attachment to Captain Warre would only break her heart in the long run. "By the time you return upstairs it will likely be true."

Miss Bunsby's gaze suddenly shifted past Katherine's shoulder. Captain Warre stood in the doorway.

"Who are you telling I've gone?"

A small voice drifted from the upstairs balcony. "Captain Warre? Captain Warre, are you here?"

"Anne!" Katherine rushed to the entrance hall just in time to see Anne's groping hands find the rail at the top of the stairs. Panic exploded in her chest. "Anne, stop!" She flew up the stairs with Miss Bunsby on her heels.

"Lady Anne, you mustn't leave your rooms alone," Miss Bunsby told her firmly. "It isn't safe."

"But I heard his voice!" Anne cried as Katherine pried her away from the railings. "He will see me, Mama. I *know* he will! Captain Warre!"

"Hush, now," Katherine scolded, watching Captain Warre take the stairs with a grim mouth and measured precision. "Do you remember our rule about you going on deck? You must always be with someone. *Always.*"

"But I heard his voice!" Anne's lip began to tremble, and Katherine's heart squeezed hard.

"I'm here, Anne," Captain Warre said, reaching the top of the stairs.

"Captain Warre!" Dearest Anne—heart of her heart and soul of her soul, with her olive skin, black hair and exotic Barbary eyes—threw her arms toward him with delight. "Oh, I'm so happy you're here!"

He lifted her away from Katherine with a hundred questions in his eyes, daring her to object. "What's all this fuss?"

"I've missed you," Anne said, patting his shoulders and winding her arms around his neck.

His arms tightened around her. "I've missed you, too."

"And I miss the ship. Mama says we can't go back, but I want to. I want to so much! I hate London. Millie went away, and my dresses are stiff and tight, and it smells bad all the time." Her pouting lip trembled, and she buried her face in the crook of his neck.

A familiar, strangling helplessness closed around Katherine's throat.

"Well, I won't deny the smell," Captain Warre said. "But your dress is lovely. You look like a little princess."

"Mr. Bogles is locked in Mama's dressing room because he climbed the drapes in my bedchamber and they tore," came Anne's muffled voice. "He's been very bad."

"I don't suppose he's used to being inside a house. But surely *something* good has happened since you've been in London."

"No. Nothing."

"Oh, I can't believe that," he said doubtfully, and began to question Anne in detail as he started toward Anne's rooms. By the time he set her on her bed they'd come up with four good things that had happened in London.

Katherine watched him brush Anne's hair from her face with the same hands that had directed men to fire at the *Merry Sea,* and a deep yearning curled around her heart and squeezed.

HE WAS SINKING.

James stretched out on his bed, fully clothed, and stared up at the brown drapery while his valet fidgeted nearby.

"Your lordship, shall I—"

"Leave me. I shall take care of it."

"Your shoes—"

"Will be fine. That will be all until I'm ready to dress for the evening, Polk. Thank you."

A few more fidgets, a long hesitation and Polk left him in blessed solitude. The canopy's fringe hung lifelessly, more beige than gold in the muted afternoon light.

James breathed in as much air as his lungs would hold and held it. Held it. Held it. Exhaled slowly. Inhaled again. Exhaled.

And wished, to his shame, that he had informed

Katherine about the committee in a note. He could still feel Anne's small arms winding a strangling sense of responsibility around his neck, even as his mind raced to think of something—anything—he might send her to add to her list of good things about London.

Katherine had been prepared to lie to keep him from Anne. That fact rankled more than anything. He pushed her from his mind, only to have her reappear, trickling inside him the way water seeped through a hull that needed fresh tar.

He'd lost control last night at Lady Carroll's. It was inevitable that he would. A devil inside him had driven him to follow her into that arbor, knowing damned well what would happen. *Wanting* it to happen. He was no better than any of those whoremongers Honoria had dredged up.

Worse, in fact. Because he could see the smoke and the flames, the listing *Merry Sea,* the bloodthirsty corsairs wreaking terror on board. He could hear the screams. Smell the gunpowder. He *knew* what she'd gone through, how terrified she must have been. And still it didn't stop the fire in his blood every time he saw her.

He needed to forget about the captain who studied the horizon with a practiced eye and knew when a line should be snubbed or cast loose and threatened disembowelment without batting an eye. He needed to forget about the woman who turned her face to the sun while the breeze molded shimmering Ottoman textiles to her body and toyed with the ends of her hair.

He didn't want to see any of them. Not the frightened girl, not the shrewd captain and definitely—*very* definitely—not the woman. He didn't want to care whether she married. *Whom* she married. He didn't want to care if she bedded every damned lord in the House. He was damned tired of caring about her.

He stared at the underneath side of the canopy above him. If she were here now... God. He felt himself grow hard and tried to shove the thought away, but it was too late.

He rolled over and groaned into the mattress. A month ago, he'd thought only of escaping the sea. Now the thing he needed to escape was her.

How in God's name would he find her a husband when he couldn't stand the thought of another man touching her because he wanted to touch her so damned badly himself? Something had to change. Immediately.

He breathed into the bedding, and an idea resurfaced.

Maybe— No.

But—

God. It wasn't as if he hadn't thought of it before. Planned on it, even.

He lay there, perfectly still, while the idea came to life in his mind: a bride. It wasn't as if he wouldn't need one eventually. Beginning the search now could be just the thing.

The right kind of bride could divert his attention. Cool his misplaced lust for a woman he as good as condemned to slavery and ruination. Let him do his duty, and give him a new sense of purpose. Give him something to think of instead of Captain Kinloch.

The idea propelled him out of bed, and he paced to the window. The right kind of bride—

Yes.

Yes, it was time. Past time. He would find a girl who'd been on the shelf so long she'd given up hope.

Someone with the right skills to look after the household at Croston, who would happily give him an heir.

A girl who was thoughtful and quiet.

Who wouldn't even know *how* to hold a cutlass.

A young lady who was biddable, and who would never, ever argue with him.

Yes. He would find Katherine a husband, and himself a wife. Then, finally, he would go to Croston and forget he'd ever set foot on a ship named *Possession*.

CHAPTER TWENTY-TWO

JAMES PUSHED THROUGH the crowd at Vauxhall that night, for once separated from Katherine, while the orchestra played a hellishly cheerful piece that only darkened his mood.

All of London had come to the garden tonight, and Honoria was determined to introduce her to every last one of them. He'd spent the past hour doing what he could on her behalf, but now he had other plans.

He worked his way through the crowd, pretending he didn't hear the calls of well-wishers eager to foolishly proclaim his heroics. Let them regale each other with tales. He flexed his hands at his sides to ease the tension curling inside him. With so many people in attendance, this was the perfect opportunity to set his new plan into motion.

The crowd surged and eddied like a strong current through a strait, illuminated by countless globe lamps hanging above. He spotted two old friends, Vincroft and Berston, and headed straight for them. Neither one had married yet. Without a doubt they would have their fingers on the pulse of the marriage mart. Besides that, he needed liquor.

"You look like you're about to do someone a harm, Croston," Vincroft said when James finally reached them.

James grunted. "I'm going after a drink."

"Do allow me!" Berston said jovially, already moving away. "Back in a moment!"

Through a break in the crowd a woman with near-black hair caught his eye. His pulse surged, but it wasn't Katherine. Thank God. He flexed his fingers and forced himself to study the crowd in search of matrimonial possibilities.

"Looking for someone?" Vincroft asked.

"Mmm," he replied. "Female, marriageable, on the shelf."

"Good God! Don't let that be known, or you'll be crushed to death before anyone can finish celebrating the fact that you're alive."

"Forgot to mention mild-mannered, biddable and quiet." *Or shrewd, fiery and combative,* a voice taunted. The essence of Katherine sizzled through him. The idiot between his legs got a brilliant idea about finding her and taking a walk down one of the gardens' darker paths and—

"Here you go." Berston returned with a glass of arrack. "Ought to do the trick."

James downed half the glass in one swallow.

"They all fit that bill when they're marriageable," Vincroft snorted. "Don't find out the truth till afterward."

"Ye gads," Berston said. "Who's getting married?"

"Croston here. Gone mad, if you ask me."

Bloody hell. He should have kept his mouth shut.

"So sorry!" Berston offered an expression that was both resignation and pity. "Got to be done eventually, I suppose. Think about it myself if it wasn't bad for my health. Hives and all that, every time I hear the word *matrimony.*"

James managed a laugh. At least Berston hadn't changed. "You'll suffer through the hives unless you want that pasty nephew of yours to inherit," he said.

Berston took a drink and shook his head. "Just so, just so."

"Who's that?" James asked, nodding toward a young-ish thing in an elegant yet subdued froth of beige. "Blond curls, pearls in her hair."

Vincroft frowned. "No idea. Never seen her before."

"Yes, you have," Berston said. "Lady Maude. Been at every do the past five seasons. Linton's daughter. You don't want the likes of her, Croston. You're probably the first one to notice the poor thing. Do better with Miss Greene—there she is, talking to Lady Trent and Lord Ponsby. In front of the supper boxes, to the left. Blue dress, full breasts." Berston grinned.

Miss Greene's false beauty mark stood out even from this distance, and her bold gaze fixed playfully on the men gathered around her. "Whoever is unfortunate enough to wed Miss Greene will be cuckolded within a week," James said, and returned his attention to the unremarkable Lady Maude. Pale hair, passable face, polite smile… His mind transported her to a chair by the fireside at Croston—in one of the upstairs drawing rooms. It wasn't a stretch to imagine her dozing off with a book in her lap and one of his hunting dogs at her feet.

"Ho, look there!" Berston suddenly pointed out. James followed his gaze through a break in the crowd, and his heart slammed into his gut.

Katherine shimmered in the lamplight like a forbidden idol. Tonight she wore a gown of deep midnight-blue, veed at the waist to reveal a petticoat and stomacher decorated with silver embroidery, ribbons and beads. Her breasts threatened to spill from the top of her stays, and a few lengths of her dark hair played at her neck in artful curls.

"Ye gads," came Berston's barely audible exclamation.

Vincroft made a noise. "Heard *she* might be on the marriage market. No doubt you've got an advantage in that corner."

James clenched his jaw and raised his glass to his lips, only to remember it was empty. "Think I'll go see if I can manage an introduction to Lady Maude."

Berston shook his head. "I'm going for another drink."

"Cracked," was all Vincroft said.

Within minutes the introductions had been made, and he had Lady Maude at his side strolling down the South Walk. She had large brown eyes, a graceful demeanor and a polite smile. A small hand, which had likely never touched a cutlass, was tucked into his elbow.

Even better, he hadn't the least inclination to drag her down one of the notorious lovers' walks and ravish that serene little mouth.

He asked whether she was enjoying the company this evening. She told him she was, but that she was much looking forward to a visit to her cousin in the country, where life was quieter.

She asked whether he was happy to be home at last. He told her he was, but that he was looking forward to the excitement of his return dying down so he could spend his time with a peaceful read and perhaps a putter in his father's old conservatory. She replied that both sounded like an improvement over the hustle-bustle of the Season, and that she had recently read a fascinating essay on the botany of Greece.

Botany. Perfect. He double-checked the color of her eyes. Yes, brown—a solid, sensible brown, without any wild flecks that made them take on odd colors in sultry lights.

"Forgive my forwardness, Captain," she said as they came to the end of the walk and turned back, "but I don't suppose…" She gripped her fan anxiously. "Well, I don't suppose you would consider introducing me to Lady Dunscore."

Just like that, his hopes crashed.

"I so long to meet her," she continued, "but I know nobody with the right connections. And Mother is little help under the circumstances, naturally— Oh, dear. I see I've offended you."

He forced a smile. "Not at all."

Those sensible brown eyes came frighteningly alive. "She is such a fascination! How I would love to see her in action, holding a spyglass to her eye beneath great, billowing sails."

The image exploded unhelpfully into his mind. "Your mother will have my head on a platter for encouraging such imaginings. Tell me, Lady Maude, have you done any reading about pigeons?"

"I doubt anyone could have your head on a platter, Captain. Pigeons? No, I daresay I haven't." They were nearly back to the grove and she was looking ahead, searching the crowd. "Do you see her? Lady Dunscore, I mean."

"Afraid not." Seeing Lady Dunscore was the last thing he needed at the moment. "Would you care to stroll down the Grand Walk?"

"Forgive me, Captain. How terribly rude of me. Indeed—let's do see the Grand Walk." They started through the crowd in the grove toward the other side. "If you don't find a satisfactory treatise on pigeons, my lord, I highly recommend this botanical essay. Greece is so fascinating! Stories of exotic places are so diverting. No doubt you would agree, given that you've spent your life visiting— Oh!" Her grip tightened on his arm. "There she is."

Katherine was laughing up at some man who had his back turned. Marshwell? Adkins? Everyone looked the same in these bloody wigs. Katherine, however, was a goddess shimmering in torchlight, and her brilliant smile shot straight to his gut.

"Oh, do let's take the Grand Walk later," Lady Maude begged. "Do you mind terribly? I promise I won't let Mother cut off your head."

"You are too kind," he said, and grimly crossed Lady Maude off his list.

THE NEXT MORNING at Westminster was a disaster.

As James had expected, Ingraham's tale of Katherine's threats had made its rounds, which meant James was peppered with questions about her loyalty to the Crown and whether or not she had, in fact, turned renegade. He managed to deflect the more outrageous inquiries and tried to inject a bit of reason into the debate about her, but he gained little ground.

He arrived at the theater that evening with renewed determination.

It didn't last.

"I want a meeting with her, Croston," Vincroft declared in a hush from the seat next to James, his eyes fixed across the balcony at Katherine's box. "Tried to get an introduction last night, but there was no getting near her. Should have had you do it before you disappeared with that mouse. My God, she's a magnificent creature!"

James stretched his fingers, checking a driving desire to wrap them around Vincroft's throat. But Vincroft was a lesser of evils, so he reached for a vaguely disinterested tone. "As a matter of fact—"

"Can't imagine her dressed like a Barbary pirate," Vincroft interrupted. "Can't imagine it at all." James clenched his jaw, and Vincroft lowered his voice. "Fearsome sight to behold, eh?"

"Terrifying." James beheld her now as she half watched the performance, half chatted with Honoria and Philomena. Tonight she sparkled in a gown the color of the sea at dusk, with her hair frozen in a pile of curls decorated with jewels that winked at him in the stagelight. The baser part of his nature preferred her the way she'd been dressed yesterday morning. But then, the baser part of his nature would prefer her dressed in nothing at all.

The sudden rumble of the theatrical thunder machine startled him. Just then she turned her head straight toward him, and a bolt of an entirely different kind shot through him.

He had to find her a husband. And by God, she would marry the man if he had to hold a pistol to her head. And then he would wash his hands of this whole damned mess. He leaned toward Vincroft. "No doubt you are aware—"

"Winston's been staring at her for most of the first act," Vincroft said through his teeth. "I demand that you take me there at once before he makes himself at home in her box. For God's sake, Croston, have pity on me. You know how I—" He turned in his seat as someone entered their box. "Wenthurst! Good to see you! And Pinsbury!"

"Don't get up, don't get up," Wenny said, sliding into the chair on the other side of James and taking a pinch of snuff. The direction of his gaze told James exactly why Wenny was there.

James got up, anyway, because Pinsbury was crowding into the box with three women—Lady Pinsbury and, James soon learned, Lady Pinsbury's sister and niece.

"Here from the country, you know," Pinsbury explained. "Joys of the Season and all that. Not so many diversions in Sussex, are there, my dear?" he jovially asked his niece.

Miss Underbridge offered her uncle what could only be termed a perfunctory smile. "Not of the sort to be found in London, Uncle."

"We thought some time in London would do her good," Lady Pinsbury added. *Would find her a husband, more like,* James thought. Lady Pinsbury beamed at Miss Underbridge, whose perfunctory smile was now pasted to her lips. They were rather full lips, James noticed, set beneath a handsome-enough nose and sturdy cheekbones. The dim theater left the color of her eyes a mystery, but he could see enough to understand the source of Lady Pinsbury and Mrs. Underbridge's pointed enthusiasm for her presence in London society: Miss Underbridge was quite clearly on the shelf.

He took a closer look.

"Such a miracle, your safe return," Pinsbury was saying. "Can't be more pleased."

"Indeed, I have to agree," James said. Miss Underbridge had already seen her twentieth birthday—he'd wager Croston Hall on it. She seemed to have a calm enough disposition, with no trace of the eagerness lighting the faces of her mother and aunt. "Have you been enjoying the play, Miss Underbridge?" he asked.

He got the full brunt of that pasted-on smile, along with a moment of surprise at having been noticed. "I have, Lord Croston. It is quite entertaining."

He applauded her effort, but her tone told him she would prefer to be elsewhere. "Of course," he added as an experiment, "I generally prefer a quiet fireside read to the noise of the theater."

"I quite agree." Her tone lost some of its falsity. "Reading is a most enjoyable pastime."

Indeed. He wondered whether, unlike Lady Maude, Miss Underbridge had a sensible disposition to match her calm demeanor.

The back of his mind teased that a reactionary demeanor and biting disposition was vastly more interesting, and a shiver slid over the back of his neck as though Katherine was watching him from her box. His senses began to churn, stirred up the way a hard rain roiled a stagnant pond. Everything in him wanted to leave his box and go to hers. Be near her. Listen to her wild, acrimonious opinions about London and its inhabitants. Find out what she thought of the gift he'd sent Anne.

He shoved the longing away and discreetly assessed whether Miss Underbridge appeared built to give him an heir.

"You will have to dine with us one evening," Lady Pinsbury said to him.

"Yes, yes," Pinsbury said, breaking away from the conversation he'd been having with Vincroft. "We'd be delighted!"

"As would I," James replied. If he accepted an invitation in the next week, he could have the business arranged by the time the committee made its decision and be ready to travel to Croston without delay. He could return to London for the ceremony, then let her decide whether to remain in London or come to Croston. The idea's simplicity was vaguely comforting.

After assuring him that an invitation would be forthcoming, the Pinsburys and Miss Underbridge left the box. James returned to his seat, where Wenny still stared openly at Katherine. James resisted the urge to do the same. He needed to get rid of Wenny so he could talk business with Vincroft.

But just thinking about it edged him a little closer to madness.

"Listen here, Croston," Wenny said the moment James sat down. "It's good to have you back—truly it is. But you'll understand if I get straight to the point. Lady Dunscore, old friend. What can you tell me that will give me an advantage?"

Vincroft leaned forward and looked at him. "You'll have to climb over me and half a dozen others first," he said. "You're not the only one with an eye on her."

Wenny snorted. "True enough. But if it's Winston that gets her, I won't abide it. Now tell me, Croston, will you give me an introduction? Will she think it an affront if I introduce myself?"

"*Lady* Wenthurst will likely think so." The frayed edge of James's control wore thinner.

Wenny snorted. "Good God, she's a beauty." He wasn't talking about his wife. "I want her, Croston. Bloody hell! There's Winston now, bold as balls."

James watched Winston enter Katherine's box without so much as an escort. Another thread snapped.

"She didn't even curtsy," Vincroft said. "She's— My God, I think she's rebuffing him. Yes—yes, she's given him the cold shoulder!" He grinned at Wenny. "Perhaps there's a chance for us, after all."

"For me perhaps," Wenny scoffed, pinching more snuff. "There's little doubt she'll go to the highest bidder, and you've never been one for high stakes."

James didn't move. Didn't sit forward, didn't take his eyes off the stage. "The next time I hear you imply that Lady Dunscore is for sale to anyone," he said quietly, "you will meet me on the field, and I will kill you." Through his rage, he heard his own words as though listening through water.

The two men at his sides fell silent. Still he did not move.

After a moment, Wenny stood up. "Understood, Croston," he said. "Understood. My apologies—I didn't realize."

Realize? What the devil— "The only thing to *realize* is that the countess of Dunscore is a lady, not a whore, and the 'highest bidder' is likely to find his head— *both* his heads—rolling on the floor." He looked up at Wenny. "Perhaps I will offer you an advantage, after all," he added, "and advise you that Lady Dunscore is particularly adroit with a cutlass."

"Good to know," Wenny said, offering a stiff bow. "Good to know. Again, my apologies."

He didn't want Wenny's apologies. He wanted to tear Wenny apart with his bare hands. A sound like the ocean rushed in his ears for long moments after Wenny had left the box. Finding Katherine a decent husband would be impossible. The ones with financial liabilities hoped to wed her and suck Dunscore dry while they rutted between her thighs every night. The ones who didn't need money only wanted to pass her around as their mistress.

"For God's sake, Croston," Vincroft said. "You'd better have a care, calling men out. If you've claimed her for yourself, you'd best let it be known. Not fair to challenge a man when he's got no idea."

"I've got no claim on her. I simply will not sit by while someone questions the honor of the person to whom I owe my life."

Vincroft hesitated. "Of course not. Didn't think of it that way. But still—"

"But nothing. They don't have to see her as a lady, but they'd damned well better act like they do," James shot back, and crossed Vincroft off his list of possibly acceptable husbands for Katherine. Which left exactly...no one.

CHAPTER TWENTY-THREE

KATHERINE WAS LOSING the battle.

She pushed past Dobbs after the awful evening at the theater and charged toward the staircase as quickly as her enormous skirts would allow, dragging in panicked breaths, keeping her hood pulled low so no one would see her tears.

Marriage!

Once you're safely wed, I hope you might consider joining me for some more interesting entertainment than the theater.

Never mind the Duke of Winston's disgusting proposition. He assumed she would marry. *Expected* her to marry.

And what had Captain Warre been doing meanwhile? She could have sworn one or two of the visitors to her box had been in his first. He'd done no better the night before at Vauxhall, going off on a turn with some young girl...which, of course, there was no reason why he shouldn't. No reason at all.

She gulped for breath against fresh tears, hurrying up the stairs. Marriage. It was out of the question. Dunscore was hers, and they would not take it from her that way. When she reached the landing, that giant portrait enticed her with its promise.

One day, Katie, you will be mistress here, and the very waves will tremble at your footsteps.

The waves *did* tremble at her feet, and she hadn't needed Dunscore to make it so. Hadn't needed the Lords, or committees or *marriage* to make it so.

Upstairs in her room, she stood impatiently while her maid unfastened her gown and stays and took down her hair. Katherine dismissed her quickly and finished the rest herself, putting on her own nightgown and sitting wearily with her brush, staring at her reflection in the glass.

If the bill passed, Holliswell would benefit. But if she married, then one of their own would reap Dunscore's reward. Was that their logic?

Her throat tightened, and a trenchant longing crept out of hiding.

When I pass away, Papa, I shall be buried right here in Dunscore's courtyard.

Good heavens, Katie. Nobody wants to play ninepins on a person's grave. Damned macabre of you. Impractical, too.

This couldn't happen. This grief—it was all in the past, and it would *not* resurface.

She got up and paced to the fireplace. What was rightfully hers had been taken a long time ago. There was no reason to feel so deeply for it now. Growing attached to places, to people, could only lead to heartache. Hadn't she learned that well enough?

Come, Papa—you must come see what the rain has done. Dunscore's walls are glistening in the sunset like they're made of jewels!

He had indulged her that time, letting her take his hand and lead him outside and show him how the battlements shone like fiery diamonds against dark storm-clouds to the east.

A sudden urge gripped her to dash off a note to Captain Warre asking for reassurance, and she clenched her fists to keep from rushing to the writing desk. Using Captain Warre for his influence—that was the plan. Not relying on him. Not leaning on him in her moments of weakness.

Her fingernails bit into her palms.

Stupid, stupid female that she was. Even now, she could feel his arms around her as if they still stood in the shadows of that arbor. She could feel his strength.

His cannons had once nearly killed her, but now he worked for her security.

He'd lied to her aboard her own ship, but now she knew him to be driven by honor.

Slowly her hands went slack. She turned away from the fire and paced a few feet, briskly, and stopped. Tried to pretend she still held him responsible for her fate. That she hadn't forgiven him entirely in that single moment, standing in Lord Deal's ballroom with a confectionery ship bearing down on them full sail.

He was pigheaded, yes. Driven to bend anything and everyone to his will, including her. He may have been many things, but devil take him, he wasn't to blame.

And she could not let him know, because his sense of guilt was the only thing keeping him on her side.

"A DUEL!" KATHERINE practically barked the word, then wished she hadn't as a couple enjoying a morning stroll in the park looked over to gawk. "Impossible," she whispered to Phil and Honoria as the sunshine struggled through high clouds. "It can't be true." What could possess him to do something so irrational?

The possible answers slid hotly through her like a sip of hard liquor.

"It is absolutely true," Honoria said. "Lady Poole sent me a note just this morning. She heard it from Lord Poole, who heard it from someone who heard it from Lord Vincroft himself, who, of course, was there."

A duel. For her honor. Deep inside, the idea of it lured her like a shimmering pearl. "Captain Warre is far too pragmatic for such nonsense," she told them.

Honoria and Phil exchanged a look.

She *needed* him to be pragmatic. Because yesterday a set of intricate toy ships had arrived, and for the first time since they'd arrived in London, Anne's face had lit with excitement. And Katherine had imagined, not for the first time, what it would be like if Captain Warre was always there to lift Anne in his arms and make her think of happy things.

If not for the scare Anne had given them that morning, Katherine would have been the one in his arms.

And it would have led to disaster, because she didn't *want* to be in his arms. He made her volatile. His fiery kisses, his murderous flashes of outrage—they needed to stop. She couldn't have him acting as though he was...as though he was...

"A man in the grip of passion," Phil said, "is anything but pragmatic." She slid her twinkling, damnable eyes toward Katherine. "I daresay you chained his heart as well as his hands when you shackled him to your bed."

"Shackled him to your bed!" Honoria stopped short, all curiosity. "La, do tell!"

She was going to kill Philomena. "Phil exaggerates,"

she managed calmly. "It was a simple precaution. He was a stranger, and one cannot be too careful at sea."

Phil gave Honoria a look. "A very...*aroused* stranger, shall we say."

"Aha! I *knew* you were not his greatest misfortune, Katherine. Forgive me— Oh, now I see what he meant by combative. Do stop looking at me like that."

"Without knowing his identity," Katherine explained impatiently, "we had no idea what he was capable of."

"I see." But still Honoria's eyes danced with other imaginings, and Phil's expression was positively triumphant.

Things were spiraling out of control very quickly. "I shall have Madame Bouchard design a space in my skirts this afternoon for my cutlass," Katherine snapped. "If anyone is to duel on my behalf, it shall be me."

"A splendid idea," Phil said. "Men like Winston and Wenthurst might not be led so slavishly by their anatomies if they feared their precious organs might be lopped off." She laughed in that sultry way of hers. "By now I'm sure all the *ton* knows you threatened to cut off Winston's cock in his sleep."

"Which was fabulous, but unwise given that he will chair the committee," Honoria said, and then laughed. "La, how it must have shocked Winston to have his proposition so violently rebuffed!"

"It wasn't *that* proposition that offended me," Katherine told them. "It was his assumption that I would soon be accepting a *different* kind of proposition." A couple rode past on horseback and waved a greeting to Honoria. Katherine lowered her voice. "What is everyone thinking of with all this talk of my marriage? Can they possibly be serious?"

Phil waved the idea away. "Dearest, it's only natural for men to think of marriage when there is a propertied woman to be had. You mustn't let it upset you. They cannot force you into wedlock."

Honoria frowned. "They could, indeed, if they make it clear the bill will move forward if she doesn't marry."

"They could at that," Phil agreed.

"But will they?" Katherine's question shot too loudly into the air.

Honoria took Katherine's arm. "Tell me, suppose a man did show honorable intentions—a tolerable man, naturally. Would you be interested?"

"Certainly not."

"A handsome man, of course. Strong. Of good breeding and titled, naturally. Honorable, steadfast, loyal—"

"Someone has been reading too many novels!" Phil laughed.

"Oh, hush. Your Pennington was such a man, Philomena." Phil fell silent, and Honoria tightened her grip on Katherine's arm. "In all seriousness, Katherine. If marriage does become your only option—"

"It can't."

"—have you not considered that perhaps it would solve everything?"

She wasn't a fool—the well-bred, titled man Honoria spoke of was her own brother. "Find me a man who obeys orders instantly, who will never question my authority even in his own private thoughts, and I shall consider it."

"Ha!" Honoria exclaimed. "If I find such a man, rest assured I shall keep him entirely for myself. Oh! Look there." Honoria grabbed Katherine's arm and her voice dropped to a whisper. "Isn't that Miss Holliswell? Who is she talking to?"

Katherine looked in the direction Honoria's nose pointed, still contemplating the too-real possibility that the price for Dunscore would be her freedom.

"It looks like Viscount Edrington," Phil said, and made a noise. "Most foppish bore in London."

"Oh, dear," Honoria said. "Look how she's in earnest. Poor girl—such a timid thing. How *could* Nicholas harbor affection for her?" After another moment she said, "Do you think she could be afraid of him?"

"Of *Edrington?*" As they watched, Miss Holliswell glanced over her shoulder and shifted a little. A prim young woman who could only be Miss Holliswell's maid waited nearby, wringing her hands.

"You don't suppose he has a tendresse for her," Honoria said doubtfully. "*How* are we supposed to discover anything when she carries no fan?"

"I should hope she doesn't have a tendresse, for both their sakes," Phil said. "The last Viscount Edrington drained the estate nearly dry. He hasn't nearly enough income to satisfy her father's expectations."

"La, look at that! She tried to walk away, but he followed her. Should we go rescue her, do you think? It's obvious she's being accosted."

At that moment, Katherine spotted Captain Warre and his brother striding purposefully toward Miss Holliswell and Lord Edrington. "I don't think we'll need to," she said. "Look."

The men hadn't seen them, and the reason why was clear: Nicholas Warre had his entire attention focused on Miss Holliswell. As they watched, he broke away from Captain Warre and strode toward her and the viscount. Captain Warre's thunderous expression was visible even from this distance.

"Good heavens, the poor girl is liable to faint dead away," Honoria said. Just then, Captain Warre spotted them. Honoria waved. "Come—let's go find out what's going on."

Katherine would have preferred not to, but yet another pair of men was strolling in their direction, so she followed Honoria and Phil. They met Captain Warre—whose heart she had absolutely *not* chained—beneath a tree.

"I know nothing more than that Nick had heard Miss Holliswell was in the park when I arrived," he told them irritably, "and that if I wanted to speak to him, I had to come along."

"Oh, what do you suppose he's saying?" Honoria asked with frustration.

Whatever Nicholas Warre said to Viscount Edrington, it had the effect of causing the viscount to bow, mount his horse and ride away.

"Well, pooh," Honoria said.

Phil's lips twitched mischievously. "He could at least have challenged Edrington to a duel."

Honoria's eyes danced in Captain Warre's direction. "Duels are all the rage these days, are they not?"

Katherine glared at her.

"Oh, look," Phil exclaimed now, taking Honoria's arm. "There's Lady Pollard. Honoria, were you not just saying this very morning that you wished to speak with her about her pair of greyhounds?"

"Indeed!" Honoria said. "And there she is, with both of them on leads. What a remarkable coincidence!

Quickly—we must catch her before they run off with her."

They scurried off toward Lady Pollard and the two greyhounds Honoria had likely been unaware of until this moment, leaving Katherine alone with Captain Warre, who still scowled at his brother.

A duel. She looked at his profile, chiseled like the most perfect statue carved by the greatest master, and her blood pulsed a little faster. It was easy to imagine the way his eyes would have turned stony when he threatened those men at the theater, the way his voice would have iced over.

A flutter took wing in her belly.

"Illegal activity is beyond the scope of anything that might repay the debt you owe me," she informed him.

"Sometimes I forget how quickly news spreads in London."

"Do not call a man out on my behalf again."

Now he turned and leveled those green eyes at her. "Rest assured, it was a momentary lapse of judgment."

A tiny, irrational disappointment grabbed her. "As were the boats," she said, when she should have thanked him. "I'll not have Anne relying on you, only to have you forget all about her after your debt is repaid."

Anger lit those eyes. "I would *never* abandon Anne."

You're my princess, Katie. Father had used to say that, too, but it was a lie. She hadn't been a princess—just a naive young girl like every other naive young girl, nothing more nor less special than the rest, expendable in the end when something more fun came along.

"Do not back yourself into a corner, Captain. It is inevitable. You and I have an acquaintance by necessity—

one that, by the grace of God, may end very soon."
Before she—not Anne—became the one in danger of
relying on him.

CHAPTER TWENTY-FOUR

Dear Sirs,
Observed Lady Dunscore at theater and Hyde
Park. No sign of unlawful maritime activity, but
recommend increasing naval budget to defend the
Serpentine as a precaution.
In your humble service,
Croston

NICK WATCHED HOLLISWELL stuff a piece of bread half the
size of a man's fist into his mouth and fought to keep
from curling his lip in disgust. The man had no bloody
business being an earl—Scottish or otherwise. Nobody
else at the table seemed to care, but then, every last one
of them had reasons to curry Holliswell's favor.

It was fitting company, considering Nick fell into
that category himself.

Next to him, Clarissa poked at her stuffed pheasant
and lifted three peas on her fork, casting him a quick,
uncertain look from beneath long, dark lashes.

Bloody Christ. Holliswell could stuff an entire roast
suckling into his mouth for all he cared—Clarissa was
the one who mattered.

"Have you recovered from this afternoon?" he asked
her under his breath.

"I have, Lord Taggart. Thank you."

The sooner he could get her out from under Holliswell's thumb, the better. She was so damned fragile. How in God's name had she been allowed to go to the park with only her maid?

"I shall make sure Edrington doesn't bother you again," he told her.

Her hands faltered as she sliced a morsel of pheasant. She nudged it a little, sliced again.

He would have to teach her something of life or be driven to an early grave watching out for her. It would be easier to explain the dangers once she understood the intimate details of a marriage. But in order for *that* to happen—

God. He would have to be very, very careful on their wedding night. Incredibly, unbelievably careful. He could hardly stand to think of it. What a girl like Clarissa really needed was to be cloistered away in a convent somewhere on the Continent where no man's hands could ever defile her.

He would bloody well need a mistress. Because aside from what was absolutely essential—if he could even bring himself to do that much—he could never expect Clarissa to endure—

Holy Christ.

He attacked his pheasant with new purpose.

"...cousin caused quite a stir at the theater last night," a Mrs. Tinningsworth was saying to Holliswell across the table.

Holliswell reached for another hunk of bread. "I would imagine my cousin causes a stir everywhere she goes," Holliswell said. "She is an oddity, after all."

"I heard she removed all the furniture from her house

and replaced it with Moorish cushions on the floor," someone else said. "Could it be true?"

Nick imagined that it probably was. He was so bloody tired of hearing about Katherine Kinloch. He'd give his right testicle to see this whole damned business finished today.

"I meant what I said," he murmured a little too sharply to Clarissa. He would find a way for them to marry even if the bill did not pass.

"Yes, I know." Her eyes never left her plate.

"No matter what we have to do." Even if they had to resort to something improper. Better to see her reputation sullied than her delicate body defiled by the likes of Oakley or Adkins.

By God, he'd bloody well take her to Scotland if he had to.

BY ALL THAT was holy, James was going to bed her. Just once—just enough to put an end to this fascination that led him around by the balls. Enough was enough. He was finished with wanting. It was time for having.

James tore off his coat without waiting for his valet and threw it on the bed. Five days. Five hellish days of thinking of practically nothing but Katherine, and thank God—thank *God*—the committee would meet tomorrow, because he couldn't take much more of this. Laughing, talking, dancing… If he had to feel her hand on his arm one more time, instead of on his cock where he wanted it, he wouldn't be responsible for his actions.

He wasn't growing more rational, finding a new sense of purpose, finding a cure for what ailed him. He was burning up with lust. It could not continue. One good tumble with her—that was what he needed. After that, he could find a suitable bride and live in peace.

A thought of Anne snuck in, and he kicked it aside. He didn't want to think of Anne, or what Katherine might ultimately have to do to keep Dunscore. The only thing he wanted to think about was Katherine's legs wrapped around his hips.

This entire business was nothing less than a debacle. Men he'd once considered friends slathered over her as though she were a succulent roast they couldn't wait to devour. An evening at Lord DeBarre's, a card party at Lord Kilbourne's, another night at the theater after he'd sworn he wouldn't go again and more strolls in the park than he'd ever hoped to take in his life. Each event felt specially calculated for his particular torment.

Tonight they'd dined with Lord and Lady Pelsworth. The only—*only*—redeeming value in the evening had been his introduction to a Miss Lydia Ridgeway. Miss Ridgeway was a perfect marriage candidate—on the shelf, he'd been told, well mannered and passably attractive. Not that he could find out anything else about her with Katherine constantly at his side.

Katherine—ill-mannered, insanely beautiful and far too convincingly amused by the damnable Earl of Tungsley—was the devil in silk. And he was no closer to finding her a husband now than he'd been the day she'd dragged his sorry arse from the water.

Because you don't want *to find her a husband.*

He did. He *did* want to find her a husband. Just not before subduing this madness inside him, because he was halfway to losing his mind. *More* than halfway.

Well, he had a solution for that. James braced his hands on the edge of his dressing table and stared at

the preservative he'd just pulled from the top drawer.
It would let him do all he wanted to Katherine without
fear of consequences, and then he could remove himself to Croston with the likes of Miss Ridgeway or Lady
Maude or Miss Underbridge.

With any luck, tomorrow the committee would put
an end to all this. The only event left to endure was tonight's ball at the Rogersfields'. And there was a good
chance he could turn that situation to his advantage. He
would simply watch for the right moment, get her to the
right part of the house and then he would seduce her. It
wouldn't be difficult. He could have had her on board
the *Possession* if William hadn't interrupted them, and
it would have saved him the torment now. He could still
feel her breasts as though he held them in his hands
this moment. If William hadn't burst in, he would have
pushed those damned trousers over her hips and—

He inhaled sharply and pushed away from the dressing table, gripping the back of his neck. He stared at
the preservative. Finally snatching it off the table, he
stalked to the armoire and slipped it inside his jacket
with a mercenary sort of relish.

Oh, yes. He would have every last inch of her open
and quivering beneath him, hot and ready for him. He
would have her at his mercy, to do with as he pleased,
and by God there would be no bloody cutlass to get
in the way. He would taste her and touch her until she
screamed his name.

Not *Captain*. Not *Lord Croston*.

James.

His beautiful, piratical emasculator would beg for

him, and he would satisfy her. He would satisfy them both, and their "acquaintance by necessity"—as she so coldly put it—could go to the devil.

CHAPTER TWENTY-FIVE

IF ONE MORE Lord So-and-so put his hand where it didn't belong, by God, she would lop it off and laugh while blood pooled on the ballroom floor.

Katherine faced her partner and applauded the orchestra, imagining the satisfaction of drawing her cutlass from its new hiding place in her skirts and showing the lecherous rat how much she appreciated his groping.

The stifling ballroom air cloyed her lungs as desperation began to set in. All her flirtations and imprisoning dresses were going to be for naught. There were bodies everywhere—tall ones, short ones, slender ones, plump ones. *Male* ones. If opinions could be swayed by "accidentally" touching her breasts, she would have little to worry about tomorrow. But the truth of the matter sat cold and indigestible in her stomach.

"You're a splendid dancer," the latest Lord Whatsit told her, steering her through the crowd by her elbow as the orchestra struck up another tune. "Splendid!" For all she knew, he didn't have any influence at all. But he did have a fascination for her cleavage.

What would he think if he knew that a foot below, her cutlass hung inside a secret opening in her skirts? How gratifying it would be to introduce the two of them and rid him of that sickly smile.

"Allow me to bring you some punch," he suggested eagerly.

"I'm not thirsty." She could find the punch herself—just as soon as she located Phil and Honoria and asked whether committing murder would be a strike against her with the committee. Judging from this crowd, she would find them sometime tomorrow.

Suddenly a hand wrapped around her arm, and Captain Warre materialized at her side. "Excuse us, Denby," he said. Excellent—perhaps he would challenge this imbecile to a duel.

Lord Whatsit backed away with a startled bow. "Of course. A pleasure, Lady Dunscore." His eyes weren't on her breasts now. She nearly smiled.

"You look pale," Captain Warre told her.

She was more glad to see him than she would have wanted to admit. "One can scarcely breathe in here, and I'm dying of thirst."

"We can't have that." He shoved a mostly full glass of red wine into her hand. Hardly a thirst-quencher, but she drank deeply anyhow. A drop of liquid clung to the glass where his lips had touched it, and a tingle awakened low in her belly as she drank. "I know where we can escape the crowds," he said, and navigated her through the milling hordes.

"Have you found out anything?" she asked.

"A little." He guided her out of the main ballroom and into a second, equally crowded, side room off which branched a large connecting hall, from which stemmed several smaller passageways. By the time they started down one of these, they were alone. "We can find privacy here," he said. His hand stayed on the small of her back even though the crowd was gone. Several doorways opened on either side of the passageway; as they passed one, she caught a glimpse of a couple intertwined on a couch. Quickly she looked away.

"Here," he said, and let her walk ahead of him into a small, empty salon. Behind her, the door shut with a solid click.

Across the room a pair of French doors leading outside stood ajar, and a waft of night air reached her. She inhaled deeply for the first time all evening. "Finally," she said, "I can breathe."

He took the glass from her hand, drained the wine she hadn't finished and reached to set it down on a tiny marble-topped table.

"These disgusting imbeciles," she fumed. "Tonight is nothing if not a waste, and a detriment to my feet— never *mind* my dignity. I don't even know who half of these men—" Captain Warre's mouth came down on hers before she could finish the sentence.

—*are.*

His tongue swept past her lips and parried fiercely with hers—hot velvet demanding a response—and whatever she'd been thinking about her dignity vanished. He tasted of wine and power, smelled of spice and sin. She put her hands on his chest with no thought for her cutlass and found rock and fire beneath her palms.

His hands framed her face, skimmed down her neck, cupped her shoulders. Found her breasts. This was no accidental grope. And when his hands closed around her, she had no thought of lopping them off. She heard herself moan. Felt herself succumbing like a drowning man to the undertow. Desire snaked through her deeply. Intimately.

It wasn't by chance that he'd brought her here. His

intention was clear. He would make love to her here, and she would welcome him, give herself to him, and there would be no going back, and then—

She tore her lips away. "You said you had a little news," she said, breathless.

"Later." His eyes were the dark green of water churning beneath a storm.

"Now."

His nostrils flared, and his jaw tightened. She watched him debate whether to comply. "Very well." Desire roughened his voice. "Hathaway, Edrington and Zagost have all assured me they'll not support a recommendation against you."

"That's three." And hardly news. She'd expected more.

"There are others."

"Who?"

"I've spoken with all of them. They know where I stand on the matter."

That was hardly a commitment. The panic that had dogged her since her first night in London returned, seeping through every crack like water through an unsealed hull. "They're going to vote against me, aren't they."

"Not if I can help it."

She stared at him. What if he *couldn't* help it? "Nobody knows me," she said. "My father's friends, my old acquaintances—they've no reason to support me." And plenty of reason not to.

"Don't be irrational. These are reasonable men. They'll not take this issue lightly." He bent his head to kiss her again, but she pulled away and paced toward the drapery fluttering in the breeze. Behind her, he exhaled sharply.

"To come to London and attempt to navigate society, when I barely remember my own debut—"

He gave a derisive laugh. "The melodrama returns. Show me the woman who doesn't remember her debut, and I'll show you a corpse twenty years in the crypt."

His sarcasm couldn't staunch the flow of her fear. Her feet began to move. "What effect did I think I could have? What did I think I would accomplish besides letting all the world witness my humiliation?"

"This is senseless. You've already made inroads into society, and I've talked with dozens of men. I'm sure I've changed more than a few minds."

But what if he hadn't? "What if they don't stop with pains and penalties?"

"Oh, for God's sake."

"What if they press charges against me?" She paced by him to the fireplace in a panic, her fear in control.

"You are not a pirate, and there will be no charges."

"The questions people ask me—"

"Impolite, certainly, but reflecting a curiosity that works to your benefit."

"The conversation we overheard, the invitations—"

"Katherine, stop."

"The odds that they'll decide to let me keep Dunscore without any conditions—"

"*Stop.*" This time he grabbed her arm as she walked by. She jerked to a halt and shot her attention to his face.

Please help me. Please do something. She couldn't beg for help. She wouldn't.

"It's too soon to give up," he said. "Which isn't to say there's anything easy about surrendering your fate into someone else's hands—especially when you're used to being in command." His voice was low and calm. It filled the cracks in her resolve like soft tar. Oh, God—she was staring at him the way he must have stared at the *Possession*'s hull as he'd floated in the water.

"No. No, it isn't easy," she said woodenly.

"You'll have to be cautious about what you tell the committee. You mustn't lie—"

"Of course."

"—but you should be…prudent."

Prudent. A hundred unanswerable questions crowded her tongue. He stood there like Gibraltar, strong and constant, and the desire to be in his arms again nearly overwhelmed her. Instead, she paced toward the fireplace. She'd promised herself she would not lean on him. She needed to say something to distance herself, but now her tongue felt leaden and all she could think was, *Please tell me it will be all right.*

"What will they want to know?" she asked.

"Everything, no doubt. Things they have no business knowing."

"And I risk their disapproval if I refuse to answer, as well as if I tell them what they want to know."

"Unfortunately. Except…"

She spun back. "What?"

His brows were furrowed, and he watched her with troubled eyes. "There's more than mere high seas drama to your story, Katherine. I would never suggest that you exploit your unfortunate circumstances, but if it would elicit even a small measure of sympathy from the committee members to remember that you were just a girl, and—"

"You want me to describe my capture."

"It might be helpful."

"And my captivity."

"If the story might affect the outcome, yes." In his eyes she could see that he wanted the story not just for its effect on the committee, but for himself. He wanted every detail, every tragic turn of events, so he could add them like stones to the weight of his debt. Everything he was doing was because of his own guilt—not affection, not even lust.

The past yawned open and began to suck her in, and she fought back hard. She didn't want his pity. More than anything, suddenly, she wanted his understanding. But she wasn't going to get it.

He hadn't moved, and neither had she. They watched each other from several yards away. "You should know that I've forgiven you," she said flatly. "You did what you thought best at the time. I understand that."

His eyes sparked, and his lips curved mirthlessly. "An ill-timed absolution, given that I'm likely to be instrumental in front of the committee tomorrow."

"Nonetheless. There is nothing you could have done to stop what happened."

"You don't know that," he said sharply, then calmed. "We can do no good rehashing this. We should return to the crush. I shall do all I can tonight, and tomorrow in front of the committee. I'll not walk away until everything is settled."

I don't want you to walk away ever.

But he hadn't brought her to this room to calm her fears. The truth of that still burned in his eyes. If she reached for him right now, he would put his arms around her, pull her to him, and she could lose herself in his strength and forget about everyone in that ballroom, if only for the time it took to—

To what? Show him how weak she really was?

She forced her lips into a stiff curve, straightened her skirts and moved toward the door. "Excellent. Then by all means, let us go see what more can be done."

NOTHING MORE COULD be done. She knew it in her gut as sure as she could sense the tide changing.

Captain Warre stayed nearby, close enough to lend his influence at the right times, but far enough not to interfere when someone asked her to dance. With each passing minute, she could sense his frustration growing. It was a palpable thing that could not be drowned out by music and laughter.

All was in vain. She knew it to be fact two hours later, after a string of new dance partners, a dozen introductions from Honoria, two very improper suggestions from men who were not even on the committee and a direct cut from Lady Wenthurst. Yet still she kept trying. Hoping. And all the while her breath grew more labored and her smile grew more brittle.

If she did not escape immediately, it would shatter.

She managed to evade Captain Warre while he was talking to a group of men. Desperate for air, for something to soothe her throat, she found a fresh glass of wine and escaped to the private rooms. Within minutes she found the open French doors she'd seen earlier. Unnoticed, she stepped onto the far end of the stone balcony that stretched along the back side of the house. Far to her left, where a set of doors opened into the ballroom, a crowd of people stood talking. Silently she retreated even farther into the shadows.

She set her glass on a stone cap and gripped the railing, desperately inhaling the cool night air. The wine warmed her blood, but a scream pushed at the back of her throat. What in God's name was she doing here? All this judgment was exactly what she had chosen to avoid by making her life on the *Possession*.

Was she really going to subject Anne to this now after protecting her from it all this time?

Earlier today she'd almost been able to forget all this, riding with Anne in Lord Deal's phaeton, hearing Anne squeal with delight. Feeling Lord Deal's reassuring gaze on them both. For a short time, it had seemed as if everything might turn out all right.

She stared into the darkness as she might have done aboard the *Possession,* except this railing was stone and the only view was a shrouded garden at the back of the house. Instead of crashing waves, small crescendos of laughter reached her ears. Everything was not going to be all right.

She imagined Captain Warre stepping onto the balcony behind her. Taking her hand and sweeping her away—her and Anne both, to a magnificent ship that they would sail to an exotic land, perhaps the West Indies or China, where they would—

She inhaled sharply. Good God.

Honoria's voice lilted through her mind. *Suppose a man did show honorable intentions—a tolerable man, naturally.*

No. Honoria was a fool if she thought Captain Warre had anything like honorable intentions—or that Katherine wished he had.

A shiver feathered her skin. If she hadn't been so preoccupied by tomorrow's hearing, would she have thrown caution to the wind and made love with him in that room?

The answer flamed through her blood, and her skin flushed hot in the cool air.

"Pray tell, Lady Dunscore..." A male voice startled her from the shadows between the great columns that lined the outside of the house. "What has given you such an air of agitation?" The Duke of Winston stepped into view, accompanied by another man she recognized as Lord Wenthurst.

She faced them with her chin high. "Good evening, Your Grace. Lord Wenthurst." She didn't bother to curtsy. This was the man James had been prepared to duel for the sake of her honor. She raked him with her eyes. One flash of her cutlass would send the poor earl scurrying back to his wife.

The duke, however, was another matter entirely.

The earl cleared his throat. "A pleasure, as always, Lady Dunscore. I, er..." His gaze shot past Winston in the direction of the ballroom. "If you'll excuse me." He gave a quick nod of his head and ducked past Winston.

The duke remained, observing her, demonic in a coat of such deep red that it looked as black as his hair.

"Tell me what can I do to ease your distress," he said smoothly.

"Your powers of observation deceive you," she told him. "I am not distressed. You are free to return to the festivities."

"And leave you here alone? Forsooth, madam." He moved in next to her. "I was sorry not to receive a response to my invitation." The breeze toyed with the queue at the back of his neck.

"I have received so many such invitations, Your Grace. I confess they have become a blur."

He smiled, a flash of white teeth in the shadowy night. "Have they? Then please—allow me to refresh your memory."

She could allow him to do more than that. He chaired the committee. His influence would be enormous. The scent of his cologne reached her and for a crazed moment she imagined offering a smile instead of scorn. Inviting him to pay a call. Taking him to her bed.

The thought had barely formed before it made her want to be sick. "I will save you the embarrassment of propositioning me again by issuing a standing 'no,'" she said, furious with herself. "Let me be perfectly clear. I will be no man's mistress." A brisk gust of wind stripped the heat from her skin and gave her a sudden chill.

"Such directness, Lady Dunscore. You shock me."

"I very much doubt that anything could shock you, Your Grace."

His laugh was a rich sound in the night that had probably melted the knees of dozens of romantically misguided girls. He leaned one hip casually against the thick marble railing. "Perhaps not, but I'm always up for a challenge. I have a feeling that *you* could shock me most extraordinarily given the right circumstance."

"What a pity you will never find out. Good evening." She needed to leave this ball. Now.

"You do realize, of course," he called after her quietly, "that I chair a committee that may hold a very particular interest for you."

She froze. Slowly she turned back. "Am I to understand," she began coldly, "that you are using your influence on the committee to blackmail me into a seduction?"

"Perhaps to bargain for a kiss, if that's what it takes. One touch, Lady Dunscore—" he laughed even more wickedly, lowering his voice to a near-whisper and leaning toward her "—or shall I say, one *stroke,* and after that there won't be any bargaining necessary, I assure you." His eyes burned across her breasts.

"Such confidence, Your Grace." Voices drifted behind her from the crowd gathered outside the ballroom. "You must be very sure of your skill."

Apparently sensing victory, he pushed away from the railing and took a step toward her. "I'm very sure when I meet a woman who would appreciate my strengths." There was just enough light filtering from the windows to see his *strengths* bulging hard inside his breeches.

"Oh, yes. I certainly can appreciate them." She feinted with her left hand as though she meant to touch him.

"Then by all means, let us— *Bloody hell!*" The duke jumped back three feet when she whipped her cutlass from its hiding place in her skirts.

She smiled. "Tell me again about your strengths, Your Grace. I want to be able to appreciate them fully." A few startled voices grew louder behind her as people began to notice something out of the ordinary was happening. They would draw a crowd, of course. She didn't care.

"For God's sake, woman, put that thing down!" he bit out.

"Only if you put yours down, as well." She lowered the tip of her cutlass to his crotch, and someone behind her gasped. Her blood sang with satisfaction. "Oh, but look how quickly you comply," she added.

"Good God, she's going to emasculate him," someone muttered.

The duke gave her that smile again and held his hands up. "You have me entirely at your mercy, Lady Dunscore. Only have a care for my future family." A few nervous laughs erupted.

"You've made such a point of telling me how eager you are to share your family assets with womankind, Your Grace—"

"Katherine!" Captain Warre called out from somewhere behind her.

"—that I would feel remiss if I didn't help you." Lightning-quick she moved her cutlass to a chorus of gasps and cries of alarm, and in the blink of an eye two delicate cuts left the duke's manhood on the edge of being exposed to the world. To his credit, he didn't flinch.

"Well, now," she said, smiling. "It looks as though I *can* shock you, given the right...circumstance. Say the word, and I shall deliver the coup de grâce."

Behind her, the crowd was in an uproar. A hand curled tightly around her wrist. "Put that away," Captain Warre growled in her ear.

Winston calmly held the gaping fabric in place. "I should have heeded your warning, after all, Croston," he said lightly. "The lady is certainly a threat to one's anatomy."

"I rather suspect you are your own worst enemy, Winston." Captain Warre's voice was flinty.

Katherine tore from his grasp and dove through the crowd.

"Wait!" Captain Warre's command barked behind her, but she didn't stop. This was it—she'd had enough. Knots of people backed out of her way in a chaos of talking and questions. She heard him calling to her but kept going, hurrying faster, running now as people scattered to her right and left, until finally she realized that she did not hear his voice anymore. She made it to the entrance and ordered the footman to get her a hack instantly. There wasn't time to wait for her coach. Within moments she was clattering toward her house.

She had actually considered him. For a moment she had actually considered taking the duke to her bed in exchange for his support.

This entire business had gone too far. There was no reason for this desperation, no reason that she should consider debasing herself, no reason for any of this. It was time to end it—now, before the Lords ended it for her.

"THERE IS A gentleman waiting for you in the salon, your ladyship," Dodd announced in a hushed voice the instant she walked through the door.

"Send him away. And have our trunks brought from the attic. Anne and I will be returning to my ship. I want our things packed within the hour."

Dodd's eyes widened, and he opened his mouth but wisely shut it again. "The *gentleman* has refused every request to leave, your ladyship."

There was no time for this. Whoever it was, she would show him that the spectacle was over. "Then he shall meet with my cutlass." She veered from the staircase and headed for the salon.

"I think it important to advise your ladyship that

the man is intoxicated," Dodd said with great disapproval, hurrying at her side. "Extremely so. Although perhaps, by now—"

"William!" Relief slammed through her when she saw him sprawled on a sofa.

He sat up. "Good evening, Captain."

"That will be all," she said to Dodd. One look told her everything about why William hadn't called before now. "You're drunk."

"Maybe a little."

More than a little. His hair stuck out at all angles. His clothes were disheveled. His eyes were bloodshot, and his face was as unshaven as his worst day at sea. "I've been worried, and Anne has been beside herself." Fear warred with fury at the sight of him.

"I've bought a house," he said, running a hand through his hair, looking at the sofa as though he was trying to decide whether to flop back down.

"You could have sent a note."

"Could have," he said. "Too drunk to write."

The only other time this had happened—it had to have been at least four years ago now—she'd spent three days alone in Valencia with no idea where he was. "A *house?*"

"Figured I ought to do something with all that money." He gave a laugh. "Hardly made a dent in it."

A whiff of tawdry perfume reached her nose. "You've been whoring."

He paced away, and she let him go. "I'm told it's in excellent condition." He sank into a chair and dug his fingers into his hair. "Old country estate—got a mind to go look at the place." He looked up at her with haunted blue eyes. "Marry me, Katherine. Be my wife and come live with me in my godawful house."

"William, please don't do this." It was Valencia all over again, and her heart ached for him.

But pain ripped across his face—that same pain she knew was always there, lurking just below the laughing surface, just out of sight where nobody could see it. He stood up, pressing a hand to his forehead. "I shall never be free of what happened in Barbary. Never. Bloody Christ, Katherine, you're the only one who'll ever understand."

He was wrong. Even she couldn't really understand, because his captivity had been so much different from hers. She'd become a member of a household, made friends, been cared for. Not so for William. He'd told her of the underground prisons, the crushing labor, the beatings. But she couldn't begin to imagine the hell he'd been through.

He needed the freedom of the sea as much as she did.

"I'm taking Anne away from here," she told him. "Tonight."

"Away!" He faced her abruptly.

"Will you help me gather the crew? Ready the ship?"

"What's happened?" he demanded.

She told him briefly about her failures, the outrages, and fresh anger flared up. "They will never give me Dunscore. I'll not allow the committee to humiliate me, only to strip me of Dunscore, anyway. Anne and I will return to sea where we belong."

He absorbed that news. "Yes." He paced a few steps away. Turned back. His lips curved a little drunkenly. "God, Katherine—excellent idea."

A nerve pulsed in her temple, and she started toward

the door. "Quickly—let us go upstairs. Help me ready Anne for the journey."

"God," he repeated as they crossed the entrance hall. "This is perfect. What I wouldn't give to feel that Mediterranean sun on my face again."

"To hear the shouts of the linemen when we raise the sails in the morning," she agreed, already feeling a surge of anticipation. Those shouts were the sounds of freedom.

"The taste of Spanish cerveza." New purpose fleeted through William's haunted eyes. "I shall scour the taverns until I've found every last one of the crew, else I'll hire others," he said as they climbed the stairs. "With luck we shall set sail in the morning."

"We *will* set sail in the morning." Anything less was unacceptable. "In a month's time, we shall pass through the strait." And once they arrived in the Mediterranean, she would decide what to do next.

Now he gave a laugh. "Should we free India from her father's prison and take her with us?"

"Ha. I'll not have Cantwell sending anyone after me. Poor India will have to make her own way, I'm afraid." She began to feel a little giddy, drunk like William, but with anticipation. The first order of business would be to strip off this gown and put on her tunic and trousers.

Anne would be so pleased. She hated London. She would never have to wear a stiff dress now.

But when she topped the stairs, there were voices coming from the direction of the rooms. In front of Anne's chamber, two trunks sat on the floor and Dodd stood arguing with Miss Bunsby, who blocked the door with her arms folded across her chest.

"What is this?" Katherine demanded.

"Anne is asleep," Miss Bunsby said.

"I gave orders for our things to be packed immediately. Move aside." Katherine pushed past her and reached for the door. It was locked. The nerve in her temple became a vicious pounding. "Unlock this door at once."

Miss Bunsby was unmoved. "You'll not take her to your ship, only to raise her hopes and then realize you've made a mistake. It would be cruel."

"How *dare* you." Katherine turned on her. After what had happened tonight she would never, ever change her mind.

The faint ringing of the bell sounded below. "Someone is here, your ladyship," Dodd said.

"Do not answer." She held out her hand to Miss Bunsby. "The key."

"She has hidden the key, your ladyship," Dodd said irritatedly. "My set is below stairs."

"Uppity baggage you've got here," William said.

Miss Bunsby scorched him from head to toe with disapproving eyes. "I am Anne's governess."

"And *I* am her mother," Katherine snapped. Below, the bell rang incessantly. "You will bring me the key, get your things and leave this house at once."

"With all due respect, your ladyship has tried that before."

"I shall have you thrown bodily into the street!"

"Keep your voice down. You'll wake Lady Anne," Miss Bunsby hissed.

Katherine turned on Dodd. "Answer the bloody door and *kill* whoever is on the other side. And bring your keys."

"You mustn't do this," Miss Bunsby said firmly as

Dodd hurried away. "What will she think when you tell her you're returning to the ship? Anyone can see you're in a state, your ladyship. Please—wait until morning when you've calmed yourself."

William grabbed her by the arm. "Best show me where that key is—"

"Unhand me!"

"—then I'll escort you out, bags or no."

As if the devil himself were orchestrating some hellish play, Captain Warre strode down the hallway with Dodd on his heels. "I'll be bloody damned if I'll let you return to that ship," he said to Katherine, pointing that finger at her. "What in God's name do you hope to accomplish by this?"

Miss Bunsby was still trying and failing to pull herself from William's grasp.

"Sailing back to the Med and having done with all this nonsense," William told him. "Perhaps you have a mind to join us?"

"*William*," Katherine said sharply.

Captain Warre looked at him. "You're drunk, Jaxbury."

"Perhaps." William shrugged a little. "Wouldn't get in her way if I was you."

"Make her see reason, your lordship," Miss Bunsby begged. "Do not let her wake Anne for this."

Captain Warre glared at Katherine. "Is what happened with Winston what's prompted this? For God's sake, the man would proposition a stone if he could figure out how to get his cock inside it. It's nothing to take personally."

"Mama?" Anne's faint cry came through the locked door.

"Now you've done it," Miss Bunsby whispered harshly.

"Mama?"

"Get the key." Katherine's voice was ice.

William released Miss Bunsby, who disappeared into an adjoining room and returned seconds later with the key. Katherine snatched it from her and shoved it in the lock with shaking fingers. Like night settling over the city, reality slowly chilled her temper. Behind her, Miss Bunsby and Captain Warre and William crowded in.

"Your ladyship, *please,*" Miss Bunsby begged.

She shut the door in their faces and went into Anne's room alone.

"Mama?"

"I'm here, dearest."

"I heard shouting."

Katherine went to the bed and gathered Anne in her arms, suddenly fighting back tears. "A small disagreement. Nothing to worry about." She imagined the servants streaming into Anne's darkened room in the middle of the night to pack her things, waking Anne to dress her quickly and whisking her away to the ship...

What on earth had she been thinking?

"Is something happening?" Anne asked.

"No, sweetling. I've just returned home later than expected." She smoothed Anne's hair from her face and held her close, breathing in her comforting little-girl scent. No sound came from the hallway now. "I'm sorry I woke you."

"It's all right, Mama." Anne sighed. "I had such fun today. Do you think Lord Deal will really take us in his phaeton when we get to Scotland?"

"I'm sure he will, darling." Anne had loved the phaeton ride they'd taken with Lord Deal earlier a bit too much, but it was the first time Anne had laughed since leaving the ship. Just like her grandpa, she'd wanted to go faster and faster. It made Katherine want to take her in a phaeton every day, just to see the light on her face.

Katherine's chest felt so tight it was hard to draw breath. She would do *anything* for Anne. Anything in the world.

Even marry?

"Miss Bunsby says a phaeton is dangerous, but I think it is such fun." Anne snuggled against Katherine's side. "Miss Bunsby always worries."

"I know she does." And thank God for it. Katherine had come so close to failing Anne again with her impulsive decisions. So close. But this was the end.

Tomorrow she would go before the committee. There was a small chance they would simply dismiss the bill as ridiculous and allow her to keep her birthright. But more likely, they would exact some kind of price in exchange for dismissing the bill. They wanted to control her, and they thought they knew how to do it.

Marriage. The word ripped her like a cannonball tearing through wood. Everything inside her rebelled at the idea of willingly entering captivity again.

But the time was past when she could simply abandon whatever could not be had on her own terms. For Anne's sake it was time to accept what needed to be done in order to keep Dunscore and secure Anne's future.

If they wanted her to marry, then she would—but she would bloody well do it on her own terms.

CHAPTER TWENTY-SIX

"'LADY DUNSCORE HAS become a dire threat to London male ego at large. Recommend gentlemen button coats in public. Lady Dunscore's threat expanding in scope—seems a matter more suited to the army.'" Admiral Wharton looked up from the letter and glared at the committee. "*That,* your lordships, is the kind of report Captain Warre, Lord Croston, has seen fit to give us."

James looked from the committee toward Katherine and knew it was only by the grace of God that she was here and not sitting in gaol, which was exactly what the admirals would have ordered if she had attempted to follow through with her plan last night.

Thank God—thank *God*—this would end today.

All nineteen lords to whom the bill had been committed for consideration were gathered around the table, backlit by a tall bank of windows that arched all the way to the high-vaulted ceiling. Others crowded into the room—the Scottish contingent of peers, a few lords he knew were hopeful they might somehow secure Dunscore for themselves and a handful of members from the Commons. Jaxbury had been summoned as a witness, along with several others of the *Possession*'s crew.

Against a side wall, standing a foot shorter than the

paneled wainscoting, Holliswell, the greedy bastard, watched the proceedings stone-faced.

From the committee's table, Edrington raised a brow at Admiral Wharton. "Pray, what did you expect Croston to learn from his assignment? That Lady Dunscore was pirating barges on the Thames?"

Wharton shot James a thunderous look, and James nearly smiled. "We do not perceive Lady Dunscore to be a threat to His Majesty's realm at this time, your lordship," Wharton said.

"Indeed," Edrington said sarcastically. He turned his attention to Katherine. "Tell us, Lady Dunscore—when exactly did you make the decision to return to England?"

James caught Nick's eye and sent him a silent message. *Withdraw your support.*

Nick looked away.

"When I received news of this bill," Katherine answered.

"Why did you not return sooner?"

"There was business to attend to."

"Why not return *the moment you were able,* Lady Dunscore?" De Lille asked sharply. "*Before* you had any 'business' to attend to?"

James tensed and fixed his eyes on Katherine.

"I had just spent four years in captivity, your lordship. I preferred to have my ostracism on my own terms." She smiled, but mirthlessly. "I do not play the pianoforte and I've never been good with a needle, and there are only so many books a young woman can read."

Her answer was met by scowls and a few raised brows.

"I know at least one young woman who would beg to

differ with you on that point," Linton remarked wryly, bringing a grunt from Marshwell and a sharp look from De Lille.

"How remarkable that you've never mastered the pianoforte, Lady Dunscore," De Lille said, "yet you've apparently grown proficient at captaining a sixteen-gun brig."

Katherine raised a brow at him. "Is it, your lordship? I suspect if you ask Captain Warre, you'll find he has the same affliction."

Good God. "Indeed," James told them. "I confess I couldn't plunk out a minuet even on my best day."

At one side of the table, Winston sat casually in his chair. "So instead of returning home to your family," he said to her, "you chose to captain a ship."

"Yes."

"What funds did you use to purchase the ship?"

"I had a trade route between Egypt and Venice. I bought the *Possession* with the proceeds."

Ponsby sat forward. "The *Possession* was not your first ship."

"No."

"Lady Dunscore," Gorst said evenly, "it does not help this committee if you do not explain yourself fully. Tell us how you came into possession of a ship after escaping from captivity. You did escape, did you not? You were not released?"

She didn't answer immediately. James stretched his fingers. Forced himself to relax. It wasn't as though he didn't already know she'd been through hell.

"My captor passed away in the nighttime," she finally said. "Chaos went up in the household, and I went into the city."

"Alone? Unseen?"

Her nostrils flared almost imperceptibly, and a delicate cord in her neck tightened. "Forgive me, Lord Gorst," she said, "but I fail to see what the details of that night have to do with the issue at hand."

"Agreed," Edrington said, and a few others muttered a general concurrence.

Gorst scowled across the table. "I am trying to ascertain how it could be possible that a woman held captive in a Barbary state could find her way aboard a ship."

"There were ships anchored in the harbor," Katherine told him evenly. "Ships the corsairs had taken as prizes. It was simple enough to take one of the longboats tied to the docks and row out."

James frowned. There could have been nothing simple about that at all. The currents would likely have been strong and the harbor far from empty.

"Row out in the harbor at Algiers?" Ponsby asked incredulously. "A woman alone?"

"I was dressed in men's clothes. And it was after midnight."

Good God.

"And in fact, you were not alone, were you, Lady Dunscore," De Lille said. "You were with Sir William Jaxbury." He shifted his attention to the back of the room, where Jaxbury stood with a group of onlookers. "I presume you were the force behind such a suicidal escape?"

"Only if by 'force' you mean oarsman, Admiral," Jaxbury said. "Lady Dunscore is a most determined woman, and braver than I."

All eyes shifted back to her. Then again to Jaxbury.

"I understand you were in captivity, as well, Sir Jaxbury."

"Yes," he said darkly.

"And I presume you escaped from your captor, as well."

"Yes."

"And the two of you met where, on the streets of Algiers?"

"Yes."

A stark scenario coalesced in James's mind. Katherine, alone and with child on the nighttime streets, dressed, most likely, in the clothes of one of her captor's male slaves. She crosses paths with Jaxbury. The two of them scrape by on whatever they can, ducking into doorways and avoiding the sultan's henchmen, plotting a way out of the country, toward which end Jaxbury draws on his experience at sea to suggest a dangerous plan.

"And the two of you, alone, snatched a prize out from under the corsairs' noses?" Winston asked. "I find that exceedingly difficult to comprehend."

"It was a small prize," Katherine told him. "Only eight cannon."

"Lady Dunscore," Nick said, finally speaking. "You will understand, of course, that some of my colleagues are concerned about a member of the peerage who has demonstrated a tendency toward the unlawful."

"Unlawful?" she said. "This is the first I've heard of it."

"You deny you have taken ships unprovoked?"

"I certainly do not deny it. But I was always justified."

"By the promise of silks and spices? That smacks mightily of piracy, Lady Dunscore."

"By the knowledge that my prey had come by its spoils by being a predator."

"A questionable activity at best," De Lille interjected.

"But one that resulted in the liberation of more than one Englishman, as this committee well knows. My prize-taking activities have been strictly limited to ships far more questionable than mine. As for my present circumstances, rest assured I know nothing about robbing stagecoaches or burgling slumbering widows."

"Relieved to hear it, Lady Dunscore," Rondale declared from the end of the table.

"At least our travelers and widows may rest easy," Edrington said, glancing down the table at Winston, "even if gentlemen hopeful of producing children may not." Uneasy laughter went up from the gallery.

"I have only the deepest respect for Lady Dunscore's skill with a cutlass," Winston replied with a half smile.

De Lille tucked his chin and assessed Katherine over the top of his spectacles. "What of your plans to marry, Lady Dunscore?" he demanded. "Certainly you do not plan to manage an estate the size of Dunscore alone."

Around the room, half the men both on and off the committee had turned their attention to Katherine, no doubt salivating at the thought of having both her wealth and her body at their disposal.

James's blood ran cold.

But Katherine merely offered that smile he was becoming too familiar with, one he'd seen night after night watching her fend off every lecher in the *ton*. "What a creative suggestion, Lord De Lille. My only regret is that *you* are not unattached."

A member three seats away erupted in a fit of coughing. Lord De Lille's face dove into a wrinkled scowl.

"Perhaps Croston ought to marry her," Winston suggested, shifting his attention to James. "He seems to take her in hand well enough."

Damn the man. "A ship can only have one captain," James said dryly, "and I prefer to be it."

Ponsby barked a laugh. "You've taken enough prizes in your day, I'll avow you know how to master *that* situation."

"You have a point." Somehow he managed to form his mouth into what he hoped was a pleasant smile. "But may I suggest the committee return to a more salient topic."

"Indeed," Edrington said, leaning forward to look down the table at his colleague. "The basis of this folly of a bill has no foundation in Lady Dunscore's marital status."

"Perhaps not," De Lille replied, "but its resolution may."

"We are not here to arrange Lady Dunscore's marriage," Edrington shot back. "We're here to get at the facts!"

"Precisely," Nick agreed, for once doing something to steer things in the right direction. "Lady Dunscore, I have here a list of a number of your exploits in the Mediterranean. Perhaps you can give us the details of each—"

"Blast the bloody details!" Edrington exclaimed. "I fail to see why this bill lives on in the face of the fact that this woman saved Croston's life. Do we have any evidence at all that she has acted against the Crown?

Violated the law of the sea? Has anyone made a complaint?"

"She sailed under her own colors," Nick reminded them, and James wanted to grab him by the throat to keep him from speaking. "And we do have evidence that she took prizes from across the Barbary coast."

"Then by God, give the woman a medal!" De Lille exploded.

"Need I remind you we are trying to maintain peaceful relations with the Barbary states for the safety of our merchant trade?"

"Peaceful," Edrington spat. "Those bloody curs have no honor. They'll agree to peace with one hand and take our ships with the other. This woman has saved not only Croston, but other British subjects—the dowager countess of Pennington, for one, and Cantwell's daughter Lady India, for another. Clearly she has acted not against the Crown, but in its interests."

"Has she?" Ponsby demanded, staring down the table at Edrington. "I believe Lord Edrington has information relevant to this discussion that he planned to withhold from us today."

Edrington's expression turned stony. "I brought no information."

"No doubt you didn't," Ponsby scoffed. "But I believe this committee should know that not three days past, Lord Edrington shared with me an affidavit he'd procured from one of Lady Dunscore's crew alleging that she did not, in fact, intend to save Croston at all. Rather, her initial order was to leave him to die in the water."

James looked at Katherine. A moment of fear in her eyes confirmed the truth. Bloody hell, this could ruin everything.

"Is it true, Lady Dunscore?" Ponsby demanded.

"Taking a stranger aboard a ship with a skeleton crew was a foolish thing to do," James told them before she could answer. "My respect for Lady Dunscore's judgment as a sea captain would seriously decline if I thought it might *not* be true. She had no way to know whether I was friend or foe, as the wreck happened at night when I was not wearing my uniform. There was nothing to mark me as British—quite the opposite, in fact, given my natural coloring. Moreover, I could have been carrying any number of diseases that might have killed everyone on board. Whether we like it or not, there is no duty to rescue."

"Don't like it," De Lille muttered. "Never have."

Ponsby frowned at him. "And it doesn't bother you, Croston, that you might have been left to perish?"

"By all rights, I should have perished the night of the wreck," he said flatly. "This line of inquiry has no bearing on the bill before this committee. If anything, it shows more clearly the risk Lady Dunscore was ultimately willing to take to help another." *You should know that I've forgiven you.* Now he had a good idea why.

Winston spoke up, addressing Jaxbury. "What have *you* to say about that day, Jaxbury?"

"Only that Lady Dunscore was acting out of care and concern for her crew. And that a young child was aboard."

"Your daughter," Winston said to Katherine.

"Who also has no bearing on this discussion," James said. He'd be damned if he'd allow them to drag Anne's legitimacy into this.

Ponsby studied Katherine. "Ultimately, you chose to take the risk and bring Croston aboard. Why?"

"My ship's surgeon was of the opinion that the man in the water had been adrift for several days, and that a diseased person would not have survived that long without food and water."

It sounded cold, even though the reasoning was sound. Fear of what might have happened gripped him, and he pushed it away.

"For God's sake, I've heard enough," De Lille blustered. "If Croston says he should have been left behind, who are we to disagree with him? I, for one, would be prepared to dispense with all this if Lady Dunscore will agree to find a husband."

James's lungs constricted. There was a murmur of agreement, punctuated by a snort of derision and more than a few sharply worded dissents. Winston, chairing the committee, cast long glances to his right and left, then looked at Katherine and smiled. "You will be informed of the committee's recommendation on this matter, Lady Dunscore. Prior to that, if it does so happen that you should enter into a marriage contract…clearly, the committee would be most interested."

Bloody living hell.

"This committee is adjourned!"

Nothing had been resolved. Not one bloody thing. They could not force her to marry, but it was obvious they hoped to try. He looked at Katherine, hoping to see her reaction, but she wasn't looking at him. She was looking at Lord Deal.

CHAPTER TWENTY-SEVEN

MARRIAGE. KATHERINE STRUGGLED to draw breath even though Winston's words only confirmed what she'd already known. A husband was the only way to put an end to this. She simply hadn't wanted to accept the truth.

The committee room erupted in commotion with the bang of Lord De Lille's gavel. She didn't dare look at Captain Warre. Instead, she pushed to her feet and made straight for Lord Deal with the weight of decision closing around her.

The committee's implication was clear, and only a fool would ignore it. She needed a husband, and she would have one—but not one of the libertines who hoped to use Dunscore's wealth to finance their excesses while slaking their lust in her bed. And not someone who might yet live thirty or fifty years before setting her free.

A man who would not interfere with her running of Dunscore.

Who would be kind to Anne.

Who would only have the strength for the marriage bed twice yearly.

"Don't worry, Katie," Lord Deal said close to her ear. "Just come to Scotland. It's past time you returned to Dunscore anyhow—we shall both journey north, and once we're there we'll work out an arrangement that will be to everyone's satisfaction."

Yes, they would—but not in the way he meant. It was all but certain he was imagining pairing her with any number of eligible young Scotsmen. But once safely at Dunscore, she would make sure Lord Deal understood there was only one arrangement she would accept.

She looked into those kindly brown eyes and imagined being with him the way she'd been with Mejdan. "I can be ready in a matter of days," she told him, even as something inside her curled up tight.

William pushed in next to her and gripped her arm. "The offer I made last night," he whispered urgently. "I will renew it, if it will help."

"I am honored, William," she murmured, "but there is no need. I plan to work out a solution with Lord Deal." Marriage to William would be a disaster, and would hardly satisfy the Lords—he was as suspect as she.

His expression hardened, and she watched comprehension dawn. "Don't like it, Katherine. There's got to be a better way."

Just then Captain Warre joined them. "A better way than what?"

William's mouth clamped shut, and deep inside, something began to keen. "Anne and I will be traveling to Scotland shortly." William was wrong. There was no better way.

"Hell of a thing, Croston," Lord Deal said, shaking his head. "Never seen anything like it."

"Indeed not." Captain Warre lowered his voice. "I'll call on you later today," he said. "We'll discuss what to do next."

But she already knew what to do next, and it didn't

help matters to be standing here next to him, looking at him, yearning so deeply to reach for him, to touch him just one more time before—

God help her, she needed to get away from here. Longing for Captain Warre would only weigh her down. "We should travel as soon as possible," she told Lord Deal. "I must go home at once and begin preparations. Please excuse me."

"Katherine—"

She ignored Captain Warre calling after her as she hurried away. Whatever debt he thought he owed her, certainly now he realized he was free.

And it would be fine. She'd done this before—or near enough—and she could do it again. At least Lord Deal wasn't a stranger, and he was kind. And, as Mr. Allen had so mercilessly implied, soon enough she would be free. May God forgive her.

She rushed into her waiting coach, chased by the reality that her association with Captain Warre was finally over, and that Papa's best friend would shortly become her husband.

But she had barely settled against the seat before the door wrenched open again and Captain Warre lurched inside as the coach pulled away. Her heart thrilled at the sight of him for one beat, then two, before a cruel hand reached into her chest and squeezed hard.

"Suppose you tell me about this 'offer' William made to you, and about the 'solution' with Deal that makes it unnecessary."

Heartache spread like fire. She couldn't have smiled if she wanted to. "Instead, suppose you explain why you chose to waylay my coach instead of paying a call."

"What solution?"

She couldn't discuss this with him—not when she knew he looked with pity on her time with Mejdan. Not when she could barely stand the sinking feeling of leading herself into captivity even as everything inside her wanted something more.

"As you saw for yourself last night," she said, deliberately addressing the first part of his question instead of the second, "William was drunk. And anyhow, not even the soberest offer of marriage from William could ever be serious. Surely you know him well enough to agree."

"I would have thought so."

"A ship can only have one captain, after all." She reminded him of his own words. "And William is not anxious to place himself under a woman's command."

The corners of his eyes creased, but only just. "Understandably so. I had the impression this offer was serious, however, because he feared the alternative."

"For no good reason. The committee only confirmed what I've suspected and what I imagine you've known—that marriage would put a quick end to all this. I can't believe you have any objection, as news of my engagement will certainly release you from your debt to me."

Something deadly flashed in his eyes, but he merely shrugged. "Interesting plan."

It hurt too much to look at him, so she turned her face to the window. This was not the way to her house. "Where are we going?" she asked sharply.

"I've ordered your coachman to take a detour through the countryside."

Her breath turned shallow. "And your own coach?"

"Sent it home."

"I see." Dangerous possibilities careened through her imagination. Dangerous yearnings. "I don't suppose you know of anyone looking for a wife?" she said, because Captain Warre on the defensive was so much easier to deal with.

"Not anyone willing to face the blade of your cutlass every time he wishes to bed you."

The look in his eyes said clearly that he would find her cutlass no obstacle. Heat flooded her most secret places. "But, Captain, what kind of wife would I be if I did not allow my husband to bed me whenever he wishes?" It was imperative to keep him at arm's length, because every part of her wanted to be *in* his arms. The reaction in his eyes was exactly what she'd hoped for. "And I intend to be a most dutiful wife," she added, just to goad him. "In fact, I doubt my cutlass will play much of a role in the marriage at all. I don't plan to marry a man who requires such measures to form, shall we say, a meeting of the minds."

"Only the feeblest man would fit that specification." The moment the words were out, he narrowed his eyes. "Good God. That's precisely what you're thinking, isn't it. This 'solution' William objects to—you're planning to marry someone too old to care about your reputation or your fortune, who will soon leave you safely widowed. Good God." He stared hard now. "You're going to marry Deal."

She hadn't wanted him to find out until after she'd left for Scotland. "You make it sound so mercenary."

"It's nothing if not that. Bloody hell." His eyes turned that familiar stormy green. "No wonder William renewed his offer. I would offer for you myself to keep you from such a disgusting plan."

A horrible pain caught her in the chest even though his cruel words only confirmed what she already knew. "And I would refuse you as I refused him." And wouldn't he be relieved.

It was impossible to look at him without an assault of memories: his mouth on fire against hers, his hands burning her flesh, his words giving her strength when she'd had none. The keening inside her broke into a silent wail.

He leaned across the coach, his mouth set in a grim line. "I'll not allow you to throw yourself like a bone to some old limpstaff who doesn't deserve you." A simmering fury in his eyes told her he was imagining Lord Deal in her marriage bed. His face was inches from hers, so close she could see the flecks of brown in his green eyes. So close she could feel the warmth of his breath on her lips. She wanted to taste them, just one more time. Just once, she would have liked to give everything to a man *she* chose.

"If I intend to have a legitimate heir, I can't afford to waste my time with a limpstaff," she scoffed, goading him. "Rest assured I will make sure of Lord Deal's virility before the marriage takes place."

"Bloody hell." It was the last thing he said before he pulled her to him and kissed her. His mouth was brutal, punishing, and the taste of him poured across her tongue like heaven. "Half of London lays awake at night thinking about how to get between your thighs," he said against her lips. "I want to kill every last one of them."

His possessiveness made her shudder. "There's no need, Captain. None of them will succeed."

THEY MIGHT NOT, but James would succeed, and he was through waiting.

He half stood and leaned across the coach, pulling her to him more forcefully than he meant to, crushing his mouth down on hers again to drink the heady taste of her. She responded instantly, and his body surged. Her lips were soft, and her tongue slid across his like velvet, stoking the fire inside him. A small voice whispered no, this wasn't the place, but then her hands touched his face and the rush of blood in his veins silenced the warning.

He had the preservative in his pocket, and this torment would end here. Now.

The coach jolted and he fell back to his seat, taking her with him in a mass of skirts that drowned his legs. The cold sheath of the cutlass hidden inside all that fabric tapped his leg, but she would have no desire to use it. He would see to that.

He invaded her mouth more and more deeply, trying to get enough of her, but it was impossible. Her scent drove him mad. He kissed her throat and neck, ran his tongue along her jaw. "I want you at my command, Katherine," he breathed against her ear, knowing full well the effect it would have, and she did not disappoint.

Her fingers dug into his shoulders. "I will be at no man's command ever again—" he nipped the base of her neck and she gasped "—Captain."

That was up for debate, but one thing was sure: he was through being "Captain" to her. He pushed her gown off her shoulders and slipped his hands inside her stays, freeing her breasts. Christ, the sight of their creamy perfection nearly pushed him over the edge. They were proud like she was, sitting high over the top of the stays, and their round softness filled his hands. Puckered, dusky areolas bewitched him and he took one in his mouth, sucking hard, satisfied when her head fell back on a ragged gasp. He pulled with his lips, nipped with his teeth, rolled her between his fingers until she was clinging to him, breathless and crying out with need.

He was so hard he could barely think. Her fingers dug into his hair, holding him to her breasts one moment, sliding down and gripping his shoulders the next. She was half-crazed, fire in his arms, and he had to touch her. Madly he yanked at her skirts until he freed her legs and had her seated open-thighed across his lap. He reached behind her, fighting yards of fabric to find her skin. His hands skimmed across silky buttocks, and he found home between her thighs. She was wet. Hot. He pushed one finger inside her, then two. Her opening constricted around him.

"Touch me, Katherine," he rasped, but she was already there. Her hands moved over the front of his breeches—too slow, too soft. His breeches were so tight it hurt. Ah, God—he undid the fastening and his erection sprang into her hands and he groaned. Her fingers tightened around him and he fought for control, gasping into her mouth on a kiss deeper than the ocean. Faster, deeper he stroked her. It wasn't enough. He needed more—needed to be inside her. When her hands slid down his shaft and cupped his sac, he snapped.

He withdrew his fingers and grasped her buttocks, kissing her hard as he lifted her over him. He felt his erection breach her opening. Felt her tight heat swallow the rest of him in one, hard stroke when he pushed inside her. Ah, God—God—

He couldn't go slow. She cried out against his lips, but he devoured the sound with his kiss and thrust into her hard and then harder, fast and then faster. Finally she was his. *His.* And still it wasn't enough. Her hips matched his savage rhythm, taking him to the hilt with every thrust, but he wanted more. He wanted every bloody thing she had.

She panted against his mouth, clinging to him. He looked at her lips, wet and swollen from his kiss. Fixed his gaze on those half-closed topaz eyes, drunk now with desire. And then he felt her begin to tighten around him and knew he was about to make her come to her peak.

He drove into her even harder. "Katherine," he rasped. Ah, God—he watched her face as the pleasure took her and she tightened around him harder, harder, convulsing in waves around his shaft.

Her fingers gripped his shoulders. "James!"

And that was all it took. The sound of his name on her lips drove him over the edge. He dug his hands into her buttocks and surrendered, buried deep inside her. The release ripped through his body and into hers and left him mindless. Voiceless.

And still—*still*—it wasn't enough to satisfy him.

CHAPTER TWENTY-EIGHT

KATHERINE SHUDDERED, GRIPPED by waves of pleasure so intense they entirely controlled her. She tried to think, tried to regain her senses, but they'd been lost—stolen, along with her breath.

She'd never known.

She closed her eyes and felt herself pulse around him tightly. Intimately. Felt him throb in reaction.

"Never known what?" he asked in a rough, throaty voice, and she realized with dismay she'd breathed the words out loud.

Another shudder, this one less intense. She opened her eyes, only to have her gaze land in the space between them where her bare breasts jutted out above her stays.

"Nothing," she said, unwilling to let him know how much of what they had just done had been new. He expected her to be experienced—assumed she was, and there was no reason to let him suspect how little she really knew.

His hands closed possessively over her breasts, and his thumbs circled her nipples. The touch sent pure pleasure shooting down through her belly, straight to the place where their bodies were joined. His eyes were dark and on fire as he watched his hands move against her flesh. "Never known what?" he asked again.

Instead of answering, she inhaled deeply and let the breath push her breasts closer to him. The distraction worked. His mouth closed around one distended nipple and she let her head fall back again. The female breast, she'd learned, carried much power.

This is Captain Warre, a voice reminded her, as though it mattered anymore. *Captain Warre.* It didn't matter. Soon enough he would be another part of her past. She would be married to Lord Deal, and there would be no reason to see Captain Warre again.

He didn't have to know that here, in the privacy of her own thoughts, she had just given herself to him in a way she would never give herself to another man as long as she lived. This was for herself, and nobody could ever take it away from her.

It was enough. It would have to be.

Already she could feel him stirring inside her, and already her pleasure began to build again. He nipped her with his teeth, and she gasped. His touch, the fire between her legs—she may as well have been a virgin for all she'd known about passion. She tried rocking against him and had the satisfaction of hearing him groan against her breast. He moved inside her, suckling and thrusting at the same time, and she barely recognized her own ragged cry.

He may have been Captain Warre. But here, now, in the secrecy of her coach with his body joined with hers, he was simply James, and his passion was madness. She put her hands on his face. Traced the bridge of his nose, the angle of his cheekbones. With that unruly, silver-streaked hair, those green eyes, those arrogant brows—he was the most beautiful man she'd ever seen. And he was inside her.

She felt his rough jaw beneath her palms and the soft give of his lips beneath her touch. Watched him take her fingertip into his mouth, felt his tongue circle it hotly while below he withdrew a little, then pushed deep, filling her completely. The penetration touched her very core.

His thrusts grew more powerful. Deeper. Faster. Instinctively she braced her knees into the seat cushion, lifting her hips and pushing herself down as he drove his shaft up. He let her finger go and used his mouth elsewhere to bruise her lips, bite her neck, ravage her breasts. She raked her fingers into that glorious hair, dug into those powerful shoulders. He commanded her now, despite everything, and the pure pleasure of him washed over her like waves crashing over a deck.

She heard herself whisper his name, then gasp it louder as the urgency began to build. It was happening—the pressure inside her that fought for release anew. He leaned his head back, and suddenly she was staring into those green eyes at the same time as she drove herself down on him.

"James—"

"Yes—" The word hissed from his lips. "Ah, Katherine."

And then that explosion of bliss took her, only this time she was looking into his eyes when her body clenched around his throbbing erection, squeezing him so tight she could feel every pulse.

"Katherine," he breathed again, the cords in his neck taut, his hands gripping her bottom. She could tell he hadn't found his release again—not yet. He leaned forward, kissing her breasts, the base of her throat, the curve where her neck met her shoulder, where he nipped and suckled her skin until she gasped with the sting of it. He pulled her against him and kissed his way to her jaw, her ear. "Katherine, marry me," he whispered into it.

Everything inside her went still. "What?"

He nipped her earlobe, played his hands over her bare buttocks, lightly stroking a finger over their cleft so that she could hardly think beyond the feathery touch. "Marry me," he said again, this time against her lips. His tongue slipped between them, simulating the intimacy they still shared below.

Marry? Instinctively she twined her tongue around his, drinking the taste of him even as she grew keenly aware of the complete, utter way he possessed her— his tongue in her mouth, his arms around her body, his hard length buried between her thighs as she'd ridden him the way a ship rode a storm.

A ship can only have one captain...

And he was proving, at this precise moment, that he would be that captain. A sharp, painful regret lodged somewhere behind her heart. "No," she said into his mouth.

His hands stilled on her buttocks. "Don't be a fool, Katherine." He kissed her again and groaned, and again his hands moved on her skin, his fingers seeking and finding that place where they were joined. "It would solve everything." His voice was rough. Languid.

"Where one problem would be solved, a dozen more would appear." It was hard to think with his tongue caressing her lips. "More the fool, you, for thinking anything different, Captain."

His face turned to stone. "I won't be 'Captain' to

you—not anymore." He looked at her with his eyes on fire.

James. She straddled him with his erection thick inside her, more vulnerable to him now than she'd been ten years ago when he'd let fly with his cannons. He didn't understand, and he never would.

His gaze raked over her face, swept across her breasts and shot back to her eyes, unsatisfied. He began to move inside her, pushing up with a long, heavy stroke. "I want to hear my name on your lips, Katherine. Say it again."

She did, but it wasn't enough. She wanted to repeat it two, five, ten times. Instead, she kissed him and met his thrusts with her hips.

After today there would be no reason to ever say his name at all.

THE MADDEST OF mad dashes from her carriage to the house should have been enough to protect her, but the clop and creak of a coach and four left no time for escape and Katherine knew, even as she rushed past Dodd so quickly she nearly knocked him over, that her tryst with James in the carriage was as good as discovered.

"Katherine!" Phil's voice called out, still a few houses away.

Hang it all, Phil needed a quiet domestic hobby very, very badly. With a desperate tug Katherine pulled her cloak's hood more tightly over her horribly dislodged hair and tried to make it up the stairs before Phil could get to the doorway.

"Katherine!"

Like a burglar caught in the act she froze on the landing and turned—just a little—as Phil swept past Dodd into the house. In the center of the entrance hall Phil stopped and looked up. "For heaven's sake, Katherine, did you not hear me calling?"

The entire neighborhood had likely heard her calling. "What is it, Phil? I'm feeling ill and I need to lie down."

"Dearest, of *course* you're feeling ill. I heard what happened and I've called twice to see you already—did you not come directly home?" She came to the foot of the stairs. "Tell me you haven't done anything rash."

Katherine swallowed a hysterical laugh. The soft flesh between her thighs felt sweetly raw and damp, and her still-sensitive nipples pressed tightly inside her stays. Her entire body thrummed with sensations that nothing in her past—except that fiery encounter in her cabin—had prepared her for. Rash? No, she hadn't done anything rash.

"I had to speak with Lord Deal," she said.

"Not about marriage. *Please* tell me not about marriage."

"About traveling to Scotland. Now please, Phil, I really do need a rest. My head aches like the devil." She started up the second flight of stairs and hoped Phil would let her go. It was not to be.

"Something's happened."

"Of course something's happened," Katherine snapped. "I've been all but ordered to marry." Good God, now Phil was climbing the stairs after her. "I told you my head aches and I need to rest before it's time to dress for Lady Effy's." God help her, she didn't know how she would meet James's eyes tonight after what they'd done.

"What you need—" somehow Phil managed to fly up the stairs twice as quickly as Katherine "—is to tell me whatever you're not telling me."

"I don't know what you're talking about."

"Rubbish."

Pit her against a shipload of bloodthirsty corsairs, or a gale that pushed thirty-foot swells over her deck, and she had courage aplenty. But confess to Phil what she'd done in the carriage? That was another matter entirely. She strode toward her rooms as though they would provide some kind of safety.

"Are you all right?" Phil asked, all concern as, naturally, she followed Katherine into her dressing room. "Have you been crying?"

"Certainly not." Blast it all, the looking glass on the dressing table was right there, letting Phil see her face. She turned, but there was nowhere to hide.

"Are you sure? Katherine, your hair! I can see from here that it's—"

"Enough!" Katherine turned, finally facing Phil. Anger surged through her but fizzled into something weak and soft and suddenly she feared maybe she *would* cry.

Marry me, Katherine. Oh, God.

"I got caught in a gust of wind," she explained, removing her hood. It sounded reasonable enough. "One of those powerful blasts that comes up between buildings."

Phil raised a brow. "Powerful enough to fling a bit of debris against your neck and leave a mark?" She came forward until their skirts touched, searched Katherine's face, and looked Katherine right in the eye. "You've taken a lover, Katherine, and if it was Lord Deal I shall run you through with your very own cutlass."

"Devil take you." Katherine turned away and wrenched open one button on her cloak, then another.

"It's *you* that ought to be run through." The looking glass proved that sure enough, there was a tiny red mark where her neck curved into her shoulder. "I must have scratched myself."

"Your lips are swollen."

"Nerves. I've been chewing on them all morning."

"Your cheeks are red and abraded."

"Did I not just tell you I got caught in a gust?"

"Your dress is torn."

"It isn't!" Katherine frowned into the reflection. Good God, it was. Right there—right above her breasts, a bit of trim had torn away and hung limply down. Warily she met Phil's knowing eyes in the looking glass.

"Captain Warre," Phil guessed.

Oh, God. Phil's softening expression brought the full weight of reality bearing mercilessly down. The urge to tell Phil everything—the lovemaking, the proposal—came up hard and fast. She swallowed it whole.

Phil came up behind her and brushed a fallen lock from Katherine's shoulder. A line creased between her delicate brows. "He didn't hurt you…"

Katherine shook her head and thought of Mejdan. He hadn't hurt her, either. But that was where the similarity ended.

"Quite the opposite, I suspect," Phil said with a little smile. "But tell me—the hearing ended not two hours ago. How can you have returned from his bed so quickly?"

Katherine's face warmed.

Phil laughed, soft and comprehending. "Ah, the carriage. I should have known. My, but he's clever. And impatient. But I suppose there will be plenty of time to explore the joys of a bed after the wedding."

Katherine turned from her and went to the window. "You of all people cannot possibly believe that I would marry Captain Warre." She imagined exploring the joys of a bed with him every night as his wife, and her heart squeezed so hard she couldn't breathe. No limpstaff, he.

"Katherine, don't be a fool!" Phil cried, following. "If not him, then who? Good God, you *are* thinking of Lord Deal."

She could not belong to James and still belong to herself, and one captivity in a lifetime was enough. Lord Deal was someone she could control. "The union makes sense."

"For a woman of mature years who isn't already in love with another man! You cannot possibly believe this will make you happy. For heaven's sake, Katherine—" Something in the street caught her attention. "Someone's coming to the door." A figure in a gray woolen cloak was painstakingly making its way up the walk below. "Katherine, I think it's Millicent!"

Katherine recognized her the moment the words left Phil's mouth. She spun away and strode out of the dressing room with Phil in her wake. For Millie to have returned here after the way she left meant something must have gone very badly. A dozen possibilities hurtled through her mind as she hurried down the main staircase as quickly as damnable fashion would allow, leaving the topic of her folly with James behind. They had reached the main landing when Dodd led Millicent into the foyer, where she pushed her hood onto her shoulders and clutched Dodd's arm, nearly collapsing against him.

"Millicent!" Katherine called out. She ran forward, already seeing the dark bruises covering Millicent's face. One side of her face was puffy, giving her a grotesquely asymmetrical appearance. "Who did this?" A deep fury rose up, making her words come out like barks.

"Gavin," Millicent breathed through a lip that was swollen and cracked.

Gavin, her brother. The physician. If he were here, she would put Gavin beyond any physician's help. "Get two footmen to carry her upstairs," Katherine ordered. "Quickly. Call for a doctor and ring for Mrs. Hibbard. Have her bring soup and a compress."

"Right away, your ladyship." Dodd hurried away, and within moments two young men from the mews rushed into the foyer. Upstairs, Katherine directed them to the room Millicent had occupied before she'd left, and by the time they laid her across it she had lost consciousness.

Immediately Katherine began pulling at Millicent's clothes. "I will kill him."

"We'll do it together," Phil said, moving in to help. There were more bruises on Millie's arms and chest, and Katherine heard Phil breathe a prayer.

"I should have stopped her," Katherine said.

Phil tugged at a sleeve, freeing Millie's arm. "You know better than to think you could have, stubborn as she is."

"I could have *ordered* her to stay."

"And she would have defied you. We're not on the ship anymore."

And Millicent would scarce have listened to her even if they had been. But the bruises and cuts were horrible, and the blood— "Perhaps she *would* have been better off in Malta," Katherine said in despair.

"Now you're being ridiculous. Even if she was admitted to that school in disguise, it would take nothing more than a man determined to avail himself of what he *thought* was some fresh, male flesh to discover the truth, and then she would be out. She would have fallen into prostitution within the week." Phil peeled away one stocking, then the other, revealing more bruises on Millie's legs. "The bastard ought to be skinned alive and hung on a pole."

Mrs. Hibbard whisked into the room followed by a maid who set down a tray with a teapot, soup tureen, cups and bowls. The maid left, and Mrs. Hibbard bustled to the bed. "It's a terrible, terrible thing, this. I've got compresses, but little good they'll do for all this. Lord above." Her soft, round face was pinched and angry. "Whoever done this ought to have twice as much done to him." She laid a compress across Millie's black eye and another across a nasty bruise on her shoulder, but it wasn't nearly enough. Millicent would need a compress for her entire body. "I'll go make up some more," Mrs. Hibbard said, shaking her head. "Let's hope the doctor gets here right quick."

A hole opened up in Katherine's chest as she stared at Millicent's battered body. "I'll never let her out of my sight again."

"She'll be delighted to hear that, I'm sure. She's a grown woman, Katherine."

"She's not yet twenty." And her time aboard the *Possession* may have sturdied up her muscles, but she was still short, and slightly built, and more delicate than a country physician's daughter should be.

"Which is plenty old enough to be acquainted with the ways of the world," Phil pointed out. "She's not as delicate as she looks, Katherine. You know that. She's got the spirit of ten sailors."

"Which didn't save her from this."

"But it will." Phil reached for Katherine's hand. "She'll survive this. I know she will."

CHAPTER TWENTY-NINE

HE'D FORGOTTEN THE preservative.

At home in his bedchamber, James stood with his waistcoat in one hand and the preservative—pristine and unused—in the other. What utter stupidity to have thought he could touch Katherine and maintain enough coherence to take precautions. She'd been pure intoxication from the moment he'd set eyes on her.

Hell and damnation! At this very moment, his child might be growing in her womb. Enraged, he flung the preservative across the chamber. It hit the wall with a soft thwack and fell to the floor.

And even his own stupidity didn't keep him from growing hard—*again*—at the memory of being inside her.

His "solution" had been entirely, completely illusory. Rather than slaking his thirst and clearing his head, making love to her in that coach only made him want her more. He had buried himself inside her, possessed her as completely as was physically possible, and still he wasn't satisfied. He wanted her naked. Here. On his bed, without stays and hoops and yards of fabric.

Instead, within the hour he would see her at this bloody rout Lady Effy was giving, where he would smile politely and make conversation with the very devils who dreamed of foraging inside her skirts exactly as he had. It was not to be tolerated.

He paced the length of the chamber, restless and unsated. There was a chance she hadn't conceived. His thoughts strayed into the queasy territory of a woman's monthly flow, and he sat on the edge of the bed. Even if she had, within weeks she would be married to Deal. He leaned forward and covered his face with his hands.

Marry me, Katherine. The whisper of his own words taunted him.

Good God—what had he been thinking? The answer, of course, was that he hadn't been. Thinking. He'd been rutting like a stallion in heat. Katherine was everything he didn't want in a wife. She was combative where he wanted peaceful, commanding where he wanted submissive, fiery where he wanted mild.

He got up and snatched the preservative off the floor and tossed it into the drawer in his dressing table. He should be thanking every bloody star in the sky that she'd rejected his reckless proposal.

In the looking glass, the man who had so blithely anticipated resolution before mocked him now. *You'll have a high time lying awake nights while Lord Deal tries to sink his half-wilted cock into that tight, wet heat.* He slammed the drawer shut and glared at himself. The staff in his breeches wasn't the only idiot in this bedchamber.

Was that it, then? A hasty farewell as he buttoned his breeches and stepped out of her coach two streets away to avoid being seen? Sod it all, he'd made a bloody mess of things. He needed to talk to her.

About what? his reflection sneered. *Arranging another tryst before she becomes Lady Deal?*

About…them. Their relationship. The debt. Yes—the debt! He pushed away from the dressing table and turned, shoving his hands through his hair. That bloody, goddamned debt that he'd failed to repay. The one she said she'd forgiven him for. The one, in fact, she didn't truly believe he owed—that much had been there in her eyes this morning when the truth behind his rescue had emerged.

There was a knock on his door—Bates's knock—and he let his hands fall. "Come in."

The door opened, and Bates handed him a small, sealed note. "This just arrived, your lordship."

"Thank you." He ripped open the seal and read Philomena's words. Tossing the note aside, he rang for his valet.

AN HOUR AFTER sunset, Katherine sat by Millicent's window in the fading light with Anne playing cat's cradle on her lap with a length of yarn. Millicent lay with her black-and-blue face stark against the white pillows and a dark prognosis. The doctor had done what he could—which was bloody little—but speculated that she might have sustained internal injuries and that only time would tell. Phil had sent their regrets to Lady Effy, and all that was left was to wait.

William paced back and forth in front of the fireplace, while Miss Bunsby dabbed Millie's forehead with a damp cloth and cast him frequent looks of disgust. That alone should have been reason enough to dismiss her—to *actually* dismiss her, this time.

"Doctors," William muttered, jabbing at the fire with an iron. "Never have an answer about anything."

Anne leaned back against Katherine with a sigh.

"Maybe Millie will feel better if Mr. Bogles sleeps with her."

Katherine stroked her hair and pulled on the yarn to help Anne thread it through her fingers. "He might walk on her, sweetling. That wouldn't feel good at all."

"You're right, Mama." Anne let her hands fall into her lap, and the yarn went limp. She wrinkled her nose at the smell of bitter herbs wafting from fresh compresses Mrs. Hibbard had brought up. "If I get a bruise, I don't want any compress."

Katherine touched her nose. "If you get a bruise, I'll make sure Mrs. Hibbard makes you an *extra big* compress to make it go away that much faster."

Anne made a face and a noise and wiggled on Katherine's lap just as Dodd appeared in the doorway. "Lady Ramsey is downstairs, your ladyship."

"Send her upstairs," Katherine told him.

Moments later she and Phil met Honoria in the adjoining dressing room. She swept into the room wringing her hands. "Katherine, I had no idea— I didn't mean to intrude! Is she going to be all right?" Upon hearing what the doctor had said, she gasped. "Poor, poor thing! I *do* hope she pulls through quickly. I never would have come if I'd known, except that I *had* to come, because Katherine—" she gripped Katherine's arm "—you didn't tell me we are to be *sisters*."

Phil's brows rose. "Sisters!"

"I was out shopping for ribbons when I saw Lady Ponsby, who said she had it on good authority from her husband after this morning's hearing that it was so. I was already obliged to drink tea this evening with Lady Kirby and Lady West—the most excruciating thing imaginable—and I wasn't able to confirm until now!

Your house was closer than James's, so I came here straightaway."

Things had gone utterly out of control. "Imbeciles! Have the rumormongers nothing better to do than spread lies?"

"In London?" Phil laughed. "Ha! But I *am* sorry, dear," she said, taking Honoria's arm, "unfortunately, the rumor is false."

"La, I was afraid of that! Forgive me for being indelicate with your friend in such grave danger, but *when* is my brother going to see reason and ask for Katherine's hand?"

The sound of Dodd's scolding carried in from the hallway. "Your lordship, I beg you, you absolutely must not—"

As if on cue, James stalked into the room—heedless, as always, of what he must or must not do. "How is she?" he demanded.

"Lord Croston, your ladyship," Dodd announced disapprovingly from the doorway.

Yes, she could see that plain enough. "At death's door," she told him. In a single heartbeat everything they'd done in the carriage flowed over her like hot water in a bath. Her pulse pounded in her throat. "Apparently her elder brother wasn't as keen to welcome her home as he might have been. We know nothing more. She arrived at the door barely able to stand— How she made it all the way here, I don't know."

With a quiet oath, James crossed the dressing room to the bedchamber and looked in. "What does the doctor say?"

"Very little," William said with barely concealed disdain as James entered the chamber. "They may be superficial bruises, or they may be life-threatening. Naturally, he cannot tell."

Katherine scowled at Phil. "I see you've occupied yourself with pen and paper."

Phil merely shrugged. "No need to thank me, dearest. I was already writing to India—it was nothing to dash off one more."

"Such an awful tragedy," Honoria said. "Absolutely terrible. I shall go to Lady Effy's and quell the inevitable rumors that will arise with both you and James absent."

IT WAS THE MIDDLE of the night when Katherine opened her eyes to find that she had dozed off on the daybed in Millicent's dressing room. A figure stood facing the fireplace.

James.

She pushed herself up, and he turned. "William and Philomena are sitting with her," he said. "She's still sleeping. There's been no change." His coat lay over the back of a chair, and he'd rolled up his shirtsleeves to his elbows the way he used to do aboard the *Possession*.

She fought her way out of the sleep she hadn't meant to fall into. Memories of the carriage ride exploded into her mind before she could stop them—his mouth on her lips, his hands on her breasts, his body buried in hers. The hasty buttoning, fastening and tucking as the carriage rolled to a stop.

He brought her a glass of water and she took it from him, careful not to touch his fingers. "You needn't have stayed," she said, letting a sip of cool water slide across her tongue.

"True enough." The clock on the mantel *tick-tick-ticked.* In the fireplace, logs cracked and snapped.

He was so beautiful it was all she could do not to stare. And the more she tried not to think of their love-making, the more the memory grew, pulsing and breathing with a life of its own. "There's nothing more to be done," she told him. "You're free to leave if—"

"I'm not leaving."

"Very well." Her fingers remembered the hard ridge of his jaw, the solid muscles on his torso rippling beneath his shirt.

His eyes lighted on her, smoldering with what they'd done together. "Was there bad blood between Millicent and her brother before she went to the Continent?" he asked.

"She didn't like him, but that was all I ever knew." Katherine stood and paced a few feet away, but the room was too small to offer the distance she needed. "When I met her in Venice she would have done almost anything to join my crew. Three years later, she was determined to stay in Malta and attend surgical school. When she learned we'd sailed from Malta while she slept, I had to order an extra watch for three days and nights for fear she would go over the rail with an empty cask and try to make it back."

"A fool's errand that would have left her dead."

"She wanted to attend that surgical school so badly."

"Another fool's errand. Did you learn what made her so desperate to join you at the first?"

Katherine made a noise. "The father of the children she'd been hired to care for. Apparently he didn't believe her duties should end once the children went to bed. I still don't know if she was running from a threat or a *fait accompli*."

"Christ." James rubbed his forehead.

"I shall take her to Dunscore with me." She prayed it would be soon, and not just for Millie's sake. "I cannot turn her into an acceptable candidate for a school of medicine, but at least there she'll be safe."

His gaze shot to her. "Nothing about your plan has changed, then." *After what happened in the carriage,* hung in the air.

"I intend to do what I must."

Marry me, Katherine. The choice she'd rejected taunted her. He did not repeat it.

"You said nothing about your captivity at the hearing. It might have made a difference. It still could. I shall speak with Winston and ask him to reconvene the committee."

"Good God." She almost laughed. "Those men cared about nothing more than preventing my return to sea and putting me under the control of a man's hand. I could have set forth every detail and the result would have been the same." James stood in front of her now. Secret places she'd hardly been aware of before grew warm and moist beneath his gaze.

He was remembering, too. It was there in his eyes, along with the torment of his wild imaginings about her life with Mejdan al-Zayar.

"It might have elicited sympathy," he said.

"Nothing could have done that after Lord Edrington's revelation," she said mirthlessly. "In the face of which you defended me." Which only proved the depth of his guilt. It all seemed so ridiculous now. Nothing in the past could be changed.

"Yes."

"Because of the debt."

"Because I should have perished with the *Henry's*

Cross, and because everything I told the committee was true. Anyhow, I'm alive because you did *not* leave me to die."

"I gave the order to do it."

"You are an experienced sea captain, Katherine. Unlike the committee, you don't need me to explain what that entails." His tone was dark. Rough. "The kinds of decisions one has to make."

She could see what he was thinking as clearly as if he'd told her. "Such as whether to engage the corsairs over the fate of a small merchant ship," she said. The two decisions—his and hers—should have made them even, except that she had changed her mind about hers, and nothing he could have done differently would have changed the outcome of his. "Your regret is wasted on that. My experience would have been the same had you never happened upon us."

A muscle worked in his jaw. It was a perfect time to tell him the truth about life with Mejdan al-Zayar—about crowded market vendors hawking bright scarves and sparkling bangles, about screaming with laughter as the dogs snatched Tamilla's new silk slippers from the harem and left the slobbery pieces beneath the tangerine tree in the courtyard, about Mejdan's daughter Kisa and her telescope. His torment would be better directed toward any number of English girls married off to men of their fathers' choosing, who ended up slaves to a marriage bed that brought only pain and disgust.

"I am sorry I gave that order," she said instead.

"You shouldn't be," he whispered harshly. "I am not sorry I gave mine. Only that I failed to execute it properly."

"You nearly killed me, and I you. The score is even, Captain—" his eyes blazed at that "—and now that there is a solution, we may finally be free of each other."

CHAPTER THIRTY

"You're going to *marry* her?" Nick's outrage exploded into James's library at half past nine the next morning.

James didn't bother to look up from the desk. He'd returned from Katherine's at four, and a few hours' restless sleep left him in no condition to deal with an outburst. "Marry whom?"

"Katherine Kinloch." Nick walked right up to the desk and braced his hands on the surface. "You could at least have told me before you let it fly all over London."

"I assure you, I have no plans to marry Lady Dunscore." He kept his voice cool, but a hot sensation snaked down to his loins.

"No? Everyone at Lady Effy's was agog with the news—and the fact that neither you nor Lady Dunscore were present. I don't suppose that was a coincidence."

An excuse not to be at Lady Effy's last night was possibly the one good thing to come of all this. "No, it wasn't. We were both needed in aid of a mutual friend."

Nick glanced at James's crotch and snorted. "Mutual friend."

Quick as that James reached across the desk and grabbed Nick by the lapels. "Do not insinuate where you are not informed," he bit out.

"Damn you," Nick shot back without flinching, and shoved James away. "I need some kind of leverage. If *you* marry her, I'll have none." Nick glared at him. "I've tried every bloody thing I can think of. I'm running out of options. She won't go to Scotland."

"*Scotland.* And you fear *my* marriage to Lady Dunscore? For God's sake, do let's get Honoria involved in some bloody scandal and drag the whole family into the mud."

"You have no idea what this means."

"Are you in love with her?"

"Of course I'm in love with her. What man wouldn't be? She's a goddamned angel. Every time I so much as think about her with Adkins or Oakley or Stalworth— It simply *can't happen.*"

James watched his brother wrestle with the fact that there could be no way to protect Miss Holliswell from her father's aspirations. "My previous offer still stands," he said. Forty thousand to resolve this—it would be worth the price.

"Bloody lot of good it would do me, even if I could accept it, which you already know I can't. He'd never consent." Nick paced the length of the room and turned back. "Why in God's name won't she go to Scotland?" He exhaled, pinching the bridge of his nose. "All right. If the rumors are false and you're not planning to marry Katherine Kinloch, then there's still a possibility of my securing a second hearing. Or—God help me—putting a new bill on the table."

"For Christ's sake, Nick, I can't let you do that."

"Do you or do you not have intentions toward Lady Dunscore?" Nick demanded.

"I do not." Liar. "But I do owe her my life, and as long as her future is uncertain I shall do every bloody thing I can to help her. As for my intentions…I've all but settled my mind on Miss Underbridge."

"Pinsbury's niece?"

James nodded, wondering when the hell he'd settled on any such thing. Just now, apparently. And why not?

His mind answered the question with an erotic image of Katherine with her breasts pushed over the top of her stays, and he cursed silently. Vilely.

"God." Nick sank into an armchair and rested his forearms on his knees, staring holes into the carpet. "There must be something I can do for Clarissa. *Something.*"

"Are you absolutely certain she isn't pretending a greater naiveté than she possesses?"

For a second it looked like Nick might lunge across the desk. "If she is," he said tightly, "then she's a masterfully accomplished actress."

They looked at each other. Plenty of women were accomplished actresses. "I have no doubt Miss Holliswell is exactly what she appears to be," James said for Nick's benefit. "And I can't think of one damned thing you *haven't* done. Perhaps it's time to be sensible." He rose and stalked to his brandy snifter, grabbing hold of this liberating idea, and poured two glasses.

"Sensible." Nick muttered the word. "I'm not sure I know what that means anymore."

James handed Nick a glass and ignored the uncomfortable feeling wriggling in his chest. "Then here's to finding out," he said.

THREE DAYS LATER Millicent was out of danger, and James decided that being sensible started with refusing to concern himself with Katherine's plans. To simply forget her.

Forget what happened in the coach.

Forget whatever the hell al-Zayar might have done all those years ago.

Forget her infuriating attempt at forgiveness. Damn it all—forget he *needed* forgiveness.

It was time to move forward, and moving forward started with finding a bride. The sooner he could come to an understanding with someone, the better.

"Forgive my bluntness, my lord," Miss Underbridge said as he drove her through the park in his open carriage the next day, "but I was led to believe that you have an understanding with the countess of Dunscore."

"And you believe, despite such an understanding, that I would ask you to accompany me on an outing?"

"Would you?" The blasted woman regarded him calmly with the most direct pair of brown eyes he'd ever had the discomfort of meeting.

"Perhaps, Miss Underbridge, you would fare better during the social season if you honed your skills of discernment," he said with an irritable flick of the reins. "There is no such understanding."

"Hmm. Thank you, my lord—I believe my skills are being honed even as we speak." That calm expression did not so much as falter. "I would like to go home, please. Now."

THERE WAS ALWAYS Lady Maude. Perhaps he'd judged her too quickly. Her fascination with Katherine may have been nothing more than a girlish curiosity that had faded by now. James received her response to his invitation the next afternoon and opened it immediately.

Lord Croston,
I am in receipt of your kind invitation for a picnic.
However, I fear my powers of discernment force
me to decline. Perhaps Lady Dunscore would
enjoy going in my stead.
Respectfully yours,
Maude Linton

James crushed the refusal in his fist and threw it into the fire.

"La, James," Honoria said that evening, whisking into his library, "what are you about? I'm hearing the most dreadful things!"

James relished the angry scratch of his pen across paper and didn't bother to look up. "I don't wish to discuss it."

"Well everyone else wishes to, and if you don't have a care you'll go from hero to laughingstock before the month is out. I've come to tell you that Lady Dunscore has left for Scotland. I want to know what you plan to do about it."

"If she's gone, there's nothing anyone can do."

"Sometimes you aggravate me to distraction, James. You're in love with her, and now she's gone, and you're pretending you don't care. Which makes your fumbling attempts to court these other young women all the more pathetic."

He jabbed the pen into its stand and stood up. "Pathetic?"

"Yes."

They faced off across his desk. And then James smiled. "My dear Honoria, your female sensibilities have taken you too far this time. Why women insist on seeing love whenever a man so much as glances at a woman, I'll never fathom."

Honoria laughed. "La, James, I daresay you've done far more than glance at Lady Dunscore—but that's neither here nor there. Tell me this, if you're not in love, then why did you stay up all hours when Miss Germain was injured? Do not say it was for Miss Germain's sake. And why have you gone to such lengths to help Lady Dunscore's cause? I hear things, James. I know what you've been about." She narrowed her eyes and studied him too intently for comfort. "You *are* in love. You're just too mutton-headed to see it."

HE WAS NOT. In love. It was the refrain that repeated in James's head as he drank his coffee in the morning, sorted through correspondence in the afternoon and, instead of attending every blasted social event in London, played away his cares at White's in the evening.

He'd succumbed to lust, but that was behind him now. It was what he told himself as two more days passed with all the haste of a bit of flotsam on a calm sea. A few more loose ends, and he would go to Croston. He met with his accountant, his solicitor, his banker. He compared figures, reviewed plans, studied reports.

Lust was an easy enough state to ease should he decide to do so. It was what he reminded himself in the middle of the night when he woke up in the darkness with a raging erection and a sheen of hot sweat on his skin.

God knew it would be a simple enough matter to find someone willing. There were plenty of women equally as beautiful and half as contentious. He could make an acquaintance in the country. Find a sensible woman, come to an understanding while he looked for a suitable bride. It was the fantasy he was indulging in, overseeing the packing of his valises on morning seven since the disastrous carriage ride home from Westminster, when news came that the committee would present its report that afternoon.

CHAPTER THIRTY-ONE

"YOU STUPID BASTARD!" Holliswell raged under his breath, yanking out a chair next to Nick at the coffee-house where Nick was coming to terms with the vote that had taken place not an hour before.

Nick glanced up from his paper and took in the red face and outraged eyes. "Oh?"

"This is *your* fault." Holliswell shoved a crumpled note in his direction. "She's gone," Holliswell said, eyes blazing.

"Gone." Nick set his paper aside and picked up the note. Instantly he recognized Clarissa's feathery hand.

"Run off with Edrington," Holliswell spat.

Edrington. Nick raced through Clarissa's words.

Please forgive me, Father. We are so much in love, and my fear was great that Lord Taggart would attempt to follow through on his own proposal, or that you would force one of your other perni-cious choices upon me.

One of Holliswell's *other* pernicious choices? For a moment he could only stare as the truth hit him like a full frontal assault: he'd been played for a fool.

"My Clarissa, my dearest angel—" For a moment Holliswell looked as if he might cry. But then he swallowed, and his fury returned. "I see now the plans you were making behind my back, filling her head with ruinous notions."

"I would think Edrington's title would carry some weight with you." That day in the park—she'd told him she was out for a walk and did not know why Edrington wished to speak to her. That she'd only spoken to him once before at a dinner.

"*Empty* title. Scotland—with a penniless pissant!"

Clarissa, not so opposed to Scotland, after all. Just not with Nick. He'd practically sold his soul to the devil, fighting his own brother to save her, and she'd been perfectly capable of saving herself.

Accomplished actress indeed.

Nick reached for his coffee and took a sip. The tepid brew slid bitterly down his throat. "Yes, I suppose you're right. As the daughter of an earl, she might have done much better." He set the cup down. "In case you haven't heard, the committe made its report this afternoon. The Lords voted against a third reading. The bill is dead."

Holliswell looked as if he might suffer an apoplexy. "You worthless bastard."

The man didn't know how right he was.

"As of this moment," Holliswell said through gritted teeth, "I am calling in my notes. Sell Taggart or assign it to me, but I'll not coddle your debtor's arse one more minute. Do I make myself clear?"

Another sip, and Nick leaned back in his chair. It was no less than he'd expected. He would lose Taggart, and he would start over with nothing. There was a moment of agonizing pain in his chest, followed by a peaceful numbness.

"Indeed," he said. "I understand you perfectly."

IT WAS OVER.

It was the fact that thrummed through James's brain all evening as he fixed his mind on port and cards at the club. The committee had made its decision. He'd raised enough support, after all, and Katherine would keep Dunscore. His debt was paid, and he was free.

Good riddance.

It was the lie he told himself as he emerged, half-drunk, from the club that night and onto the dark street. The rank, misty air hit him full force at the same time as the realization that Katherine and Deal had no way of knowing the committee's decision. It would take days for the news to reach them in Scotland. She could well end up married to Deal before learning the marriage wasn't necessary.

Katherine. Married. To Lord Deal.

No.

Bloody, sodding, *hell* no.

He ground to a halt right there on the pavement. There was no way in hell he could let that happen.

It was the truth that blazed to life inside him right there beneath a sputtering lamppost: He wanted her. Age, insanity, illness—whatever the cause of this flatness inside him, it didn't matter. She brought him to life, and he didn't care why. Misguided fascination, carnal lust—none of that mattered.

He wanted her for himself, and he didn't have to be in love to make it happen. Lust was more than enough. God knew plenty of marriages had been based on less.

Not that she would agree. Katherine would never consider marrying him or anyone else if she knew she held Dunscore outright.

But she didn't know. Had no way of knowing, until someone brought the news.

God.

If he got there in time—even a day in advance of the post or a messenger—he might be able to...

God. He couldn't really do it.

Could he?

He imagined how she would rejoice in triumph when she learned of the committee's vote in her favor. How coldly she would smile as she turned away in disdain from all the men who'd imagined they could tame her.

From *him*.

Resolution impelled him forward, twice as quickly as before. Oh, yes. He could do it. He would leave for Dunscore immediately. Tonight.

He'd gone no more than twenty paces when someone grabbed him around the neck and yanked him into a dark alley.

"Bloody—" James cursed and fought, but the assailant had caught him by surprise and a moment later James felt his back slam against a wall. "Goddamned blackguard," a familiar voice growled in his ear. "I ought to kill you right here."

"I would prefer that you didn't, Jaxbury. I'd always hoped to die in my bed." James's breath came hard and his heart pounded out of his chest. He struggled to inhale past the arm pressing into his throat. "To what do I owe this honor?"

"I told you what would happen if you seduced Katherine." Clearly Jaxbury had the advantage of sobriety. "You thought I was bluffing?"

"I thought you were smart enough to stay out of

other people's affairs. I don't know what you think you know—"

"Everything! Phil never could keep a secret worth a damn." Jaxbury's arm tightened, he sneered. "Bastard. Didn't know I needed to see Katherine safely home from the hearing. You knew she'd be forced to marry, so you took advantage for your own designs."

A rush of fury gave James a momentary advantage and he pushed hard against Jaxbury, breaking the hold. He slammed his fist against Jaxbury's jaw, half-blind with rage, almost welcoming the pain of Jaxbury's counterattack. He threw another punch. Jaxbury grabbed him again and together they stumbled from one side of the alley to the other. James gave a nasty kick to Jaxbury's leg and Jaxbury threw James against the wall. James launched himself against Jaxbury, hurtling the man's body across the narrow alley and against the wall on the other side, but Jaxbury was back immediately with another hook to James's jaw. James returned the favor, reeling, and managed to grapple on to Jaxbury's shoulders at the precise moment Jaxbury grappled on to his.

They stood there, locked eye to eye, breathing raggedly. In the faint lamplight coming from the street, James could see fury in Jaxbury's eyes. "Bloody coward," Jaxbury spat, "hiding in White's while Katherine offers herself up in captivity once again. Some gentleman, you, but I'll make one out of you yet. We're going to Dunscore. Tonight. You plowed the field, Croston—you'll damn well bring in the harvest."

James wrenched himself away. "You want me to *marry* Katherine?"

"And you're going to do it if I've got to hold my sword to your balls."

"She'll never agree."

"Got to marry someone, but then, you already know that. Sure as hell isn't going to be Deal. Not if I have anything to do about it."

Apparently Jaxbury didn't know about the committee's decision. James stared into that hard-edged, sea-weathered face and wondered if Jaxbury might prove an ally in his plan.

Perhaps. But more likely, if Jaxbury knew Katherine did not have to marry at all, he would abandon this protective outrage. All hope of marrying Katherine would be gone.

"As it happens," James said, "I had already come to the same conclusion on my own."

"Oh, aye," Jaxbury said sarcastically, wiping at a trickle of blood at the corner of his mouth. "I can see how you've spent the evening thinking of her."

James crushed a fresh surge of temper. "I leave for Dunscore immediately. Good evening, Jaxbury. It's been a pleasure." He turned to go.

"Not a chance," Jaxbury laughed, falling in step beside him. "We'll go to Dunscore together."

"I don't require an escort."

Jaxbury gave him a friendly slap on the back. "Then think of it more as an insurance."

THEY WERE IN James's stables when a footman arrived, breathless. "Message for Lord Croston!"

James took the message and tore it open. It was from Admiral Wharton. He read the contents and looked sharply at Jaxbury. "You lying bastard. You would have let me go to Dunscore knowing of this."

Jaxbury narrowed his eyes. "Don't have the first idea what you're talking about."

James thrust the note at him. Jaxbury took it. Read. Visibly paled. "Good God."

"She's fled," James said flatly.

"No. Not Katherine."

"Of course, Katherine."

"I'm telling you," Jaxbury ground out, "she would not have done this."

But she must have. "Who else would sail the *Possession* out of London in the dead of night, bold as balls?"

CHAPTER THIRTY-TWO

KATHERINE FACED THE wind coming off the sea and tried to pretend its cold bite was what stung her eyes to tears. Damnation. She was stronger than this. She knew better. Clouds churned in the sky, and whitecaps chopped the gray, restless water. A cool, salty breeze whipped her hair and chilled the damp tracks on her cheeks.

"Are you crying again, Mama?" Anne asked.

Sometimes it would be nice if her daughter weren't quite so perceptive. "A little. But you mustn't worry."

"The sound of the waves makes me happy, Mama. If you listen, they might make you happy, too."

Katherine reached for Anne's hand and turned, pulling strands of hair from her face to stare at the fortress that was Dunscore. "Perhaps they will at that." But the sound of waves on Dunscore's shore only brought the memories back more strongly. Yesterday this place had been a ghost—as lost to her as the girl she'd been the last time she stepped over its threshold. But the moment the coach had rolled to a stop outside Dunscore's massive doors, what was dead had sprung to life.

Home. Home. Home.

Her heart thundered the word she knew better than to reach for.

"Mama, you're squeezing."

Katherine loosened her grip. "I'm sorry, dearest."
Where the east tower once stood, a pile of rubble now sat.

*Fortify the east tower! What a silly muffin you are,
Katie. That tower has stood for six hundred years, and
mark my words, it will stand for six hundred more.
Come—let us order the phaeton. I fancy a fast ride
and a visit to Deal.*

Oh, Papa.

Across the velvety landscape that hugged Dunscore's
walls she spotted the housekeeper Martha marching toward them, her crisp white apron billowing in the wind.
Katherine already knew what the message was: Lord
Deal had arrived.

One night's reprieve was all she could afford. Today,
she and Lord Deal would discuss an arrangement. It
was imperative that she marry before the committee
could decide against her. Lord Deal was the only one
she would consider, and she would need to make that
very clear to him.

Lord Deal, I insist that we marry. No, that didn't
sound right at all.

*Lord Deal, I assure you I would make a most bid-
dable wife.* He would never believe it.

Lord Deal, you are my only hope. Pathetic.

Nothing sounded right. Nothing *felt* right. But of
course it wouldn't. This was a last resort. A desperate situation.

And you are in love with another man.

She pushed the thought of James away. "Come," she
said to Anne, tugging lightly on her hand. "I see Martha." Martha's disapproving scowl, to be precise. Its
sternness matched the imposing gray walls behind her

as she met them partway along the trail that led from the castle to the sea.

"Ach, Katie!" Martha cried, fisting her hands on her hips. "You canna see him looking like this!"

"Will I scare him away, do you think?" She looped her arm through Martha's, honestly unsure whether to hope for or dread the possibility. She should have been inside preparing for Lord Deal's visit, having her hair carefully coiffed and powdered and her face brightened with a subtle layer of paint. Instead, she would receive her future husband looking as wild as this place where the rocky shore touched the North Sea.

"The most terrible demon would be scared away by the likes of you," Martha humphed, and Anne giggled. The three of them headed back to the keep, Anne's hand in Katherine's, and Katherine's arm in Martha's, the sea wind pushing at their backs. With each step, Katherine's nerves swirled in fearful eddies in her belly.

Once she and Lord Deal came to an agreement, all this unpleasantness would soon be finished. And Anne's place would be secure.

Miss Bunsby met them outside the door and took Anne. "But I want to greet Lord Deal, Mama," Anne complained.

"Next time, dearest. I have business to discuss with him now." If only she could put off the inevitable forever.

"Will you ask him about the phaeton?"

"I will ask."

Martha still clucked and fussed after Miss Bunsby took Anne upstairs, brushing at Katherine's dress and trying to pull her hair together. "At least have your hair done up, Katie," she begged, clearly distressed. "What will he think of you like this?"

"He will think I've been enjoying the wilds of Dunscore. He's seen me in gowns and jewels, Martha. It will be all right."

"Humph."

Katherine looked down the stone corridor that led toward the main hall. Light streamed into the arched passageway through a row of windows down the east side. A line of unlit sconces disappeared into the shadows.

Catch me, Papa! The ghost of the little girl she'd been ran headlong toward the end, laughing, pounding her feet on the stones.

Her grown-up feet did not want to move. Martha's hands stilled and went to her face. "Don't worry, Katie. They won't dare take this place from you," she said forcefully. And then, more softly, "Maybe his lordship can do something to help."

A wild laugh rose up in her throat. She wanted desperately to put her arms around Martha and tell her everything just like she used to do after Mama died. But she couldn't afford to break down now, so she kissed Martha's cheek and gently set her away. "Perhaps he can at that." She would tell Martha soon enough that Dunscore would, indeed, remain hers.

Anne's voice drifted down the corridor. "Wait, Miss Bunsby. I want to feel the floor. I think it is made of great, giant stones!"

I shall step on every stone in the corridor, Papa. How long do you suppose it will take me?

Finally her feet moved.

"WELL, KATHERINE, WHAT do you think of your old home?" Lord Deal's voice rang out but was quickly absorbed by the main hall's vastness. Fires crackling in four fireplaces barely touched the cool, damp air, and he stood near the closest one holding out his hands. He turned now, and behind him the hall arched toward the sky.

"I think it is in dire need of repair." Katherine walked toward him, her footsteps silent on the wide carpets, then muted on ancient wood planks. Giant paintings lined the walls—hunting scenes, battle scenes, scenes of Dunscore itself. Each one was like a piece of her, she knew them so well even after a lifetime away. On the opposite side, narrow windows rose toward the ceiling and let in the cloudy day's muted light. Great iron chandeliers hung from the ceiling. Only two were lit, but the glow from dozens of candles helped chase away the gloom. "There was a time when I had great plans for it." Plans that had included an addition to the north wing drafted by her great-great-grandfather. How many hours had she spent studying those old yellowed plans while Papa was away at his card games?

"Surely that time has come again," Lord Deal said. She held out a hand that threatened to tremble, and he kissed it. "A pleasure, as always," he told her kindly. "You've been outside. The weather's a bit chill, is it not? Oh, but the sea is lovely on a day like this."

"Yes, lovely." His hand was warm and firm.

"And how is dear Anne faring?"

"Very well, except that I haven't a moment's peace with her asking when we might ride in your phaeton again."

"She has but to say the word," he declared, laughing.

"I will caution you now to set limits, or you'll be spending more time in the phaeton than you ever dreamed possible." She tried to smile, but fear made it too hard.

Lord Deal must have seen it, because his laughter faded. "I'm very sorry things weren't resolved in precisely the way we'd hoped," he said soberly. "But all will be well as soon as you marry—the committee will have no reason to rule against you then—and I feel certain it won't be as bad as you think." He smiled and patted her hand.

"Of course," she said, and tried to return his smile. "Now please, do sit down and let's discuss the details."

He let go of her hand. "Of course, of course." They settled into two oak armchairs by the fire. "Now, I'm not sure there are any details to discuss yet, of course, but I do have some thoughts. McGowan, for one. A bit older than you, but not by too much, and he's an earl. A solid fellow—never been married. And there's Arran, of course. Perhaps a bit flowery for a woman like you, but he'd do. And there's Weogh—"

"Lord Deal." There was no sense allowing the conversation to move any further in this direction. The time was ripe. "When we agreed to come to Scotland and discuss the details," she said carefully, "I assumed—" A lick of panic flared. It would be so easy to fail. "I had no idea you intended to introduce me to someone else."

A moment of genuine confusion knitted his brows.

She pressed on. "I assumed you and I would work out some kind of arrangement."

"You and I!" Now there was genuine surprise. He managed a kind of half laugh edged with horror. "Good God, Katherine, you're Cullen's little girl. Bad enough to be patching you into a hasty marriage to a stranger, but *me*— Ach." He rubbed his chin. "I'm afraid that possibility never crossed my mind."

"Well perhaps it could cross your mind now," she said flatly. "It makes good sense, given your relationship with my father and the proximity of the Deal and Dunscore estates."

"Katherine—"

"I do not want to marry a stranger."

"Of course not. But under the circumstances…" He cleared his throat. "You'd like McGowan. I'm sure of it."

If there was one thing she could be sure of, it was that she would *not* like McGowan. Or Arran, or Weogh, or any other bloody pillock Lord Deal got it in mind to marry her off to. The fear that he might refuse to marry her made it difficult to smile. "My apologies, Lord Deal. I never meant to shock you. I had no idea we were not of the same mind on this subject." It was only a small lie.

"No apology necessary, my dear." He tried another laugh. "Such flattery, so early in the morning."

"Let me assure you, I would do everything in my power to make you a suitable wife. I would be on my very best behavior. There would be no more scenes like the one at the ball." His hand was warm and dry, with loose skin that wrinkled a little in her grasp. A knot in her stomach screamed for attention, but she ignored it.

"What a pity that would be, my dear." He laughed again, perhaps a bit edgily. "I daresay the duke will think twice before he gets a mind to press his attentions where he's not wanted. You may well have done womankind a favor."

"I can't say I regret it," she admitted. "But I also understand the importance of propriety. I wouldn't want you to think I can't behave myself."

He pulled his hand away. "Ach, no—no, I would never think that. But, Katie, you can hardly expect me to be inclined toward matrimony with a girl who once served me mud biscuits and seawater tea."

"I promise I shan't serve them again." She laughed lightly, the way Phil might have, but his kindly brown eyes didn't quite crinkle.

"My dear, when I look upon you I see a girl Anne's age."

Which was one of the reasons why he would make the perfect husband.

She leaned forward and reached for his hand again—slowly, deliberately—knowing full well her low-cut gown would give him a glimpse of more than it should. "I doubt that, my lord." She was rewarded when his eyes flicked downward. No, he was not entirely immune.

His lips thinned.

"You can't really intend to see me forcibly married to one of those men—a complete stranger."

"They weren't strangers to your father."

"But they are to me." Fear ate through her seductive pretense. "I can't bear it. I can't."

"You *must* bear it," he said sternly. "You can't allow Holliswell to take Dunscore. For Cullen's sake, *I* can't allow it. But God help me—" He stood suddenly, and so did she. He was thinking now. Considering. There was hesitation in his brow.

She took a chance and brazenly lay her palms against his chest. If appealing to his male nature would change his mind, she would fire all guns. "Would it be so terrible to have me as your wife?" she asked, in a voice Phil would have been proud of.

He looked down at her as though this was the Garden of Eden and she was offering him a bite of apple. "Cullen would call me out, and rightfully so."

"My father isn't here," she reminded him quietly. "And I'm a woman long since grown." She smoothed the front of his waistcoat the way a wife might do. "My days of mud biscuits are far behind me."

"Not so far."

"Far enough."

He circled her wrists with hands that were stronger than they looked. "I can't believe I'm even considering this," he said brusquely. He wanted to touch her. She could see it in his eyes, and she fought the urge to back away as her pulse sped and a nerve ticked wildly in her throat.

She'd already decided on this. And she would see it through. Their marriage bed would be no different from the day she'd finally been sent to Mejdan's bed. Lord Deal was kind, and he would be gentle. He was kindly to Anne, and, most important, wouldn't try to shackle Katherine down.

"Little about your life would need to change," she told him. "I would ask nothing of you. You would be forced into nothing you didn't wish to do."

He laughed a little. "Except one thing. I don't even know if I could— Good God." He shook his head. "I really don't think I could do what you're asking."

"Marriages of convenience are hardly uncommon."

"Is there nobody who would meet your approval?" he demanded, looking her hard in the eyes, giving her a glimpse of the man he'd been thirty years ago. His hands tightened on her wrists. "You must have met dozens of eligible men while you were in London. Am I to believe nobody caught your eye? Are the gentlemen in London so blind that nobody so much as hinted at an offer? Ah, I can see there is someone. Who is he?"

"Nobody acceptable." But the image of James exploded to life—his face, drunk with passion inside her carriage, while his hands laid claim to her body. *Katherine, marry me.* "You know as well as I what kind of interest I garnered in London. Lord Deal, I am quite serious. You are my only hope."

"Tell me about this unacceptable gentleman in London. What was the objection? No doubt you outrank him significantly."

She was not going to discuss James with Lord Deal. But before she could tell him as much, he softened. "You've had your heart broken, haven't you, my dear?"

"Certainly not."

Lord Deal's brows dove. "He's wronged you, then?"

"No." This was not the discussion they were supposed to be having. "Lord Deal, please." Now she'd been reduced to begging. She schooled herself to soften her voice. "Please consider this."

"Honestly, Katherine, I'm hard-pressed to think of anything that would seem more wrong."

Marrying one of Lord Deal's "suggestions" would be more wrong. But it was obvious that continuing to press the issue now might lead to failure, so she just looked at him.

He watched her with tight lips and troubled eyes that sparked with the beginnings of indecision.

After a long moment he let go of her and stepped away. "I can't give you an answer now."

Suddenly she could hardly breathe. "I wouldn't expect you to."

"It would be a betrayal of Cullen beyond anything I could have ever imagined."

"I am convinced he would rather *you* be the one to save Dunscore than anyone else."

Lord Deal did not seem to share her conviction. "Give me a few days to at least satisfy myself that I've thought of every other possibility, and if you haven't thought of a better solution by then—" Something outside caught his attention, and he frowned toward the windows. "Are you expecting visitors?"

Visitors. Katherine turned abruptly and spotted two riders coming up the drive—riders she recognized even from this distance. "It's William Jaxbury." She clenched her jaw. "And Captain Warre."

"Croston?" Lord Deal peered harder. "Ach, it is. And from the looks of things, they've ridden fast and hard."

What were they doing here? This could ruin everything.

"Are you all right, Katie? You seem displeased by their arrival. Sir Jaxbury is a dear friend, is he not?"

"My dearest friend. And I am not—"

"Then it is Croston whose presence displeases you?"

"I am not displeased." She tucked her hand in Lord Deal's arm and urged him toward the door. "Let us go and greet our visitors," she said in the most pleasant voice she could manage.

"Mama!" Anne's voice called delightedly from the staircase in the entrance hall. "Mama, I hear horses! Miss Bunsby says it is William! And Captain Warre! Mama, Captain Warre has come to visit us!"

Her fingers tightened around Lord Deal's arm before she could stop them.

"Mmm," he said. "I daresay young Lady Anne has made a friend."

It was a full twenty minutes before Katherine had the heart to tear Anne away from her *friend* and send her upstairs with Miss Bunsby. Something was wrong. Very wrong. When James told them what day they'd left London, there was no doubt they'd hardly stopped at all.

"What's happened?" she demanded the moment Anne was out of hearing.

"Millicent and India have taken the *Possession,*" William told her. "Slipped out of the Thames in the dead of night."

An invisible hand closed over her throat. "That's impossible."

"Apparently it's not," James said flatly. "We went to your house after hearing the *Possession* was gone and found no trace of Miss Germain," James said. "We checked with Cantwell, and India was gone, as well. Snuck away somehow, and in her infinite wisdom, left a note. Wouldn't be treated like a child, or something to that effect."

William snorted.

"That is quite an offense," Lord Deal commented gravely.

Suddenly things made sense—why Millie had been so adamant about not feeling well enough to travel, why she had begged to stay in London instead of accompanying them to Dunscore. With her face so pale and yellowed with bruises, it had been impossible to deny her. Katherine had allowed her the use of the London house indefinitely.

But *indefinitely* had lasted only as long as it had taken Millicent to put her plan into action. Katherine's hands began to tremble, and she made fists to keep them still. "You must go after them," she said to William. "I will commission a ship in Edinburgh and pay for a crew."

A gleam came into William's eye. "An easy guess where they're headed."

Malta. But what India planned to do with the *Possession* while Millicent tried to gain admittance to that surgical school was anyone's guess.

"It'll be a damned business, bringing up Cantwell's daughter on charges," Lord Deal said.

"There won't be any charges," Katherine said. Her thoughts churned, struggling to make sense of this development. "I only want the *Possession* returned."

"Aye, Captain," William said.

She did want it returned. Right now. Today. This instant. It belonged to her, with her, where she could see it every day and hold on to its promise. It made her who she was.

"What of the committee? Has there been any word?" she asked.

"I daresay it's too soon to expect any," James said. And then he turned to Lord Deal. "Have there been any developments here?"

He was windblown from the ride, looking more like a sea captain than he had for weeks, and it was hard to keep from staring. A lock of his hair curled over his forehead. A shadow of beard roughened his jaw. Those calculating, sea-captain eyes watched her carefully.

She wanted to throw her arms around him the way Anne had done.

Instead, she reached for Lord Deal's arm. "Indeed, Henry and I have just been discussing the arrangements."

James's tight lips curved. "Have you."

Lord Deal cleared his throat. "Yes. Well. We have indeed been discussing a variety of possibilities—attempting, naturally, to think of some gentlemen who would be appropriate and, of course, to identify those whom Lady Dunscore finds objectionable." He patted her hand. "And I do believe we have identified at least *one* of the gentlemen in question."

CHAPTER THIRTY-THREE

JUST AFTER MIDNIGHT, a knock sounded at the door of her bedchamber.

The sound caught Katherine standing with her hands pressed against the cool, bare stone of her bedroom wall. In the quiet room with her palms against rock, she could almost feel Dunscore's heartbeat. It pulsed through her as though they were one.

She ignored the knock and let her hands fall. Went to stab at the fire, watching the sparks fly, calling up memories of her life—her *real* life. The one she'd built herself, not the one of her girlhood fantasies. William, grinning in the sunshine while porpoises played in the water. Young rigger Danby, dangling from the main yard after slipping from the footrope and nearly causing her to succumb in a fit of apoplexy in the process. That hot rush of anticipation that gripped her when she sighted a corsair xebec through her glass.

The sound of Anne's screams above the cannon-fire, and the knowledge that one small mistake—one single misstep—could change her life forever. Or end it completely.

Jab. Jab. She attacked a burning log until it fell into crumbling, hot orange pieces. *That* was why she was giving up her freedom. For Anne's sake. And marrying Lord Deal was the most tolerable answer.

There was a second knock, more insistent this time.

It is the answer only because you refused a proposal from the man on the other side of that door.

Proposal? Ha. What she had refused was a lust-drunk misjudgment that had tumbled from his lips in a moment of passion.

A third knock, and this time, the hushed bark of her name. She unlatched the door and opened it a crack. "You've already received all the hospitality I plan to offer, Captain."

"Open the bloody door." The hallway was nearly dark, but the glow from her room lit the murderous expression on his face. He stood there in only his breeches and shirt—no waistcoat, no stockings, no shoes. Nerves tangled in her belly even as her ire rose.

"Devil take you," she said, and started to shut the door, only to have him shove it open. "Get out!" she hissed, fearful of waking anyone.

"Are you engaged to him?" he demanded.

"That's none of your concern."

"Everything about you is my concern."

He grabbed her around the waist and crushed his mouth on to hers. The shock of instant fire in her blood had her gasping against him even as she tried to push him away, but he was immovable and her parted lips only gave his tongue free entrance into her mouth. He smelled like spicy soap and tasted of temptation. She felt him try to push the door closed and she tightened her hand around the latch to prevent him. He turned her back against the door and used their bodies to push it shut.

"Leave," she gasped, and cursed him. He only kissed her more savagely, and even her outrage could not fight the fire that tore across her skin. She shoved at him and pulled him closer all at the same time, and suddenly it was like the first time they'd touched in her cabin aboard the *Possession,* except this time there was no reason to stop.

"I ask you again," he said harshly. "Are you engaged to Deal?"

"I shan't reveal the intimacies of my relationship with Henry." His face was so close her lips brushed his when she spoke.

James barked a laugh. "Intimacies." He kissed her again, deeply. "That man has as much desire to be your lover as he does to tup a wild boar. He looks on you quite as his own granddaughter."

She couldn't force him to leave, but she could goad him. "Perhaps. But he's agreed to help me nonetheless." She paused. "In every way."

This time James's kiss was ruthless. She knew she'd said those words to push him over the edge of control, so he would make love to her and leave her no choice but to give in to what her body desperately wanted. He did not disappoint. He tore away her nightdress, and as his hands took possession of her breasts she imagined how it would be if things were different. She imagined him lifting her gently and carrying her to the bed.

Instead, he pinched her nipples and bit her neck. She swallowed a scream of intense pleasure and fisted her hands in his shirt. Ran her palms down his solid chest, his hard stomach, to the thick bulge at the front of his breeches. Impatiently he worked the placket and freed himself. He was hot—satin and iron in her hands. She stroked his length with both hands and he groaned. She loved the power her touch had over him and she stroked him again and again while he worshiped her breasts, suckled her already-puckered nipples, molded her flesh in his hands.

But then he moved lower, out of her reach, burning his mouth across her belly, pushing her legs apart with his hands.

She balked, but he was having none of it. He dipped his tongue into her navel and drew a hot, moist line with it to the top of her woman's hair, as though he was going to—

Oh.

She gasped when his tongue found her slit. His hands held her in place, urging her legs apart. Letting her thighs fall open while he tasted her most secret places was an act of submission she almost couldn't bear— there was nowhere to hide. His tongue feasted on her pleasure spot and found her entrance, thrusting inside. He found another pleasure spot there—one she hadn't known existed.

Her control fled. She strained her legs wide, submission forgotten, trying to push herself closer to that wicked tongue. Pleasure ripped through her in breathless convulsions. He made an inarticulate sound against her flesh as her body clenched hard, hard, hard in release.

He stood up, and she felt his erection against her.

Already she wanted the rest of him. "I don't think I can stand," she whispered.

"I have no intention of letting you try," he rasped against her ear as he lifted her up. "Wrap your legs around me, Katherine."

She did, and cried out into his kiss when he entered her in one thick stroke. He turned with her in his arms and carried her to the bed with their bodies joined, hiking one knee onto the mattress as he laid her down.

His eyes lit with unholy fire. "I don't want to be outside you even long enough to shed my clothes," he told her fiercely, already finding a rhythm, thrusting long and deep. She worked the buttons on his shirt, desperate to touch him the way she hadn't been able to in her coach.

After a moment he cursed. "Damn these breeches," he growled, and withdrew from her completely to strip them off and yank his shirt over his head. His full erection glistened with her own moisture. In a heartbeat he fell over her and pierced her again, stretching her, filling her, sliding deep.

It wasn't enough. She returned his kiss madly, running her hands down his back, digging her fingers into his pumping buttocks, tilting and lifting her hips to meet his thrusts. He made an inarticulate sound against her mouth and rolled with her so she straddled him, with her hair spilling over them and his hands grasping her hips as he thrust up, up, up. Restless need coiled inside her, tightening, building. He lifted his head and caught her right nipple with his teeth, sucking hard, and her release exploded violently. Every intimate muscle convulsed around him as he kept thrusting, pushing, until finally she felt him let go, too.

Her body was still shuddering when he rolled them back and lay with his full weight on top of her and his length still buried in her. He pressed hot kisses to her jaw, her throat, her collarbone. She hooked her legs around his as if, somehow, it would pull him closer.

He lifted his head and looked hard into her eyes.

"Did you really believe," he breathed raggedly, "that I would sit idly by and allow you to marry another man?"

Her pulse leaped. With his body buried in hers, all her defenses were down. But something had caught her eye that was impossible to miss: a simple necklace of twine and beads circling his neck.

She ran her finger along the beads. "You still wear it."

He searched her face, her eyes, and said nothing. Suddenly she wanted to cry. She traced the curve of his lips, and he caught her fingertip in his teeth. "And you have fresh bruises," she said.

"Your guard dog is nothing if not tenacious. Apparently someone told him that I compromised you." The corners of his eyes creased, and he arched a brow. "You surprise me, Katherine."

"Phil waylaid me the moment I returned from the hearing." And she was going to get an earful about her loose tongue.

"With your hair falling down and your lips red and swollen."

"I didn't stand a chance."

"I would imagine not." He kissed her again. Deeply. Thoroughly.

Her tongue trembled with things she wanted to tell him—things she didn't know how to put words to. Even if she could find the words, she wasn't sure she would speak them.

You fill me. Not just physically. He filled her heart. Her breath.

"William should not have hit you," she said between kisses.

"I deserved it. I should never have let you out of my

sight." With his elbows braced on either side of her, he framed her face in his strong hands. "Understand me well—I do not intend to do so again. God, Katherine—" He breathed the words against her mouth, and she looked into his eyes. They were so beautiful, so green, and filled with the fierce possession of a man who had what he wanted.

What if…

She gripped his solid buttocks and urged him closer, as though it was possible for him to be even deeper inside her than he already was. As though she could have more of him. He groaned and held her even more tightly.

"James," she whispered, wanting to hear his name on her lips. Her own name echoed back on his breath.

What if…

She threaded her legs through his and pressed her mouth to the cords of his neck while he held her as though she were the only woman in the world.

He'd made it clear he wanted her for himself, and now she felt herself falling, tumbling out of control.

What if she let herself surrender?

CHAPTER THIRTY-FOUR

THEY SPENT THE night making love. Even after James fell asleep pressed against her back with his hand on her breast, Katherine lay awake with her body rippling and pulsing with sensation. The musky blend of James's spice and the heady scent of their lovemaking filled every breath. His breathing came deep and even in the darkness, while invisible stones of truth piled up and crushed the air from her lungs.

In the early morning half light she slipped out of bed, found her discarded nightdress and went to the window. Offshore, two ships slowly rocked with the waves, anchored in the bluish-gray mist.

There were places in her heart that had surrendered without awaiting the command.

She closed her eyes and saw his face, drunk with desire and emotion as he sank himself into her. The memory of it shuddered through her. Only half of their lovemaking had been a quest for sexual pleasure; the other half had been a desperate attempt to crawl inside each other's skin, as though—as though this fierce yearning inside her chest couldn't be satisfied by something as simple as the stroke of his body.

She was falling in love.

The thought made her shiver. It couldn't be love.

Love would be too…binding. It would make her too vulnerable.

The solid bed didn't creak, so she didn't realize James had gotten up until his voice sounded behind her. "Dreaming of better days?" he asked softly, putting his hands on her shoulders.

She trembled beneath his touch. Had he always been capable of such gentleness? Of course he had. It had been evident enough in his relationship with Anne. "They'll be weighing anchor soon," she said of the ships.

Surrender…

"Yes." His hands were a whisper on her skin, brushing her hair aside. "Out with the tide." He pressed a kiss to the curve of her neck and shoulder, soft and sweet.

"Headed for the West Indies, perhaps. Or the Levant."

"Or Sunderland." He laughed quietly, running his hands down her arms. He stood naked behind her, solid and strong. If she were a different kind of woman, it would be so easy to lean on him. To let him take care of her.

"How do you suppose Millie and India are faring?" she asked.

"That depends on the crew they've hired. But they'll be no match for William."

"No." She watched the ships offshore and imagined the *Possession* there, empty and waiting.

He pressed more lazy kisses to her skin. Found a sensitive spot behind her ear.

"Dunscore is magnificent, Katherine," he whispered. "Frozen in time. Every time I enter the main hall, I expect to see a group of knights strategizing for battle.

It would make an excellent fortress." Low and teasing against her ear, he added, "Or pirate's lair."

"Hush," she scolded, smiling a little. "It would make a terrible pirate's lair. The coastline is flat for miles. Nowhere to hide the ship."

"Ah, well. A retired pirate's lair, then."

A retired pirate and a retired naval captain. She craved his presence the way some men craved strong drink. She wanted to see him laugh, hear him talk, watch him lift Anne into the air. "I'm not a pirate," she reminded him.

Another kiss burned her neck, and another. "Please— allow me my fantasies at least occasionally," he said against her skin.

She had her own fantasies. She imagined standing at the potting bench with James, showing Anne how to poke her fingers into tiny pots of soil and plant seeds. Walking the beach with Anne between them, stopping to pick up stones and shells and little crabs that would pinch Anne's fingers and make her squeal.

"Is Croston anything like Dunscore?" she asked.

"Nothing. Croston is a modern monstrosity, a mere hundred and fifty years old, give or take a decade or two. Built by my great-great-great—" he paused "—great-grandfather."

"But certainly you love it."

"I suppose I do. Haven't spent any time there since I took the title, though. Been at sea the entire time."

He must have looked magnificent standing on the deck of a gigantic frigate with his uniform gleaming in the sunshine. She didn't know that man at all, but she knew another—a swarthy, square-jawed sailor holding his face to the sun while the sea breeze played idly with his hair. "Do you miss it at all?" she asked. "The sea?"

"No." His hands caressed delicious circles on her shoulders and arms, and she felt him press his face into her hair. "Maybe a little," he amended. "The sea air doesn't smell the same from shore."

"No, it doesn't." All she had to do was lean back and close her eyes and ask the question that burned inside her. *Is your offer of marriage still open?*

"But it would take a press gang of a hundred men to force me back into service." His voice took on a bitter edge. "Thank God there are a dozen young officers lined up behind me, eager to take their turn at making a name for themselves. The admirals will soon turn their attention to someone more promising."

"I doubt any will earn your reputation."

"They will if they're ruthless enough."

He didn't have to say more. She could read his thoughts in the tone of his voice. He was remembering a career defined by horror. One violent incident after the next—often instigated by his own command—culminating in the wreck of the *Henry's Cross*. He'd never admitted it aloud, but she knew he counted that among his personal failings. "What kinds of decisions do you suppose a captain bound for Sunderland has to make?" she mused.

"At which tavern he'll take his grog, for one," James answered with a nip on her shoulder. Humor returned to his voice. "And with which whore he'll pass the night."

A wicked shiver passed across her skin. "Weighty decisions indeed."

"You never answered my question. What do you see

when you look at those ships? Do you think of returning to the Med? Dream of the West Indies?"

The dark shapes on the water grew more distinct
with every passing moment. Even from this distance
she could see the sails going up. "I've always dreamed
of them."

"And yet you never went."

"There was fortune aplenty to be made on the Mediterranean. I had no reason to cross the Atlantic and face
the unknown. Especially not with Anne." She watched
another white sail billow to life, and another. "I see a
thousand ways for Anne to be injured," she said. "That's
what I see when I look at those ships."

His arms came around her and he held her tight. Her
throat closed over at the terrifying safety of his embrace. After a moment, she let herself lean back. He
was solid, immovable.

Marry me, Katherine. If he said the words again,
would she accept? She imagined his ring sitting with
heavy finality on her finger, and she tasted fear.

"As long as I draw breath," he whispered, "I shall
do anything in my power to keep her safe. Wherever
I am, whatever I'm doing, one word and I'll come for
her. You have my promise."

Disappointment stole her breath. Those were not
the words of a man with a proposal on the tip of his
tongue. "Anne is my responsibility," she said quietly.
"Not yours."

He was quiet for a moment. "My promise stands,
regardless."

Marry me, Katherine.

He wasn't going to repeat those words now. Instead,
he drew up the hem of her nightgown and caressed her

thighs. Desire flamed across her skin, mocking the turmoil in her heart. "You should return to your room before the household awakes," she said.

"Agreed. And I will." His fingers began an intimate exploration. One finger slid home, then two. "Soon."

THEY MADE LOVE once more in the predawn. It was five o'clock when James returned to his room. Moments after he left, Katherine silently let herself into the hallway and crept up a back staircase and down an upper corridor, up more stairs and out onto the ramparts. A brisk, humid wind caught her in the face and snuck its fingers down her shawl and nightgown to nip places still warm from James's touch.

She needed to find some sense. Some sanity.

Love was hurling its cannonballs at her, destroying her resistance. And just like a cannonfire attack, one didn't need prior experience to tell when it was happening—or how destructive it could be. The rubble shifted and settled in fits and starts every time James defied her expectations.

She hadn't gone five paces when a body stepped around the corner ahead of her. "William!" Her heart leaped, then settled. "If you'd startled me this way aboard the *Possession,* I would have had you flogged," she snapped.

He flashed that white-toothed grin of his that had no business appearing in the predawn hours. "Makes me miss the sea something fierce when you talk that way."

"Well, you'll be going back to it soon enough," she said irritably. "Maybe you ought to start today. Now, in fact."

"A few extra days' delay in securing a ship and provisions isn't going to make a difference. I'm not leaving here until I see you wed to James."

"William!"

"I would say wedded and bedded, but I can see the second part's been taken care of already."

"You see nothing," she scoffed.

He laughed, leaving her wondering what had given her away, and whether anyone else would notice it. Beyond him, the surf crashed against the rocky beach and the two ships she'd seen from the window were tiny white dots in the distance. "If it's a wedding you came to see, you'll have to satisfy yourself with seeing me wed to Lord Deal."

"The hell I will."

"We've already made arrangements."

"The hell you have," William said. "Never would have let Croston into your room last night."

"Arrangements are forthcoming." Guilt gnawed at her. It was one thing to present herself to Lord Deal as the victim of unfortunate circumstances. It was something else entirely to go to him in marriage still warm from another man's attentions.

Yet maybe it didn't matter. If Lord Deal agreed to marry her, it would not be for love. And he certainly didn't expect to find her chaste.

"Sounds to me like Croston's babe might well be forthcoming. What will you do then? Pass it off as Deal's?"

Katherine looked away, turning her face to the wind. The plan was damning, phrased that way.

"Good God," William said. "Even you aren't that ruthless."

"Lord Deal is kind. And amusing," she added, ignoring his question. "I like him." All she had to do was refuse to open her door tonight when James knocked—and there was no doubt that he would—and make sure what they'd done never happened again.

If only it were that simple. If only what she and James had done had just been...what they'd done.

William reached out with a familiar gesture and pulled a strand of hair from her face. "You could never do what you're suggesting. Know you too well."

Sudden emotion welled into her throat, and by the time she felt the tears burning her eyes it was too late to stop them.

William's hands clamped over her shoulders. "Did Croston hurt you?"

She could only shake her head and gulp a breath of air as a tear leaked out. "I do not want to talk about this," she said fiercely. "William, about the *Possession*—"

"Don't worry, pet. I'll bring her back safe."

"No, do not bring her back here." Her breath shook, but she forced the words out, anyway. "When you find her, William, she shall be yours."

"Katherine—"

"I mean it. I shall have no need of her now." It hurt to say the words.

"That's not a choice that needs making. I will return her to you regardless. You and Croston can decide what to do with her." He brushed a wisp of hair from her face. "Consider her return my wedding gift to you. Now, suppose you tell me why you don't want to talk about Croston."

The gentleness in William's voice was too much, and the words tumbled out. "He makes me...want things... I can't have."

"What things?" William asked, pulling her close. "And why can't you have them?"

She buried her face against his shoulder and breathed his familiar scent—that exotic, Ottoman oil he favored. She wanted to give James everything. She wanted to offer him her heart and have him accept it like a precious jewel. She wanted to hear Anne call him Papa. She wanted to take him to the ramparts and show him how the land stretched for miles and miles and tell him of her plans and dreams.

They were so fragile, those plans and dreams. Yet with the slightest encouragement, she would tell him everything. The most secret longings of her heart.

"He makes me want to surrender," she confessed on a fresh wave of tears, and she felt William tense.

"Surrendered already, haven't you?"

"He makes me want to surrender *everything,* William. My heart, my mind—I've become the foolish, romantic girl I've always scorned."

William set her back and framed her face. "Katherine, listen to me. I'm all for you marrying Croston—"

"He hasn't renewed his proposal."

"Renewed."

Katherine looked away.

"You are the most stubborn woman in creation. He'll renew it in the morning—stake my life on it. But think twice before giving him your heart, Katherine. You'll only regret it. Worked too hard for your freedom."

"I know." But leaning against James this morning felt more like entering a safe harbor than admitting defeat. Another tear leaked out, and another. She knew all about safe harbors. There weren't any.

William searched her eyes. "Haven't seen you cry in years."

She tried to remember another time she'd cried in front of William, but the only one she could think of was the time they'd nearly lost him to infection when he'd taken that wound in his cheek. She'd loved him so much, and the thought of losing him— "I can't love him, William. I *can't*."

"Love?" His grip on her tightened.

"I'm so afraid. The things he makes me feel— It's gone too far. He is overpowering my will."

"Lust, Katherine. Pure and simple. I promise."

"How can you be sure?"

"Done it a few more times than you, I daresay. Good God." He pressed a kiss against her forehead. "You're not the type to succumb to love, Kate. Been in slavery once already—won't let it happen again. You're too strong."

But this didn't feel like slavery had. It was something entirely different—more of a softening. An opening. "I don't know."

"Listen to me. Don't let Croston turn you into a spineless featherhead. Give him your body, your respect even, but don't give him what's inside you."

She stared at him, unable to believe it. She'd given James her body, and now she'd all but lost control over it. And she was at risk of giving, and losing, so much more. "What if it's too late?"

"It's not too late. Didn't you just threaten to have me flogged?" His grin was a momentary flash that hardened almost instantly. "Your threats only prove the Katherine I know is still here."

The only thing her threats proved was that William was still capable of aggravating her to no end.

"My ferocious, bloodthirsty corsair," William murmured, catching her tears with his thumbs. "You're a powerful woman, not a foolish child, and you're much too shrewd to succumb to this kind of romantic fluff. Take him to your bed, if it pleases you. Marry him because he's the best of your choices—I won't see you married to anyone less, mark my words—and God knows he'll make an honest woman of you or he'll answer to me. Enjoy the bastard's company, even. But don't let it be more than that."

It was already too late for that. She broke away from him and went to the rampart wall where it faced the sea. Below, the east tower's ruins sat in a wretched heap. She ran her hands over the cold turret stone, letting her fingers play in the pocks left behind by Papa and his friends the night they'd decided to fire their pistols at a row of bottles.

How could Dunscore have meant so little to him, when it meant so much to her?

William joined her at the railing. "Didn't hear you agree," he said quietly.

That was because she was too afraid he was wrong. It would be impossible to marry James and not lose herself to him. "If only there were some word from the committee," she said.

"I heard nothing before we left London. Croston himself said it was too soon."

"Yes. I know." But there would be no mercy from the committee, and she didn't expect any.

She touched the ragged spot where an entire corner had been shot away. She would have it repaired. She would have everything repaired. Before the month was out, there would be a crew of masons rebuilding the east tower and an army of gardeners coaxing the rose garden back to life.

The two ships were barely visible on the horizon now. *A ship can only have one captain, and I prefer to be it.*

If she didn't do something to steer herself on course, everything she'd worked so hard to gain would be crushed. *She* would be crushed. She needed to solidify things with Lord Deal now—today—before she lost herself completely to James.

CHAPTER THIRTY-FIVE

THE NEWS OF the committee's decision had not yet reached Dunscore.

It was the critical fact that pounded through James's thoughts as he thundered across the countryside toward Deal Manor with the night's sensations still thrumming in his blood.

Last night had made one thing clear: he needed Katherine like a cannon needed powder. Like a sail needed wind.

The way she'd felt in his embrace this morning—he'd wanted to renew his proposal right then and there. But he wasn't a fool. He knew Katherine too well to believe last night had changed her mind about anything.

That she still believed she needed to marry was his only hope for success.

Deal Manor came into view, and a familiar feeling coursed through his veins. An old exhilaration surged up from some hidden place. His strategy unfolded before him.

With any luck, this one confrontation would be all that was necessary.

James dismounted outside Deal Manor, rehearsing his attack as he handed off the reins. Once Deal was no longer an option for her, his marriage to Katherine would be all but assured.

Inside, he found Deal comfortably seated in his breakfast room. A copy of the *Edinburgh Courant* lay open with a scattering of crumbs dusting its pages.

"Had an uncanny feeling I might be seeing you," Deal said.

"Oh?"

Deal only smiled and gestured to the empty chair at his small table nestled in a bay of tall windows. "Please, be seated. I'll call for an extra plate."

James preferred to stand, but there was no need to be an ass. "No need for the plate. I've already eaten." It was a lie. Food was the last thing he could stomach this morning. A maid poured him a cup of coffee before being dismissed by Deal, and James sipped the brew even though he would have preferred something stronger. Good Scotch whiskey, for example.

"I'll come straight to the point," James said. "Whatever your understanding with Lady Dunscore, I want you to break it. I am prepared to negotiate an incentive."

Deal took a bite of some dark bread, unperturbed save for a slight raising of his bushy brows. "And if the promise of an incentive doesn't tempt me, you'll resort to stronger measures, I suppose."

James tamped down a flare of anger. "I'll do whatever is necessary."

Deal chewed his bread and took a sip of tea. "I can see now why Katherine said you were unsuitable."

James's gut pitched sharply. "Katherine thinks anyone in breeches is unsuitable."

"But she has too volatile a nature to hide her emotions well, and when we discussed marriage it was clear her love lay elsewhere."

Her *love*. James squelched a callow urge to embark on a fishing expedition.

"I asked her if she'd left someone behind in London—someone who'd broken her heart, perhaps—" Deal gave him a pointed look "—but she said no, that there was nobody appropriate. Now I can see perhaps she was right. Do you really think to win Katherine by threats and bribes?"

"I will have Katherine by whatever method it takes. Have you come to an understanding?"

"That, Croston, is a question you should be asking her."

"I'm asking you."

"I certainly won't deny Katherine my help, though I'll admit I haven't yet decided what form it should take." There was a stubborn set to Deal's face that James didn't like.

"Perhaps I can help you decide," James said coldly. "Katherine may be carrying my child. And even were that not the case, there's a good chance that after last night it would be."

Deal set down his bread and looked James in the eye. "Impertinent bastard. I would call you out for besmirching her if it wasn't plain as day you're besotted. A man in love deserves a measure of mercy, I suppose."

In love. The idea grabbed him by the throat and for a moment he couldn't breathe.

Deal gave James a look he hadn't received since school days. "My only question is how you plan to make her say the vows. Will you hold a pistol on her?"

Somehow he managed to inhale. "I'll take care of it."

"You think to leave her no choice, is that it? Make yourself the only option? A faulty premise, my boy, as

you well know. A rich estate and a beautiful countess—
even a seafaring one—is bound to be a powerful lure.
Been thinking of a few suggestions these past days. Mc-
Gowan, for example. He's young enough. Solid estate.
Weogh wouldn't be a bad choice, either."

"I'll tell any man that tries exactly what I told you,"
James said darkly.

Deal narrowed his eyes. "You'll ruin her in your attempt to have her?"

He was in love.

In *love*. The certainty of it snaked down on the inside of him and curled up tight.

"I'll do anything to have her," he said flatly.

Wasn't that what a man in love was supposed to do?

KATHERINE STEPPED OUT of her carriage in front of Lord
Deal's house, where dozens of hoofprints in the dough-
soft mud made the ground uneven and hard to walk on
in her slippers. Obviously hers was not the first visit of
the morning. There were muddy footprints on the steps
and in the entranceway.

"My dear, what a lovely surprise," Lord Deal said,
meeting her in the entry. "Come, come—I'm just fin-
ishing my breakfast." A few crumbs on his mustache
attested to the truth of it. "Will you have anything? A
bit of fruit, perhaps? Tea?"

Brandy, more like. "Tea would be nice, thank you."
He guided her into the sitting room where his breakfast table was set up by the window. His gait was more
shuffly this morning than it had been before, and he
nearly lost his balance when they walked from the floor
to the carpet. She put out a hand to help him.

"There's a good girl. My bones just aren't what they

used to be. Been having some trouble this morning—weather must be changing." He gestured her to a chair at his table and sat down. A maid hurried over and whisked away the cup from his last visitor and replaced it with a fresh one. "Has something happened? Is everything all right with your guests?"

"Nothing has happened. William has gone to Edinburgh, and Lord Croston has been out on a morning ride." She took a breath. "I fear waiting much longer given the uncertainty with the committee. I've come to find out what I can do to help you come to your decision."

"Ah, I see." He buttered a thick slice of dark currant bread and chewed thoughtfully. "Nothing should be decided before you meet McGowan. I'm certain I can arrange something within the next few days."

"I do not wish to meet Lord McGowan," she said sharply, and Lord Deal raised a brow. "Forgive me," she said. "It's just that I have my heart set on you."

The brow lowered, and he reached for his tea. "Tell me, Katherine—" he sipped and set the cup down "—has Lord Croston made you an offer?"

She froze. "No." The lie rolled off her tongue like a sour grape.

"You're quite certain? Not even a hint? London is a terribly long journey to bring a bit of news that could have been written in a letter."

She hesitated a moment too long.

"He did make an offer, then," he said.

"Anything Lord Croston might have suggested was not meant to be serious."

Lord Deal laughed. "My dear, if a man like Croston

offers marriage, I assure you it is serious. You rejected him, didn't you. Why?"

"He is unsuitable."

"Yes, I believe you mentioned that once already. But why is he unsuitable? He seems a solid enough fellow, and his estate is larger than McGowan's and Arran's put together. And you've got much in common. It seems a perfect match."

"It isn't."

"Why not?"

Because it couldn't be. Because she felt too much when she was with him. Because she was in love, and everything William said about that was true. "Lord Croston is too demanding. He wants to be in command—of everything."

"Well yes, I suppose I've seen that in him."

"I won't stand for it."

"Forgive me, my dear, but are you not just as commanding?"

She smiled tightly. "As you heard him say in front of the committee, a ship cannot have two captains."

"Ah, yes. Well, I suppose that's true enough." He looked at her hard across the table, letting his false senility fall completely away. "Are you in love with him?"

"Certainly not." Her cheeks flamed, putting the lie to her words.

"Is he in love with you?"

"I'm sure he's not."

"Really?"

She shot to her feet. "Enough of this. Lord Deal, I will not marry Lord Croston. And even if I would, he has not renewed his offer, and—"

"So try accepting the first one."

She stared at Lord Deal across the table, and he stared back with knowing brown eyes. God help her, this was not going the way she planned. After a moment, he pushed his chair back and stood. "My dear—" he came around the table and stood looking down at her "—I cannot in good conscience proceed with an engagement to you under anything less than the direst exigency."

"Then let us proceed."

He put a finger against her lips. "Why are you so afraid of him? You, who seem afraid of nothing."

She was a rabbit caught in the open, staring at him with the pressure of his finger keeping her silent. *I love him.*

"I've seen love change more than one man, Katie." He removed his finger, and his eyes turned deadly serious. "Tell me right now that he's been unkind to you, that he's used you badly, that he's been violent—tell me right now, in all possible honesty, that you truly wish to marry me and not him, and God help me, I'll do it."

She couldn't find a single word.

CHAPTER THIRTY-SIX

IT WAS A BLOODY close call. James had seen Katherine's carriage trundling toward Deal Manor and quickly turned his horse down a side road through a thicket of alarmingly sparse vegetation. It was almost certain she hadn't spotted him.

All afternoon he waited for the opportunity to renew his proposal, to argue his case, all the while expecting every moment to see a rider approaching the castle with news of the vote.

It didn't arrive.

And the opportunity he sought remained elusive.

The afternoon clouds burned away, and the sun shone brilliantly over the damp moors. They took Anne to the barn, sat her on a shaggy pony named Bess and walked her around the meadow. Katherine had put wildflowers in Anne's hair, laughed freely—more freely than before?—and turned her face to the breeze. James tried to guess what Deal might have said to her that morning, whether he might have said anything that would assure James's success.

It was impossible to tell.

They took Anne to the beach, followed by a goldfish feeding frenzy at the pond. Anne stuck her hands in the water and squealed as the small fish nibbled at her fingers. Katherine stuck her fingers in, too, and splashed water at him. He splashed back until they both looked as if they'd been standing at the bow of a ship in a storm, and he'd loved her so much in that moment he'd almost asked her again to marry him, timing be damned.

And now time was running out. If they came to an understanding tonight, they could marry in the morning—blessed be liberal Scottish law. He would waste no time consummating the union, and then if the news did arrive it would be too late. They would set out for London immediately on pretense of ending the whole business by making the marriage known, and he could pretend he'd missed the vote by a hairsbreadth before setting out for Dunscore. She would find out eventually, but by then she would be irrevocably his.

He would make sure she didn't regret it.

As night fell, James contemplated this with a glass of brandy clenched in his fist and heat from a blazing fire in the great hall scorching his face. She'd gone upstairs to tuck Anne into bed, but soon she would return, and then he would need to finish his plan.

But Katherine would not accept him in marriage as easily as she had accepted him into her bed. Stubborn woman. Hold a pistol to her head and force her to say the vows? If it would have resulted in a binding contract, he would have tried it already.

I'll do anything to have her. Guilt slithered through the back of his mind, but he shoved it aside. This was the only way. Other men might have tried following her like a puppy, yapping pretty words of love and devotion. Such a man would have had his hopes skewered on the end of her cutlass.

Telling her he loved her—good God. That bloody well wouldn't work, either.

No, Katherine was like an enemy ship. She would have to be captured.

He was so consumed by his thoughts that he didn't notice Katherine approaching until she stood next to him. He turned to her, feeling his liquor more than he'd realized. She was beautiful—his very own fantasy in the flesh, standing there in a simple blue gown with all that dark silk falling over her shoulders. God help him, he lost a part of himself every time he looked at her. She commanded his world, whether he wanted her to or not.

She held a glass half-full of wine. In the firelight, the liquid glinted the same dark pink as her most intimate flesh. "Come," she said quietly, holding out her hand. "I have something to show you."

His pulse leaped. He was in no mood for surprises, but he would follow her anywhere. He took her hand and she led him out of the main hall, down the main corridor, up a back staircase. They turned down another corridor, climbed narrower staircases and followed narrower hallways. Finally she pushed open an ancient wooden door, and they emerged onto Dunscore's ramparts.

The view stole his breath. Above them, the night sky glittered with stardust. A slender crescent moon hung over the horizon to the west, where a faint blue glow was quickly fading. To the east, the shadowy ocean surged against the beach in shimmering crashes of froth.

She released his hand and went to the waist-high rampart wall, setting down her glass and laying her hands flat against the stone. "Lovely, isn't it?"

He stared at her back. Something had changed. "Magnificent."

"This is where I always came to think. Or sometimes, just to look at the stars." She tipped her head back and looked up. "Sometimes I would talk to my mother and imagine she was up there somewhere, listening."

Her mother. James's pulse ticked hard in his throat. There was only one reason she might be telling him this. Wasn't there?

"I have no doubt that she was," he said, and joined her at the rampart wall. His tongue was thick with the need to ask about her visit to Lord Deal. Perhaps— God. Perhaps this was her way of turning to him now that Deal had ended things. He took a drink of brandy and swallowed his questions, keeping his eyes fixed on the sea.

"Do you ever watch the stars?" she asked him.

He didn't give a rat's arse about the bloody stars. Not right now. "At sea," he told her. "On the night watch."

"Mmm. The stars are beautiful at sea."

Marry me, Katherine. He would have to say it sometime.

"Sometimes we watched the stars in Algiers," she said quietly. "Mejdan's fourth daughter had a small telescope that she would set up in the courtyard, and we would take turns viewing the stars and planets."

Every muscle tensed. She noticed, and he felt her tense, too. "You don't wish me to speak of that," she said.

"You may speak of whatever you damn well please." Sick apprehension caught him in the gut, but whatever horrors she revealed, he could withstand it.

But why now? Here?

"I declined Lord Deal's offer of marriage," she told him instead.

"His *offer*." For a heartbeat the world froze.

"It was pure kindness," she said quietly. "Lord Deal is a dear friend—he would do anything for Papa. For me."

Despite their conversation earlier. James's heart thundered in his chest. If she had accepted, he would have killed Deal with his bare hands. But then—

"You declined?" A powerful sense of victory surged through him.

"He wasn't what I wanted." Hope flooded him, but then she added, "Not that it wouldn't have been... tolerable."

"Tolerable."

"Living with a kind man is not so awful." She looked him straight in the eye. "Anne's father was such a man."

That quickly, they were back to Algiers. He tried to digest her words but couldn't. "You describe your captor as *tolerable?*"

"No. I describe him as kindhearted."

Kindhearted. James thought about the time he'd spent in Salé trying to negotiate her freedom, only to discover she'd been gifted to al-Zayar.

"Full of smiles and laughter, if not vim and vigor," she went on quietly. Directly. Softly, with something like nostalgia in her voice. "His physicians said he had a bad heart. But he loved to play in the courtyard with the children, and he treated his dogs like royalty. No creatures were ever so pampered."

"His dogs."

"Spoiled. Each and every one."

"And his slaves?"

Even in the darkness, he saw her eyes flash. "The

dreadful tale of ravishment and horror you imagine is the stuff of novels."

"Anne's existence says it isn't."

Her hand flew up to slap him. He caught her arms and held it firmly. "I meant no insult by that." Bathed in starlight, her face looked like porcelain. He felt her arm relax, and he released it.

"I need you to understand," she said desperately, gripping his shirt. "You *must* understand."

Ah, God. He framed her face, pushed his fingers into her hair. "I do. I do understand. God knows, we tried to convince al-Zayar to accept a ransom." The futility of it stung bitterly even now. "I can only imagine how you must have prayed—"

"No—that's not it at all. Don't you see? Can't you see how much better my life was with Mejdan than it would have been if I'd been ransomed and brought home?"

"Better!" He tightened his fingers in her hair, wanting the impossible: to kill a man that, according to her testimony before the committee, was already dead.

"You know bloody well the life that awaited me here. The whispers, the ostracism, the kind of man who would have offered for poor, ruined Lady Katherine."

He forced himself to inhale. "And the alternative?"

"Studying the stars through Kisa's telescope." Her expression softened, and her fisted hands uncurled against his chest. "Savoring pomegranate seeds on a hot day. Trying not to laugh when Mejdan's mother scolded us for talking too much." She searched his face. "Please understand, James. I thought I would live there forever. It wasn't a large household. We all lived together— Mejdan's wives, daughters."

Concubines.

"They were my friends. My family, even."

"Until al-Zayar died."

A shadow darkened her eyes.

"You *grieve* for him." He caught himself before sharper words shot from his lips.

"He never mistreated me. It could have been so much worse. Would have been, if his mother hadn't helped me that night. James, *please*—"

"I know. I know." He struggled to calm himself in the face of something he couldn't change. "I understand."

KATHERINE COULD SEE it was a lie. Even in the near-dark, his murderous expression was clear: he wanted to raise Mejdan from the dead just for the pleasure of killing him. Perhaps it had been a mistake to entrust James with this. But if they were to be married…

Oh, God.

Perhaps this entire thing was folly. He still had not renewed his proposal. *Marry me, Katherine.* The words were so simple. Why had he not said them?

She needed to make him understand about Algiers. "Without Riuza's help, I would have been trapped when Mejdan's son took over the household, and all could have been exactly as you imagine." James's chest was taut beneath her hands, rising and falling with his angry breath.

"You should have gone to the consulate."

"With Anne in my belly?"

"At least you would have been safe!"

"I *was* safe."

"Rowing out with William to steal a ship from the harbor? Good God. When I think what you must have endured…" His arms came around her, and he held her tightly against him.

His furious heartbeat thudded in her ear. "*Endure* is relative. You know that."

"You never should have had to endure anything," he said against her hair. "And I intend to see that you never do again."

Never again. She pulled back a little and tried to read his thoughts, but couldn't. She made herself take a chance. "I don't want to spend the rest of my life seeing pity in your eyes and knowing you see me as a tragedy."

"That's not what I see, Katherine. Not at all." She saw the moment he realized what she'd said. His hands came to her face. "Then you'll marry me?" The words might have sounded like a command if not for the uncertainty coloring them.

"I will." She barely managed the words.

His hands tightened a little on her cheeks. "Immediately. Tomorrow morning."

It was mere hours away. Her pulse danced wildly. "I suppose that would be wise," she said, cursing the nerves in her voice. "Under the circumstances. Do you not agree?"

A muscle flexed in his jaw, and triumph flashed in his eyes. Instead of answering, he kissed her.

CHAPTER THIRTY-SEVEN

NICK SAT ACROSS the desk from Lord Cantwell, negotiating his own future with all the warmth and excitement of a shipping transaction. In fact, it *was* a shipping transaction—a bloody irregular one.

"I have good reason to believe my daughter is headed for the Mediterranean," Cantwell was saying. "You would agree to pursue her all the way there, if necessary?"

For fifty thousand pounds, he would pursue her to the bloody interior of China. "I will."

"As a condition of this marriage, I shall expect nothing less."

"Nor shall I."

Cantwell exhaled. Bushy blond brows dove over bright blue eyes, and he assessed Nick over steepled hands. "It's not in my interest to say this, but my daughter is a wild harridan. Marriage to her won't be easy."

"Under the circumstances, I didn't expect that it would." But it would be profitable, and that was all that mattered. "I shall find her and bring her back to England, where I assure you I shall keep her under control."

Cantwell gave a laugh. "I assure you, Taggart, if it were that easy, *I* would have kept her under control. In any case, I intend to obtain a special dispensation.

Although I expect the marriage to be performed at the earliest opportunity once you find her. I don't care how you get it done—only that you do. You won't find any challenge from me on that point."

"Understood." Cantwell had no cause for concern. It was either this or lose Taggart to Holliswell, and Nick wasn't going to risk letting the answer to all his problems slip from his grasp. He would marry Lady India the moment he found her.

"And in the meantime," Cantwell went on, "I shall speak with Mr. Holliswell." Cantwell smiled. "You won't need to concern yourself there."

Nick might have smiled, too, under other circumstances. Already his thoughts hurtled forward. He was engaged to be married, after all—this time, to save himself.

THE HASTY WEDDING and hurried coach ride hardly left time to think. At the same time, there'd been too much time to think, staring for hours and hours at the passing countryside, unable to speak of important matters in front of Anne and Miss Bunsby.

Married. To the man who had sunk the *Merry Sea.*

Now Katherine stood in her new apartment in James's London house, feeling as if she'd been tossed for days by high seas.

Married. To Captain Warre.

A warm feeling snuck through her—the same warm feeling she'd allowed herself to sample each time she'd looked at him in the coach. Each night at the inns where they stayed, when she watched him climb into bed with her. Each morning when she woke to find herself in his arms.

Every moment she expected to realize she'd made an enormous, irreversible mistake. But then he would look at her with those green eyes full of satisfaction, on fire for the woman she was, with no trace of the pity she feared. And a little more of her resistance would slough away, leaving behind something new and hopeful and alive.

He strode into her room now, all outrage. "Good God—I'll dismiss every last one of them!" A maid scurried out, and she watched him bolt the bedroom door against the savage hordes masquerading as footmen bringing in their trunks.

"Would you rather the trunks had stayed on the coach?" she asked.

"I would rather not have to think of trunks at all," he said darkly, coming toward her. "Or footmen. Or—" he waved the letter Bates had given them on their arrival "—emergencies at Croston. I would much prefer to think exclusively—"

"Wait, what are you— Put me down!"

"—of you." He carried her to the bed and pinned her to it with his weight. "Very well. I shall happily keep you down for as long as you like." He bent his head for a searing kiss, and she drank it in hungrily.

This was no captivity.

That warm feeling worked its magic again, and she suppressed a bubble of laughter. The Lords would hardly attaint her now.

"It's late," he said, resting his forehead on hers, "but I'm determined to see Nick tonight, and a few others, as well."

"We probably have ten minutes at the most before

your sister learns we're in London and calls round," Katherine said.

"That long? Really? I'd say five, more like, and that's if your friend the Dowager Lady Pennington doesn't learn of it first." He raised a wicked brow. "One can accomplish much in five minutes."

"You're insatiable."

"I could say the same of you." He tugged on her lower lip with his teeth and kissed her again.

There was a knock. "Bates," he muttered, rolling off her and stalking to the door. He cracked it open with a terse suggestion for Bates's permanent holiday destination, and she heard poor Bates announce that Honoria was waiting in the salon.

James glanced over his shoulder at Katherine. "Six minutes. She's losing her touch." And then, to Bates, "Tell my sister we're not receiving."

He closed the door in Bates's face, but before he'd crossed the room there was another knock.

"That'll be Honoria herself," Katherine said, smiling at the expression on his face.

James wrenched the door open. "The Dowager Lady Pennington was just admitted below," Bates apprised them.

"Tell them *both* we're not receiving."

"James—" Katherine started.

"I mean it. I do not wish to be disturbed," he told Bates, and shut the door again.

"Refusing them now will only put off the inevitable," Katherine pointed out, and sat up. "I should go satisfy their curiosity. And you're going out anyhow."

"Their curiosity can wait," he said sharply, and a firm hand came down on her shoulder. For a moment she thought he might actually order her to stay, and all her defenses flared to life. Instead, he kissed her. A devilish curve tugged his lips when he pulled back, and he hooked a finger inside her stays to peek into her cleavage. "Mine can't."

That warm feeling sizzled, and she hooked a finger inside the top of his breeches. "Then let them wait."

She let him push her back onto the bed and stoke that feeling into a blazing fire.

"You've made a deal with *Cantwell?*" It was enough to make James forget—but only for a moment—that his entire marriage was on the brink of crashing down around him. He stared at Nick in disbelief through the coffeehouse's smoky haze.

"A damned profitable one, too. I only hope the girl isn't such a terror that the money pales in comparison. Even Cantwell admits she's a bloody harridan. And after two years at sea, there's little chance her virtue is intact." Nick's lip curled in mirthless appreciation. "Could be an enjoyable benefit, though."

James looked at him sharply. "I have it on good authority that her virtue *is* intact. So have a care."

"Good God." Nick took a long drink. "That makes it worse."

James smiled a little. "India isn't such a bad girl."

"She ran away on a ship. *Twice.*"

"I didn't say she wouldn't be time-consuming."

Nick cursed. "I'll be leaving England as soon as I plan my strategy for finding Lady India and organize passage. But if you'd like me to go to Croston first and take care of things, I will."

"No need," James said. "I want Katherine and Anne

to see the place." The tenant issue at Croston could not have been timed more perfectly. He could whisk Katherine away from London first thing in the morning and buy himself more time to figure out how to tell her about the vote.

If he hadn't succeeded in keeping her away from Honoria and Philomena earlier, there was no doubt she would have learned the truth from them. He'd be damned if he would allow that to happen. Fortunately for him, Honoria and Philomena cared for nothing if not romance, and they would not return tonight if they thought he and Katherine were occupied in bed.

"As far as passage, though, you ought to know that William Jaxbury is in Edinburgh outfitting a ship to chase after the *Possession*. It's the ship he's after, not the women—but that makes no difference for you. Your simplest chance may be to join forces with him."

Nick cursed again. "I'd thought to travel through France."

"Easier to scour the ports if you've got a ship." Unfortunately, Nick had fallen prey to seasickness his entire life. "Jaxbury will make a seaman out of you in no time."

Nick made a noise. "My one earthly desire."

"Are you certain it's worth it?"

Nick just looked at him.

"For God's sake, Nick, you don't have to do this." James didn't need to explain. Nick knew exactly what he meant, and reacted exactly as James expected he would.

"I won't take your money." Nick's eyes were so cold that James felt a little sorry for India. "Honoria tells me congratulations are in order," he said now.

"The king ought to put her to the task of improving

overseas communication times," James said irritably. "I've no doubt she could do it."

"You wish it to remain a secret?"

James rubbed his finger back and forth on the table, then looked at Nick. "I've done something unforgivable, and I don't know how to fix it."

Nick frowned. "What have you done?"

James sat back and exhaled. "Katherine doesn't know about the committee vote."

Nick stared at him, not comprehending.

"Because I didn't tell her," James clarified.

Nick's brows shot up. "You didn't *tell* her? But the committee voted before you— Good God." Another long stare, while the implications settled in. "So she thinks she's married you out of necessity."

James tightened his lips. For the millionth time he rechoreographed that day in Dunscore. This time, instead of going to Lord Deal, he'd gone to find Katherine and told her everything.

But if he had, he'd be alone now.

"And I fancied myself a fool with Clarissa," Nick said, shaking his head. "You'll have a hell of a time hiding it now. Too many people know what happened and when." He reached for his coffee. "Can't you simply grovel and tell her you love her?"

"She'll hardly believe it now."

"More likely she'll skewer your testicles with that cutlass of hers and hang 'em from her mainmast as she sails back where she came from."

And wasn't that the truth.

"But if there's anything I can do," Nick added.

James shook his head. "I have to tell her. If she

doesn't hear it from me, she'll hear it from someone else. And I definitely don't want to face the result if *that* happens."

CHAPTER THIRTY-EIGHT

NEARLY AN HOUR after James left, Katherine was on her way downstairs when someone called at the door. It would be Honoria and Phil, of course, returning to learn every last detail.

Instead, Bates admitted the Duke of Winston.

"May I offer my congratulations," he said as Katherine descended the stairs. "It would seem London's most ravishing pirate has finally been captured."

She surveyed his rakish black hair, his burgundy coat embroidered with a gold-and-black geometric pattern, and the sword that hung at his side. "I prefer to think of myself as having made a strategic defensive move," she told him.

He glanced at her hip as she joined him in the entrance hall. "At least reassure me you are unarmed this evening?"

She raised her brows and curved her lips a little.

"Very well." He grinned. "I shall be on my best behavior."

"And instead of your congratulations," she added meaningfully, "I would prefer your apologies."

He laughed. "Very well. You may have those, as well. And if there is ever a way I can make it up to you, you have only to name it. I confess to being on the blackguard side of things when it comes to beautiful women—and you are spectacularly beautiful, Lady Dunscore." His eyes flashed wickedly. "Forgive me. Lady *Croston*. Would seem Croston's a bit on the blackguard side of things, too. Should have suspected he fancied you for himself, for all he kept trying to fob you off on everyone else."

Fob her off?

"Never would have suited with any of them, I daresay. Although, if you should ever grow tired of Croston and care to, shall we say, expand your horizons..."

"I shall certainly keep you in mind," she said.

"Excellent. I need a few words with Croston. Is he at home?"

"No. He's gone out."

"And left you here alone? The man must have lost his mind." Wicked thoughts sparkled like dark jewels in his eyes.

"Either that, or he wishes to make sure the committee is in no doubt as to our marriage."

His brows flicked downward, but he smiled. "Rest assured, the committee was quite adamant in its decision. And for the record, I voted in your favor."

Voted? In her favor? Her mind scrambled to make sense of what he said. "I am flattered, Your Grace," she managed. "The committee has made a decision already?"

He cocked his head. "Surely you knew."

Her blood ran cold. "News is sometimes slow in traveling to Dunscore, and I was only there a few days." Her mind reeled. "You're saying the committee reported in my favor."

Something like alarm lit his eyes. "I would hate to

rob Croston of the pleasure of telling you himself," the duke said smoothly.

"When was the decision made?" she demanded.

He held up a hand. "Please—Croston will have my head if I discuss this with you further."

"When was the decision made?"

"If you'll excuse me, that light in your eye makes me damned nervous." He bowed hastily. "Good evening— a pleasure, as always."

LONG AFTER SHE and Miss Bunsby had put Anne to bed, Katherine waited in the library at James's desk. She sat in near darkness in the giant leather armchair that had been crafted for comfortable arrogance. The only light came from a fire that had burned low but still cracked and flickered. She smoothed her hands across an expanse of mahogany that screamed of power. Command.

Her own power and command lay buried beneath a heart that ached so badly she could hardly breathe.

That night on the ramparts, she'd told him things she'd never thought she would tell anyone. Things she hadn't even told William because he, with the brutal captivity he had suffered, would not understand.

James did not understand, either. She'd been thinking perhaps that was all right. That perhaps it had been unfair of her to ask him to try.

No, not unfair.

Unfair was James lying to her. Taking advantage of her ignorance after she'd given herself to him so completely.

A footman carrying a note to her solicitor had quickly confirmed the date of the committee's decision. Bates had claimed not to remember when James had left for Dunscore, but one of the stable boys had proved less forgetful.

James had known. He'd bloody *known* what it meant to her, and he'd still tricked her into marriage.

She brought her hand down hard on the desk, relishing the sting. James may have thought himself powerful, but starting tonight the power in this marriage belonged to her. What she had given James of herself she would take back.

An hour passed—perhaps more—before she heard him talking to Bates in the entry. She tensed. Her throat constricted so tightly only the thinnest ribbon of air could pass. Her heart pounded so hard she could feel its beat in her legs.

When he came through the library door, he didn't see her at first because he was reading something in his hand. The urge to go to him rose up, but she squashed it. He was almost to the desk when he glanced up. When he saw her, he stopped.

She leaned back in the chair with her palms flat on the desk. "Good evening, Captain."

"Likewise." He paused. "Captain." The look in his eyes changed from pleasure at the sight of her to the guarded calculation that had marked the first weeks of their acquaintance.

A ferocious urge to forget everything welled up inside her. Whatever he might have done, they were still married. She could let it go.

Except he'd taken her independence, her birthright, and now she could not get them back.

"How were your visits?" she asked. "Is everything finished?"

He tossed the sheaf of papers in his hand onto the

desk and stood opposite her. "I suppose you could say that."

She stared at him silently across the mahogany expanse, partly to see what else he would offer without her prompting, and partly because her throat was too tight to speak.

"Katherine—"

"I suppose I *could* say that, couldn't I," she interrupted, suddenly not wanting to give him an opportunity for more lies. "Especially given that the committee had already decided not to attaint me when you left for Dunscore."

There was a barely perceptible change in his eyes, and her belly dropped. "I see Honoria and Phil returned, after all," he said darkly.

I didn't know. I hadn't heard. That was what he was supposed to say. Heaven help her, she wished it were true so badly she would almost be willing to accept a lie. Thank God—thank *God*—she hadn't told him she loved him.

She stood up suddenly. "Bastard," she spat. Damn him— No *I'm sorry,* no *Let me explain.* Just *I see Honoria and Phil returned, after all.* "*This* was why you sent them away. And then you made love to me in order to cover up your lie."

He leveled those green eyes at her. "*That* isn't true."

"I should kill you right here." She came around the desk and drew her cutlass, so enraged that her vision hazed over.

He didn't move.

"Draw, damn you!"

"I won't draw on you, Katherine."

"Why not?" she demanded, and saw the truth in his

eyes. "You *do* pity me. Even now." It wasn't to be borne. "Draw!"

He just stood there, watching her.

She raised her blade to his neck. "I should slit your throat for what you've done."

"When I left London for Dunscore, I had every intention of telling you about the vote."

She stared at him and wondered how her heart could keep beating when it hurt so much.

"I'd planned to tell you, Katherine. But when I saw you—"

"I don't want to hear any more of your lies."

"I don't expect you to believe me."

"After all this talk of helping me, of winning over the committee— God. After all that talk of guilt—"

"Do *not* tell me how I feel." He pointed at her, heedless of the blade.

"Dunscore could have been mine. It *was* mine. And you *stole* it!"

"The trusts we woke Deal's solicitor in the middle of the night to draft say otherwise. Dunscore remains in your name."

"You *betrayed* me!"

"Would you have agreed to marry me under any other circumstance?"

"Yes!" The answer shot from her lips on its own, stunning them both into silence.

He blanched, and his mouth thinned. "If we would have married, anyway, then I fail to see why it matters now what ultimately brought us together."

He may as well have stabbed her through the heart. She forced her mouth into a curve. "No. Nor would I expect you to." Finally she sheathed her blade.

"Katherine..." He came toward her, but she backed away, ready to draw again. He held his hands up, but his eyes blazed. "I would do it again," he said harshly. "If it was the only way to have you, I would do it again."

Katherine could think of only one reason for him to say such a thing. "God, I'm a fool. Croston is in debt, isn't it? I should have known."

"Croston is *not* in debt." Anger raged across his face. "Enough of this. We're leaving for Croston in the morning, and I haven't had time to prepare."

"You may go to Croston," she told him stonily. "Anne and I shall stay here. In a few days, after she's recovered from the journey, we will return to Dunscore."

"You will do nothing of the kind."

"I make my own decisions, Captain. I am the countess of Dunscore."

He jabbed his finger at her. "You are my *wife*."

The words struck like blows. "Yes," she said. "And you managed it with deceit as your grappling hook and lies as your cannon fire." The pressure in her chest and belly ached so badly she nearly doubled over with it. It hurt to look at him. "I've been taken captive before, Captain. I may not be able to escape, but this time I will have my captivity on my own terms."

CHAPTER THIRTY-NINE

"MOVE OUT!" PHIL exclaimed the next morning, as Katherine's coach trundled toward Madame Bouchard's. The sunshine had burned off the mist, and its rays glared through the windowpanes. "You'll be responsible for sore tongues all across London."

"Let them talk till their tongues fall out, for all I care." Katherine shook out the old coat Dodd had found in the attic—Grandfather's, most likely—and held it up. "It won't stop me from attending the masquerade, which you said yourself is the most important event of the Season. I'm envisioning a pair of breeches in beige silk. *Nude* beige."

"Katherine..."

"And something very scanty on the top." Phil didn't respond. She would go to the masquerade alone, and why not? Let James see what their marriage meant to her now that she'd learned of his betrayal—and his lack of remorse.

"The swine," Phil muttered, as if reading Katherine's mind.

"Thank you."

"I can't believe he didn't tell you."

"Nor can I." And her heart felt like a rag in a scullery maid's hands, but she'd be damned before she ever let him find out.

James had hoisted his flag on her mast, and all of society knew he had conquered her. Now he was her captor. Her liege lord. The past days' delight was gone, as there was no delight in being someone's spoils. She may as well have been a cask of Italian wine or a bolt of Ottoman silk.

She would show all of London she was nobody's captive. Not anymore.

"The blackguard. Not—" Phil pointed her finger at Katherine "—that I think you should move out, because I absolutely do not. But that doesn't mean he wouldn't deserve it if you did. No—you must punish him some other way. Something that will bring him crawling on his knees to declare his undying love."

"He has no undying love to declare," Katherine said shortly, even as her imagination played out the scene Phil described, and she found herself wanting very badly to hear such a declaration.

"Breaking your heart with his deception—"

"He has *not* broken my heart."

"Darling," Phil said in that you-can't-hide-anything-from-me tone, "do you think I can't see?"

"Lust. William said so."

"Ha! And what would our dear scoundrel William possibly know about matters of the heart? Tell me you didn't listen to him. I assure you, lust does not cause the heartache I see in your eyes right now."

"Whatever I may have felt for Captain Warre died the moment I learned of his betrayal," Katherine said, and wished to God it was true.

Phil rolled her eyes as the carriage slowed to a stop on the busy street in front of Madame Bouchard's shop. "You love him, and there's no sense denying it."

"Don't be ridiculous." Katherine made herself laugh even as invisible hands wrung another drop of pain from her heart. "I can be grateful I never succumbed to that frippery, at least."

"Now who's being ridiculous?" Phil laughed, and then added, "You aren't *really* going to move out."

"I am. Just as soon as I've shown him the consequences of his lies." It would break Anne's heart. Katherine's fingers tightened into the coat, and she wadded it in her lap. During the journey from Dunscore, Anne had already begun calling James "Papa." It would be cruel to drag her away from James now.

But it would be more cruel to keep her with a man who viewed the two of them as little more than chattel.

HALFWAY THROUGH THE fitting at Madame Bouchard's, Katherine got an idea. It was a perfect, vengeful idea that made her heart race, then ache with satisfaction, then grow strangely numb. James thought he could control her? She would show him he could not.

The moment she parted company with Phil and returned home—flush with success at having arranged a costume that would have everyone from London to Venice talking—she put her plan into action.

"You mentioned that if there was ever a way you could right your wrongs against me, I had only to ask," she told the Duke of Winston a short time later, seated in the entirely red first floor drawing room of his town house. "I require your assistance."

One dark brow ticked downward. "A matter with which Croston is unable to assist?"

"Very much unable."

"You have only to name it, Lady Croston."

She smiled past the hurt. James and all of London would see exactly how she took to captivity. "I want you to pretend to have an affair with me."

The duke barked a laugh. "You're trying to get me killed. My apology wasn't enough? You hope to lure me in so Croston will cut me down?"

She smiled. "Not at all. If you'll recall, you did offer to expand my horizons."

"Then perhaps Croston has done something unforgivable, and *I* am to be your revenge on *him*."

Precisely. Making her point to James by flirting her way outrageously through London might have been ideal, but the chance was too great that someone would take her attentions seriously. As ridiculous as it was, Winston was the only one she could trust. And his reputation made him the perfect partner in revenge.

"So many questions, Your Grace." She laughed. "I would not have expected you to be so scrupulous."

"Strictly self-preservation. I'm no match for Croston with a sword. And much as it pains me to say it, I doubt I'm a match for you, either." He assessed her through those devil eyes. "So you propose what? Dances together in public, walks in the park, carriage rides—"

"No carriage rides." God save her, carriage rides were the last thing she wanted to think of.

He smiled wickedly. "Must I reassure you that my carriage is very…comfortable? But I believe I've conveyed that fact to you already."

"I'm not interested in the comfort of your carriage. Dances, yes. Walks in the park, certainly. And I suppose you could linger in my box at the theater."

Now he laughed. "A sham affair, indeed. And my answer, dear Lady Croston, is no."

"No?" The word shot out with all the sharpness of an on-deck command.

He only smiled. "No," he repeated.

"Not so much on the blackguard side of things, after all," she said angrily.

"Not so much on the *suicidal* side of things. Tell me…" He closed the distance between them and took her chin in his fingers. "What has that arrogant bastard done?"

She chose not to turn her face from his grasp. If James were here now and saw Winston touching her like this, blood would spill.

She smiled. "That, Your Grace, is none of your concern."

"If you're asking me to take part in this sham, I daresay it is. Bloody fool hasn't taken a mistress already, has he?"

"No."

He lowered his voice. "Is he demanding…eccentricities?"

"No!" Not that she knew precisely what he meant, but—good God.

And then, "The vote." His eyes narrowed, and she could see he'd finally guessed. "When I came to your house the other night, it was the first you'd heard of the committee's conclusion."

Anger flared fresh. "You extricated yourself quite neatly."

"I'm normally quite adept at escaping conflict," he said. "He didn't bother to tell you."

Stonily she looked a him.

The duke cursed and let his hand fall. "Where is he now?"

"At Croston."

His lips thinned, but he looked at her askance. "Are you determined that it would be *entirely* a sham?"

"Entirely and completely." Her heart beat a little faster. He was about to change his mind. Her thoughts raced ahead to the theater, the park, the Pollards' grand masquerade. James would get wind of her dalliance through the grapevine, and when he did, it would cut him to the bone—just as he had cut her.

"I'll do it, then," he said, with a mix of resignation and relish. "If only to teach Croston a lesson about leaving his property unattended."

"His *property*—"

"Now, now, darling." The duke touched her cheek and smiled. "Any more of those combative looks and I may have to put an end to our torrid affair."

HER CAPTIVITY. JAMES slouched in a chair in the library at Croston with his shirttails untucked and his feet propped—shoeless—on a footstool, nursing a glass of cognac while the rest of the world sat down to dinner.

He wasn't hungry. Perhaps he would eat this evening. Or perhaps he wouldn't.

Sounds of the crew on the roof drifted in through the windows even though they were closed. His arrival at Croston had opened Pandora's box. He'd resolved the disagreement between his tenants, only to have a dozen other issues crop up. The two days he'd planned to spend had turned into a week.

A week's worth of nights alone, remembering Katherine shooting daggers at him with those topaz eyes while she held her blade at his throat.

He took a swallow and leaned his head back, closing his eyes while the liquid slid down his throat. On his lap, the book he'd been trying to read began to feel heavy. He opened his eyes and looked down at it.

A Treatise on Domestic Pigeons: Comprehending All the Species Known in England...

He set his glass aside and searched for the last sentence he'd read. This was the moment he'd been looking forward to for months. Years.

Relaxation was what he really wanted, anyway. Not marriage to a woman who would always make him feel a little bit mad, who would always keep him listing to one side or the other. A woman who saw him as her captor, when all he'd ever done was—

He inhaled sharply and flipped a page. Never mind about that.

He reached for his cognac.

If only she *were* his captive, he would truss her up like a Christmas goose and keep her in his bed until she gave up her will to fight him.

He felt himself grow hard, and cursed.

"Brother?" Honoria's voice called from somewhere inside the house. "James! I know you're here, you ridiculous man."

Oh, of all the bloody—

She swept through the library door from the morning room. "There you are. La, you look a fright. I realize this is the country, James, but there *must* be limits."

He downed another swallow of cognac. "What are you doing here?"

"We've lost our polite manners, as well. Excellent. I've torn myself away from London in order to save your marriage, brother dear, and convince you to return posthaste."

"You needn't have bothered. The marriage is beyond annulment."

"Of that I have no doubt, but is it beyond adultery?" He looked up at her.

"Oh, do forgive me. That was much too strong a word." He recognized that look in her eye too well. "I only meant that Katherine is enjoying the Season, which is as it should be. I'm certain that despite your absence so soon after the wedding, Katherine is confident of your continued love and affection, and would never do anything to cause you a moment's alarm."

From the moment he'd landed in a sodden mass on the deck of her ship, she'd caused him nothing *but* alarm. "Don't be coy with me, Honoria. Have out with it."

She assessed him shrewdly. "I'm certain, for example, that her new friendship with the Duke of Winston is exactly that—friendship."

"Winston." His blood ran cold.

"People are forming all kinds of acquaintances these days," she said with a careless wave of her hand, and smiled. "Perhaps she is teaching him how to defend himself more effectively against a sword. Oh, now, don't look like that, James. Murder isn't the answer. Besides," she added, growing serious, "this is all your fault."

"What," he said slowly, "is happening between Katherine and Winston?" Merely saying those names in the same sentence made him feel sick.

"Likely nothing. But one can never be sure. You must return to London and fix it."

"Fix it," he bit out. "As though I can simply charge into London and wave a wand and force her to love me."

"Love you! Is that what this is about? You have a fine

way of showing it, lying to her about the vote. Why in heaven's name— Never mind. I know why. James, you are blinder than a mole. She would have accepted you if you had but asked."

"You speak where you are not informed."

"Pooh. I've never seen a woman more heartbroken than Katherine. She loves you—of that you may be sure."

"Has she told you as much?" he demanded. "Do you have proof?"

Honoria huffed in exasperation. "Thank goodness you haven't called for tea—most rudely, I might add— because I shall certainly need something stronger before this conversation is finished. Of course she hasn't *told* me. This is Katherine we're talking about. But it's true. She hasn't been pleasant company at all."

"Irrefutable proof indeed."

"Sarcasm is so ugly, James." She perched on the arm of his chair. "She has one of those awful trinkets—the very one you teased me about, with your likeness."

That awful brooch?

"She doesn't know I saw it," Honoria confided. "There was a drawer ajar on her dressing table, and I spotted it inside."

"Along with myriad other odds and ends, I'm sure."

"Why would she have it if not to possess a likeness of the man she loves?"

"Why indeed. To think how your talent for scientific reasoning has been wasted all these years." It could have been a gift. Or a memento of her own heroic act of saving his life. "Perhaps she plans a ceremonial desecration."

Honoria snorted. "You *are* an ass, James. A blind ass. It's your choice, of course, whether to come to London and set things right, or leave Katherine and the duke to their devices. I don't think I shall stay for any refreshment, after all—thank you for offering," she added dryly. "The masquerade is tomorrow night, and if I leave immediately I can still get a decent night's rest tonight. Katherine is planning to attend as a pirate, by the way. I haven't seen her costume, but I'm told it is positively scandalous. I'm sure I shall envy it more than anything." She reached for his hand, her expression darkening. "James, it frightens me to see you like this."

He didn't want her frightened. He just wanted her to leave him alone. "After years of exacting discipline, you can hardly begrudge me a few days of sloth."

"Sloth, James? Really?" She searched him deeply, and he looked away. "You've slunk away to Croston the way an animal goes off on its own to die." She was quiet for an uncharacteristically long moment.

"Go back to London, Ree. I'm fine."

"You aren't."

He looked her in the eye and called up all the clarity he could muster. "I am. I've been looking forward to this for months and now, finally, I'm home."

She pursed her lips. "Very well," she finally said. Impulsively she reached for his arm. "Anything can be fixed, dearest. Have you tried everything? And I do mean everything, James."

There was one thing he hadn't tried. *I love you.* He imagined saying those words to Katherine, but could only imagine her scorn if he did.

HIS HEAD POUNDED like the devil after Honoria left. Winston! Bloody hell. He needed to return to London now. Today.

But what good would it do? It was far too late to fix anything. He'd acted with complete disregard for Katherine's feelings—there was no way to change that now. And in the process, he'd robbed himself of ever knowing whether she might have chosen him of her own free will.

Yes! Her sharp answer shot through his head. He set his glass down and sat forward, cradling his head in his hands. If he'd just renewed his proposal instead of assuming he knew what she was thinking...

Perhaps he would return to London. God only knew what he'd do when he got there, but he would think of something. He was her *husband.* And he'd spent years issuing commands. If nothing else, he could order her never to see Winston again.

There were footsteps outside the library, so he called out. "Hodges! Have Finley pack my bag. I ride for London in twenty minutes."

"Don't know who Hodges is," came a voice he recognized too well, "but if he was supposed to be at the door, he's abandoned his post. Let myself in—hope you won't hold it against me." Winston ambled into the library as if he owned it.

James was across the room in two seconds with Winston shoved against the wall by his shirt. "Bastard! Is Katherine with you?"

"God, no," Winston choked out. "And if you tell Lady Croston of this visit, I shall deny it. I have ten men prepared to swear I've been in the country inspecting a prime piece of horseflesh."

From the sound of things, the only prime piece Winston had been inspecting was Katherine. James tightened his grip on Winston's throat. "If you've touched her, I shall kill you. Honoria has told me everything."

"Clearly not," Winston said, shoving back at James powerfully enough to break his hold. "I had to run my horse into the brush to avoid being seen by your sister not ten minutes ago. Now listen here—" He held up a hand when James took a step forward. "Damned unsporting of you, not telling Lady Dunscore about the vote. I don't know what you were thinking—and I don't care—but I intend to see that you fix things immediately. This business of pretending to have an affair with your wife is playing hell with my ability to pursue legitimate amorous liaisons."

"*Pretending* to have an *affair* with my *wife?*"

"I never should have agreed to such a ridiculous plan." Winston tugged at his sleeves and stalked into the room. "Tried to tell her no, but she was so clearly aggrieved I thought it was the least I could do. Had no idea it would drag on close to a week without you turning up to call me out. And now we've got that bloody masquerade tomorrow evening, and I've been hearing talk of a pirate costume that is rumored to be de trop— and I doubt they're referring to the volume of fabric— and quite frankly, Croston, it is indeed too much. I'm a man, not a saint, though God knows for your sake I've been trying. I demand to know whether you plan to come to London and call me out, or whether my sacrifices have been in vain."

"Are you asking me to believe," James said quietly, stalking toward him, "that Katherine suggested that the two of you *pretend* to have an affair?"

"God, Croston, you're a slow one. Is that cognac over there? I could use a slosh."

James grabbed him again. "You have no idea how satisfying it would be to obliterate you once and for all," he said between clenched teeth.

"I'm half tempted to oblige you," Winston drawled, "as it would extract me from my current misery. But I daresay all this enthusiasm would be much better spent between your wife's legs. Although at the moment, one would be hard-pressed to determine that you have a wife at all."

The temptation to bloody that curled lip was overwhelming. "Have you touched her?" James demanded.

"Only to hand her in and out of my curricle. Ride back from the park—perfectly innocent."

"Nothing with you is innocent." The idea of Katherine riding anywhere with Winston in anything curdled his stomach.

"The memory of my humiliation at her hand is ever with me. You're more of a man than I am, taking that virago to wife. Good God." Winston curled a hand around James's arm. "If you're going to take a swing at me, then do it. Otherwise, release me before I decide to take the initiative myself."

If he took that swing, he wasn't sure he could control himself. He let go. "Get out."

"You're obviously in love with her," Winston said. "Even I can see that much, and I've got exactly no experience with love, nor do I wish to ever gain any. So what you're doing hiding at Croston while your wife and her charms are back in London, I cannot begin to imagine." He went to the door, still adjusting his shirt. "I must return to London immediately. From what I've heard of that pirate costume, tomorrow's masquerade is not to be missed."

"Get. Out."

Winston flashed a damnable grin and disappeared, leaving James behind to contemplate the significance of Katherine's pretend affair. But it didn't take much contemplation because he knew exactly what she was doing: showing him she would not be taken captive.

He had failed her. On the *Merry Sea,* in Salé, in London, at Dunscore. He had failed her in every possible way. But devil take it, he loved her. And she was still his wife whether she liked it or not. Whether he deserved her or not.

Yes. Yes, he bloody well *was* going to go to London and fix this, and he knew exactly how he was going to do it.

CHAPTER FORTY

"YOU MUSTN'T BE angry with me," Honoria said as she swept into Katherine's dressing room, which Katherine knew could only mean she *would* be angry with Honoria the moment she spilled whatever news had pruned those barely painted lips. "La—is *that* your costume?" Honoria stopped short, staring at the bed.

There was a certain satisfaction in answering, "Yes."

"It's…" Honoria shifted wide eyes from the costume to Katherine's face. "Quite daring."

"You disapprove?"

"Not at all." Honoria went to finger the flesh-colored breeches. "I am undone with envy, in fact."

"Ridiculous. Your costume is fabulous." But Honoria hadn't come here to discuss the masquerade. That much was clear, and it was a good bet what Honoria did want to discuss.

Honoria turned her back on the costume, and Katherine held her breath. "Katherine, I've been to Croston— No, do not be angry. James is my brother, after all."

It was the one drawback of their friendship. "I am sorry for your misfortune, but in this case I do not wish to be company for your misery."

"I'm worried about him, Katherine."

Honoria's tone gave her pause. She ignored it. "Your worry is wasted. He may not be accustomed to losing, but you may rest assured he knows from experience that underhanded battle tactics do not always succeed."

"It isn't like James to be underhanded," Honoria said quietly. She took Katherine's hand and squeezed it. "I can't condone what he's done—he was a fool, and nothing less. If he wasn't my brother, I might even say he's done the unforgivable. But, Katherine, I've never seen him like this."

Like what? "If he appears to be suffering, you've come to the wrong person with your concern." But her mind conjured up all sorts of imaginings of the state James might be in. She tried to feel pleased.

"Hear me out. Please." Her gravity was a little alarming. Katherine tried to ignore it. "He'd been drinking when I arrived. It was only one o'clock."

"Hardly uncommon, and hardly cause for worry." Though not like James, but she hardly cared.

"He was half-drunk, Katherine. Rumpled clothes, unshaved, hair a mess—he was reading a treatise about *pigeons,* Katherine. Pigeons!"

"In other words, he is enjoying the retirement he's been speaking of since he first came aboard my ship. Honoria—"

"No. You don't understand. There was a quality in his eyes, Katherine. I've never seen it before." Her voice faltered, and Katherine looked hard for any sign Honoria was putting on a performance. "It was as if he didn't care whether he lives or dies," Honoria said with difficulty. "Katherine, you must do something. If not for him, for me. I've already lost one brother—I don't think I could stand to lose another."

Now she was being melodramatic, but it would have been cruel to say so.

"I realize how much I'm asking," Honoria added. "And that he's been a complete, utter ass. I told him as much."

"Yes, he has. He stole my inheritance, Honoria. He lied to me, betrayed me—"

"I know, I know—"

"—after everything he knew, everything I told him! I trusted him."

"He loves you, Katherine— No, don't scoff. Please. I've never been more certain of anything in my life."

"If he loved me—"

"I know, I know. He never would have done any of this. But Katherine, this is *James*. You know as well as I how he's accustomed to thinking. Orders, commands— if he could have commanded you to marry him, I am convinced he would have. Because he loves you, and he doesn't know any other way."

IF HE LOVED her, he would have found another way, Katherine fumed on the way to the masquerade. Such as *telling* her he loved her, which he'd never done—not when she'd agreed to marry him, not after their wedding, and not when she'd confronted him with his treachery.

Lord and Lady Pollard's grand masquerade was a glittering sensation, a mass of fabulously costumed people swirling through an endless ballroom beneath painted ceilings and sparkling chandeliers. Dancing, laughter, drinking, gaiety—all of it closed in around Katherine while she tried in vain to forget what Honoria had told her.

I've never seen him like this.

Katherine caressed the handle of her cutlass, which for once hung prominently at her side. *I won't draw on you, Katherine.* Coward. If he truly respected her, they would have met on the field for what he did.

Let him waste away at Croston. Tonight she felt powerful. Beneath her tricorne hat, her hair hung in loose, shining curls to her waist. Madame Bouchard had altered Grandfather's old coat so that it hugged her curves. She'd let it hang open in front, revealing a corset and breeches in soft beige that gave the perfect illusion of nudity.

"There isn't a man here who's taken his eyes off you all evening," Honoria said under her breath, giving the white drape of toga across her breasts a little tug— downward. "I ought to send you home."

"If your toga dips any lower," she said to Honoria, "you'll have the attention of every man *and* woman when your female charms go on public display."

"I would never allow such a thing to happen." Beneath her ivy-edged mask, a wicked smile curved Honoria's lips. "At least, not in front of the *entire* party."

Phil, barely concealed in a patterned tunic that was supposed to make her look like an Egyptian goddess, made a noise.

An ill-concealed Duke of Winston ducked through the crowd and joined them. "You look magnificent tonight," he said to Katherine from behind a sleek black mask. "Positively terrifying—and damned tempting."

"How impolite to imply that you've guessed my identity, Your Grace," she scolded.

A sparkling white grin appeared below the mask. "My apologies, Madam Pirate. And may I add, I have a great deal of respect for your costume accessories."

"Perhaps a chain mail tunic should have been your choice for the evening," Phil told him.

He laughed. "Chain mail is much too tedious for the kind of unexpected situations one finds oneself in at these events." Even as he spoke, he surveyed the crowd with a glint in his eye.

"Searching for prey, Your Grace?" Katherine asked. He was tiring of their arrangement. So was she, but for entirely different reasons. Her gaze strayed toward the entrance, and she yanked it back. James would not be here tonight, nor did she want him to be.

Above the mask, Winston's dark brow rose with interest as he returned his attention to her. "Why would I search for prey when I have such a delectable morsel right here at my side? Perhaps you and I could find a secluded alcove and—"

"And nothing," Honoria snapped. "This has already gone too far."

"Oh, I don't know," Katherine said, eyeing Winston. "It might be an enjoyable distraction to cut someone to ribbons this evening."

The brow disappeared. "Naturally," he drawled. "Very well, then. No secluded alcove. A dance, perhaps?"

She didn't want a dance any more than she wanted an alcove—unless both were with James. But that was folly, so she let Winston guide her into the crowd. They took their places in a line of couples that seemed to stretch for a mile. Music filled the room, and she turned with him, stepped aside, stepped together.

Her heart began to ache. *He loves you, Katherine.*

No. He'd tricked her. Lied to her. Stolen the freedom she could have had.

Step, turn, change partners. She took the hand of a man dressed as Henry VIII.

James knew what freedom meant to her. He knew she valued it above anything, that she would give it up for nothing.

Step, turn, duck, and she was back with Winston.

He knew.

A fledgling realization tumbled through her mind, and she faltered the next step. Winston righted her, and she kept on.

Turn, duck, turn.

He knew.

They turned again, but this time she missed a step because the couples were suddenly moving the wrong direction. She reached to the side to grasp the gentleman's hand for the next sequence, but nobody was there. The couples had scattered. It took a moment to realize what was happening as the crowd backed away and one by one down the line couples stopped dancing.

A second pirate had joined the masquerade.

A burgundy tunic hung casually over broad shoulders and a solid chest. A length of black linen covered his head and was tied in the back, letting dark waves shot through with silver peek out below. Gold hoops flashed at his ears, and loose, black linen trousers flowed around his legs.

A Royal Navy officer's sword gleamed at his side.

Winston raised a brow at her and melted into the crowd. Silence descended over the ballroom in a wave that radiated from the center outward. And then a great murmur went up. The same word was on everyone's lips.

Croston.

He watched her with ruthless green eyes. There was barely a moment to savor the joy that leaped in her pulse before his hand went to his side and, with a smooth shink of metal, he drew on her.

A collective gasp went up through the crowd.

With lightning instinct she matched his motion, and in a heartbeat they faced each other, sabre to sabre.

His stoic expression revealed nothing. Through the corner of her eye she could see people retreating, backing up into each other, at once escaping and giving them room. But her entire focus homed in on his blade.

Whatever this spectacle of a marriage was to become, it would become it right here, right now.

He lunged. She parried. Metal clanged against metal. He circled around, stalking her like a lion hunts its prey. She lunged this time.

Clang. Clang. Clang. *Bastard. Liar. Wretch.*

She drove him back, back, nearly into the crowd before he regained the advantage. She whirled then and met metal with metal. He held nothing back and soon she forgot all about the crowd. All of her rage at his betrayal exploded to the surface.

There was a sharp sting when his blade nicked her shoulder. A clean bite when her blade sliced his arm.

"Good God, they've drawn blood!" someone shouted.

Her breath came fast and hard.

How dare he withhold the committee's decision from her.

Clang!

Let her marry him believing she had no choice.

Clang! Clang!

They turned. She sidestepped. Parried. Thrust. Lunged—

Froze.

With shock, she realized the point of her blade rested

at the hollow of his throat. And the point of his rested at the hollow of hers.

Stalemate.

The ballroom was deathly silent. The stench of perfumes and powders filled her nostrils.

She stared at him. The rise and fall of her breath pressed the point of his blade into her skin. A bead of perspiration trickled down the side of his cheek. His hand was steady, his lips hard. He faced her as an equal now, and her heart pounded as she held his gaze, waiting. Waiting.

He was so beautiful her heart hurt.

I love him. The words leaped from her aching heart into her thoughts, an unexpected jab and parry. *God help me, I still love—*

He moved suddenly, and with a quick flick of his wrist he knocked her sword out of her hand. It clattered to the floor.

A deafening cheer went up from the crowd and there was barely time to realize what was happening before James had sheathed his sword. Fresh anger welled up. He had seen her distraction and taken the advantage. He stepped forward, taking hold of her arm.

"Unhand me." The commotion made her command nearly inaudible.

"I don't think I will." Instead of letting go, he lifted her into his arms.

"Put me down! Wait— No!" He lifted her higher, up and over his shoulder, tossing her like a sack of flour so that her hat dropped to the floor amid feminine shrieks and gasps that were audible even among the commotion. "Put me *down!*" She grabbed the hem of his tunic and thumped her fist against his back. "I shall kill you in your sleep if you don't put me down this *instant!*"

His reply was impossible to make out, but his unconcerned tone reached her perfectly. Already they were halfway through the ballroom, headed toward the doorway as the crowd closed in behind them. Then they were outside in the damp darkness. She fought and struggled, but his arms held her fast as mooring lines.

Even as people spilled out of the doorway he forced her into his waiting coach, somehow managing not to bang her head against the side. And then the door slammed shut and the coach lurched forward.

"Devil take you, James!" She pushed against him, but he held her fast by his side. "I swear on my life, if you don't release me right now I will consult an apothecary, and you won't like the result!"

He was still breathing hard from their fight. "If you still wish to murder me after I've had my say, I invite you to try."

"Where are you taking me?"

He looked at her—inches away from her face—and smiled a little. "I've ordered the coachman to take a detour through the countryside."

"You've gone mad."

"No." With his torn shirt and his earrings glinting in the darkness, he looked exactly like the fearsome corsair he portrayed. "I'm in love with you."

She stared at him. Every emotion she'd spent the past week fighting tooth and nail threatened to overcome her. Whatever she'd thought he might say, this was not it.

"I don't believe you." She didn't *dare* believe him.

She knew better. "You *knew* what Dunscore meant to me. You knew how I valued my freedom."

"I did."

And that, she'd realized in the ballroom, was exactly why he'd done it. Because he feared he'd never win her without taking her.

She pushed away from him. "Let me out of the coach."

"Damn you, Katherine." In the dim light she could see the frustration in his eyes. The pain. "I'm asking your forgiveness."

"No—damn *you,* James. You say you love me, but you—" her voice caught "—all you want is to own me. Possess me."

He trapped her face in his hands. "You're damned right I want to possess you," he said harshly, so close she could feel his breath against her lips. "For Christ's sake—you possess *me,* Katherine. Down to my very last drop of blood. You own me, body and soul. You want to know why I did what I did? *That* is why. Because I love you, and I don't want to live without you, and I knew that given the chance you would turn away from me and never look back." His voice tore. "And now I will never know if by some bloody miracle you might have chosen me, anyway."

He was such a fool. "I chose you *days* ago. *Weeks* ago." She paused. "I *love* you." She practically spat the words.

His hands tightened. "Katherine—"

"But I can't surrender. I can't."

"I don't want your surrender," he said roughly. "I want your choice."

Her heart ached as if it should be mangled and dead, but it pounded fiercely with life.

Her choice. His feelings were unmistakable, and yet—

"A ship can only have one captain," she said. "Or so I've heard."

He searched her eyes. "Then I shall be your captain," he said, smoothing his thumbs across her face, "and you shall be mine." The raw hope in his voice said more than he ever could have—this man who had once nearly killed her and then appointed himself her savior, and failed at both. This man, who made her senses come alive and made her hope again, who made her daughter find the happy things.

"I love you, James." A great weight lifted off her heart as she spoke the words.

Her name exhaled from him as he pulled her into his arms and held her as if she were the only thing keeping him alive.

She closed her eyes and let herself relax in his embrace.

* * * * *